THE COST
OF
BETRAYAL

THE COST

OF

BETRAYAL

THREE ROMANTIC SUSPENSE NOVELLAS

BETRAYED BY DEE HENDERSON

DEADLY ISLE BY DANI PETTREY

CODE OF ETHICS BY LYNETTE EASON

BETHANYHOUSE
a division of Baker Publishing Group
Minneapolis, Minnesota

Betrayed © 2018 by Dee Henderson
Deadly Isle © 2018 by Gracie & Johnny, Inc.
Code of Ethics © 2018 by Lynette Eason

Published by Bethany House Publishers
11400 Hampshire Avenue South
Bloomington, Minnesota 55438
www.bethanyhouse.com

Bethany House Publishers is a division of
Baker Publishing Group, Grand Rapids, Michigan

Printed in the United States of America

Library of Congress Cataloging-in-Publication Data
Names: Henderson, Dee. Betrayed. | Pettrey, Dani. Deadly isle. | Eason, Lynette.
    Code of ethics.
Title: The cost of betrayal : three romantic suspense novellas.
Description: Minneapolis, Minnesota : Bethany House Publishers, [2018]
Identifiers: LCCN 2018018555 | ISBN 9780764231735 (trade paper) | ISBN
    9780764231773 (cloth) | ISBN 9781493416059 (e-book) | ISBN 9780764233067
    (large print)
Subjects: LCSH: Suspense fiction, American.
Classification: LCC PS648.S88 C67 2018 | DDC 813/.08720806—dc23
LC record available at https://lccn.loc.gov/2018018555

Scripture quotations in the novella *Betrayed* are from the New Revised Standard Version of the Bible, copyright © 1989, by the Division of Christian Education of the National Council of the Churches of Christ in the United States of America. Used by permission. All rights reserved.

Scripture quotations in the novella *Code of Ethics* are from the Holy Bible, New International Version®. NIV®. Copyright © 1973, 1978, 1984, 2011 by Biblica, Inc.™ Used by permission of Zondervan. All rights reserved worldwide. www.zondervan.com

Cover design by Studio Gearbox

Dani Pettrey is represented by Books & Such Literary Agency

Lynette Eason is represented by The Steve Laube Agency

18 19 20 21 22 23 24   7 6 5 4 3 2 1

CONTENTS

BETRAYED

DEE HENDERSON

ONE

ANN FALCON

ANN FALCON EASED TOWARD the front of the crowd. The auctioneer working his way down a line of tables was presently selling off kitchenware. She felt a light touch at the small of her back and glanced around to find her husband had rejoined her. She leaned toward him to be heard. "That was fast—find anything interesting?"

"Most of the paintings are too modern for my taste, but there's one item, a Chicago-skyline print from the '40s," Paul replied. "They'll be starting the art auction in about ten minutes, but it's going to be an hour before they reach that print. How about you?"

"There are some silk scarves and half-used perfume bottles in a box of miscellaneous dresser drawer items that might make a nice painting arrangement. If the box doesn't go over twenty dollars, I'm interested. That dumpy one with the green stripes on the side."

He looked across the tables and nodded when he spotted her choice. "The third auctioneer has finished with the garden and patio items and is moving over to tools. No surprise, the largest crowd is there. I'm going to scope out the furniture, then look through the industrial and professional section. It looks like several businesses are clearing excess inventory. The FBI lab is always looking for the basics in volume. Maybe something there will be useful to the bureau."

"I'll find you," Ann assured him, and with another nod her husband disappeared into the crowd. She liked spending weekends with Paul doing non-crisis things like wandering a big auction looking for hidden treasures. Twice a year this former aircraft hangar near O'Hare Airport filled with merchandise brought in by area auction houses. A day-long sale by professional auctioneers kept the crowd active and buying. She always found something interesting at this December sale to give as a gift, like the odd toy or the unexpected book.

She lifted her number as the box she was interested in got hoisted on high, quickly realized she was bidding against four people, and two dropped out at ten. The woman to her left still had the box when it reached sixteen. Ann hesitated, let the auctioneer call for the raise twice, looking to her for another bid. Ann saw brief regret rather than pleasure on the high bidder's face—she must not have really wanted it at sixteen. Ann nodded to the auctioneer and wasn't surprised when he called it "sold" to her at seventeen.

Three dollars under her limit gave her a nice deal. She accepted the box and the sales ticket from the staff. Twenty dollars on items for herself, now it was time to find something for either Paul or one of his family members with another twenty. She paid for her first purchase at the exit gate, hauled it out to the car trunk, and went back to shopping.

TWO

PAUL FALCON

MONDAY NIGHT PAUL FOUND HIS WIFE working at her desk in their shared home office, not surprised she was still up waiting for him. "Sorry I'm late."

"What? Oh, yeah, it is late. You called, didn't you?" She came swimming out of what it was she was doing to focus on him and smiled.

He leaned over her desk and kissed her. The conference call that had cost him a spaghetti dinner and movie with his wife had ended just after eleven. Some aspiring young bureaucrat in Washington, D.C., had thought it worth cutting corners to get a wiretap on a federal judge. Being the neutral party first hearing about the problem now, Paul would be spending the next several days untangling the current NYC investigation mess in order to tell his boss, the director of the FBI, what could be salvaged and who should be fired.

The big black bear of a dog at Ann's feet rolled over and planted his paw across Paul's left shoe, yawned, and shook

11

his head violently. Paul glanced down. "You were dreaming, weren't you?"

The dog merely rested his head across Paul's other shoe and tried to go back to sleep. If it wasn't such a typical greeting, Paul would have laughed. "You've been here awhile if Black has taken up station under your feet."

The auction-purchased box was on the floor beside Ann, the collection of perfume bottles now on her desk in a basket, the silk scarves neatly folded, along with a jewelry box and some rather unexpected items: a small sewing kit and a bulky pink pocketknife. He'd figured at this late hour he would find her upstairs painting, but she hadn't taken her auction haul up to the studio yet. "Did the jewelry box have anything in it?" It didn't look particularly old, but it had a highly polished cherry finish and a nice appearance.

"A man's ring, probably missed when the box was emptied, as it was in the lower compartment and kind of stuck. There are initials on the jewelry box." Ann closed the lid to show him. "A cursive *T.C.*, which makes me think female. The pink pocketknife has the name Janelle Roberts engraved on it. I got curious and was doing some research."

"Think you can trace where the box came from?" he asked, interested.

"I'd like to return the ring if it turns out to have sentimental value. A woman's dresser items suggest someone who died recently, so I started with obituaries. So far the initials T.C. has yielded only men. Jane or Janelle Roberts has yielded three obituaries, but none who seem likely to have carried a pink pocketknife or used this collection of perfumes. These are on the expensive end of modern fragrances. And the scarves have contemporary patterns. I'm thinking a rather young woman."

"I buy that logic." It was so like his wife to reason out how to track down a jewelry box in order to return a ring, and then go the long route of original research. "Or you could call the auction company tomorrow."

"What fun would that be?" she joked back.

He laughed. "I've got an early call with D.C. that I need to take back at the office. I'm heading to bed."

"I'll be—" she glanced at the items, the screen, and guessed— "twenty minutes?"

He interpreted that to mean an hour if she found something interesting and could live with that. "Sounds good." He kissed his wife good-night and wished the evening had unfolded differently. Then he eased his feet from under the dog and leaned down to ruffle fur. His life had been boring without a wife and a dog in it. He left Ann to her search.

Understanding realities, Paul packed a bag in case he needed to be on a flight to New York or D.C. tomorrow, took a fast shower, and crawled into bed. He was tired physically and mentally. Running the Chicago FBI office had a predictable order to it, but there hadn't been enough Saturdays to just wander around at an auction or similar event and simply decompress. The year always ended hard in the FBI as December brought personnel moves, attempts to tie off investigations so the numbers could be counted in this calendar year, and higher crime rates as criminals seemed to operate with a desire to finish whatever was going on by year's end as well. He put work out of his mind, turned his thoughts toward God. He was asleep before he'd finished his prayer for his large extended family.

||||||||||

"Paul."

He woke enough to realize his wife was sliding into bed. "Hmm?"

"I found a murder."

If it was anyone other than his wife, he would have struggled to come the rest of the way to full consciousness. This was Ann. She'd worked as many murders in her career as he had before she retired to marry him. "Okay," he murmured.

"I'll show you in the morning."

"That works." He wrapped an arm around her, glad to have her beside him, and dropped back to sleep.

He was more alert six hours later. He thoughtfully didn't turn on the overhead light, though it was dark outside, just shifted the bathroom door so a comfortable amount of light spilled into the bedroom.

"You said 'murder.'"

Ann mumbled something but didn't stir. He finished shaving, and she still hadn't turned over. They had a deal; he didn't wake her on the way to the office, and she would be a wife that didn't get snippy because she was exhausted. On her bedside table was a stack of printed pages that had not been there when he turned off the light. They looked like printed newspaper articles from—what was it?—six and seven years ago. He carried them into the kitchen, popped a bagel into the toaster, started coffee. He read through the material she'd printed, the items she'd underlined. He came back with coffee for both of them and took a seat on the side of the bed, turned on the bedside light. "You did indeed find a murder." He kept his voice low, conversational.

"Give me the coffee," she mumbled. He made sure she was propped up on an elbow and steady before handing over the second mug.

"Janelle Roberts murdered her boyfriend, Andrew Chadwick, the night he broke up with her," he summarized. "Stabbed him once and pushed him down a steep flight of stairs at the beach. She got twenty years for second-degree murder." He set the printed articles on the bedside table. "You found not just a murder, but an interesting one."

"Can you send the pocketknife through the lab for me? I put it in an evidence bag on your desk."

"You think we've got the murder weapon?" Paul asked, genuinely surprised.

Ann shrugged. "It's pink, has her name on it. By Janelle's own admission, she had the pocketknife in her purse two days before his death—she pried a cork out of a bottle for her friend Tanya. The fact she couldn't produce the pocketknife was used against her at the trial because the model was consistent with the blade that stabbed Andrew. It makes sense it was the murder weapon, hidden somewhere cops didn't locate during their search. They turned up her tennis shoes with faint blood traces in the treads, but not the pocketknife."

Paul considered Ann's request. After six years in prison, winning an appeal was unlikely, yet having the murder weapon would impact a DA's decision on how to retry the case should the need arise. "Okay, I'll send it through the lab."

"Thanks." Ann drank more of the coffee. "The friend Tanya, by the way, is the sister of the dead man. Janelle had a particularly bad night. She stabbed Andrew with a pink pocketknife that has her name on it. I imagine she was afraid to throw it in a dumpster—hey, it's pink!—someone probably retrieves it. She could bury it, but if someone finds the knife years later, it's still got her name on it. If she doesn't get it cleaned well first, there might be traces of blood left, and there's no statute of limitations on murder. She would have needed to melt it down to truly dispose of it safely." Ann paused, thought a moment, and added, "That's not so easy to do. She'd need a blowtorch or something like it, since I don't think putting it in the oven would get it hot enough to reshape metal."

Paul smiled as his wife gestured with her mug. "Anyway, cops are on her doorstep that night," she continued, "serving a warrant to search her place. So now Janelle's afraid to go near where she stashed the pocketknife while cops see her as their primary suspect. She gets arrested, can't make bail, and the trial renders a guilty verdict. Her landlord ends up hiring two guys to box up her apartment because her friends have all deserted her and she's no longer paying the rent. The missing pocketknife falls out of the ceramic Christmas tree she had stored in a neighbor's locker area—or some other similarly odd hiding place. It gets tossed into a box, everything heading toward the cobweb-end of an unused basement, while the landlord sorts out if he can legally sell Janelle's possessions or not. Years later, everything gets cleared out and that box ends up at Saturday's massive sale."

Paul could easily envision the kind of scenario Ann had laid out. "The initials on the jewelry box, T.C., that would be Tanya Chadwick, the dead man's sister?"

"It is. Good memory." Ann shoved pillows around to get more comfortable. "We know from the news articles Janelle and Tanya were best friends since second grade. I can see that jewelry box being passed along. 'I don't need this anymore, as I've got a larger one—do you want it?' and Janelle ends up with Tanya's jewelry box. They reach their twenties and Janelle starts dating Tanya's brother. Then the bad breakup happens, Janelle kills the brother, and there goes the friendship. I haven't tracked Tanya down yet. I don't know if she's still in the Chicago area or not. Not that I plan to say anything if we've found the murder weapon. I just want to hand it to the DA in case an appeal results in a new trial."

"We're of like minds on that," Paul agreed, but wondered how awake she was and proposed an obvious question. "Have you considered the fact this box of items could instead be Tanya's things, rather than Janelle's?"

Ann blinked twice, her face registering her surprise. Then she handed him the coffee and collapsed back, pulling one of the pillows over her face. "I just wanted an interesting collection of dresser things to paint."

He set the mug on the side table with a smile and rubbed her arm. "It raises an interesting question. How did the sister of the dead man come to have the pink pocketknife in her possession? And why doesn't she say anything about it while her friend is on trial for murder and they are talking about the fact they can't locate that very pocketknife?"

Ann sighed as she lowered the pillow. "You figure out if it's the murder weapon. I'll figure out where that box came from—if it's Janelle's belongings or it's actually Tanya's things."

He leaned over and kissed her. "Enjoy your puzzle."

"You're heading somewhere? I saw the bag by the door."

"I sincerely hope not, but if so I'll make it a lightning trip."

"Take a good book for the flight."

"I will. Go back to sleep."

She nodded and rolled over to hug his pillow. He shut off the side table light. The dog was still snoring, resting on his back, feet in the air, guarding the bathroom door. Paul gave him a belly rub and whispered, "Take good care of her today." Black's tail swished back and forth. Paul collected his luggage, stopped in their shared office to pick up the pocketknife now in an evidence bag, and headed downstairs to the waiting car.

||||||||||

"Miss me?"

The dog darted away to bring back a mangled fuzzy bear that growled when he bit down on it hard enough. Paul set down his luggage, gave the bear a solid tug to confirm its special place as the favorite toy, and rubbed Black's head. "Where is she?"

The dog turned his head and looked toward the office rather than the stairs to the studio. "Thanks."

It had been a long two days. A federal judge was taking bribes to sway his rulings, and not much of a case was left that could prove it, given how tainted the investigation had become. The Chicago office would be taking over the matter from the New York office, which meant he had to figure out who he could give up for the next six weeks from among the best of his investigators. Probably Sam and Rita, as he trusted them to get it right, but it was going to mean that what they were managing now would land back on his desk.

Paul paused in the doorway of their home office. "I'd ask if you missed me, but I recognize the look that says you're not even sure what day it is."

His wife turned from the whiteboard, now a case board, set down the marker she held, and walked into his hug. "Welcome home," she said with a satisfied sigh.

"You've been busy."

"Don't want to talk about it," she mumbled against his chest. "I want spaghetti and a movie and your feet up on the coffee table beside mine."

He rubbed her back and chuckled. "That sounds perfect. Are you fixing that meal or am I?"

"We'll call your sister and ask for a delivery from the restaurant. You can choose the movie so long as it's not one of the X-men ones."

"Deal."

They ate dinner at the kitchen counter, tabbing through the family messages and photos of the last couple of days to share updates before retreating to the living room to enjoy a movie and decompress together from what life had already tossed at them this month.

Their month would only get busier. Paul didn't want to think about how many holiday parties were stacked on their social calendar for the next few weeks. His extended family would start arriving to town. And between Christmas and New Year's they were hosting a gathering here that the governor was likely to attend. Ann would handle it, but every year at this time he regretted that they couldn't make December about half as complex as it inevitably turned out to be.

He idly twisted a strand of her hair around his finger, glad for at least one evening in their week to reconnect. They still functioned best as *us*, and he wanted more than anything to protect that. Not for the first time he thought about retirement, mulling over his working assumption it was more than five years and less than ten years away. He could feel himself getting closer to the day when he would say more than two but less than five years.

When the movie was over, and even Black had decided he'd had enough popcorn, Paul steered the conversation to the details of Ann's last few days. He knew she really didn't mind talking shop. She'd retired, and he'd been promoted too high to take the lead on a case anymore, but they still kept their hands in the investigative side of things by working the occasional cold case together. "I heard the pocketknife came back as a positive match for the murder weapon."

Ann stirred enough to uncross her feet and sit up. "There was blood on the longest blade, and the DNA is a match to Andrew Chadwick."

"Your whiteboard looks a lot like an investigation."

She glanced his direction. "Just preliminary thoughts. You were right. The box of items belongs to Tanya Chadwick."

He was surprised to hear his brief suggestion had turned out to be right. "You found an obituary? She's dead? Or did you track the box ownership down through the auction company?"

"Tanya is very much alive and now living in New York City. I've learned the box I purchased was brought to the area-wide auction by Mark's Auction House. They had bought fifty-eight boxes of household goods, twenty-three pieces of furniture, and eight floor rugs from a Michelle Rice, a woman who turns out to be the former house manager for the Chadwick family. Tanya sold the family home this year, and Mrs. Rice has moved on to new employment. I spoke briefly with Mrs. Rice today. She said she would have packed the items that were taken to the auction house. I'm having coffee with her tomorrow under the guise of showing her the jewelry box and ring so I can confirm I'll be returning the ring to its rightful owner. I should be able to guide the conversation around to learn how that varied collection of items, including a pink pocketknife, made it into the same box. I went ahead and put out requests today for the trial transcript and the case file. I'll give the materials a few days of my time and see what I can learn."

"Want some help?"

"Do you honestly have an extra brain cell right now?"

"I'm burned to a crisp."

She rubbed a hand across his hair and smiled. "Still just smoking gray showing up. You begin turning active flame and I'll start to worry. I'll take a preliminary look at the files and let you know." She reached for her glass sitting on a coffee-table coaster. "I don't expect to get very far. The knife probably showed up after the trial was concluded, and Tanya couldn't convince herself to throw it away but didn't want to talk to cops ever again, so she dumped it in a drawer. Janelle was already in jail for the murder. Six years later, Tanya decides she's going to stay permanently in New York and makes arrangements to sell the family home back here in Chicago. The house manager is directing a crew of people, boxing what is going to Tanya in New York, what is going to the auction house, and what is being left for the house stagers to use in showcasing it for sale. In the process, the pocketknife that had been dropped in a forget-me drawer ends up in a box of dresser items heading to auction rather than the trash."

Paul could hear the cop in her putting the pieces together in logical order. "The common-sense answer does tend to be what happened," he murmured. He knew she'd look until the question was resolved to her satisfaction. "Ready to call it a night?"

"Been ready since about the second half of the movie. I don't sleep as well without you."

He reached for her hand and pulled her to her feet. "Now you're just being kind. I'll walk the dog tonight if you tackle unpacking my bag. I'd rather not see a reminder that I might get pulled away again."

"How deep is the snow?"

"They're saying ten inches by morning, mostly lake-effect."

"You can walk the dog."

Paul laughed. The dog enjoyed fresh snow, liked to crash through drifts and climb mountains when it got piled. The walk that would take twenty minutes in the summer would take forty in winter. "Black, want to walk?"

The dog shook himself awake and headed out to the entry for his leash.

Paul kissed his wife, content this one corner of his life was in good order, and went to join their dog.

THREE

"TANYA IS AN INTERESTING WOMAN, although possibly in a bad way," Ann said from the closet, looking for a pair of shoes.

Paul straightened his tie and picked up the watch he still preferred to wear rather than pull out his phone to check the time. "How do you mean?"

Ann found the shoes to go with her dress and sat down on the bed to slip them on. "She was considering taking her brother to court over his decisions about the family's trust."

Being the eldest son and future trustee of a sizable family business, the one being groomed to provide direction for brothers, sister, and cousins on any number of enterprises the family owned, the comment caught Paul's attention in a personal way. "She was, what, in her twenties?"

"Yes. There's a desperate need for money in Tanya's history, and her brother had been doling out their parents' estate in a too-little, too-late fashion in her estimation. She'd lost out on a boutique franchise, a clothing-line launch, the upper-tier design school. Tanya wanted better than a comfortable allowance. She wanted New York and fashion and had looked at taking her brother to court over the matter. I got that from Andrew's college buddy, who is not a fan of Tanya. Andrew was a business major, finishing up his MBA."

"How sizable a trust are we talking about?"

"Four to five million. They both were drawing eighty thousand a year."

"She wasn't going to win a complaint in court," Paul assessed.

"I suspect legal counsel told her the same. Her brother was a healthy young man destined to live a long life. The trust did not sunset when she reached a particular age, plus there was no exit to the terms while Andrew was alive. She had a problem that was never going to go away. And money is a big motive for murder. Why split it when you can just have it all?"

Paul glanced over, hearing in Ann's tone a cop who had caught the scent of something tangible. She was fixing the ankle strap on her shoe. "A good motive isn't proof of murder."

Ann sat upright, gave him a distracted nod. "I know. She'd been considering taking the trust matter to court but hadn't taken that step yet, hadn't fully breached the relationship with her brother, and on other matters they were apparently still on good terms. Tanya was living at the family home, while Andrew would be back at the house between college terms. The house manager said they got along as well as a brother and sister would a few years apart in age, different groups of friends, interests—but family.

"And what the jury heard makes sense," Ann continued. "Janelle and Andrew broke up that night, and Janelle was furious about it—her own words. The break-up fight was at the beach where he was found dead. There were traces of blood in the treads of her tennis shoes. And we now have her pink pocketknife with his blood on it. There is plenty to say Janelle did this murder." Ann crossed to the dresser and selected a necklace, earrings. "But I think Tanya did this, Paul, and framed Janelle."

He studied her reflected face in the mirror as she slipped in the earrings, met her gaze. He knew his wife. She didn't make a statement like that if there wasn't a certainty inside that she had found a thread connected to the real truth. *Sister kills brother, frames his girlfriend.* Put it in a newspaper headline and it would get nods like any other murder case. It happened. Only rarely, though, did it actually succeed.

Ann wouldn't set the case aside now until she had figured out if she could prove it. "I'll find time for you to walk me through the details," Paul offered. He held out his hand as she was ready to go. "A party is calling our name."

"What number is this one?"

"Three."

She squeezed his hand. "Deal still in effect?"

He grinned. "No shop talk at a holiday party. Kids, vacations, sports, even politics if necessary, but not a single tangent related to work. That goes for both of us."

Ann smiled. "It's a good rule. I like parties for the food, the music, and the fact we're mostly surrounded by interesting people I've met before. We need this." She picked up her purse.

"We need an extra few hours of sleep even more, but I like dancing with my wife; you're beautiful tonight." He trailed a finger down her cheek, pleased with the fact she still blushed easily.

"Thank you."

"You're welcome." He would make sure they were home by eleven so they could have a reasonable night. "Which of us tells Black he's being left behind?" The dog was already trailing them down the hall, ears perked up.

She laughed softly. "There's one of his favorite jerky treats by the entryway statue, so we can say goodbye with kindness. He'll forgive us. He likes the party cookies I've been smuggling home for him."

"Smart thinking." Paul held her coat for her, then slipped on his own. She said goodbye to their dog, and they headed out for the evening. If his wife was right, someone was sitting in a prison cell who hadn't committed a murder, and someone who had was enjoying the holidays. He couldn't justify diverting someone from his office to look at a concluded state case, but between himself and Ann, there was more murder-case experience than anyone he could assign. He'd find the time to help her take a deeper look at it.

|||||||||

It had been a nice party, the kind that reminded Paul why they said yes to the varied holiday invitations. He was able to meet the spouses of those who worked for him, see photos of kids, hear vacation plans, enjoy some laughter as "Did you hear about?" stories circled the room. The value was in the connections renewed, the new ones formed.

He glanced over at Ann as traffic halted at a red light. She had enjoyed herself by all appearances, but now rested with head against the headrest and eyes closed. He reached over to slip a strand of tinsel from her hair. She'd become a princess for twenty minutes, sharing with a child how to make a handmade Christmas crown. They were of like minds that parenthood had passed them by, but she was good with other people's children in a way he loved to watch. He held up the tinsel and got a smile.

"I'm going to show the kids how to make them when we host your family. I was practicing."

"They'll enjoy that." He could hear the fatigue in her voice and planned to make sure she slept in tomorrow morning. Traffic began to move again, so he turned his attention back to the road ahead.

"The lights are pretty tonight," she mentioned. "Those who put out strands of Christmas lights do a favor for the rest of us."

"It is beautiful," he agreed. The fresh white snow and colored lights made a festive combination. He gave her a brief glance. "I don't like to dampen what is a relaxed mood, but we have twenty minutes at the pace traffic is moving, and I have a feeling Christmas lights are not the only thing now on your mind. Tell me about the murder scene."

Ann reached over and squeezed his free hand. "Thanks."

"I prefer doing the hard stuff with you." Taking apart a solved murder where a jury had already convicted on the crime was the picture of a hard undertaking.

"The murder happened at a beach north of Lake Point. You don't think of the Chicago area as having such interesting places—we spend so much of the year in this snow. But during the summer months, there are destination beaches around the lake. This one is a long stretch of sand and not one tourists visit often. You can't carry your chairs and blankets and coolers from the parking lot directly to the sand. Instead you have to traverse several staircases to reach the beach or else use the steeper direct staircase about a mile from the parking lot. But if you want to take your date for a walk on the beach, or see a full display of sunset colors reflecting on the water and in the clouds, this is where the locals go. I can see why Janelle and Andrew ended up there that Friday night. By late August it's cool in the evenings, plus there's a wind off the lake to deal with. But it's a place to walk and talk with some privacy."

Paul could visualize the scene. "So what played out that night? How did Janelle end up in prison?"

"Tanya found her brother's body. He had mentioned the plans for the evening with Janelle were dinner and a walk on the beach, then home. It's getting late. The beach closes after the sunset hour. Tanya is in a snit because her brother was supposed to help her finish up paperwork for a meeting on

Saturday morning and she needs his signature. Neither Janelle nor Andrew is answering her calls, so Tanya drives over to the beach. Her brother's car is still there. Tanya walks down the steeper stairs and discovers Andrew at the bottom. She calls 9-1-1 at 10:46 p.m. Cops are on scene at 10:58. It's faint moonlight, and she's been using a penlight on her keychain to move around. She's desperately trying to stop his bleeding, thinking it's flowing and Andrew's alive. Cops have to tell her that her brother is dead.

"She's hysterical that Janelle can't be found. 'She was with my brother. They were on a date tonight. Is she dead somewhere around here too? Look for her!' And cops are spreading out to do that very thing, bringing in more law enforcement on the possibility it was an abduction. Janelle was grabbed, and Andrew was stabbed and pushed down the stairs in the ensuing fight.

"Calm descends when a patrol officer discovers Janelle at her apartment. She'd walked down to the pizza place and called a taxi to take her home after Andrew dumped her. She didn't want a ride from him. And she'd been ignoring her phone because she didn't want to talk to anyone. The officer brings her out to the beach to talk to the detective in charge. Things spiral downward from there.

"They get a warrant to search Janelle's place, recover the clothes she had worn on the date, look for a knife. Her tennis shoes have traces of blood in the treads. It doesn't help that Tanya wails 'What did you do?' and tearfully tells the cops and later the jury that her friend had a crush on her brother for years and wasn't going to let him dump her and move on to another girlfriend. The jury buys it and convicts Janelle of second-degree murder." Ann went quiet for a long moment. "It's a neat case . . . on the surface."

"You don't think that's what happened?"

"I think we're looking at something well scripted and carefully staged."

Paul considered his wife's words. "Show me. Lay out the photos, the transcripts, the details. I need to see what you have." He was asking as her husband, but also as the head of the Chicago FBI office. His agreement with her conclusion would be a significant step in determining what happened next.

Ann nodded. "I mostly see Tanya, her actions, and hear her in the interviews and trial testimony. Maybe it's too many years of murder cases, but there is a serious false note."

The traffic had thinned, and they now were nearing home, so he purposefully lightened things. "Were you able to smuggle home a cookie or two?"

Ann smiled. "Two sugar cookies. I nearly brought Black an oatmeal one, but he would give me that look that says 'Really? *Oatmeal?*'" She laughed. "You know he's been sleeping the entire time we've been away. We get home, feed him sugar—the walk tonight is going to last a good hour."

Paul thought she had it pegged. "We'll change and both take him for a walk. The fresh air will do us all good, and then you can sleep in for hours if you like."

"I like that plan."

Paul parked the car and came around to offer his arm for the short walk to their building. In their building lobby and elevator, he used his key to override the security lock, then pressed the button for their private floor. "Will he be asleep or waiting?" he wondered aloud.

Ann laughed. "Oh, definitely waiting. He's learned when the elevator is slowing to stop on our floor."

Ann was right. Black sat and promptly lifted a paw to say hi, which Paul accepted so as not to disappoint him. The dog wound a figure eight between them as they slipped off their coats, trying to lean and love on them both at the same time.

Paul gave him a bear hug in thanks. "I'll be back for a walk in a minute, buddy." The dog's attention snapped to Ann holding cookies, and his tail about knocked Paul over. With a laugh Paul cleared the field for Ann and went to change clothes for their walk. It felt good to be home.

||||||||||

Paul dropped the medical examiner's report back on the stack of case materials that had migrated from their home office to wherever he might have a moment. He heard Ann moving around in the bedroom. He turned to the breakfast he had prepped and checked that the waffle iron was hot, poured the first one.

"You should have nudged me awake." Ann joined him in a flurry of plaid flannel over jeans, having pulled on her favorite painting shirt and shoved up the sleeves. "Our Saturday breakfast is turning into brunch."

He kissed her good morning. "You needed the sleep."

He pulled blueberry syrup from the microwave, avoided the steam rising from the waffle iron, and placed the syrup on the counter. "Would you prefer something else?"

"Blueberry is fine." Ann brought out glasses, poured orange juice, and set one by each place setting. She slid onto a stool. "What time is the car picking you up?"

It was telling that she simply assumed he'd be heading into the office. He glanced at his watch. "Forty-five minutes." Work requiring some of Saturday was a fact of his life in December. "The New York matter is resolved if Sam can get the judge to take a new bribe and we get it on the record, preferably both audio and video. To our good fortune, a case got assigned to the judge this week that has organized-crime overtones. The defendant would have both the means and motive to offer a bribe. We just need to find a reason he would like to cooperate with us, unrelated to the case going to trial. We'll be looking through his past for that leverage today." He forked out a finished waffle and placed it on her plate.

"Thanks." She reached for the syrup. "If you can connect him to anyone now in witness protection, there might be an avenue of information you can tap there," she offered.

Paul nodded, pouring more batter. "I've already got Lori in mind. One has to approach carefully when asking her a question like that one. Risk the reward of taking down a federal judge versus protecting Lori's past? It's not even a close call."

"Well, I wish you a quick answer, for when you get home today I'm thinking we take an hour and go build a snowman somewhere, freeze our fingers, maybe toss a few friendly snowballs at each other, with Black to umpire."

Paul laughed at the image. "I'm game. Party number four is tonight?"

"It's late, eight to whenever, at the Marriott. It's mostly your parents' friends, so I expect the party to go into the early hours of the morning, but we can duck out at a reasonable time." Ann nodded toward the crime photos. "Switching cases—anything surprise you?"

He reached to pick up his orange juice. "If it were not for the fact Andrew was stabbed with a pocketknife, I could make a good argument this was simply an unfortunate Friday night for him. He breaks up badly with his girlfriend, stays stewing over it on that beach after she leaves, it gets dark, he gets robbed on the way back to his car, and rather than hand over his wallet he throws a punch because he's in the mood to hit something. He gets stabbed once, stumbles back, and tumbles down that steeper set of stairs. The robber either already had his wallet and phone or hustled down the stairs after him and takes them."

Paul plated his waffle, sat down beside her, reached for the syrup, and continued with his thought. "The injuries were not fatal. If Andrew hadn't knocked himself out, his evening would have ended with a bad headache and some stitches. But the fall knocks him unconscious and he bleeds to death from the stab wound before he's found. According to the ME, he'd been on a mild blood thinner since he was in his teens, and that stab wound wasn't going to clot and close on its own since it had nicked his liver. It reads as mostly a very bad night. The problem is the stabbing . . . it's with a pocketknife. No self-respecting robber is going to use a pocketknife as his weapon of choice. You bring a knife rather than a gun to a robbery so you don't do a decade in jail if convicted of taking a wallet with forty bucks in it, but you do at least bring a decent knife."

Ann nodded. "I see a pocketknife, I'm liable to just kick the guy, and I'm a girl. Andrew's a young athletic man, tall, giving him good reach, from all accounts confident in himself. He would have gone for the fight that night."

Paul sliced into the center of his waffle. "So . . . probably not a robbery." He gestured with his fork. "Then there's the blood on Janelle's tennis shoes, and the fact we now have a pink pocketknife that has both Janelle's name on it and Andrew's blood. Which are also saying not a robbery."

"There's that too," Ann agreed. She had finished her waffle and reached for her juice. "I think we've got a stage set for us, and a stage manager. Tanya stabbed her brother with Janelle's pocketknife and sent him tumbling down the beach stairs. She confirms he's dying satisfactorily fast, makes it look like a robbery, gets blood on a pair of Janelle's tennis shoes, leaves him there, and goes to establish her alibi. She slips those tennis shoes into Janelle's closet either before Janelle got herself home by taxi or while Janelle is out walking her dog that night, and then Tanya waits for it to be late enough in the evening she can go 'find' her brother dead." She paused. "I think this was planned, premeditated for months."

31

Paul forked the last of his waffle through syrup and felt like he'd walked into that one. He thought through what he had seen so far of the case and couldn't come up with a single time-line item that said she was wrong. "You deliberately leave me with hours to ponder that statement before I can walk through the details with you."

His wife gave him a small, wise smile. "Guilty." She leaned her head against his shoulder. "Remember our first meal at this counter?"

"Cheeseburgers, I think it was. It was raining. You were piloting a borrowed plane from one case to another."

"Our lives are always going to be moments together like this between cases."

He laughed and tipped her chin, kissed her. "I can deal with that kind of marriage if you can."

"We'd be bored if the topics of conversation were limited to family, books, painting, and business," Ann replied. "We're going to enjoy retirement, but let's give it a few more years. So long as no one's shooting at me, I rather like the occasional case."

"You do realize you're mostly hiding out with this one. You don't have a book idea for what to write come January first, and you're avoiding that problem by hiding in this one."

Ann playfully slapped his arm for the reminder, then slid off the stool to collect dishes for the dishwasher. "That's the pleasure of not having a contract or deadline. When I come up with something that stirs my imagination, I'll turn my attention to writing another book."

"Good, because for all the recent activities, you're actually getting bored. I recognize the signs." Paul glanced at his watch. His driver would be downstairs waiting soon. "Snowman, friendly tossed snowballs, dinner delivered in, and you can walk me through your Tanya theory on either side of the party. I'll do my best to be home by three."

"It's a plan." Ann shot a warning finger at the dog considering if he could reach into the dishwasher to lick a syrupy plate. Paul chuckled and headed out. Ann would have a good morning. He hoped he would be able to say the same about his.

FOUR

PAUL FELT LIKE SNOW was still melting down the back of his neck and shook out his shirt collar as he entered their home office. Ann was already settled on the couch with an oversized mug of hot chocolate. She tossed a couple of minia- ture marshmallows for Black, who barked with delight as he pounced on them. "He thinks I won the snowball fight," she told her husband with a grin.

"Yeah, he knows you've got the bribes going." Paul settled in his office chair, coffee in hand. Ann didn't often let her inner child show, but he'd heard a few giggles during the snowball battle that had made the last hour and a half well worth it.

Ann tossed another marshmallow to the dog. "Tanya gave Janelle that pink pocketknife, had it engraved, called it a birth- day gag gift."

Paul felt his attention snap toward the case. "Talk about burying the lead. Okay, that's interesting."

He set his coffee aside, considered his wife. Her cheeks were still the rosy red of cold and snow. She had a good arm when she was tossing even friendly missives his way, and he'd been effectively shellacked. "I've been wondering what was tipping you toward Tanya setting this up. An engraved pink pocketknife is something people remember, something a jury would latch on to."

Ann nodded. "You'll need a murder weapon one day, so you give it as a gift—to your best friend, a pink knife, her name on it, hard to miss. Then you use it to kill your brother." She closed her eyes and quoted, "'Where's your pink pocketknife, Janelle? The one with your name on it? You had it in your purse two days before his death. The ME says that model of knife is consistent with the stab wound. You say you didn't do this. Produce your pocketknife so we can see it's not the weapon and believe you.'" She opened her eyes and glanced over at him. "Not verbatim from the trial transcript, but close enough."

"And she can't produce it," Paul said simply.

"That fact crucified her at the trial. The jury probably gave the missing knife more weight than if it had been sitting there in evidence with Andrew's blood on it. The jury likes the logical answer. *Murder weapon?* Of course she got rid of it." Ann sipped her hot chocolate. "Tanya took the knife, uses it, tucks it away as her insurance. If the cops start looking beyond Janelle, that pink pocketknife can turn up in the beach sand, bearing Janelle's name and Andrew's blood. If subtle evidence doesn't get the job done, blunt will."

He needed maybe sixty hours just to read the materials Ann already had been through in depth. The odds of that happening soon were not promising, but Paul thought they might be able to get a solid four hours in on it tonight. Where the next hours after that could be found was tomorrow's problem. He'd go through the case, and somewhere during that process he would find the information he needed to make a conclusion of his own.

Paul pulled off damp socks and put on the dry ones he'd taken from his dresser drawer. "I need to see the trial transcript first, then probably the first interview with Tanya. You don't like her."

"I viscerally don't, mostly because of what I'm uncovering. I think Tanya planned this for months in advance. The first step was convincing her best friend and her brother they should date, knowing eventually there'd be a fight or a breakup, something to give her cover to kill her brother, and give the cops an obvious viable suspect in Janelle. Tanya took the person who trusted her most and walked her into a guilty verdict for murder."

Paul stopped the sock thief with the snap of his fingers. Black dropped the sock and decided to roll on it instead.

Ann smiled. "He can't help it. Smelly socks are his favorite."

"He ends up smelling like one too."

"I'll face his wrath and give him a bath this week. He'll need one before our party anyway."

Paul considered the dog, now upside down with four feet in the air, watching them, tail swishing, obviously hoping to hear his name and the word *play*. "He'll be okay for a few days. There's probably a rule that guys should smell like guys occasionally. At least he hasn't tangled with a skunk this year."

Ann laughed at the shared memory. "There is that."

She dug out the trial transcript and handed it to him. "The fact Tanya gave Janelle the knife, it gets used in a murder, and Tanya has that knife in her possession years later—that's nearly evidence."

Paul appreciated the nuance of her using the word *nearly*—it reflected reality. For all his wife's passion for digging through the layers toward the truth of a matter, she was still at the heart of it a cop who understood reality. What was true and what was provable were not always the same.

"Let me start reading. We can pick it up again after the party tonight."

‖‖‖‖‖‖

Their lives were a constant refrain of conversations put on hold and picked up again in the next block of time until the topic was satisfactorily covered from all angles. Paul could list a dozen such conversations he and Ann were currently having on topics of various importance and urgency. The pattern worked for them.

The party was not a distant memory, for his mother had sent home a box of the confectionaries, but the work was absorbing them both again. Ann was sitting on the office floor now, case materials piled around her—interviews and the detective's report—methodically taking him through the record piece by piece.

Paul considered what he was reading, paused, and changed directions on the question he was going to ask. He studied his wife for a long moment. "Argue the other side for me."

Ann gave him a slight tilt of her head, a hint of a smile, and did just that. "Janelle did it, killed her boyfriend because he broke up with her. Heat of the moment, pure tragedy, she didn't mean to do it. 'I was going to stab the tires of his precious sports car and walk myself home. Only he tried to take the knife away from me when I told him that, and I got knocked off-balance, fell into him, and accidentally stabbed him. I didn't mean for him to stumble back and tumble down the stairs to the beach. I tried to grab him and stop his fall. He crashed down the stairs, and I started down after him, but then I heard voices yelling at the base of the stairs and I panicked. I ran. I rushed home and prayed it would be only a nightmare, that Andrew wouldn't give me up to the cops as the one who stabbed him. I was certain he had help as soon as he fell. That's why I left the beach in such a hurry. I didn't rob him. I wouldn't do that. Then the cops came to my apartment. . . .'"

Paul nodded as Ann drifted to a stop, not surprised she gave him her strongest theory for Janelle having done the crime.

"Well argued. Knifing his car tires—that's what an angry ex-girlfriend would do. It's authentic. And it puts the knife in her hand without premeditation."

"Yeah. The knife tumbles and gets lost in the beach sand when Andrew falls. Tanya finds the knife in the sand after the trial is over, can't stand the thought of talking to another cop, so drops the knife in a forget-me drawer—can't let herself throw it away, just holds on to it in case Janelle gets a retrial because it's tangible evidence of what happened. Similar with the ring I found in the jewelry box. Andrew didn't always wear it; Tanya found it in his things and held on to it as a keepsake. She moves to New York right after the trial because she can't stand to be in the house without her brother. Years later she sells the family home, and those items end up in a box at an auction."

Paul looked at the photos of the pocketknife with Janelle's name it, the jewelry box with Tanya's initials. "Ann, it's possible to argue both answers convincingly. Janelle had a fair trial by her peers. Nothing here is conclusive enough to do more than get her a retrial."

"It's Janelle's knife with Andrew's blood on it. She's got no chance of a retrial," Ann replied. She shifted and moodily poked at the trial binder. "I can argue both scenarios, but only one is actually true, Paul. And it's that Tanya killed her brother and framed her friend. It's there in the interviews of Tanya and Janelle, in the way the trial transcript reads. Tanya's leading people to the conclusions she wants made even as she's flowing tears at the idea her best friend killed her brother. She convincingly sold the story she wanted people to follow.

"Janelle was furious and devastated that she was getting dumped by the guy she was in love with. But she didn't have reason to kill him. She wanted him to change his mind. She's worked in restaurant kitchens since she got a work permit at fifteen. She's not someone who makes a mistake with a knife.

If she intended to hurt him, he would have been stabbed in the heart or hit multiple times. And the cynic in me says if you want to betray someone, the best person to target is the one who trusts you the most. Tanya killed her brother and set up her best friend."

Paul wasn't there yet. He was seeing beneath Tanya's emotional language and tears, hearing the calculation in what she said in the interviews. He could see instances where she was leading the conversation in subtle ways and how she was directing the cops, DA, and jury. But the cold calculation to murder a brother, betray a best friend—that was a long last step. "I need to see the Tanya interviews again, the third one in particular."

"It's late." Ann leaned forward to check the time and winced. "Very late. We can pick it up again another time."

He conceded he was running on fumes, and the reality of it being a Saturday night factored in. They both attempted to give church and those they met for lunch after the services the best they could offer. He closed the transcript he held. "For Janelle, time is running by very slowly. We'll find the time, Ann."

She got to her feet and offered him a hand. "We will. As you've shown me, the best way to live life is to do what you can and expect God to do the rest."

|||||||||

They carved out more time Tuesday night. Ann set a fresh cup of coffee beside Paul on his desk and curled up with hers on the couch. "I've been thinking today about the hardest piece. The coldness this implies has to be in Tanya. I can give you a variation on the theme that might be easier to accept. Tanya killed her brother because he was already dying, tried to get the cops to see it as a robbery, and only sacrificed her best friend to keep cops from looking beyond Janelle to herself."

Paul set aside the detective's report. "It's interesting already. What are you thinking?"

"Andrew simply had an accident. He tumbled down those stairs because it was dark and they were damp, and he knocked himself out. There's no initial robbery, no stab wound. Just a bad breakup with his girlfriend. She'd stormed off for home, and he'd stayed on the beach fuming until it turned dark.

"Tanya's waiting for Andrew to get home, for Janelle to call. Neither do. She comes to the beach looking for him. She sees her brother at the bottom of the steps and thinks he's dead. By the time she gets down there, she's realized her own life is so much better off if he *is* dead. And that idea seals his fate.

"She instead finds him badly injured from the fall, but alive. He's lying there probably with a broken back, broken neck—he could be crippled for life, and the family trust prioritizes health expenses over everything else. She's seeing her future disappear. If she calls 9-1-1, she's hurting herself. She can walk away, but the cops will find him when they check the parking lot and see the car still there. If he hasn't died already, odds are good he'll live another day or two just lying there. She can't risk smothering him, having the ME put that as the cause of death. She wants her freedom, not to walk herself into a prison term. He has to die before he's found, and she has to be protected from any blame. She needs to give the cops a stronger viable suspect. And with that thought Janelle's fate is now sealed too.

"No one saw Andrew go tumbling down the flight of stairs or they would have called for help. So she's gambling no one can say it *wasn't* Janelle who pushed him. And if Janelle can push him, she can stab him. Do it right, given the medication he's on, he'll bleed to death quickly. Janelle's got a pink pocketknife with her name on it. Tanya needs tangible evidence Janelle did the crime. It doesn't get more direct than if she uses that knife. With Janelle on a date, odds are good she's carrying a clutch purse that matches her dress, and her handbag with the pocketknife will be hanging on the inside of her closet door. It means risking that no one finds Andrew in the thirty minutes it is going to take for Tanya to go fetch the knife and get back, yet it protects her from being blamed for his death.

"So Tanya gets the pocketknife from Janelle's apartment, also grabs a pair of her tennis shoes, and then rushes back to the beach. She stabs her brother while he's lying on the sand at the bottom of the stairs, only once as she's trying to sell stab-and-fall, and she's afraid multiple stab wounds risk making it apparent he was lying down. She's nicked his liver, and he's bleeding steadily. She gets blood on the shoes. She takes his wallet and phone and ring so it can be argued a robber did this. She makes sure some blood drops get left at the top of the stairs where the so-called robbery happened. She then slips away from the beach and creates an alibi. She returns the shoes to Janelle's closet, keeps the pocketknife as her insurance policy. If cops don't buy robbery, if they don't focus on Janelle and find the tennis shoes, then the pink pocketknife can turn up in the sand—with Janelle's name on it and Andrew's blood. She's protected any way this moves forward.

"The only thing that doesn't work out for Tanya is that the cops don't find him. It's getting late with no officer knocking on the door. She's worried if it goes past midnight with the cops not focused on Janelle. If so, she has to shut this down fast. So she goes back and 'finds' her brother dead. The ME report is inconclusive because of two critical points: that he's stabbed while lying on the ground, and that the stab wound took place at a different time than the fall."

Paul thought it was an insightful variation. "It softens Tanya into being an opportunistic murderer, so it's got serious merit. Why don't you prefer it?"

"It's two trips to the beach—one to find the brother, the

second to return with the knife and shoes. Then there's getting the shoes returned to Janelle's apartment. The timing is tight."

Paul thought about that timeline aloud. "After Andrew and Janelle break up at the beach, Janelle walked to the pizza place and called a taxi. She had to wait for it to arrive . . . then you add the drive time to her apartment. After she arrived home, she went back out again when she took her dog for a walk. Janelle is away from her apartment for a considerable amount of time after she has left Andrew. Tanya is driving, can eliminate those delays. So it is possible. I wouldn't say probable. It's doable, but tight."

Ann nodded. "But now add in the sum total of what transpires next. Tanya handled her reactions when the cops arrived, the interviews, without ever stumbling on what she wanted to say. She didn't fumble and need to repair a statement in a later interview. What transpires is too neat for a plan put together in a matter of a couple hours. She was leading everyone right to the conclusions she wanted them to reach, from the detective at the beach that night to the jury at trial later on. She didn't figure out those nuances on Friday night in the two hours she had to prepare for what would unfold. She had spent months getting ready for that performance."

He understood Ann's point. "I agree. I'm reading interviews which on the surface are emotional sister-of-the-victim statements about her brother, her best friend. But then you take a look at the information she's laying out, and it's lining up like ducks in a row, everything cops would need to view Janelle as the guilty party. There was one recorded statement in particular." Paul flipped back through the detective's report. "Tanya mentions that pink pocketknife in her first conversation with the detective while still at the beach. Quoting her, 'You think Janelle did this? That's crazy. I know my brother was stabbed, but you said he was also robbed. Ask Janelle for her pocket-knife. You'll see she didn't do this—she's got it in her purse.'

42

The detective asks Janelle for it, she says 'sure,' reaches for her purse, and the pocketknife isn't in it. That was a risky leading statement on Tanya's part, but she sold it with the right emotion, defending her best friend while also driving the knife home—pun intended. Every statement Tanya gives after that is more subtle, nuanced, but she knew the core sentence she had to provide the detective that first night, how to set this unfolding in the direction she had planned. She'd practiced how to deliver it to get the job done."

Ann gave him a nod. "It's calculated, Paul. Planned. Rehearsed. I concede it's the fact I don't like her that makes me willing to say she's cold enough to plan the crime far in advance. The truth is probably kinder to her. She found her brother that night and said, 'No, I'm not letting his fall ruin my life,' so she came up with a way to kill him and keep attention off herself. She's a selfish woman capable of killing her brother and framing her best friend to protect herself. But maybe she's not so cold that she planned it months in advance."

Paul rested his head back against his office chair. "Does it matter?"

"Not really. I simply want to understand her. Because if I'm right, for six years she's let her best friend sit in prison."

"Friendships rupture. Even those who have been best friends since second grade have periods where they're at odds with each other."

Ann shook her head. "Putting this kind of blame on a friend, it's not normal behavior. You might do it under stress, but you feel guilty about it afterwards and try to fix it. That's what bugs me the most. I see the betrayal, but it's foreign to me how you get to that point. Friends protect friends. It's the friendship code."

"Maybe Tanya lives with what she did by warping that friendship code to suit what she needs—she reframes this as 'Janelle is protecting me. She doesn't know that, but if she did, she'd agree to do this for me. She knows why I had to get free.' People can justify anything to themselves."

"That's true."

Paul shifted his focus. There were two people in this case, and he was still developing what he thought of each of them. "Let me see the interviews with Janelle again, the first night in particular."

Ann sorted out the case materials and passed them over.

"Are we in agreement on one thing, Ann? If Janelle did this, it was spur-of-the-moment. She fights with Andrew, intentionally or not stabs him once, he tumbles, and she flees the scene. There's no premeditation on Janelle's part, no planning of what happened, just a bad breakup that she didn't see coming. Andrew ends up hurt, and she runs away from the scene?"

Ann smiled. "Our first full agreement. Even the DA wasn't pushing any consideration that Janelle thought about this in advance. The two argued, she stabbed Andrew, he falls, she panics, ditches the knife, tries to cover herself and say she didn't do it. But it's all a breakup fight and its aftermath."

Paul felt something click as Ann spoke, something resonating with what he had read earlier. *Finally.* Just as Ann had her sense of when she had the right thread to pull, he had a point when something jelled, and it had just done so, deeper than his conscious mind. It would surface.

"What time is it?" he asked idly.

"Just after midnight."

"I could use some more ice cream if you were inclined to want some yourself."

Ann smiled. "Butter pecan?"

"Is there any other kind worth mentioning? Thanks, Ann."

She squeezed his shoulder as she went past. The dog rolled to his feet to follow her.

||||||||||

Good people committed murder. Paul had long since accepted that. He'd put a significant number of them in prison. But a good person didn't often plan the murder in advance, requiring rapid decisions on what to do afterward, leading to mistakes, panic. Janelle had not planned what happened that night. That was what had clicked. Paul leaned back to ponder that thought.

Guilty people gave themselves away—sweating, minds racing, desperate to get rid of the evidence, establish an alibi, spin a story out to friends to cover the time period. Good people who committed murder were unable to walk away and *show no signs of it*. As an investigator, you didn't make a decision based on behavior. You worked from the evidence. But the evidence backed up behavior. He had two people in this case file, and they were handling events very differently.

He accepted the bowl of ice cream from his wife, waited till she was seated. "Ann, your best evidence that Tanya—or someone else—did this murder is Janelle's behavior. The patrol officer found Janelle at home wearing sweats, eating chocolate ice cream out of the carton, and methodically taking apart a scrapbook full of pictures of her with Andrew. The search of her home yielded some things of Andrew's: jacket, CDs, and books haphazardly thrown together in a box in the hall. Janelle had been purging her apartment of her boyfriend when the patrol officer knocked on her door."

He saw the surprise cross her face.

"I hadn't thought about that specifically."

"Character tells. It always does. Janelle isn't guilty of this. The patrol officer knocks on her door, and she's clueless that her boyfriend has been hurt, let alone is dead. If it was the detective who knocked on her door and saw for himself what she was doing, her shock and the tears, he would have kept pushing until he could find another answer.

"But by the time Janelle has been driven in the back of a squad car to the beach, has seen all the flashing lights and cops and medical examiner vehicles, she's quiet and wound tight and confused, desperately trying to sort out what happened to the man she loves after she left him. The detective sees someone saying she didn't do it, but missed seeing the physical innocence, that clueless expression that would have told him she was telling the truth. He knows they had a fight, there's blood on her shoes, the knife she can't produce is consistent with what stabbed Andrew—he had to go with what was there in front of him. The detective bought the frame."

"You believe me?"

"Yes."

Relief flowed across her face.

"It's here, Ann. It's not just your theory. The murder weapon was in Tanya's possession until the auction. That alone gets people willing to listen to this case again. You look at the money she had to gain, listen to the interviews and what she said about Janelle, with an ear for this, and it rings true."

Ann laid her head back against the sofa cushion. "I feel like I just climbed Mount Everest and back."

"I hit the summit a few days after you, but I'm looking at the same view."

"Thank you, Paul."

He understood the quiet emotion in her words. Independent climbs, but the same conclusion. Janelle wasn't guilty.

He gave her a minute to absorb it before he said, "We've got a problem, though. A new trial doesn't help Janelle. She gets convicted by a new jury because we've now got the murder weapon. That pink pocketknife has her name on it, Andrew's blood, and it is no longer missing. The jury can see it. That pink pocketknife is still wreaking havoc."

Ann grimaced. "Yeah, I'm there too. The knife that showed

up in the auction box—leading me to conclude Janelle didn't do this—is the same knife that solidifies Janelle's apparent guilt. Tanya's brilliant ace in the hole is doing its job."

"Tanya isn't likely to confess, and we won't be able to prove Tanya took that knife out of Janelle's purse. Even if we can show Tanya made more than one trip to the beach that night, it doesn't prove she actually caused her brother's death. When Tanya 'found' her brother and tried to stop the apparent bleeding, she corrupted the crime scene. The fact she had that knife years after the trial is damaging to her, but the real power of the knife is its reinforcement of the conviction on record."

"Any good news?" Ann wondered aloud.

"We'll have some allies. The original detective—it's not going to sit well with a good cop that he was manipulated like this. The DA too will have some strong feelings on the matter. There will be a concerted effort to take Tanya's story apart. You've convinced me. We'll convince others. But you and I both know that seeing it and effectively doing something about it are very different matters."

Paul dropped the report back onto the stack. "I hate to give Tanya credit, but she came up with a crime she could get away with. It reminds me of Psalm sixty-four—'Who can see us? Who can search out our crimes? We have thought out a cunningly conceived plot.' That could have been written with Tanya in mind. I don't know how to convince twelve people on a jury, or even a judge in a bench trial, that Tanya is guilty. Convincing a judge there's reasonable doubt Janelle is guilty has some merit, but even that would be hard to win. Getting her conviction overturned, that's a moon shot."

"What are we going to do?"

Paul thought long and hard about how to answer that question. "A new trial doesn't solve Janelle's problem. She just gets convicted again because the murder weapon has her name on it. We aren't going to get Tanya to confess to a crime she's ducked. There's only one person who can help Janelle, and we're going to have to convince him to do so." He reached over and picked up his phone.

Ann draped her arms around her knees. "He's going to love having us as friends."

Paul smiled at her and then turned his attention to the answered call. "This is Paul Falcon with the Chicago FBI office. And I do recognize the hour. I need you to wake up Governor Bliss and hand him the phone."

He figured it would take them a few minutes to comply and briefly thought about fresh coffee. This was going to be one of the most difficult pitches he'd made in years.

"A pardon," Ann said.

Paul nodded as he mentally did the math. "Janelle's been in prison for six years, two months, and nine days. She's innocent. Calling at this time of night says we both believe it. But he still might not agree to take the political risk. This is an unprovable truth where only one scenario is right. You just hope the person receiving mercy uses the rest of her life to demonstrate it was the right call."

"Thank you, Paul. This is."

He smiled. "I'm making the call because I agree with you. Janelle doesn't fit what happened—Tanya does. That pocketknife smells of a setup, from the fact Tanya bought it for Janelle all the way through to the fact Tanya had it in her possession years later."

The music broke as the line was picked up. "I have Governor Bliss for you, sir." Paul punched the speakerphone button so his wife could listen in.

"Paul, it's always good to hear from you when this month's emergency code word isn't the opening. What can I do for you tonight?"

"I have a problem only you can solve. My wife found a murder weapon in a box of items purchased at auction."

The governor laughed and tried to stifle it. "Sorry. Not funny. But that is so Ann."

"She does indeed attract interesting problems," Paul agreed with a smile and turned toward her. "Jeffery, I need a pardon for a woman named Janelle Roberts, who was betrayed by a friend and convicted of a murder she did not commit. On the face of it, everyone who looks at this case will tell you not to grant it. The new evidence is open to interpretation, and she received a fair trial. Both are true. But Ann and I are fully convinced she's innocent. She's been in prison for six years, two months, and nine days. She can't get relief through the courts. Her only recourse is a pardon. Hence I'm waking you up. Ann convinced me in ten hours. I hope I can convince you in less."

"You already did."

Paul was staggered by the statement, and he and Ann looked at each other in astonishment.

"Wake up the pardon attorney, tell him I'd like the papers on my desk by nine."

"Thank you, Governor."

"Let's stay with 'Jeffery.' If a person can't exercise power appropriately, he shouldn't have this job. I'd trust either of you on a murder case. Tell Janelle she found mercy from the people of Illinois, and the governor wishes her a speedy return to a normal life."

"I'll do that, Jeffery. Ann just started crying."

"I'll take that as a compliment. Good night, Paul."

|||||||||

Paul slipped Black a piece of bacon while he waited for Ann to join them. Breakfast this morning was abbreviated, events stepping on their normal routine. "Don't tell your mother."

49

The dog slapped his tail against the cabinet and looked hopefully at the rest of the bacon croissant Paul had stacked together.

Ann joined them, ruffling the dog's ears out of habit. Black leaned his weight into her knee in greeting, but his gaze stayed locked on the sandwich. Paul laughed and offered the dog another piece, then gave Ann the rest of his sandwich. "We can pick up the paperwork on the way. He's signing it now. Your choice, we can call the warden in advance or deal with it when we arrive."

She considered the question while she ate. "Wheels turn faster when you're standing there," she decided. "I vote we see the warden, talk Janelle through what happened, and walk out of prison with her—take all the shocks in one wave before the press gets wind of this."

"She's going to need somewhere to go. She has no close family. Her apartment has long since been leased to someone else. Her best friend is the one who betrayed her. That leaves possibly someone from her church or maybe a prior neighbor."

Ann pulled a postcard free from a magnet clip on the refrigerator. "She needs to be outside of press attention entirely until she has her bearings back. I'm thinking I call Greg Tate."

Paul considered that solution and found it an interesting one on so many levels. "That works, provided we can conceal her travel itinerary."

"I can fly her down and be back in forty-eight hours. Tell people I'm on a Christmas shopping trip—I'll find something I can buy and wrap while I'm there."

He smiled, knowing how she disliked shopping. "I'll come up with something better than that to cover your absence, but it makes sense for you to provide the transportation. Call Greg and see what he says. I'll give Yancey a call, put her on standby in case Janelle needs someone with her full-time as these first days unfold. Then we'll take the dog for an abbreviated walk and get on the road."

Ann nodded and picked up the phone to call an old friend.

FIVE

FOR A THIRD TIME THE WARDEN flipped pages of the pardon packet addressed to his attention. "It's a first in my career, I'll give you that. What do you need first?"

Paul purposefully stretched out his legs in a very uncomfortable visitor's chair, well accustomed to the realities of the Illinois prison system. "We'd like to have a private conversation with her—in the chapel if possible. We'll need some time, probably a couple of hours. She'll be accompanying us when we leave."

"The chapel is no problem, nor her being signed out through the system. Her possessions are going to fit in a couple of boxes, so packing will be quick enough. Her IDs will have expired, driver's license and such, but her medical records here are current. I'll have them pulled."

"She will likely want to say farewell to a friend or two," Ann put in. "If we limit the number of names she provides, can that be arranged for the chapel as well?"

"Depending on the persons, we'll try to accommodate you," the warden agreed. He turned back to Paul, studying him with interest. "The head of the Chicago FBI delivers papers like this in person, it suggests there is something beyond just 'new evidence' and 'miscarriage of justice' cited by the governor in the pardon. Anything else you can tell me?"

Paul smiled easily. "There's a need to keep news of the pardon away from the press until we've secured her safety, as a murderer is about to realize the person framed is now free. The FBI is assisting since the murder weapon has come into our possession. And we also have a personal interest in this matter." He checked the time. "She has been free for two hours and forty-seven minutes and does not realize it yet. Would it be possible to finish our conversation, you and I, once we've broken the news? And Ann and Janelle are talking about arrangements from here?"

"I see your point." The warden pushed back his chair. "I'll handle the arrangements personally. You can follow my aide to the chapel, and I'll have her escorted there momentarily."

Paul glanced at his wife and got a slight nod toward a photo on the wall. He looked over at it. "You play soccer, Jim?"

"I've been known to kick around the ball. Sports leagues are helpful in a prison; we foster them as rewards."

"Janelle was a good soccer player in high school. If you could find her an outfit like they are wearing in that picture? It's neutral enough to feel like street clothes. Timing was such we haven't yet addressed those practical matters."

"I can do that for you."

"Appreciate it."

Paul was sure the governor's name and the fact the paperwork had been signed less than three hours ago was moving things along faster than his credentials on their own. Whatever worked suited him.

He let his hand rest in the small of Ann's back as they followed the aide through corridors toward the chapel, not saying what was on his mind while there were others to overhear.

The aide unlocked the chapel for them; they were looking at

pews facing a small raised platform, some folding chairs on the stage. A round table and short counter formed a catchall for songbooks, Bibles, and a communion area, with two restrooms and a small office at the opposite end. "There are basic refreshments here," the aide said, pointing, "pretzels, tea, a vending machine with cold sodas. Several classes meet here. The phone on the wall is a direct line to the office. I can remain out here or return to the office, whichever suits you."

"We'll call as we need you, thanks."

"Sure." He left them in the chapel.

Ann let out a long breath and dumped her briefcase on a pew bench. "It's going smoother than I expected."

"The surprise arrival was useful." Paul pulled out his wallet and walked over to feed the soda vending machine. This location was probably as neutral as they could get. The chapel walls had been painted a light blue, and someone had taken the time to trim out the windowsills in a crisp white. The sunlight on the snow outside added reflected brightness to the room. He and Ann had talked over their strategy for the first half hour with Janelle. After that, topics would depend mostly on how she was reacting. Greg Tate's professional advice on that had been useful.

He passed a Diet Coke to Ann. "You still think Greg is the right call?"

"You're wondering because he and I used to be . . . ?" She crossed her fingers.

Paul laughed and tipped his soda can toward her. That Ann had dated widely in the years before they met was part of her history, which kept reappearing in unexpected ways. It no longer bothered him, for he'd been the only one she'd said yes to marrying.

"I'm confident he's the right combination of person and place," she replied. "The case details—those were always going to be our strong suit. We need him for the rest of this. No matter how wide Janelle's emotional swings are in the first weeks, he's going to have already seen stronger ones."

He opened cupboard doors, looking for the pretzels. "I'm inclined to think there's going to be the opposite problem— little to no emotion for some time."

Ann nodded. "Just as likely too. So long as we sort out what to do with Tanya before Janelle gets her equilibrium back and decides betrayal deserves payback, this can work."

"One of the values of Greg living on an island. Janelle doesn't head toward Tanya without us having early warning." He pulled a folder from his briefcase and set it on the counter, having given up on the pretzels. "She's going to have figured out by now that Tanya set her up. It's been six years. That's a lot of time to think."

"Probably, but I'm not suggesting anything near that idea unless she opens that door. But it would be fitting, don't you think, for Tanya to be here next year in Janelle's place?"

"I could live with that outcome."

At the sound of voices outside the chapel, Paul set his open drink down on the nearest windowsill and slid hands into his pockets. The corrections officer who opened the door was younger than those they had seen up to now. Beside him stood a woman a few inches taller than his wife, an athlete either by environment or choice, with light brown hair neatly French-braided and caught in the back, wearing the olive-green T-shirt and khakis assigned to inmates. A faint sheen covered her face, no doubt accounted for by the prison being hot, even in winter. He was sweltering in his suit and tie but hadn't wanted to drop the visible signs of authority until this was concluded.

"Ms. Roberts, please, would you come in and have a seat? I'm Paul Falcon, and this is my wife, Ann. We'd like to speak with you concerning your case. Thank you, Officer."

The young man gave a puzzled nod and reluctantly stepped out. Paul picked up his soda, chose a back pew that would position her in his line of sight, and sat down, stretching his legs out and offering a friendly smile. The woman was still standing where she had entered the room, looking around to assess an uncertain situation. "If you don't mind me calling you Janelle," Paul continued, voice easy, "I'll do so. Please help yourself to your choice of soda." He gestured to a row of cans on the counter. "I could only guess at your preference. In the folder beside them there is a document from the governor of the state of Illinois. He'd like to pardon you, Janelle, if you'll accept the gift from the people of Illinois. Legally it requires your signature. He's already signed the document and sent a copy to the warden. You'll be free to leave the prison with us after we're done talking here."

"You found who really killed Andrew."

She was fast to the bottom line, and he liked it. "We believe we know who killed him, yes. My wife and I are certain you did not. And the governor is an honorable man who listens to people who have a job like mine. I head the Chicago FBI office. Please, get yourself a drink, look through the papers. When you're ready to sign, I'll show you the page and line."

She glanced toward Ann.

His wife simply nodded, her smile mostly one of compassion. "It's true. The governor signed the papers three hours ago. We picked them up and drove down to walk through the bureaucracy for you. I'm sorry we're short of a civilian change of clothes we can offer, but we'll find a mall after we leave here to let you choose something appropriate. We asked if they would find one of the soccer uniforms for now. While I'm not one for much makeup, you'll no doubt do better with the makeup in my purse than I will." Another smile. "You're innocent, Janelle. We believe you. So does the governor. I'm truly sorry it has taken so long for someone like us to come and get you out of here."

Janelle walked over and picked up a can of Pepsi, popped the metal ring, then hesitated. She lifted the folder beside the sodas and chose the half pew by the stage facing into the room. Freedom began in the smallest of ways; for six years she'd been handing over the metal tab on the soda can so it couldn't be squirreled away and turned into a weapon. She drank half the soda and opened the file, began to read.

For several minutes there was no sound.

"You have a pen I can use?"

Her voice was a bit husky and not much else . . . yet.

Paul went over and handed her one of his better pens he'd selected for the occasion. "Initial the pages with the blue tabs—you'll see the governor's already there—sign the last page on both sets. Today's date is December seventeenth."

She placed the two documents on the pew bench, initialed as the tabs indicated, boldly signed her name, added the date to each document. She handed him back the pen.

"Consider the pen yours now." He offered her the case that went with it. "One of the signed documents stays with you. Later this afternoon we'll stop and get you several copies made. I'll take the other original back with me to the governor's office for you.

"This pardon sets aside all matters entered against you. If asked on any job application whether you have ever been convicted of a crime, your legal answer is no. If asked by a lawyer, police officer, or any other party if you've ever been arrested for a crime, your legal answer is no. The arrest, the charges, and the conviction have all been set aside, made null and void. A pardon is not identical to a court-overturned sentence, but legally it frees you to the same level."

She gave a long sigh and nodded. "Okay." She tried a smile. "Thanks."

He returned to his pew, being careful not to crowd her,

shedding his jacket on the way. She was still sitting with her back to the wall, not unexpected, as he would have done the same. The next hour was the real test of how she was handling matters and would determine if they needed to adjust their plans.

Ann had laid out the contents of her briefcase on the round table. She now walked over and set the briefcase beside Janelle. "Some of the materials we are going to go through with you you'll want to keep, so please consider the briefcase yours now. Whatever is going back with me can easily fit into Paul's."

Janelle ran her hand lightly across the soft leather. "I'm free. I can walk outside right now if I like."

Paul took that one. "Yes. We'll go with you now if you would like, and we can have the rest of our conversation far from here. But if you could trust us for a few minutes that you are now in fact free, we thought you might like to say goodbye to friends here first before you leave. If you give us the names of those you'd like to see, we've arranged, where possible, for them to come here to the chapel."

"There's a few."

Ann handed her a notepad. "Make a list and we'll start those arrangements right away. Later we can add anyone you might have missed."

Janelle was starting to blink back tears. She wrote down a few names, bit her lip, added another two, then offered the pad. "Those six really are it."

Ann accepted the list, walked over and picked up the wall phone receiver, and gave the names to the warden's aide. She returned the list to Janelle. "He thought it'll take about forty minutes."

"What do you have to show me?" Janelle asked.

Ann smiled and walked over to the table. "For starters, travel. We've made arrangements for you to spend the next few weeks away from the press, so you can get your bearings in peace. If you are agreeable, I have a friend, Greg Tate, who has property on an island in the Gulf of Mexico just off the Louisiana coast. It's a place with sandy beaches, a rather laid-back tourist town, some year-round residents, and peaceful this time of year. If you like the area and desire to stay for a while, it's ready-made for finding work. There are restaurants he owns that can always use talent, some retail shops too."

Janelle came over to the round table as Ann spread out photos she'd printed from the town's website. "You're talking mostly looking at the ocean, walking sandy beaches, and eating seafood that was alive a few hours before, as what to do with your time. There isn't even a grade school on the island—kids take the ferry over to the mainland. This destination is closer than I would like to your last experience with a beach, but Chicago has eight inches of snow on the ground right now, central Illinois is fighting ice, and it's bad weather most of the way down to Texas. I thought you'd prefer someplace you could be outdoors at any hour you like without having to first bundle up like an Eskimo."

Janelle faintly smiled and slid over one of the photos. Ann had dropped a recent one of their dog into the random collection. "That guy belongs to Paul and me, but the last time I visited Greg there was a similar version in white following him around. He's a dog guy rather than cats. This is Greg." Ann tapped an old photo of Greg, playing baseball on a sunny afternoon. "I've known him for nearly all my life. He's the one who hauls the cooler around when it's full of ice and handles the grill when you're trying to feed a crowd with brats and hamburgers. He truly loves to be helpful. He was married once, though it ended in a bad divorce after a work accident and rehab cost him a couple years of his life. He decided a change of location was how to best start over and so headed south until he couldn't go any farther without fins. His father was still alive back then, had lived on this island for a number of years. I think Greg's glad he's there. We talk often enough I know he's enjoying his life."

Paul was watching Janelle as Ann talked and could see her growing stress as she tried to keep up with the speed of the unexpected information. He'd interrupt, but he knew Ann was doing it deliberately. Casual conversations that bopped around topics had a unique feel and rhythm to them, and Janelle hadn't experienced the real thing for going on seven years. Freedom was an enormous culture shock—the distant memory of walking into a fast-food restaurant, driving down a busy road, sleeping in . . . it was all there in Janelle's memory of life before prison but had been dormant for years. Today shocked it back to the forefront. She would walk out of here into a new normal. The stress related to her physical safety would fade, but a fast-moving world would arrive, and that was a massive new stressor. Remembering how to acclimate to new people who were just being friendly was just the beginning of the coming adjustments.

Ann paused the information falling like rain on Janelle, and just smiled. "It feels like the first day of high school, doesn't it? All of it hitting at once?"

"Something like that," Janelle said softly.

Ann touched one of the photos. "This is the plane we'll fly to the island. I paid for college piloting aircraft around for clients. I asked to borrow this one, since it's good for sight-seeing. Greg will have arranged a place for you. I'll be staying for a day and coming back to Illinois. You'll have as long as you like to simply breathe, Janelle. The island does the Christmas thing in a big way—*Come Vacation at the Island for Christmas*—you won't miss out on Christmas trees, music, streets strung with lights, even though the 'snow' around the trees will be fake white fluff."

Paul offered from where he sat on the pew, not crossing over to the table yet, "Pardons are unusual things, and the press will learn about this one in a matter of hours, which is why we want to give you some downtime at an out-of-the-way destination. From here on out, simply say to anyone who might ask how to contact you that you'll be traveling for a while. You should be free to talk to the press on your own terms, in your own timing, and in whatever detail you choose. If you would like to sit down and have just one conversation on the matter, we can offer names of two reporters with solid reputations in Illinois whom we know personally.

"You're free to decline these arrangements in whole or part. You're welcome to take off and disappear once you leave here, or on any day of your choosing as this unfolds. We won't hold that against you or think less of you for it. We've made arrangements to draw five thousand in cash at a local bank today so you have some flexibility. If you prefer that we take you somewhere else today, we'll be pleased to do so."

Ann set a phone on the table. "It's been activated for you."

Janelle's hand immediately closed over the phone. "This is overwhelming."

"I know," Ann replied gently. "We're doing it rather deliberately because the next several weeks are going to feel overwhelming like this, even under the best of circumstances. We want you to feel that swirl of emotions while you're still in a place familiar to you so you know what to expect."

Janelle blinked at that comment and gave another glimmer of a smile. "I get it. Seems like you've thought of everything." She looked down at the photo under her hand. "You're the people with a plan, and I get dizzy at the thought of making one of my own. What else do you have to tell me?"

Paul got up and came to join them. He held out a business card with his private number on the back. "Believe it or not, Janelle, you've now heard the full wall of information you need immediately. Now we'll simply answer any questions you wish to ask. We'll let you enjoy the next few weeks in peace before we ask to have a conversation with you about what happened."

She studied the card, the embossed *Paul Falcon*, the FBI logo, then looked over at the drinks lined up. "Those sodas are all fair game?"

"Help yourself."

She picked up another Pepsi, slid over one of the chairs, and sat. Paul rested his hand lightly against Ann's back as she gathered together the island information for Janelle. He'd been studied before with the same thoroughness as Janelle was now doing, but rarely by someone who was not facing him across an interview table.

"I want to know who killed Andrew—not today, but in a few days when I'm ready to ask the question. You'll answer that, and others I have?"

"Every one," Paul agreed. "Maybe not me personally—it will probably be Ann who has the information you need, or someone else on my staff, but I'll accept any question you ask on that matter."

"Do I need a lawyer involved in any of this?"

"Not regarding the pardon. It's a finished fact. Arrangements for the next six months are all a gift. You'll never see a bill or be asked to sign anything. Accepting what's being offered will not create an implied obligation to the FBI or anyone else.

"I can recommend my personal attorney if you would like advice on who might best serve your personal needs. Or you may know of someone yourself. You'll have legal avenues of redress for the past six years available to you. When you're ready to explore those questions, we will provide the full case materials to the lawyer of your choice, so you can be advised on how best to proceed in your situation."

There was a tap on the door, and Ann answered it. She came back with a neatly folded light yellow sports shirt and black athletic pants. "These are definitely temporary. We'll stop at the mall by the airport so you can pick out better travel clothes and a few essentials. We'll seriously shop for summer clothes once we're on the island. Your friends will be here shortly. If you're comfortable with my doing so, I'll pack your things here while you visit with them. Or you can ask one of them to do that for you."

"You don't mind?"

"Consider it one of the perks. We'll leave after you talk with your friends. Why don't you get changed? Makeup is in my bag; there's a mirror with the cosmetics. They'll have your medical paperwork and some documents for Paul to sign. He'll get that done while I'm bringing your things."

Janelle hesitated, then opened Ann's purse and took out the makeup. "Thanks for sharing this."

"I'm glad I'm able to do so."

Janelle headed to the restroom with the clothing. Paul watched her go, seeing a relaxed stride that hadn't been there when she first entered the chapel. The physical strain seemed to be fading. He hoped the mental shift would grab hold as well, so she could walk out of here on her way to *feeling* free also. They could point the way, but it rested on Janelle's ability to adjust and take that path herself. He turned back to Ann. "Ask the warden's aide to escort you and carry the boxes."

"I will. I've been in this prison before. Give me an hour, though I'll do my best to be back in forty-five. Anything else we need to do?"

"Find her a non-prison-issue coat and some decent gloves. I'll have a further conversation with the warden about the additional material Greg asked to see."

"That hanging bag you carried to the car is an extra coat of mine. I didn't want to mention it until I saw if there was a chance we might share a coat size. It will be short for her, but short's in style. There's an extra pair of leather gloves in the pocket."

"Good, thanks." Paul slipped into his jacket in preparation for a final conversation with the warden. They heard voices approaching—Janelle's friends were being escorted over. The warden's aide stepped in, and Ann went with him to pack Janelle's belongings.

Paul thought it had gone remarkably well thus far. Janelle was showing mostly controlled emotions, which didn't surprise him. She'd break down soon—the uncontrolled tears, the relief overwhelming her, but probably in the privacy of her room tonight, once she was outside these walls, when the reality that she was free truly sank in.

The reaction of her friends, those not walking out of jail today, was going to be a different matter and would likely range from envy to despair, all of it conveyed in high emotions. Janelle was crossing the chapel, looking neat and heading toward very attractive. "Getting hungry?" he asked. "For a late lunch, I saw Italian, Mexican, and a decent steak place by the airport, if you have a preference."

"A decent steak sounds very nice."

Paul nodded to the group of women arriving with two corrections officers and looked toward Janelle. "I'll step out unless you would like me to stay."

She glanced toward the officers. "They'll be staying, so come and go as you like. An hour okay?"

"An hour is fine," Paul replied. "I'll make arrangements for us to go then."

"Go?" several of them said.

"Janelle?" came from others.

She looked to her friends. "I've got news."

SIX

ANN FALCON

THE CELL WAS SMALL—TWO BEDS with thin mattresses, two narrow writing surfaces and attached solid chairs, narrow shelves on opposite walls, a toilet and sink. Ann set two packing boxes on the side that was Janelle's. The wall of photos on the other side of the cell displayed a woman with two daughters. Ann assumed the cellmate was one of the friends Janelle had requested join her in the chapel.

Janelle had a single photo of her parents taped to the wall over the desk, plus a collection of twelve calendar images, large flowers, on her bedside wall. Her belongings on the shelf consisted of a gardening book from the prison library, toiletries, a worn Bible with her name on the cover, two notebooks, and a plastic-sided expanding folder labeled *Attorney*. Even aware of what life was like when minimal things were the norm, this wasn't much. Ann carefully took down the parents photo and placed it inside the Bible for safekeeping.

"It's true? She's out of here?"

It was the lunch hour for this wing of the prison and relatively quiet, with most of the women still in the dining hall. Ann removed a calendar picture before glancing over. A woman significantly older than Janelle, who looked as if all of life had been hard on her, stood by the door. Ann smiled. A paper bracelet on her wrist was braided together with alternating white-and-blue strands. "Yes, she is."

"She always said she was innocent. After a while you started to believe her."

"You've known Janelle for a while?"

The woman shrugged. "I know everyone in this wing. I'm in for life. I figure 'knowing people' is my entertainment. Everyone eventually talks to me just to stop me asking questions. My cell is three doors down, so we're neighbors of a sort." She leaned against the door's bars, watching Ann pack. Ann didn't volunteer further information, knowing the rhythm that worked best with a sociable woman like this.

"She said a robber did it, killed her boyfriend," the woman mentioned. "They had a fight at a beach. He wants to break up before he goes back to college. She leaves him there, and he ends up dead. Nearly did her in to know the last words they hurled at each other were angry shouts. She'd give about anything to be able to apologize to him for calling him a 'selfish, no-good, small-hearted man who's throwing away the person who loves him most in the world, so he can go play the field at college hoping to find someone prettier, wealthier, and of bluer blood.'"

Ann looked over, surprised, and the woman smiled. "Pretty much a word-for-word quote. She wants whoever stole his wallet, phone, and ring, then left him there to die, to face real justice someday. She prayed for that often enough, you figure God might do it just to have her quit asking."

"Thanks." Ann offered her hand. "Ann Falcon."

The woman held out her own. "Louise Amber."

"She received a pardon from the governor because we believe something like that did happen."

Louise paused for a sucked-in breath, then offered a soft, "Good for her."

Ann stacked Janelle's items from the shelf into the second box. "Are you innocent of whatever landed you here?"

"Naw, I robbed a liquor store. Wanted a bottle of scotch, couldn't afford it, figured they had plenty and I'd been a customer long enough that they ought to give me one, plus some of my cash back. Wore a ski mask, but hey, my voice, not hard to pick me out. They told the cops my name. I was just drunk enough to be extra stupid that night. I would have been five years and out, but I took an unloaded gun, had two other robberies on my sheet, and three felonies made it forever. Can't say I like the in-for-life part, but I'm sober for the first time in my life and that's marginally refreshing. I got two girls, and they come visit now that I don't smell like a distillery and constantly nag on them."

Ann offered her card. "You remember, or hear from others, any other details Janelle mentioned about that night, I'd appreciate a call."

"I'll pass the word. Got anything else I can pass on that's interesting news?"

Ann didn't mind feeding the in-house grapevine. "The rumor from the governor's office is that this prison is getting a cosmetology and beautician training school come first of the year, twenty students every six months, chosen from those within two years of their release dates. You'll be able to sign up for an appointment with the stylist of your choice. Driving in, I saw electrician trucks over at the building that houses the library, so I assume it's being set up there. The dog-training area is going to expand to forty-five dogs with puppies allowed inside the A wing. And the community garden is expanding to allow anyone who would like one to have a garden plot of their own."

"Someone likes us."

"The prior warden from Wayforth is on the governor's advisory staff. I saw her briefly, and she's of a mind that you do more of what's working in as many places as you can implement the ideas."

Ann picked up the two boxes. "Have I missed anything?"

Louise looked around after Ann stepped out. "You've got her whole life in those boxes. She really was innocent?"

Ann understood the emotion. "The toughest break of all—to not be believed when you tell the truth."

"I hear you. Wish her good luck from me."

"I'll do that, Louise."

Ann let the warden's aide carry the boxes as they walked back through the prison halls.

"Can I ask you something?" he asked when they were nearing the chapel.

"Sure."

"How do you tell the difference between someone who's innocent and those ones who just say they are?"

"Find the murder weapon in someone else's possession."

He stopped for a moment to look at her. "Thanks. I was thinking there was some magic formula I was missing."

"Just experience. I've worked a lot of crimes, and this one was wrong from a couple of different angles, but it was where the murder weapon was found that changed the outcome. My advice, treat everyone with decent courtesy, and listen. Odds are good you'll deal with another actually innocent person in your career. You find a story that catches your attention, go look at the public record of the trial, convince yourself one way or another about the matter. If you put in the time to free a wrongly convicted person, you'll do some serious good." She paused and grinned. "Besides, it never hurts to have the governor know your name."

He chuckled and nodded. "There's a point to that."

"I personally see things through a spiritual lens when a string of unusual events come together like this. I think she's a Christian that God arranged to vindicate in His own time and way. I bought a box at auction that had the murder weapon inside."

The aide gave her a second look. "How much did you spend?"

"Seventeen dollars."

"I'm not a religious man, but I'll agree that woman had someone watching out for her."

Ann paused outside the chapel door. "We should be ready to leave in about ten minutes, if you can hang around and walk us out."

"The warden is going to want that pleasure, but I'll trail behind you with the boxes."

"Appreciate that." Ann opened the door on a group hug, tears flowing. She glanced over at Paul, who was leaning against the counter, and recognized the look of a man in some pain behind the polite expression. There were seven women gathered in the chapel, most of them crying. Ann moved to him and slid her hand in his. "I see I missed some fireworks."

"One of them fainted, a couple screamed, three tried a chant, 'I want out too.' Envy—not surprising—seems to be the word of the day. Janelle has been giving advice and bucking people up: 'Finish that GED. Quit choosing loser boyfriends. Apologize to your sister. Talk to the chaplain.' Like that. I've caught a couple of hints that she's desperate to get out of here now but feels guilty walking out when her friends have to stay behind. We were just waiting on you to get back." He nodded to the file beside him. "I've got everything Greg asked for ready to go with us."

"Okay. I'll handle it from here." Ann moved over to the huddle, caught Janelle's attention. Janelle eased herself back, and Ann softly whispered, "There's a bag of farewell gifts in

Paul's briefcase. Go take a look, find something that suits each person."

She got an expression of deep relief, and Janelle walked over to the pew, opened the case, lifted out a blue sack. She carefully looked at options, chose gifts, and came back to the group. She gave a gift, a hug, and said individual goodbyes, then wiped her own tears before she picked up the briefcase Ann gave her. With a last nod goodbye to the group, she headed toward the door. And her friends let her go.

The warden escorted them out through the prison. Ann walked beside Janelle, watched her breathing catch and her hand tighten nearly white on the briefcase handle. Though the pardon papers said she was already free, the walk out of the prison was when it became real. The garment bag they'd brought was hanging on the coatrack inside the administrative entrance doors. Ann unzipped it, held out the coat. "One of mine. It's short for you, but you'll need it only for a few hours. Greg says the weather there is seventy-eight and sunny."

Janelle slipped it on with a "Thanks" and a wobbly smile. The gloves fit. Ann grabbed her own coat while Paul held the door for them. The warden led them to the guest parking area. His aide stored Janelle's boxes in the trunk. Handshakes in the cold were quick; everything had already been said. Janelle settled in the back seat while Ann took the front passenger seat.

As they drove out through the gate of the prison, Ann heard a quietly whispered "Thank you, God" from the back seat. She reached for her husband's hand and gave it a quick squeeze.

SEVEN

GREGORY TATE

GREG WATCHED ANN MAKE a smooth landing coming in west to east, reversing the airstrip's normal direction to suit the lighting rather than the wind. He strode toward the open hangar while the taxiing aircraft circled the runway, swung around into the hangar, and powered down its engines. Knowing close to the minute how long it would take Ann to work through the landing checklist before the aircraft's stairs came down, he didn't hurry.

What had once been a spacious Coast Guard air station before they moved flight operations to Florida had turned into a private airstrip for island residents. Greg removed his sunglasses as he entered the hangar, walked past his waiting SUV, and picked up wheel chocks from a nearby equipment rack. Ducking under the wing, he set the physical brakes, then moved around to the aircraft door. The small airfield was deserted but for the security officer and the fuel guy who would prep Ann's return flight. The quiet was welcome, suitable for the guest he was here to meet.

Ann's call this morning had interrupted his plan to spend the day deep-sea fishing in the Gulf. It wasn't the first time a favor for Ann had interrupted a vacation day and probably wouldn't be the last. So far in his life, Greg had never regretted agreeing to one of her requests, and this one sounded uniquely interesting. *Six years wrongly convicted* . . . that made for a long journey. He'd be able to help, he was confident of that.

The setting sun cast long shadows across the hangar floor. Berry Island off the Louisiana coast was basically a chunk of rock sticking up out of the Gulf of Mexico. One hugged by enough pulverized rock and shells, it seemed to float within a ring of wide, sandy beaches. There were a few lazy pelicans and other migrating birds, some turtles, but otherwise the island's chief claim to fame was the sun and sand. The wind here was a constant. He could feel the dryness in his eyes after spending the day on his deck, reading over the case materials Ann had emailed him.

The aircraft stairs gave a brief hydraulic hum as they engaged and lowered. Ann stepped out. Her smile bloomed. "You're looking particularly young and tanned today, Greg."

He laughed. "Tanned, I'll give you. Good to see you, friend." He hugged her in welcome and gave her an encompassing look. "Marriage agrees with you," he decided, for she looked even more relaxed than two years ago when she'd been here with Paul, still practically on their honeymoon.

"I'm loving every minute of it."

He glanced behind her to the doorway.

"Give her a minute. The landing woke her up. Hardly surprising, given the cabin is effectively soundproof and the last eight hours have been rolling stress."

"She's holding up?"

"Seems to be. The biggest surprise so far is the fact she still thinks Andrew's death was a robbery gone wrong."

"I got your text." They were going to have to break the news it had been something else, or rather *he* was. He would be walking Janelle through that truth sometime in the next few weeks. He would outline a strategy for that conversation with Ann after she took him through the full case file later tonight. "How about you finish your flight log, check the radar and weather for tomorrow, call Paul to let him know you've arrived, and give me some time with her? Janelle and I may as well get acquainted right here."

"Sure. I appreciate your taking on an emergency placement."

"What are friends for, if not situations like this?"

There was movement on the stairs behind her, and his arriving guest stepped out of the plane. Slender, athletic, hazel eyes, neatly trimmed bangs with the rest of her hair braided. The travel clothes she'd chosen for herself suited her. Nothing in his first impression gave him particular pause. He smiled and said, "Introduce me, Ann."

"Janelle Roberts, I'd like you to meet Greg Tate."

She accepted the hand he offered and shook it. "It's nice to meet you, Greg."

He saw polite wariness covering lingering exhaustion. The woman needed her life to stop moving, and that made his first decision on how to proceed with her a simple one. "Let's go for a walk, Janelle. Ann's got some flight details to finish up."

She glanced outside the hangar and nodded. Greg held out a spare ball cap as they left the building. "Not as effective as sunglasses, but you'll find yourself wearing a hat most of the time you're here."

"It's comfortably warm for this late in the day."

"Mid-seventies," he agreed. "Can you handle heights?" He pointed to the set of stairs that serviced the water tower. "The best view of the island is that first landing."

She changed course toward it.

The stairs took them up a story and a half. They couldn't see over the hangar roofs to the south, but the rest of the island was on display. She leaned against the metal railing, her gaze sweeping over the view. He leaned against the opposite railing, fished a couple of butterscotch candies out of his pocket, and unwrapped one. She glanced over at the sound of the cellophane, and he held out the other piece. She accepted it.

"That's my place," he indicated with a nod, spotting it for her to the west. "The oval track where we race go-carts, the horse barns beyond. The main house is just beyond that ridge with a view down toward the beach."

"Ann didn't mention horses."

"A recent addition." He tucked the cellophane wrapper into his pocket. After six years in prison, he doubted she'd spend more than a handful of hours inside over the next month, so he mentioned next, "You'll find there are a number of basic things to do on the island: bike riding, hiking, spending time on the beach or in the water, and boating. For my guests, add the go-carts and the horses to that list. If you don't know how to ride, I'll teach you. If you don't know how to spin out on a go-cart, I'll teach you this too—so it will be a fair race."

She looked at him and nearly laughed. "That sounds ideal."

He liked how her smile changed her face. Not relaxed yet, that smile, but on the way to being natural. "There will be full days spent just working through the list." He wanted to get her up on a horse soon, let her enjoy the unique freedom that riding offered.

He weighed how to word a request, then simply said, "Give me three hours."

Janelle glanced over, surprised.

"Ann and Paul have already hit you with a lot of changes today. But there's another waterfall of information I need to give you—about this place, about me—and then your world will truly, finally, stop moving. Give me three hours."

Janelle hesitated before she answered, "The nap during the flight helped. I can listen. But I don't think I have the capacity to be making any more major decisions today."

"Good," Greg agreed, "that works. Because I've pretty much been making all the decisions for you. Tomorrow, next week, you can tell me which ones I've made that you prefer be changed to something else."

She blinked and gave him a more alive smile. "That I can live with," Janelle said. "Okay. Three hours. I'll hold you to that."

"I'd like to give you a high-level sense of where you've landed, and then who you have landed with. The stress you're experiencing will stop forming once you have enough answers that your world returns to being something stable." He sounded more like a doctor than he would prefer with that remark, but she simply nodded and let it pass without comment. He nodded to the view. "So, let's start with this place."

He'd introduced the island to a lot of guests, and did so now for Janelle. "One hundred eighty-seven people live on this island year-round. On a typical day, there can be an additional five to six hundred guests, out enjoying the sun and the sand. To say we care about them is an understatement—they're most of our economy."

"I can imagine."

He smiled. "The faces change, but the routine is constant. People come, enjoy themselves, then head home. We islanders quickly reset for the next incoming wave of people, trying to give them all a good experience. The island caters mostly to day tourists, with some guests staying for a handful of days at our two local hotels. We're not really the two-week vacation kind of place, though there are a number of weekly and monthly rentals available.

"The east side of the island facing Florida is mostly condos with walks out onto the beach. The south side facing the Gulf would be considered the expensive side and has about twenty homes total. The west side gives the best views, but building there is tough, like drilling into solid granite, so my neighbors are rather sparse and clustered into pockets."

"You've lived here for a while?" she asked.

"Thirteen years now. My father settled here ten years before that." He looked to the north. "There's one town on the island, and you can see about eighty percent of it from here. Nice shops—clothing and gifts, a good florist, a few cafés. I own three of the restaurants, some of the food trucks that work the public beaches, and that ferry you see now crossing from the mainland back to the island. Consider me an accidental businessman. Islanders want to retire and move to the mainland, they ask me if I want to purchase their businesses, and I've been in a position to say yes. I can run a balance sheet, and I enjoy good food, but the rest I leave to excellent managers. The businesses are not my main career. The docks to the east of that ferry landing are always a busy place—a lot of fishing charters go out daily, and it's a popular mooring for sailboats."

"You sail?"

"Some. I prefer to fly. Hangar four there is mine." He pointed. She glanced at him at the comment, but he chose not to expand on it yet. "I'll introduce you to friends who love to sail, though, and also the best charter boat captains. If you want to spend most of your days on the water, it's easily arranged."

"Thanks. I haven't been on a boat in a very long time. It sounds freeing."

"And I think you'd enjoy the adventure of it."

The sunset was turning the beaches golden, showing off the island at its finest. "The public beaches on the north side of the island are the prime tourist destinations," he mentioned, "as you can walk out in the water for thirty feet with your feet still touching the sandy bottom. The shallow water warms up in the sunlight and stays comfortable year-round. The rest of the island is mostly private beaches with varying levels of drop-offs and, in some cases, persistent riptides.

"I wanted you to see the island as a whole, so when I say you can go exploring and not get lost, I mean it. The landmass is about twenty square miles. The rocky cliffs deserve your respect, and the hiking trails will challenge your endurance. You might get yourself a twisted ankle, or take a bad fall, but you really can't get lost."

"It does help to see it all from up here."

"Got a phone on you?"

She nodded.

"Dig it out and put my number in it. We get decent cell reception across the island."

He gave her his cell number, then added hers to his phone's contacts.

"The road circling the island is filled with hills and turns and offers some spectacular scenery. There are all sorts of different bikes to rent—beach cruisers, road bikes, or mountain bikes depending on your destination. But golf carts are the favored choice here, for island residents and tourists alike. In fact, I inherited from my father the golf-cart business as well as the ferry. And that ends my introduction to the island. Have any questions about the place I can answer for you, Janelle?"

"Could you show me one of the beaches while it's still light enough to walk on the sand?"

He checked the position of the sun, calculated they had about thirty minutes of light left. "Sure. I can do that easily enough. You'll enjoy the sunset."

||||||||||

Greg parked in front of his place. His house was well lit, as was the companion place just beyond it. He quickly stepped out and opened Janelle's door before she could do so, determined to begin changing her perception of herself with the return of small courtesies. Ann exited the vehicle on the other side, caught his gaze, and silently mouthed *Tell her*. There were two ways to play this evening, and Ann was indicating the harder path. *Interesting.* He would have thought she'd prefer to leave those details until tomorrow. He gave her a slight nod, willing to trust her judgment.

As Janelle stepped out of the SUV, he casually said, "Ann, dinner is arriving in about ten minutes. Catch that for us, would you? It's already on my tab. The house is unlocked. I'm going to show Janelle the path to the beach while there's still light. Then I'll get the boxes and luggage unloaded."

"Sure." Ann headed up the walk.

Greg pulled two flashlights from under the front seat and handed one to Janelle. "Just a precaution. It's not far." He pointed to where the sunset was now saturating the horizon and led the way. The beach was a three-minute walk along a path that gradually dropped toward the sea, then took one last steeper decline to the sand.

He wasn't surprised at Janelle's silence as they walked. She would have too many things going on in her mind right now to have the bandwidth to offer casual conversation. Greg filled in the silence simply to get her accustomed to the sound of his voice. "You'll want to get in the habit of picking up a flashlight if you head out in the evening. Nights on the island are like a thick, tangible darkness. What you get in compensation is a sky filled with bright stars."

"All right, I'll remember."

Twilight was descending even as the clouds overhead shifted toward a brilliant hot pink. Janelle momentarily stopped to gaze up at the color change. "Wow."

Greg chuckled. "The sunsets are one reason why you want to live here."

He clicked on his flashlight, and Janelle followed suit. The sound of water lapping ashore signaled that they were approaching the final descent to the beach. "You'll want to use the handrail I put in for this steep turn ahead." He led the way down, took the bend, and suddenly they were on the beach.

Janelle stopped, startled. "This is a really nice stretch of sand."

"Right at eighty yards," he replied with a smile, "and very private."

She immediately removed her shoes and began walking barefoot across the sand toward the water, letting the next wave lap across her toes. "It's warm!"

"Probably a few degrees warmer than the air," he agreed. "The Gulf waters hold on to the sun's heat." He could see her joy as she strolled along in ankle-deep water. "Can you swim? Be honest."

"Like a duck," she reassured. "The first item on my shopping list is a swimsuit. I love your beach. I could easily spend a month just listening to the water come ashore."

"Then I'm delighted to share it with you. You'll see turtles along here, crabs, driftwood after storms, the occasional starfish. I swim for a couple of hours most days. It's the clearest water you'll ever experience, like a highly filtered pristine sea."

"Thanks for bringing me down here tonight." She spotted a nearly intact shell with her flashlight and dug it out of the wet sand.

"Glad to oblige." Given her delight with the warm water, it was time for safety information. He pointed his flashlight out across the waves. "That big circle dial with the arrow is mounted on a floating buoy about fifty yards out. It indicates the strongest riptides measured in the prior hour. If the arrow is in the red zone, stay out of the water. If in the yellow zone, stay nearer to shore and on this side of the buoy. Green, you're safe to swim out a distance beyond it. When you're swimming, keep a general sense of that dial. The arrow starts to rise, you'll want to move in."

"That's useful, thanks."

"These dials are on all the island beaches. They've protected people and saved a lot of lives since they were installed about twenty-five years ago," he added. "Swimming is sunup to sundown, and lifeguards enforce it on the public beaches. I do the same here. We don't have much in the way of sharks in these waters—they favor being west of here—nor many stingrays or jellyfish. Still, you'll be wise to treat it as the sea it is and stay aware of your surroundings. You don't treat the Gulf casually—in the dark, it's wet feet only."

"Agreed," she said with a nod.

He gestured with the flashlight to the north. "I've got a fire ring and benches down at that end, and a sand-colored storage bin with lounge chairs, beach umbrellas—the basics to get comfortable if you want something more than a tree trunk to sit on. You'll need to bring with you towels and water bottles, sunscreen, the book you want to enjoy. There are selections of backpacks and mini-coolers in my utility room, cold packs in the freezer, to make it easier to haul stuff around."

He walked farther along the sand and took a seat on his favorite fallen tree trunk. She didn't take a seat beside him, but he hadn't expected her to. She continued to stroll the meeting place of sand and water. The sea was calm tonight, mild in its mood.

"It's helpful, seeing this beach," she called over to him. "This could have waited until tomorrow, but it's going to be nice having a different beach in my head tonight than the one that has haunted me for the last six years."

"Copy that," he replied calmly, and simply watched her enjoy walking the beach. She returned his direction after about ten minutes.

He aimed his flashlight toward the path up to the house. "See the handrail for going back up that incline?"

"Yes."

"Then I'm going to tell you something and I'd like you to just listen for a few minutes. If you decide you don't want to continue the conversation, there's the exit. I won't follow after you. I figure you can find the way without a problem from here." She stopped about eight feet away, but her gaze was on him.

"You asked during the drive from the airfield if I often have guests. Like I said, I do. I'm a doctor, Janelle. The PhD kind. I specialize in helping people deal with injuries to their minds. You're here to safely get acclimated back to freedom, to debrief what happened, and for me to help you fix what got damaged."

"I knew there was a catch—I just didn't see what it was. So you're a shrink."

He smiled at her shrewd tone. "Ann doesn't do anything without a few layers of reasons to it. I'm not a man in a hurry. We can talk tomorrow, or we can talk a few weeks from now. You've got stuff in your mind that's going to give you problems in the future if it's not sorted out. I can help. I've seen some of what you're dealing with firsthand."

He'd already noticed her glance at the scar on his arm. "I come with a pretty good story of my own. I'm a former military pilot and, for what it's worth, a Medal of Honor recipient. I flew close-air-support gunships, got shot down in Afghanistan, spent nine months in a prison on the Pakistan side of the border before people realized I was still alive. There isn't much you can tell me about incarceration that I can't personally relate to. The sounds, the uncertainty, the chaos of ending up there. It was burning aviation fuel, by the way, that caused most of the scars. It's why you'll normally see me swimming with a shirt on."

"I'm sorry to hear that, and I apologize for my 'shrink' comment."

He nodded, smiled briefly. "Appreciated—both the apology and the sympathy. In my mind it all happened eons ago, about fourteen years in actual fact. But I do speak from personal knowledge when I say the details can fade with time. My job is to apply what I know to make sure you walk away from what happened in good shape."

She sat down on the other end of the log. "Why make a big deal of this? Why someone with your level of expertise? I was convicted of something I didn't do; I'm now pardoned and free of it. There's going to be a transition period to get back some kind of a life—I get that. But I'm not particularly damaged. I'm in good health, and once I establish a job somewhere, it's not going to take long to reacquire a decent life."

He couldn't help but smile. "Janelle, that confidence is good, but the reality is you don't know yet what shape you're in, or where your head is at, or what you most need. In these first days, you're going to decompress. Your emotions are going to occasionally feel like they're shaking you apart, and other times you'll wonder if you'll ever feel anything again. It's your shattered nerves shaking off six years of stress. You're going to get the reaction from your body in whatever form it decides to take. Don't fight it, just let it pass. It's part of the process."

"That bad?"

"It will pass," he repeated. "Freedom is a process. I understand that better than anyone you'll likely ever meet. Think of me as your safety valve, your road map. I'll get you there, so that when you do leave this island, you'll truly be in good shape." The first stars were appearing. He stood to change the subject. "Why don't we head back?"

Janelle slipped on her socks and tennis shoes and walked with him. He wasn't surprised when she retreated again to silence. He eventually said, "I read some of the trial transcript this afternoon. It's your belief that Andrew was killed in a robbery that night. You still hold to that?" He turned her way.

"Yes." She gave him a quick glance.

He nodded thoughtfully. "The pardon, the reason for it, will add some details to what you know, and the truth you're going to hear will be hard to accept. The timing of those conversations is part of what we'll be sorting out, Janelle. Ann and Paul are working the case as investigators. I'm the neutral party who will help you move through the discovery process safely so it doesn't overwhelm you.

"We all want you to recover smoothly. But you're going to have to trust people you've just met, have confidence in their judgment—that is all part of the process too. So I would ask one thing from you now. Don't call old friends or communicate with people from your life before or talk to the press—not until you've had some time to acclimate and have heard what you need to know about the research that resulted in your pardon."

"Ann was stressing that point too but in a more subtle way. Why?"

"How various individuals react to news of your pardon can tell investigators more information than they had before, and right now they have some people they are watching very closely. If you speak to people too soon, the conditions change. It's simply easier if you aren't one of the variables in these first few days."

Janelle nodded. "I can agree to that, although the reason has me puzzled."

"Thanks." Greg left the topic there. Ann's chief focus had shifted to figuring out how to hold Tanya accountable for Andrew's murder. But Janelle wasn't yet aware how this case was going to turn. Walking through the truth with her would be a challenge he would handle with great care when the time was right.

EIGHT

THE RETURN WALK FROM THE BEACH felt shorter, in part because they were walking toward lights. Greg pointed to a large building to the south of the main house, now dark. "A lot of my clients are recovering military veterans whose daily therapy includes physical workouts. That building houses a full gym, with weights, stationary equipment, a steam room, and a hot tub. On the east side you'll find outdoor gear—floating boards, bikes, hiking equipment. Consider all of it at your disposal. Dad built much of this for my own particular needs as I recovered."

"All right," she said.

Rather than enter the main house, he took the breezeway to the left toward the other home and its welcoming lights. "This is one of the guesthouses. I think you'll find it comfortable."

Greg unlocked the door, and they stepped inside. He watched Janelle as she took in the sight of vases full of fresh flowers, the smell of sugar cookies, the background holiday music playing, a Christmas tree twinkling with lights and its faint smell of pine. His estate manager, Amy Juette, had lovely ideas for making things welcoming for guests.

Greg noticed Janelle's tears, saw her hand fist in an unconscious motion to assert control and stop them, watched her smile to cover her reaction. It was a good sign, those sudden emotions that caught her off guard, even if she was still trying to suppress them.

"It's truly beautiful, Greg."

"You're getting Christmas a little early. Amy Juette, my estate manager, couldn't resist doing some shopping for you at her sister's boutique after Ann had sent her a size range. The boxes under the tree are some clothes that might suit the island. Feel free to exchange any or all of them; you aren't going to hurt their feelings. The two sisters simply love clothes, and shopping is Amy's Christmastime pleasure."

Tears did escape now. "Presents I can open early. Please, tell her thanks from me."

"I will," he promised. "I'll introduce you two later this week." Keeping his tone practical, he walked her through the short list of things that would bring this evening to a close. "Everything here is for your use—towels, soap, cosmetics, DVDs, board games, books—go ahead and explore every room, closet, and dresser drawer, and enjoy whatever you find helpful.

"In a three-ring binder on the kitchen counter you'll find photos and brief bios of the people you're likely to meet—some who work for me, others year-round residents."

He walked to the front window and pointed. "See that living room table lamp at my place?" She came to join him, nodded.

"When that light is on, I'm up, company is welcome. Feel free to come over and find me. There's no need to knock, just let yourself in and track me down. I'll either be somewhere around the property or down at the beach. If I've left a note, it will be on my kitchen counter." He held out the guesthouse key. "This is the last time I enter this house unless you invite me in. You deserve a place that is both private and yours when you aren't working with me. Think of this as a borrowed vacation home—which hopefully it's going to be for you."

She accepted the key. "Thanks again."

"Come back to the main house for a bit. I've one last thing to show you, and there's some dinner if you're hungry. I'll bring over your bag with the items you picked up at the mall earlier today. You can talk over any last details with Ann, and then you're on your own until you decide to show up tomorrow."

Janelle glanced around the place, hesitating to leave, then nodded.

||||||||||

Greg smiled at who was waiting for them outside his home. "I misspoke—I have *two* last things to show you." He knelt. "This is my dog Marco." He looked up at Janelle. "If you're allergic to dogs, tell me now. Marco has a friend he vacations with when I need to make this a dog-free property. It's not a problem—he loves it there."

"I'm good," she replied.

He rose so she could better see Marco. The dog was big, his coat solid white. "Then I need you to make a decision about him. If you just don't like dogs, or are neutral to the idea of one, I can give Marco a command to leave you alone and he will honor that. He'll basically ignore you forever like you're a cat person." Janelle smiled at the analogy. "If I don't wave him off," Greg continued, "he's going to consider you part of his family and routinely come find out what you are doing. Marco gravitates to guests—he figures they're a lot more interesting than me. He will keep you company if given a choice and tag along with whatever you're doing."

Janelle crouched down to greet him. "I like dogs. Actually, I've missed them a lot. Hello, Marco."

Greg watched the two of them as they checked each other out. When she found the spot to scratch on the back of his neck, Marco fell in love and tumbled on his side to offer his belly. Greg saw the first true smile from Janelle, one that wasn't shadowed. He figured one problem had just solved itself. These two would get along just fine.

"The large green storage box on the breezeway is his toy box with dozens of his favorites. And he loves to swim. We pretend he doesn't eat people food, but he runs around enough that it's not a problem. Whatever you want to share he'll be happy to wolf down—except green beans."

Janelle smiled, and with another scratch of Marco's belly, nodded and rose. "You've got a nice dog."

"He's been with me since he was a puppy. Early in my own therapy I needed a friend, one willing to walk with me everywhere. He's good about coming when you call his name, so if you want to take him on island jaunts with you, again, feel free. There's nothing on this island he doesn't enjoy, from being out on a boat to riding around in a golf cart. He's an indoors dog too, well trained to stay off the furniture, but comes and goes as he likes. He'll bark once at your door if he wants to come in or be let out."

Greg continued on through the breezeway and into his house, adding, "The only dogs permitted on the island are owned by residents. There are twenty-three total with a yearly fee of two hundred dollars each—an amount decided by those who don't own a dog. The dogs can be off-leash and are allowed on the beaches so long as they're with somebody. Your dog gets a bad reputation, you get a talking-to by the mayor and then have to keep your dog on a leash. So public peer pressure keeps all our dogs and their owners law-abiding. The cats are much more likely to misbehave."

Janelle laughed, and it was a nice sound. "Got it."

Greg led them down a hallway to the second door on the left, turned on lights. "This is my office. You may or may not ever see it again, depending on how you like the word *office* and how this space feels to you."

Removing the wall between two bedrooms had opened up the length, and adding large windows brought the flower garden into the visual space during the day. The room held sofas, wing-back chairs, side tables, and a desk that was shoved up against the wall, its top filled with papers mostly. Decorated by Amy, the room was softer in décor than his personal tastes would have chosen to do, yet the space suited working with clients and their loved ones.

Greg leaned back against the desk, and Marco sniffed at his shoes before stretching out on the carpet. Greg wasn't surprised that Janelle had stopped just inside the doorway. He watched the openness shown earlier while interacting with his dog turn now into cautious reserve. Her arms were unconsciously folded across her chest, her expression marked by uncertainty. He had expected just such a reaction. So far, Janelle wasn't giving him anything unexpected, though he knew she would do so eventually. No client was predictable really, but he hadn't yet discovered where or in what way Janelle would show herself as unique.

"The assumption is we talk," he mentioned lightly. "When, where, how long, and on what topic will depend mostly on what works for you. You're my only client at the moment. And I'm not an office-hours sort of person."

She walked over to study the photos on the wall, the degrees he'd framed—not out of vanity but because clients needed to have a frame of reference about him before opening up about their own lives. The Medal of Honor and its ceremonial photo wasn't on that wall for personal reasons, but many other milestones of his life and career were there on display.

Janelle stopped at his wedding photo, he in uniform, his bride in a beautiful white wedding dress of lace and satin. "Ann said you were married once."

"Melinda couldn't handle the nine months I was presumed

dead, the rehab after it, and left me to marry a guy she'd known since high school."

Janelle glanced over at him. "I'm sorry."

He nodded his acceptance of the quiet words. "There are home-front casualties of war too. Though it's both a happy and sad reminder of my past, I like that picture's image of the hope-filled dreamers we both were back then. I miss her. I've survived, I've let go of the pain of her leaving as the years have passed, and she's got a good husband. She's now in a good place too. But I do miss her. When I think about the past, it's Melinda versus those months in prison that comes to mind first these days."

Janelle nodded at that remark.

He scanned the photos, then looked over at her. "The last six years of your life have just begun the process of turning into history for you, your own wall of pictures. I'm going to help you work through the land mines of that process, sort it out, and close it well. Most of that happens as we simply talk together.

"Some people find this office and a set time a useful 'box' for those conversations. Others prefer the distraction of being elsewhere, talking around the fire ring on the beach at midnight, while lifting weights in the gym, or taking hikes around the island. More than a few clients preferred to start the discussion in one place and then let it continue unfolding through meals and walks and activities until we'd worked through everything. A general rule of thumb is that the more we talk, the faster the work gets done.

"I can tell you up front you're going to cry, get mad at me, probably storm out of a conversation or two. You aren't going to hurt my feelings when you do. I won't be handing out any demerit points, think less of you, or get angry in return. If you leave a discussion, my policy is I let you go, and we don't talk about anything related to that subject for at least four hours, and then only after we've talked through a safer topic first. I'll be calibrating that approach based on how you're interacting with me.

"My hope is you'll stay long enough that you're well on the way to being whole again. Truth is, not that many clients do." She glanced back at him, surprised. "They get stable enough they want to take a break, quit working on the hard issues, see how they do with life on their own. If you reach that point, I ask you to give me three more days. I'll wrap things up with an exit interview of sorts, then help you transition to wherever you want to go next."

She nodded. "Okay."

"My assumption is you'll be around the island for at least a few months. We'll talk when you wish to do so. You're my guest for as long as you'd like to be. There are six guest accommodations in this immediate area, and it's rare for them all to be full, even when families of clients have come in at my request."

"You had no clients when Ann called you. I interrupted your Christmas break?"

"I'm good at saying no, Janelle. Having you here suits me." He gave that a moment, then added, "When other clients do arrive, I simply alternate days so you'll know that on Tuesdays and Fridays I'm working with someone else. You'll cross paths occasionally with another client at the horse barn or the gym, but this place is large enough that it's not been a concern. If you ever do desire more privacy, the island is full of rentals to choose from, ranging from apartments in town to condos on the other side. I can arrange for your accommodations with a single phone call."

"I take it you own some of those rentals."

He smiled. "More than a few. Either way, you really are welcome here for as long as you would like to stay." He gave her a minute. "We okay?"

"Yes."

"Good." He looked at the time and calculated what was left to tell her. "Thanks for listening as you have. I asked for three hours, and we're going to be done with both the conversation items and dinner well before then."

"Information is leaking out of my brain," she admitted.

Greg chuckled at the image. "You'll be amazed at what you still remember tomorrow. The last thing I have is a few general guidelines you need to know tonight.

"The first is this: call me for any reason, twenty-four seven. I don't care if you simply have insomnia, I want the call. If you're someone who likes to talk all the time, that's on me, I'll adjust and cope. You'd be one of those clients who figures things out by saying it aloud. My job becomes remarkably easy if you happen to be one of them." He caught her brief smile. "I'm going to wager a guess that's not going to be you." She fully smiled as she shook her head. "That's a shame. But seriously, Janelle, call me. You won't be imposing. Not every conversation is therapy—I'm good with small talk too. Which is useful to me in its own way, as it lets me know you've relaxed enough just to chat.

"The refrigerator in the guesthouse is well stocked. I also keep a well-stocked refrigerator and pantry in this main house and will learn your tastes. Feel free to eat and drink whatever appeals to you. It's appropriate to consider this an open kitchen. Fix meals in my kitchen rather than yours if you like—this one has more pots and pans and gadgets than the ones in the guesthouses—just expect to share if you do. I occasionally put a red *Mine* sticker on fried-rice leftovers, otherwise I'm a sharing kind of guy.

"I like company. If you want to hang out and watch a movie, bring a book over to read, or just be over here so you're not alone, you're welcome to do that. If we can become friends during this process, that's a good milestone. You'll find I'm more than willing to meet you halfway.

"And a final point. I love to fly. We'll be making day trips together as far as the Grand Canyon when the sights around here become routine." He smiled at her change in expression. "You'll find me throwing curve balls into our conversations occasionally, and that one was to judge your capacity to absorb more change. Don't worry, I fully expected that mental freeze you just showed me. We won't be going anywhere until well into next year. I'm not someone who likes crowds, but I do love to fly. I'll head up to Nashville for the day, over to Miami, or more recently I've been heading west so I can explore the Badlands. I'm open to suggestions if there's somewhere you'd like to visit.

"And with that, the dump of info hitting you comes to a close. The waterfall is shutting off. There's no more stuff to absorb from Ann, Paul, or myself. Life is going to stop moving now."

"It's all been . . . overwhelming, and so totally unexpected."

"Sleep on it, Janelle. Defer judgment on what Ann arranged. If you decide this isn't for you, I'm not going to take it personally. We'll figure something else out. I'm an adaptable guy." He opened a desk drawer and retrieved a gift-wrapped package, held it out. "One who did also, however, get you a welcome gift."

She hesitated before reaching out to accept it, not sure how to react, and carefully unwrapped it. The reference Bible was leather-bound, new.

"Ann mentioned you had a Bible among your belongings, one that no doubt reflects the last six years. God will be giving you new verses to underline, new notes to make, focused on how to deal with your freedom and what comes next in your life. Use both Bibles for a while. You'll find the contrast interesting a decade from now, reflecting on these two periods of your life."

"Thanks. It's a thoughtful gift."

"God is the best Counselor I know." He gave her a minute before turning practical again. "You get space from me from this point on. Ann leaves tomorrow midday if you have questions for her. My recommendation for tonight, do whatever suits you. You want to spend the entire night on the beach watching the stars, enjoy yourself. Marco will tag along. You want a movie marathon and want company, hang out here and I'll make the popcorn. You want to sleep for twenty-four hours, I'll see you when I see you."

"You set a nice welcoming stage."

"Can you handle it?"

"Yes." Her hands tightened around the gift Bible. "Actually, I can. I want some dinner, then I'm going to explore the guesthouse and try on clothes. Will it be a problem if I walk over to the barn later?"

"Take Marco, and a bunch of carrots or apples," he recommended. "The painted pinto is Marco's favorite. Three cats hang around the barn, so if you see unexpected motion, it's likely one of them.

"Security on the property already has your name and photo. Mike is on duty tonight; his photo and particulars are in the binder on your kitchen counter. You'll also find keys to the gym there, and a Tate courtesy card. Show the card at any business on the island rather than spend down your cash. It will be honored just like any major credit card would be. Ferry trips, meals, shopping—your stay is covered, Janelle."

"Someone is being very generous."

"They aren't afraid you'll take advantage of the offer— they're afraid you won't use it. Seriously, the financing of the next six months shouldn't be part of your concerns. You'll never see a bill. Settle in, deal with life, then turn and look at the future you want. There's time to think it all through."

"Okay." She turned to the office door. "It's a nice room, but I think you're right. I'm going to be fine with never seeing it again."

He laughed. "Thank you. I prefer our conversations happen elsewhere too."

Greg followed Janelle out and then shut off the lights, feeling mostly relief. He was ready to find Ann and get some dinner himself, then deal with the fact he still had about four hours of work ahead of him.

Ann would be giving him a crash course through the case file tonight. It was easy to sympathize with Janelle at the moment. He was about to face an information waterfall of his own. He'd likely feel as if the info was leaking out of his brain too before Ann was done.

NINE

THE NEXT DAY, Greg watched from the kitchen doorway as Janelle neatly tucked pie dough in a glass pie plate, filled it with sliced apples and cinnamon sugar, dotted it with butter, latticed the top dough, fluted the edges—practiced hands doing what her brain directed while he very much doubted her thoughts were anywhere near her pie making. She was the picture of a woman lost in thought—either unaware she'd had company join her, which was unlikely, or she was determined not to react as she would have in prison. She wore a flowered shirt and light-blue slacks, and her expression was peaceful. She pulled a second pie plate over.

"An interesting choice for your first morning," he noted, circling the counter.

She glanced over. "I thought I'd send a pie home with Ann to share with Paul, and since I'm making them one, I decided I'd make you one too." She neatly set in the rolled dough. "I thought I might have lost my touch. We'll see."

He laughed. "I'll be glad to judge the outcome."

"Your kitchen made more sense than the guesthouse. Plus I need to talk to Ann while these bake."

"My kitchen is yours. Especially when it serves up an apple

pie." He opened the refrigerator to check out snack options. He'd been on the beach for a swim at dawn, and his appetite spiked midmorning.

"Would you prefer cherry?"

His groan was theatrical. "You're killing me here, Janelle. But apple beats out cherry by, say, two whiskers."

"Then I'll make you both."

He picked out a cluster of washed white grapes. "Start with one, next week another. It can be like food therapy. You bake, I help you eat."

"All right."

"Sleep okay?"

She shrugged. "So-so, but that's fine. Too much quiet, too soft a bed, too much to think about. Those hours—it was the best night of 'not sleeping' I've had in years."

He smiled at her phrasing, the doctor in him glad to see she was already beginning to thrive. A few days like this would help temper the inevitably hard days ahead.

He had interesting guests every year, but it had been a while since he'd had a naturally inclined baker around. "The grocery list is on the side of the refrigerator. Fill it in with whatever I'm missing that you need."

"What are the odds I can get decent chocolate on this island?"

He ate more of the grapes, tapped his finger on his shirt. "Pilot. I'll fly it in. Just be specific and print so I can read your handwriting."

She grinned. "This could come in handy."

"As long as you're willing to share your creations, you've got a willing gofer." Ann joined them, and Greg beamed at her. "We're getting pies, thanks to you, so nice goin'. Weather still holding?"

"If I take off before two o'clock, I should be in the clear. And my pie is getting its own seat on the flight home. Paul is going to love homemade dessert tonight." She helped herself to some of his grapes. "We're going to hit the shops after the pies come out of the oven, look for swimsuits and other things. You want to come with us?"

"Shopping? No thanks. I'm taking Marco for a swim in place of his bath. He'll semi-tolerate the freshwater shower afterwards." He glanced around. "Where is he, by the way?"

"I gave him the ham bone," Janelle answered. "It was small, he was pleading, so I hope that was okay. He grabbed it and vanished toward the barn."

"He can have whatever he can mooch. We're having ham?"

"Scalloped potatoes, ham, corn casserole, and fresh rolls. I want my own home-cooked meal, and I thought I'd make enough to share. A pie deserves a first course."

"I'm already enjoying it just hearing the menu." The three laughed, and Ann tugged at his sleeve.

"I'll get him out of your hair for twenty minutes, Janelle," she said, "while you finish up here. Come on, Greg. We need to take a walk and figure out a strategy for the news media."

"I want to avoid any news for now," Janelle offered at his questioning glance, "and all comments, please, from your friends who might recognize my name."

"Got it. I'd want the same," he reassured her. He worked hard to give his guests anonymity when they needed it, and his employees and friends honored that request.

At Ann's nudge they left Janelle to complete work on the pies. He slipped on his sunglasses as they headed outside. "She's in the kitchen on her first morning. I am going to be a well-fed man," he commented. "Good for her and good for me." He turned to Ann. "What's the real topic?"

"Tanya learned about the pardon late yesterday afternoon. She's quoted in a breaking-news article on the *Chicago Tribune* website as pleased her friend has been cleared of this crime, and she hopes law enforcement will be able to use the newly discovered evidence to locate and arrest the man who robbed and murdered her brother."

"She's telling the same story Janelle believes. That's intriguing on quite a few levels."

"Paul put out a statement that the FBI requested the pardon based on further evidence, and that the matter of Andrew Chadwick's death was now an active investigation by state and federal authorities. Nothing is out there yet regarding what the new evidence is, and we'll try to keep it that way."

"Tanya's going to be frantic for information."

Ann nodded. "I've been tracking some of those moves already. She's reached out to Janelle's trial attorney, the governor's office, and she tried to reach the pardon attorney. We can assume that Tanya's also been contacting mutual friends of Janelle, looking for information on where she might be. No one has that answer, and as long as Janelle herself doesn't call anyone, there won't be."

"How well disguised was your flight here?"

"I played some sleight of hand. A good reporter may put the dots together as far as Kentucky. But it would take a *great* reporter to figure out the redirect past there."

"You do like your skullduggery, Ann." He couldn't help but chuckle.

She shrugged. "I've been doing this a long time. You can try to stay dark, but that only causes people to dig harder. It's better to let people think they've found the answer. Once you discover the plane I'm flying and the airport I flew out of, you pull the flight plan. Except—oops—I filed a flight plan for Pennsylvania and didn't amend it until I was ready to take off. The amended flight plan, being verbal, was entered real time, which puts it in another system. Most reporters will stop at the flight plan. A smart reporter asks if there's an amended flight plan. That inquiry would get back a more limited entry, but enough to know my destination airport. So a reporter asking for an amended flight plan will be heading for Kentucky right now."

Greg followed her logic through and started laughing. "You called from the air with a change of plans, verbally filing a second amended flight plan?"

Ann grinned. "Every time I switched air-traffic-control grids, I was talking to a new region and verbally filed an amended flight plan. All routine entries that happen every day. But only a pilot would think to unravel my flight by checking each region. And since I was being paranoid, I touched down briefly at two of the amended airports, so the question remains as to where I actually dropped my passenger."

"Your flight here is well covered," he agreed. "What about the flight home?"

"The owner would like his plane left in Indiana. I'll borrow another plane for the last leg into Chicago. I'll amend flight plans for each leg of the trip to obscure it further."

"Okay, if Janelle gets 'found,' it'll be because she calls someone, gives out that information herself, or someone on the island recognizes her from news about the pardon and gets chatty about it on social media."

"Pretty much. I'll teach her the basics of looking different before we go shopping today, and I predict she'll be a quick study. It's amazing what a hat, sunglasses, and a change in hairstyle can do. She won't look like Janelle to the casual glance. All the media has is a nearly seven-year-old photo from the trial. A few days in the sun adding a tan, and the comparison will move even further apart."

"We'll leave it unsaid, but the fallback is always a flight out of here with either you or me, and Janelle gets tucked somewhere in Arizona or Nevada under a different name."

"A very good point, Greg. And a sign I'm reaching my own saturation point, as I should have mentioned that myself."

"You've been pressing hard for quite a few days. Right now it's a matter of simply watching what Tanya does and what reporters might figure out. Janelle needs some breathing room. We're not going to bring up the case details until she starts asking questions, so there's time to let this sit and settle."

"Paul's made some calls. We'll know if Tanya travels."

"Good. A guilty person reacts when it looks like their cover story is falling apart. You'll get some useful data out of Tanya's behavior over the next few days."

"I hope we do." Ann considered him. "I feel like I owe you an apology for asking a favor that's rapidly growing in complexity and the time it's going to demand. I'm about to head back to Illinois, leaving you on the front line."

Greg smiled. "I'll enjoy working with Janelle. So, anything else we need to discuss before your departure flight? She'll likely want to come to the airport to see you off. This is the last point before we officially transition her from being your concern to mine."

"My list is now clear."

"Mine too," Greg decided.

They had circled back to the house, and as Ann opened the door, Greg smelled the baking pies. He shared with Janelle the experience of prison, and he knew one of the best realities that came with the return of freedom was good food. He envisioned they'd be bonding over meals in the coming days, and there was certainly no hardship in that thought.

TEN

GREG SWATTED AT A PERSISTENT FLY, mildly regretting not using bug spray before they left the house. Janelle nudged her Appaloosa alongside his mount as they approached the barn. "I'm thinking fish chowder and stuffed mushrooms. There are steaks thawed out, but maybe we grill those tomorrow evening, go hot spice and Southern sweet on the glaze, and serve them alongside twice-baked potatoes."

Greg resettled his cowboy hat, his leather gloves workman worn. "If you're asking my opinion, I like the sound of all of it. I've said it before, and I'll say it again—it's nice having a real-life chef in residence."

"It's hard to beat the variety I've got to work with. The fish are so fresh they're often still flopping around on delivery."

Greg was grateful they had found her primary stress-relief outlet on the first day—Janelle loved to cook—because she was now a bundle of nerves, her body reacting as he had predicted it would. She jumped at everything that startled her, and occasionally even her own shadow. She was mostly handling the overreactions with good humor, taking his word that the jitters would one day fade just as rapidly as they had appeared. The fact she was decompressing so quickly told him she fundamentally felt safe again. It was progress . . . good progress.

She'd been hanging out in his kitchen, flipping through cookbooks, enjoying herself and, in her words, finding it useful to have someone around who liked to eat. He'd been introducing her to employees who stopped by to talk ferry business or restaurant matters. She liked small talk and enjoyed having a game of checkers going on the counter.

She was looking and feeling alive again. Greg could see and hear the transformation happening. He was content to give her more room than she knew what to do with, to decide if and when she wanted to talk about what happened. So far she wasn't going there, and that was fine with him. She'd commented a few times about prison life, but he wasn't yet asking the follow-up questions that would take her there in detail.

Janelle's arrival hadn't really changed his own plans. For all practical purposes, he was still on vacation for the holidays. Today had started with an early swim, a bike ride, and moved into the afternoon with a two-hour wander on horseback. Janelle had chosen to come along for the afternoon ride.

Greg swung off his horse and held out a hand for her reins. She liked being around the horses and his dog—they were providing another good stress-relief outlet for her. She dismounted and followed him into the barn to help brush the horses.

Back at the main house, he picked up a book to read while Janelle retreated to the kitchen. They were in the habit of eating leisurely meals on the patio, not on any particular schedule. An hour later, he was enjoying fish chowder and stuffed mushrooms. Both were incredibly good. "Thanks. I love these."

"My pleasure."

Janelle neatly crossed her fork and knife on her plate after she finished her last mushroom. "Tomorrow I want to talk about the pardon and what happened to Andrew."

When the topic hadn't come up by day three, he'd figured it would be into the month of January before she asked. Greg reached for his glass of iced tea, leaned back in his chair. "Okay. Interesting timing. Any particular reason?"

She tried to make it a casual shrug, but he could tell her nerves were rippling. "I hear the details, I think about them. Then Christmas gives me a day to think about something else. The calendar steps on any impulse to brood."

He thoughtfully nodded. "We'll talk about it tomorrow, then."

She picked up her spoon and turned her attention to the custard she'd made for dessert. "I'm not going to like what I hear," she said, testing for his reaction.

He was careful with his words, but truthful, knowing with the question she was beginning to sort out what working with him would be like. "You've handled worse things than the truth that set you free," he remarked. "They found your pink pocket-knife, Janelle. Ann happened upon it at an auction in a box of miscellaneous dresser-drawer items."

Surprise stilled her hand. "Finding my knife set me free?"

"Yes, and the dominoes that fell from locating it." That one fact was enough for now. He nodded to the paper beside her plate. "Have you narrowed down the movie for tonight?" Which one in his DVD collection would fit her mood on a given evening was always an open question.

She let him change the subject and scanned her list. "Would you mind a sci-fi movie?"

"I only keep movies I like. Which one strikes your fancy tonight?"

"*The Martian.*"

"Both long and good. I'll have an excuse to open the caramel-corn tin."

She rose to gather the plates, then stopped. "Can I ask you something?"

"Ask."

"All this—the last several days—how much of it is normal you, and how much of it is you being nice?"

He didn't answer her for a long moment, then half smiled. "You're constantly surprising me, Janelle. I'm simply enjoying your company for the most part. I do accommodate myself to people—it's a necessary piece of hosting ever-changing clients, all of whom arrive in traumatic seasons of their lives. You haven't needed much accommodation on my part, which is really weird in a way. You don't smoke, swear, criticize, or even show a down mood very often. If anything, the prison stay didn't touch your character as it should have, and when basic predictions are upended, it's a highly interesting mystery to my professional side."

She flushed faintly. "I was God-conscious, I think. I was aware that Jesus was with me, literally. So what I said was always circumspect; I mostly kept my mouth shut. What were you expecting?"

"Moody, withdrawn, not sleeping, flashes of temper, frustration—the darker side of the color palette as your emotions are finally free to deal with the fact you endured prison for something you didn't do."

"I think I'm still in the relief side of the picture. The anger over the injustice hasn't had space to rise up yet. I imagine it will."

"It would be a normal reaction. But you can skip entire pages of what is normal and still be processing things just fine. I'm going to get concerned only if I see you getting stuck on some step."

"Like I mentally start spinning my wheels?"

Greg smiled. "Once I figure out how you brood, most of my work is actually done. I see you brooding, that's my cue to step in and help you shift the way you're thinking about something."

He rose to help her clear the table. "Let's start that movie, then later go watch the sunset from the beach. Marco loves to end his day playing in the sand."

She looked down with amusement at the dog, still hoping for table scraps to fall his way. "He'll try to steal and bury my tennis shoe again."

"His version of hide-and-seek. My guess, he's playing the game in your honor."

She laughed and headed into the kitchen. Greg ruffled the dog's fur. It helped to get her to laugh, and Marco had been doing an impressive job assisting him with that.

|||||||||

Food had become a theme of Janelle's stay. She had the fixings for BLTs laid out for breakfast. Greg decided it suited him fine. He stacked bacon on a piece of toast, piled on lettuce and a tomato slice, then picked up a knife and the peanut butter jar to liberally coat the other piece of toast.

He found her on the patio, tossing a bite of bacon to Marco, who had obligingly backed up to the other side for a long toss. Greg smiled, watching them. He'd never known Marco to miss, no matter how long the toss.

He pulled out a chair and settled in across from her. Adapting to her wasn't a particular hardship thus far. Janelle didn't eat inside if she could be outside. And she was showing a not-unexpected skittishness about being completely alone. He was thinking he'd buy her a good pair of cowboy boots for Christmas. She'd already picked up a cowboy hat at an island shop and was wearing it now. Her nose had sunburned and peeled, her shoulders and arms had tanned, spared the burn by ample sunscreen. She was adapting to life on the island. It was overcast, but the threat of rain had passed. It would be a nice day for a horseback ride.

"I take it you know the pardon and case details well enough to tell me what all happened."

Greg nodded, not surprised that she would immediately bring up the topic. Having gathered the courage to ask this morning, waiting until later would only increase her tension. "I do." He'd played out variations of how the next minutes would go and wondered which way Janelle would take them. He was as prepared as he knew how to be for this conversation.

"Then let me just ask: Who killed Andrew? Do they know?"

"Tanya."

She blinked, then erupted. "That's crazy!" Her chair landed on its side behind her, startling Marco.

Being well trained, rather than bolt, the dog immediately dropped down and stayed low. Greg used a hand gesture to command *comfort*, and the dog was instantly up again and into Janelle's space, under her hand, leaning into her knee. Her hand curled into Marco's fur. "Sorry, Marco. I'm sorry."

Greg leaned over to set right her chair.

Her instantaneous reaction he'd expected, but the surging, adrenaline-driven anger that followed, flushing her face, was stronger than he'd anticipated. Okay, one question answered. Janelle's instinct was to both mentally and emotionally defend her friend. Loyalty ran to the core of her personality. Greg didn't follow up with another comment, as he needed to see how she'd process something she intensely rejected. He let his dog be the distraction and comfort she needed right now.

"Ann found my pink pocketknife."

He nodded at her restatement of the fact from last night. Her tone was confused, softer now. She was desperately trying to rein in the anger. Janelle carefully sat back down. He gave her as much of a verbatim quote from Ann as he could recall. "She was at an auction with Paul. There were silk scarves and half-filled perfume bottles in a box of miscellaneous dresser-drawer items she thought might make a nice painting arrangement. She bought the box. When she unpacked everything, she found your knife in the bottom."

"Tanya's fingerprints were on the knife, Andrew's blood? They concluded Tanya did the murder off that new evidence? Because Tanya handled that knife all the time for innocent reasons—it had a corkscrew and nail file, any number of other gadgets she used."

"Your fingerprints were found on the knife, Andrew's blood," Greg corrected.

Janelle began to run her fingertips back and forth on the tabletop in an unconscious gesture. "Then how . . . ? That doesn't end up at a pardon. It proves the jury verdict against me," she added, still confused.

"Ann traced the box. They were Tanya's things. There was a sewing kit, a jewelry box with the initials T.C. on it, the scarves and perfume. It turns out your knife was in Tanya's dresser drawer."

That stopped her hand motion. "Her dresser drawer . . . Tanya's dead?" Janelle whispered, a horrified look on her face.

He'd miscalculated, not anticipating that question, and so quickly shifted gears. "Tanya's alive and well and living in New York. She owns a high-end dress boutique, holds a partnership interest in a fashion magazine."

Janelle shook her head. "I don't understand."

"Were you aware that Tanya moved to New York after the trial?"

"Yes. That was always her dream," Janelle replied, her voice softening again. "It was good that she went, that she got away from the tragedy of Andrew's death."

Greg offered a piece of his bacon to Marco as a reward for the dog faithfully staying at Janelle's side. "Tanya recently sold the Chadwick family's Chicago home. She sent a few things to New York, but the rest of the contents went to auction. The house manager boxed up Tanya's bedroom dresser—the box of items Ann purchased." He waited.

"Tanya killed Andrew." Janelle wasn't processing the fact so much as repeating it.

"Yes." He gave her another long moment. "Someone put those bloody shoes in your closet, Janelle. Tanya had a key to your apartment, right?"

Her gaze lifted to meet his. "She had a key," she whispered.

She wasn't seeing him. She was thinking, thinking hard. He'd just blown her understanding of the world into confetti pieces. The growing pallor of her face worried him, yet her hand on the table was still opened, not fisted, nor had she stiffened in the chair. Her original denial was so strong a response, he wasn't sure she could absorb the facts the first time she heard the news. She wasn't processing the facts yet, for none of it was real to her; they were just words.

"She set you up, Janelle," he said gently.

She swallowed so hard, she looked sick. When the denial broke, she would desperately need to see what was real. He gave her the truth he needed her to stand on so her mind would process this through rather than get stuck.

"There are a few different theories as to why Tanya did it. The most kind is that she found Andrew at the bottom of those stairs, knew his medical bills would eat through the family trust, and made a terrible decision. She used your knife to stab him and let him bleed to death. She tried to make it look like a robbery. But if the cops didn't buy that, you would be her fallback. Tanya used the fact you had fought that night with Andrew. She put the bloody shoes in your closet for the cops to find so they would start with you rather than her."

Janelle held up her hand to halt his words. "Can we . . . stop this conversation now?" She was already more calmly pushing back her chair.

"Of course."

Confusion, shock, bewilderment . . . all the emotions painting her face were easy to read, but he wasn't seeing even a trace of reluctant acceptance as her mind fought it out with her heart. "I'm sorry, Janelle, that this was a betrayal by a lifelong friend."

She put her paper plate on the stone pavers as a thank-you to Marco, who pushed aside the tomatoes with his nose but gladly snapped up the bacon. She wiped at tears with the palms of her hands. "I'll be at the beach."

He nodded and let her go. Marco looked up as she broke into a jog. Greg nudged him with his foot. "Comfort," he said. Marco considered matters, devoured the last piece of peanut-butter-covered bread, then ran after her.

Greg rubbed his hands down his face. There were times this job was simply miserable. He pulled out his phone and made a call. "She just asked the question, Ann. She may not be able to accept it." Twenty minutes later, he ended the call, sighed, reached down for the plate, and wadded it up with his.

He couldn't help Janelle, not yet. She'd hopefully storm that beach, kick up sand, do some yelling, then crying, and when the emotional storm ran out, she'd sit down on a log, her emotions numb, and replay their conversation.

She would either be able to quote his words verbatim or wouldn't remember much of anything beyond the statement that Tanya did it. Her mind would deal with the news however it had to, either shutting down or going to the opposite extreme of examining each word in an endless loop. He'd adjust what came next based on which coping mechanism had been triggered. He hoped she would smile again in the next week. It wasn't likely, but he could hope for it.

One small blessing—Janelle had left her phone on the table.

She wasn't calling someone from her past right now, wasn't calling Tanya. She was alone, thinking, denial and truth locked in a fierce battle, her heart and mind at war with each other. If denial won, the next conversation was going to be particularly difficult. He looked at her phone and left it on the table. Marco would come bounding back here to get him if Janelle needed help. He went to fetch a book, settled back at the table, and waited for her to return.

ELEVEN

GREG COULDN'T READ HER FACE; it was as impassive as granite. But she'd cried so hard that her eyes were swollen, and he could only guess at an acute tension headache. She came to a stop beside the table and picked up her phone. "Ann found my pocketknife, and tests showed it had Andrew's blood on it. Ann reasoned Tanya did the murder because she had possession of the murder weapon and had motive because of the family trust money. Then Ann considered what had happened to me and determined the evidence against me had to have been planted by Tanya, who set me up to take the blame. I have it right?"

"Yes," Greg said.

"I want to see the case file."

He nodded. "It's in the conference room—past my office, second door on the right. Some of it's video interviews, various investigators' notes, the trial transcript. The photos are not there—I'd like us to talk before you look at them. Do you want me to walk you through the material? Would you like Ann to do so?"

"It's written down, how the pardon conclusion was reached?"

"Start with the blue folder with Ann's card stapled on the front. Her pardon note runs about sixty pages."

"I'll come find you if I have a question." She hesitated, then handed him the phone. "So I won't call a reporter, do something I might later regret."

"Thank you." He pocketed her phone.

"They're wrong about Tanya."

"I know you honestly believe that. You'll find Tylenol and Ibuprofen in the cabinet with the coffee filters. I'd recommend you guzzle a sports drink after your choice of painkiller. I'll bring you food in a few hours that you can share with Marco if you can't stomach eating anything yet."

She looked at the dog, swishing his tail at the sound of his name, politely sitting beside her. She gently ruffled his fur. "I'll bet he puts on weight around your more emotional clients."

Greg smiled. "He loses it just as quickly by tagging along when they go exploring."

She turned toward the house, but then stopped, turned back to face him. "I didn't kill Andrew," she said simply.

"I know."

"Do you?"

He'd read the transcripts, watched the videos of the interviews, had just seen Janelle's immediate reaction to the idea Tanya was the guilty one. There were two women in this case. One was a liar, the other loyal, honest but bewildered. Janelle hadn't stabbed her boyfriend.

"I know it, Janelle." He tried to offer her some safe ground. "My job is to help you, not be another investigator. I'm officially neutral to the question of whether Tanya did this, or if it was a robbery committed by a stranger, or something else entirely. But for your own well-being, denial can't be where you stop. If Ann is right, the implications going forward are very dangerous. You don't have to agree with her conclusion, but you do need to accept the possibility." And Greg could tell that acceptance was still a long way off. "I'll be here when you're ready to talk."

Janelle nodded and went into the house.

||||||||||

Janelle had been reading through the materials for several days, and Greg hadn't interrupted. He thought it was now time, however. She was brooding, edging toward being stuck. "I've got clam chowder simmering. Come eat."

Janelle left the conference room to join him in the kitchen. She'd lost most of Christmas to those case files, along with her smile, that joy he'd found so delightful. He'd been able to pull her attention away only for an abbreviated hour on Christmas Day. She'd opened the packages with her name on them with pleasure—a watch and earrings from Ann and Paul, cowboy boots from him—and accepted his lavish thanks when he opened her gift and found she'd made him a cheesecake. But the case details had sucked her right back in. The one saving grace: she was still eating and sleeping, and letting Marco tag along as her shadow.

Janelle settled onto a stool at the counter, blew on the first spoonful of chowder, then reached for the canister of crackers. "I don't buy it. I understand their theory; they're just plain wrong."

Greg slipped Marco a piece of salami as a way of thanking the dog for keeping Janelle company. Her anger was abating, which was good. Yet the stubborn certainty was still there, set in stone. At the moment, he put Tanya's guilt at around seventy percent. The professional in him recognized a skilled liar in the interviews, and all kinds of flags had gone up. Still, he was willing to discuss with her either side of the argument as needed—a reasoned conversation was the only way to help Janelle, rather than offering a particular set of facts.

"I can tell you what Ann is going to say." Greg didn't say anything further. Instead, he just waited.

"Tell me," Janelle said moodily.

Greg couldn't help but smile. He rather liked this person she was when pushed into a corner, asked to believe something she didn't agree with. The backbone that had gotten her through the trial and subsequent mistaken verdict and sentence was still as strong as ever. She wasn't about to cave to an idea she couldn't accept. So he gently used that strength to help her.

"Ann would say you need to put aside the rose-colored glasses and realize the personal danger you're in," he replied. "You're fully persuaded it was a robbery gone wrong that resulted in Andrew's death. But what if you're wrong? Then Tanya *is* a murderer, and you are the greatest threat she faces. The cops are looking into Andrew's death again. Tanya is going to be in a panic about what you might remember, what you might know, what you didn't say at the time. And a second murder is considerably easier than the first.

"Ann and Paul are two very experienced homicide detectives, skilled enough to figure out you're innocent even after finding a knife that has your name on it, as well as traces of Andrew's blood. Their instincts come from decades of solving murders. They've reached the conclusion that the full evidence supports, including your and Tanya's behavior. And based on all that, Tanya is the one who killed Andrew."

Though Janelle listened well, he watched the expressions flicker across her face and could read the continued denial. It was an emotional reaction as much as a logical one. The problem was simply the fact Janelle didn't want to believe what she was hearing. She had the facts, she followed the logic, and yet she just didn't want to believe it was true.

"How about this?" Greg changed his tack. "You're innocent."

She nodded.

"Someone put those bloody shoes in your closet. If a stranger robber did the crime, how would the person know your address, Janelle? The only one who had your key, who had access to your knife and could plant those shoes, is Tanya. And don't forget—she had a strong reason to want her brother dead, rather than paralyzed for life with a broken back. She had an intense, felt need for the money his death would bring her, and that need led an otherwise good woman to commit murder. She likely convinced herself that her brother wouldn't want to live the rest of his life in a wheelchair, that what she was doing was best for him."

He slid the Kleenex box her direction. He was pushing because she was stuck, the one place he couldn't let her stay. "I know the truth is miserable. You don't want to believe it. That's fair. But, again, you need to accept it as a possibility, then deal with the emotions that come as a result."

"He was my boyfriend. He got nosebleeds. I never believed the blood on my shoes was from that night. It could have been there for ages. Tanya didn't do it. I told you, I'm not buying that theory."

She pushed aside her chowder, got up and started pacing the room, blew her nose. "I'm not helping them send another innocent person to prison. I was falsely accused, and now Tanya is being falsely accused. Don't you see that? If they take her to trial, Greg, I'll get on the stand and perjure myself, state that I stabbed Andrew and pushed him down the stairs. If they rip up the pardon, so be it. I'll do whatever it takes. I'd have to in order to stop another miscarriage of justice of this magnitude."

He took out an energy shake from the fridge, shook it, and passed it over to her. She needed something in her system if it wasn't going to be the chowder. He doubted she could lie under oath, given she hadn't done so when changing her story would have let her accept a plea deal and receive a lighter sentence. Even so, he believed she'd do what she could. "You honestly believe it's not in Tanya's character to commit murder."

"That's what I believe, yes. It's *not* in her character."

"Then convince them—Ann and Paul. She'd like to come down and have a conversation with you."

He saw relief cross her face. "Tell her to come."

"Yeah?"

"I can convince her Tanya didn't do it."

He nodded and said, "Sit back down, then, hand me that shake, and eat the soup instead. You'll ignore that conference room until Ann gets here. What you want to tell her isn't going to be found in there or you would have already shown it to me."

She blew her nose one last time, sat and picked up her spoon. She obediently spooned in more bites. "It is good chowder. What did you use?"

For the first time in days, the knot in his back relaxed. "A secret family recipe."

"Some cream, real butter, fresh clams. You called one of your restaurants for a delivery."

"Guilty."

She ate some more. "I'd give your chef a raise."

TWELVE

GREG WAS WATCHING A SLOW-MOTION COLLISION.
The two women were cooperating with each other, working
together. It wasn't an antagonistic conversation. Ann had been
patiently listening to Janelle's point of view and asking questions for the better part of two days. Greg had sat in on most
of it, pleased at how Janelle was handling it. But the most important impasse hadn't budged.

"Even if I set aside how the bloody shoes ended up in your
apartment, a stranger robbery isn't supported by what's here,"
Ann was saying gently to Janelle. "Your knife being the murder
weapon is too compelling. The only other conclusion is that
you yourself did the murder, Janelle. And since you didn't,
everything points to Tanya. She ceased to be your friend when
she wanted something else more than she wanted the friendship. She wanted her freedom from her brother, the money
that brought her, and she was willing to sacrifice you to get it."

Janelle paced. She'd paced so much in the last couple of
days, Greg suspected her calf muscles were burning and her
feet feeling bruised.

She finally nodded and turned to Ann. "Okay. I'll accept
your conclusion that Tanya could be a danger to me. I don't

117

agree with it, but your logic is rational and I will agree that it may be true. I'll live accordingly. Change my name, not get in touch with her, keep my distance from those who knew us both. When I leave here, I won't let our paths cross. But you're talking about accusing another innocent person of murder, possibly putting her on trial for that murder, and I can't live with that."

Greg felt one of his strongest worries fade. This was going to find a way to end at a compromise. The two very self-assured women were trying to reach an acceptable conclusion.

"Acknowledging Tanya as a possible danger is a big concession," Ann replied, "one I'm relieved to hear, Janelle. You want me to be wrong because she was your friend. That's the heart of a good friend. But I'm *not* wrong. And I know that if we don't stop Tanya now, the next person who crosses her who has something Tanya desperately wants, that person could die too. That's the part *I* can't live with."

Janelle went back to pacing, then stopped again. "You need more proof to accept I'm right. I need more proof to accept you're right. So let's add more facts to the table. Let's go have a conversation with her."

"You want to meet with Tanya?"

"It's time, don't you think? You said she's been aggressively looking for me, asking everyone from my trial lawyer to newspaper reporters of my whereabouts. You see that as a sign of guilt, that she's worried what I'm telling the cops, worried about the new evidence. I see it as the logical step Andrew's sister would take to the news I've been pardoned. She'll agree to meet me.

"You can record it, you can listen in. If you put what she says to me now alongside those past interviews, you'll see her in a different light, that what I'm saying is true. I know her, Ann."

Janelle came back to the table. "And I need to meet with Tanya for my own sake. We never talked—not after the detective separated us that night at the beach to get our individual statements. I want to hear what she has to say—about the knife, about that night, all of it."

Ann glanced over at him, and Greg gave her a subtle nod. A conversation with Tanya would help Janelle on a lot of levels. Even if it went an unexpected direction, it was movement.

Greg watched Ann assess Janelle, then choose her words with great care. "You could burn us badly, Janelle, by telling Tanya you did it or by confessing remorse to protect her. You could lie and face no immediate consequences for it. That audio could guarantee we can't touch Tanya for whatever role she might have played that night. I'm asking you to play fair with us."

"You'll have to trust me, Ann. I can't help you convict another innocent person, but I do want justice for Andrew. You can trust that. One of us is right. I can accept, at least theoretically, that it might be you. I'll do my best to cooperate and stay within the parameters we work out."

Greg didn't need to hear Ann's reply to know where this was heading, so he added a point of his own. "Promise me you'll never tell Tanya you are staying somewhere in the South, and never mention this island."

"She's going to notice the tan. I'll just imply I've been vacationing in the Caribbean while staying away from the press."

"Ann?" he said.

"We can fly to New York this afternoon if the weather along the Eastern Seaboard cooperates. A delay doesn't help any of us."

Janelle visibly relaxed. "Thank you."

Ann reached over to lay a hand on her arm. "I want the answers too, Janelle."

THIRTEEN

"I'M SO GLAD YOU CALLED!" Tanya reached over for a hug, but Janelle didn't move to reciprocate. Tanya then slid into the opposite bench, her hands covering Janelle's on the booth's table. "This is like a miracle squared, the news of the pardon!" Her tone bubbled over with excitement.

"It's nice to be free." Janelle returned the smile, nodded to their server, and waited as Tanya's coffee was poured. Tanya was a fashion statement—flowing sleeves, sleek dress fitted tight around a narrow waist. Not a model's figure, but the expressive presence of one. "The dress shop must be doing well. You look quite fashionable."

"I try to set the trends rather than just follow them," Tanya replied with a laugh. "Oh, I've *so* been wanting to know you were okay. No one could find you, but the tan looks recent, so I'm thinking you enjoyed Christmas somewhere nice?"

"We always did talk about a Caribbean vacation. I've been avoiding the press."

"What happened? Please tell me they found the guy who killed Andrew. I've been pestering the cops, but I can't get anything useful on the new evidence. I'm guessing they have at least a confession, given the speed the pardon happened."

"I wish I could say that was true." Janelle switched the coffee mug to her other hand. "They found my pink pocketknife, Tanya. In a box of items from your dresser drawer."

Tanya froze, eyes wide. "Janelle . . . really? You got told that?"

"How did it get there?"

Tanya closed her eyes for a long moment, opened them, spread her hands. "Which is easier to accept, Janelle—I don't know anything about that knife or I tossed it in a drawer to protect you?"

"Try the truth."

"I was out at the beach," she began slowly, "about a week after Andrew's death. I found it under some sagebrush about halfway down those stairs and maybe eight feet past the railing. The rain had practically covered it in mud. I wouldn't have seen it but for three sea gulls getting into a fight over some crime-scene tape that had blown loose and wrapped around the shrub."

Her words picked up speed. "We know the robber took Andrew's phone and wallet. I figured he must have been on the beach earlier that evening, saw you two fighting, and robbed your purse first, had the knife in his hand when he confronted Andrew later. I was in a quandary. The knife might have prints on it to show who had held it, or time and the rain had made that a useless quest and the cops would then blame you. It's your knife, and the blade was out and stained. If I handed it to the cops, I risked you getting sent to prison for the rest of your life. So I tossed it in a drawer and prayed for what to do next. In the end I just left it there, but it was to protect you."

Tanya blew on her steaming-hot coffee. "I know I caused problems for you at the trial, blabbing about the ups and downs of your relationship with Andrew, but I also told the jury a robber did it because I know that's the truth of what happened. I

121

know you. You stabbing Andrew is ludicrous. I was devastated by his murder, and later your trial—living on pills and nerves, talking a mile a minute. You know how emotional I get. I was honestly trying to get across how much you loved Andrew, and the questions the cops and lawyers were hounding me with just tangled everything up in a knot. But you must know I was only trying to help, even if I was doing a poor job of it. That's why I tossed the knife in that drawer, and that's why I didn't come to visit you after the verdict. Because it was partly my fault they didn't believe your innocence, and I couldn't fix it."

"The knife ended up in a box of your dresser things at an auction," Janelle said.

"I put everything about that awful summer into a mental off-limits and left Chicago. I hadn't forgotten I had it, but it had been years, and I didn't want to go there again. The house was getting sold, so I figured I'd just let the hired movers throw the knife away. It was the passive way to deal with it—just let it get thrown out by others."

She must have noticed Janelle's expression, which said she was having a hard time believing Tanya.

"Oh, please, you really think it was something more complicated than that? Finding the knife was one of the reasons I was so all over the map when I testified. I knew you hadn't hurt Andrew, but I've got your pocketknife that says maybe you did. I was trying to reconcile what was going on, which turned out to be impossible. If they had just caught the robber, none of this nightmare would have ever happened."

Janelle sighed and pushed over the sugar. Tanya loaded up her cup and stirred it in vigorous swirls. "I want to believe you," Janelle said quietly.

"*Do*," Tanya insisted. "I was an emotional mess, trying to help my friend. That's what my awful summer was like. And I know yours was worse."

"Fall."

"What?"

"Andrew died in August."

"See? It's still this time-consuming chaos. The trial was in late summer, wasn't it? I'm surprised I was even functional."

"You knew Andrew was going to break up with me that night. You two had breakfast together most mornings, dinner occasionally—you were living in the same house. His misgivings about college and dating me didn't just abruptly appear. He would have told you he was changing his mind about me."

Tanya vehemently shook her head. "I thought Andrew was going to *propose marriage* that night. I even had champagne ready so we could celebrate together. I was waiting for either you or Andrew to call me with the happy news. You were thinking the same, that he was going to propose that night. You'd told me so that afternoon. Hearing he'd broken up with you, that was a massive shock. To both of us!"

Tanya began rummaging through her bag. "I so wish I smoked at moments like this." She took out a prescription bottle, opened it, and dumped a pill in her hand. "It's been almost seven years and I'm still turning into a wreck just thinking about that Friday night." She swallowed the pill, sipped more coffee. "I would have alerted you had I known my brother was even *thinking* about throwing you over. Come on, you know that, Janelle. It's like girl-code 101."

"He never mentioned the possibility to you of breaking up with me, knowing you would be with me that afternoon, would maybe warn me?"

Tanya promptly crossed her heart and kissed her fingers. "Not a word. I thought you were great with my brother. I wanted us to be sisters for real."

She reached across and rested her hand on Janelle's again. "It was a nightmare for both of us, and I still feel guilty about walking away from you like I did . . . I just fled to New York. Please. This is all in the past. The new year is around the corner. Come stay with me—I've got plenty of room. We can do the city sights. Talk. I can grovel, give you the apology you deserve for my being such a lousy friend."

"It's not possible, Tanya, not with the press situation. In fact, it's probably best if we part ways now. You've been in the news a lot, talking about this. Someone will recognize you, and I want to avoid press questions for now."

"Reporters don't let up, so it's just easier to give them a quote than try to maneuver around them. I've been slipping in mentions of the dress shop so at least something about all their pressure has been useful." Tanya pulled her phone out of her purse. "What's your number?"

"I'll call you," Janelle said.

"Really?" Tanya pressed. "Not even your number?" At Janelle's headshake, she put away her phone with a pout, slid out of the booth, and stood. "Then I want a weekend somewhere outside the city with you sometime soon. Can you do that?"

"I'll think about it."

Tanya came around to hug her, and this time Janelle tolerated it. "I'm so glad to see you free."

||||||||||

Greg watched as the women parted ways. He looked over at Ann. They had been observing it all via monitors in the coffee-shop office. Janelle should have been relieved now that the conversation was over, but clearly she wasn't. "What do you want to do now, Ann?"

Ann was still watching the monitor. "Go sit with her, Greg. Whomever Tanya may have arranged to have watch Janelle will assume she isn't traveling alone, so seeing you join her isn't going to be a surprise. When you leave here, take a taxi to the hotel as planned. We'll debrief there. If I see someone following you, I'll call and warn you to divert to the airport. Or if you think you're being followed, do the same. They can't follow a private flight. Her best chance at safety is for us to leave town."

He nodded and went to join Janelle. This coffee shop was one of many businesses owned by Paul's father in New York, and it had been disconcertingly straightforward to get cameras and audio put in place during the hours they were in flight from the island. That Tanya had agreed to meet for coffee in twenty minutes at a location near her work hadn't been a surprise.

Greg took a seat on the bench across from Janelle and just waited.

"She lied to me," she said after a moment of silence. "Andrew would avoid a confrontation at all costs. He would have told Tanya he was going to break up with me. I thought he was going to propose that evening because she'd been hinting he was thinking that way. She set us up to have a bad breakup. Maybe it's denial now, rewriting her own history to live with what she did, saying she too thought he was going to propose. I don't know. I still don't think Tanya killed her brother. I don't think it's in her. But she just lied to me, Greg."

"Okay."

Janelle drew in a deep breath and shuddered as she exhaled. "Where to now?"

"A hotel, so we can talk it over with Ann, then back to the island tonight might be best, I think."

||||||||||

Greg handed Janelle a soft drink in the hotel suite, avoided the questions he would ask until Ann joined them, talked instead about New York.

Ann stepped in twenty minutes later. "Thank you, Janelle. You did very well."

"Greg said the audio and video were fine."

"Like we were sitting beside you—which, given the bud vase on the table, was practically true."

Janelle rubbed the back of her neck. "She lied. I don't know what involvement she could have had in his death, but she lied. Andrew avoided like the plague having a conversation that would distress someone. He always had someone else lay the groundwork before he would ever say it himself. Tanya set us up to have a breakup conversation that turned much more difficult than it should have been. She let me get severely hurt that night when she could have warned me with a simple caution: 'He's still thinking about getting college behind him before he makes firm plans for his future.' That would have been enough to head off much of the trouble. She didn't, and that was unkind, cruel even. And until today, I didn't think she had it in her to be cruel. For whatever reason—maybe to get back at her brother for his decisions about the trust—she let us walk into that night primed to both get badly hurt. That night was devastating in so many ways. I thought nothing could hurt as badly as being dumped like what happened during our fight on the beach, but then the cop knocked on my door . . . and the grief of knowing Andrew was dead crushed everything in me. I'm ready to say part of that was Tanya's doing. She knew Andrew was going to break up with me and didn't warn me."

Ann nodded. "Okay."

"I want to stay the night in New York, talk to her again tomorrow."

"You sure, Janelle?"

"I can push her. Nothing she said today particularly helps change what we know. But I can get her to say more than she intends to. We were friends since elementary school, and I know

126

how to push her buttons. I just never thought I'd need to do so while cops were listening in. For Andrew's sake, Ann, I need to know the truth. This is the only way I'm going to know."

"All right, we'll arrange something. Maybe suggest breakfast before you leave town, something to get her to come on short notice."

FOURTEEN

THE RESTAURANT CHOSEN was sparsely occupied because it was expensive even by New York standards and the hour was early. The breakfast plates had been delivered, coffee poured, the conversation thus far limited to Janelle's polite questions about living in New York and Tanya's animated answers.

Greg watched with Ann from the restaurant's office. Just like before, the video was good, the audio clear. Janelle pretty much ignored the food. There were a lot of clues that this meeting was going to be very different from yesterday's, but that one observation was enough to tell Greg how stressed Janelle was.

She interrupted Tanya's description of her apartment and abruptly turned the conversation to the Friday night of Andrew's death. "Tanya, there's no way you didn't know Andrew was going to break up with me that night. He avoided conflicts of any kind. He would have told you, so you could ease me toward already knowing what he was going to say. You might relish confrontations, but not Andrew."

"I was in the dark," Tanya insisted. "He knew I was elated that you two were dating. If he tells me he's thinking of breaking up with you, he would have had a confrontation on the *spot*. He'd avoid a confrontation at all costs, that was Andrew. But with us—hello, sisters bonding here—what's he going to do? He probably figured breaking up with you cold was easier than a battle with me, followed by a second one with you. You don't believe me?" Tanya shook sugar packets and ripped four open. "Whyever not? I would have felt awful giving you the news, but I would have warned you if I knew something like that was coming."

Janelle leaned back in her chair. "I was your friend, dating your brother, but I saw what was going on, Tanya. I watched you pick fights with him just to get him riled up. You would stay out until all hours, not answer your phone, go to parties with guys you knew would give him concern. You would leave him wondering if you were hurt somewhere, if he should start calling the hospitals. You were angry at your parents dying, and he was a convenient target. You often caused Andrew grief simply because you could."

Tanya flushed angrily. "We fought at times, not a surprise given he was a few years older and acting like my *father*. I thought you were on my side. I loved him, but he was my brother, not my keeper."

Janelle's voice turned icy. "I know you were there that night, Tanya. Your car was in the lot when I left Andrew—last parking place on the far side. I saw your vanity license plate. You came to see the fireworks when we broke up, to watch what you'd set in motion. I knew as soon as I spotted your car that you'd set your brother up for a doozy of a breakup, and you wanted to get it on video. You wanted to embarrass Andrew to his friends, post it on social media. That would suit how you wanted to get back at him for telling you how to live. I was just your unwitting actress in the drama you'd staged."

In the office, both Greg and Ann stiffened.

"'May we live in interesting times,'" Greg breathed out,

quoting the song lyric. He was listening not only to Janelle's words but also to the change in her tone of voice. She'd had the ability to point the finger at Tanya all along, but feeling jammed up by cops herself, the last thing Janelle would have done was to point a finger at a friend she thought was innocent too. "She should have told this to her lawyer, used it in her own defense."

Ann shook her head. "If she's right about the reason Tanya was there, saying this at the time just puts potential video of the fight in the hands of law enforcement. If the tape shows Janelle storming off, it doesn't mean she didn't come back for round two of the fight and Andrew got stabbed then. Video of it all just makes it easier for the jury to believe motive."

On the monitor, Janelle was leaning forward to make a similar point. "That video shows I walked away, proof I hadn't lied about how the fight ended. But you didn't want to admit you were there, did you, Tanya? You didn't want to chance the cops asking if you and Andrew had a conversation after I left."

"You've got it all wrong," Tanya insisted. "I didn't admit I was at the beach because I was *protecting* you. If I said I was there, they'd want to know whether or not I'd seen you two fighting. And I'm a bad liar; it would have come out that there was video. I was protecting you by not saying I was there. For the same reason I tossed that knife in a drawer after I found it, I shoved the camera in a closet after I got home and left it there. The jury would have used both the knife and the fight video to bolster their conclusion you were guilty."

"You were *helping* me, *protecting* me?" Janelle pushed her breakfast plate away. "Tanya, you and I both know you were the last one to have that pocketknife. You used the nail file to smooth off a chipped nail. You said you put it back in my purse and I believed you. Then I went to get it and give it to the cops and it wasn't there. But you *knew* that, didn't you? You knew because you still had the knife. And as it was Andrew's blood on the knife, *you* used it that night, didn't you?"

Tanya had flushed red and now went sheet white. "You're crazy. I had nothing to do with my brother's death."

"You're impulsive, you've got a flash temper, you could justify 'stab him once, let fate decide. He dies, I'm free. He lives, he's already facing a long recovery from his injuries, and one more doesn't make much of a difference.' I know how you think, Tanya. You could hurt Andrew and live with it. You didn't like your brother running your life, controlling your money, being the authority in your life. Whatever you did that night, causing our breakup to be an ultra-disaster, being involved in his death—Andrew didn't deserve it, Tanya."

"That's nuts. That is just wildly crazy *nuts*." Tanya pushed away from the table. "I did not harm my brother. We fought occasionally, but he was my *brother*! I would never do what you're suggesting, ever! How could you ever even *think* that, Janelle?" She got up and stormed away.

Greg watched as Janelle folded, covering her face with her hands, her shoulders shaking. The information she'd revealed was still reverberating. He forced himself to look away, to give her a few moments of privacy, and turned to Ann. "So, what did you take from that?"

Ann, absorbing the deluge of new information, was already shifting through the implications. "Video exists," she said simply. "We've got to find it."

"I heard Janelle speculating in several different directions. I didn't hear Tanya agree."

"Listen to it again. Tanya didn't deny her car was in the parking lot that night, that she was there. Nor did she deny the videotape. Tanya was so paranoid the cops might look at her concerning Andrew's death that she overdid the frame. She set up the two of them to have a blowout breakup, she got

131

the fight on tape, she used Janelle's knife, and she planted the bloody shoes in the closet.

"The shoes and missing knife turned out to be enough at trial to get a conviction, but Tanya couldn't throw away her insurance policy—the knife and videotape—in case of an appeal. They're her security blanket against detectives ever looking at her as the one responsible for her brother's death. 'You need more proof they were fighting that night—how about a tape of them fighting?' If she held on to the knife, she held on to a video."

The call Ann made was answered. "Paul, I need a very good researcher. We have to track down all fifty-eight boxes from the Chadwick house that went to auction. There may be video still in existence. We've got to find it."

FIFTEEN

WHEN SHE WAS HAVING A BAD DAY, Janelle switched from baking to fussing with more involved meals, and she chose background music that would make stones weep. Greg considered both to be healthy coping, so he left her to the kitchen's comfort and headed out for a solo afternoon ride. He set a vase of wildflowers on the counter when he returned. It got him a smile, and she stopped to finger a petal. "Thanks."

"You're welcome." They were having breaded pork chops and some kind of honey-glazed dessert from what he could identify on the counters. "Smells good."

"Appetizers are heating."

He settled at the counter to scan mail he'd brought in, not sure if she would want to talk but giving her the opportunity. That she was hanging out at his place and using his kitchen to avoid being alone was as readable as a first-grade storybook, but it saved him having to track her down to see how she was coping. He liked having her in his line of sight, cooking in his kitchen, and pacing. She was coping, and coping was good.

"I accused the woman who used to be my best friend of murdering her brother. I still feel sick about it. It's in Tanya, the dramatics, the self-interest, but not the premeditated violence to actually kill him. Six years in prison to mull over what happened and I never went this way, never considered it possible."

"People do what you could never imagine, what they themselves might never imagine, if given enough pressure."

She pulled the tray out of the oven, set the pan on a trivet, and pushed it his way—a stacked cracker, bacon, horseradish, olive, and cheese combination based on the tray not yet heating. He gingerly tasted one, not sure of the horseradish, and got a pleasant surprise. "This is delicious."

"Thanks." She slid the second pan into the oven.

Janelle leaned against the counter and moodily ate one of the appetizers. "Tanya would take and post video of a breakup fight to embarrass Andrew, conveniently ignoring the fact she would also hurt me in the process. I can accept the idea Tanya *did* arrange for it to be a nasty breakup. But I can't live with where Ann then takes this. She doesn't believe it was a spur-of-the-moment decision that Friday night, does she? She thinks Tanya planned it months in advance, all the way back to giving me that pink knife as a gag gift for my birthday."

Greg knew Ann thought Tanya was precisely that cold. It wouldn't help Janelle to deal further with that, so he simply took them a different direction. "Accept what you can, leave as possibly true what you can't. Denial is the danger, Janelle, not the disagreement itself on what the known facts suggest."

She nodded. "Ann's looking for that videotape, I'll bet. After nearly seven years."

"I've seen her pull off miracles. If Tanya kept the knife, then she kept the video too." He ate another appetizer. "We'll know something when Ann does. Have a movie in mind for tonight?"

Janelle let him change the subject. He hoped Ann could find answers, for Janelle's sake. Though he was only an indirect party, he felt the weight of this.

||||||||||

Ann and Paul arrived on the island late in the afternoon on December 29. Greg set the chocks on the plane's wheels and then waited as the stairs opened and Paul stepped out, Ann behind him. "You found the video."

"We did," Ann confirmed. "The twenty-third box from the Chadwick house was still packed in the back of a trailer. The purchaser bought a number of old electronics, cameras, video players. The box yielded an older-model video camera with a tape still inside it. The first minutes confirm it's what Tanya recorded that night. We haven't watched it yet, Greg. I felt it was important for Janelle to be offered a chance to see it with us the first time it's played . . . or not."

"Watch her last fight with Andrew? That's got some serious don't-go-there implications, Ann."

"I need her to trust me. If we're ever to make a case against Tanya, it will need to go through Janelle. I want to at least give her the choice."

Greg understood the gesture. He nodded to his SUV. "Let's go see what she wants to do."

He drove them from the airfield to his home.

Janelle was waiting in the living room. She put down the magazine she had been idly thumbing through. "You wouldn't both be here unless it was serious news."

Ann walked her through how they had found the tape. "We are *strongly recommending* that you let us, or Greg if you prefer, watch the video first, provide a caution for what is on it, and let you make an informed decision before you view it."

Greg nodded his agreement. "It's one thing to remember, Janelle, that you fought, to remember a few sentences which were said. It's quite another to watch the whole episode play out. Reliving it after all these years, seeing Andrew from that evening, will make your grief that much more vivid."

"I understand the concern," Janelle replied. "But I was there.

I've replayed that fight a thousand times over the years. I owe this to him. I want to see it along with you."

"Okay then." Ann set the camera on the coffee table, angled it so all three could see the small screen, and tapped the play button.

Sand. The scene wobbled around, but it was mostly sand. And then the image focused properly and they were looking down the Chicago beach. A breathless voice said, "There's my brother, Andrew, and his girlfriend, Janelle, coming down the stairs now. Andrew said he would bring her to the beach tonight—it's a favorite destination. I'm told there's a proposal coming. I want to get it on tape for Janelle. She'll love having it in her permanent record."

Janelle sighed, and Ann hit pause.

"She slipped down to the beach that night," Janelle said, "thinking to record a marriage proposal. That's why Tanya tried to hide her car. She was there because I told her I thought Andrew was going to propose."

Ann resumed the video. As the conversation on the beach turned into a fight, the emotions Janelle was feeling then rippling through her words, she showed every bit of that pain over again now as she watched. Greg squeezed her shoulder in sympathy. He had imagined a bad breakup, endured such a thing with his wife, but this one was particularly cruel. Janelle stormed away down the beach back toward the stairs.

The camera bounced around as Tanya ran across the beach. "What are you doing?" she shouted at her brother. "Are you nuts? You're dumping her? You yellow-bellied wimp! She loves you! And you *dump* her?" The confrontation went on in a similar vein as Tanya raged at Andrew, but then the image shifted again as Tanya pushed past him to find Janelle, showing mostly sand until Tanya realized she still had the camera in her hand, still recording. The image then went blank and stayed that way.

Ann stopped the playback. "We'll watch the rest to the end to confirm that's all there is. One minor point I noticed, Janelle. You were carrying your purse that night, not a clutch that matched your dress. And your purse wasn't robbed that night. You dropped it on a towel on the sand, and that general area is in and out of the video frames. The purse—from when you set it down to when you grab it up and leave—is lying the same way, with the same twist in the strap. It wasn't moved."

"Okay." Janelle took a deep breath and dashed a hand across her eyes. "Thanks for commenting on my purse rather than that awful fight. I need a minute." She walked outside.

Greg watched her go with concern. Her seeing the video had been a mistake, possibly a major one.

"Did you notice how Tanya was setting up the video to be another insurance policy?" Ann asked Paul. "It's terrifying how good she is at arranging her frame." She took the video back to the beginning to watch it again.

Greg's gaze snapped back to Ann, startled. "Wait a minute. You think this video implicates Tanya further?"

"It's too perfectly scripted not to be a frame," Ann said patiently. "It explains everything. Why she's secretly on the beach, recording—it's to record a marriage proposal. After the fight and Janelle storms off, Tanya makes sure her own fight with Andrew is on tape. 'She's loved you since the fifth grade and you dump her! Don't you dare be bringing another girlfriend home with you and be rubbing her nose in the fact you moved on!' She's waving the camera around like she's forgotten she's holding it. And she's making sure Andrew can't get more than a word in. Then she stomps away with the camera bouncing around, showing sand, and you hear her muttering to herself, 'Where did Janelle go? He drove. She's going to need a lift home. She'll key that car before she ever rides in it again, or stick a tire.' And the camera clicks off. Tanya layered together the evidence like a pro. The video of the fight preserves in dramatic fashion Janelle's motive. The knife with Janelle's name on it is blunt proof of the act. The blood on Janelle's tennis shoes is even more proof she was there. It's so well packaged it's terrifying."

Greg could feel some of Janelle's confusion. "You honestly think the video confirms your theory that Tanya did it?"

Paul moved over to the couch. "You can't see it, Greg? All the way to the muttered last four words—'*or stick a tire.*' Tanya was laying another predicate for the jury, dropping an inference to Janelle's pocketknife. This frame was months in the planning. Tanya likely already had Janelle's knife in her possession when she was filming this." He turned to his wife. "She's incredibly dangerous, Ann," he remarked, "and I'm not sure what we can do about it."

Ann nodded. "Tanya Chadwick got a taste of manipulation and murder, and her reward was a handsome amount of money. Odds are good she's still a liar and manipulator—money being a strong motivator—and a murderer when necessary."

She looked at Greg. "The New York FBI office owes Paul—they can keep an eye on what she's doing, take a long look at her history, maybe spot the next frame as it's being set up."

Greg held up his hand. "You both know Janelle is going to see all of this through a different lens. She thinks Tanya was helping her."

Janelle came back in to join them and heard the last of his remark. "She was helping me, or attempting to do so. I pushed her hard in New York, trying to fit her to what you've been thinking. Tanya said she didn't have anything to do with Andrew's death and I believe her." She dropped into a chair across from Ann. "So talking with Tanya, finding the video, it hasn't changed our basic impasse. I don't think my friend could do this. You think she could."

"I think Tanya framed you, Janelle, and didn't miss a note," Ann replied calmly.

Janelle nodded. "I can live with us disagreeing, but I know one thing after today. That knife and that video would convince a new jury I was the guilty party. If you arrest Tanya now, she plays the video and says, 'I didn't do it, Janelle did,' and the jury's going to believe her. And since you can't make the case against Tanya, you won't arrest her. That's good enough for me. Further, I'm going to guess that even if you could find my 'stranger robber' with Andrew's wallet and phone, you'd hesitate to charge him with murder because you can't explain how he acquired my pocketknife, given my purse wasn't robbed during the fight on the beach. Bottom line, no one will be charged in Andrew's death."

The four looked at each other, and Paul said, "That's probably realistic, Janelle."

"I know you don't agree with us," Ann said, "but you do need to keep your distance from Tanya, a good distance."

"After what I said to her at breakfast, that's not going to be a problem," Janelle replied. "I killed the friendship in spectacular fashion. I'll accept what you believe could be true and live accordingly." She turned to Greg. "I'm going down to the beach."

"Take Marco with you," he suggested.

Janelle got to her feet and held out her hand. "Thank you, Ann. Paul. For bringing the tape, for everything. I'll say goodbye for now, as I know you're heading back tonight. Maybe next time we meet, it's a more enjoyable occasion for me to simply cook you a good meal, and we won't have a single case-related question to talk about."

Ann smiled. "A nice plan. Take care of yourself, Janelle."

Janelle headed out. Ann watched her go, then looked to her husband. "So Tanya gets away with it."

Paul pushed to his feet. "At least an innocent person is no longer sitting in prison. Let's go home, Ann."

Greg tried to find some good news in how things had ended. "Janelle needed this, the look back at what happened. She'll close the chapter more easily now, having been through the details in such an intense fashion. The grieving can begin—for all that she's lost, for both Andrew and almost seven years of her life. Why don't you two plan to come for an actual vacation weekend in February, let her fix you that dinner? I predict you'll find her in a much more content state of mind by then."

"We'll plan to do that," Ann said with a smile. "Thanks, Greg."

"'You do what is possible, you live with the rest,'" he replied, quoting her words back to her.

SIXTEEN

GREG SETTLED BESIDE JANELLE on the sand after driving Ann and Paul back to the airfield. "A tough day."

"Another one of them," she agreed, using a piece of driftwood to drag over more sand for the sandcastle she was building. It now had walls and towers and a bridge. He nudged one tower into a more uniform shape, and Janelle stuck a twig atop it. She gave him a brief glance. "Has anyone ever considered that it might have been Andrew who took my pocketknife out of my purse?"

Greg studied her face. "Go on."

"He would use that pocketknife, since it was handy for all kinds of guy things—cutting cord, tightening screws, stripping twigs—it's why I carried something that bulky around in my purse. It wasn't for Tanya. I think Andrew took it out of my purse for something he was doing and then put it in his pocket. Then we have a fight, he's pacing the beach, and like any guy he shoves his hands in his pockets, realizes he's got the pocketknife, pulls it out, opens the blade, and starts flipping it into the sand, at pieces of driftwood—just to have something tangible in his hand as he paces. He still has the knife in his hand when he starts up those stairs."

"It's late. He's distracted. The stairs are damp, and he's in a hurry. He's moving too fast and catches his foot on a tread, trips and tumbles all the way down. With the knife in his hand, somehow he stabs himself by accident. The knife ends up buried under brush as it flips away.

"Tanya finds it, and it's like the video. She doesn't think I had anything to do with Andrew's death, so the only thing she can really do to help me is to not give the cops evidence that makes me look guilty. So she doesn't say there's video of the fight. She doesn't say she found my pocketknife and there's dried blood on it. She's a friend. Tanya tosses the knife in a drawer, the camera with its tape in a cabinet. She gives me a chance at the trial, and a chance to win an appeal. Her testimony hurt me, but she was trying her best to answer the questions without a lie and couldn't avoid some of what she said when she got asked a direct question. She told what she understood to be the truth of the matter, what Andrew or I had said to her."

Greg had been a doctor too many years to get surprised at what had now surfaced in Janelle's thoughts. "You think it was an accident?"

"You get stabbed with a pink pocketknife, a wimpy blade—no self-respecting robber carries that knife. So I accept Ann's conclusion it's not a robbery. I know it wasn't me. That video—Tanya was horrified with the way he broke up with me, was reaming him out, and that was authentic outrage in my friend's voice. Tanya didn't do this. It wasn't me, a robber, or Tanya. So who's left? Andrew. He had an accident. He fell, stabbed himself, and he died."

Greg considered that statement. "You could probably convince me. I've flipped a knife more than a few times myself at driftwood. But what's left is someone took his wallet and phone."

"A passerby finds a dead man on a beach, takes his wallet and phone, and leaves it to someone else to report the body." She said it as a casual, verbal shrug, yet he knew how deep those words went because it was Andrew.

"You should have mentioned this possibility during the trial."

"It never dawned on me before today." Janelle sighed and dug in to strengthen her sandcastle's bridge. "The thing is, we're never going to know the truth."

He let the silence linger for a long time. "You okay?"

"I will be. After I sit here for about a zillion nights watching the stars come out as the sunset fades."

He smiled at her word choice. "My beach is your beach."

"Thanks. I'm going to stick around for a few months, if it's all right with you. I'm going to need to talk with you."

He was glad to hear she would stay and let him help. "You spent six years in prison because either your best friend framed you or Andrew had an accident, which the cops misread as murder. We'll be unpacking this one for a while," he agreed.

She nodded.

He was relieved the day was ending with such a matter-of-fact tone. "You'll get through this, Janelle. And while we do that work, you can keep me well supplied in pies—cherry, apple, and that coconut one was particularly good. Whatever suits your baking mood."

"I'm thinking something dark suits this day, like a good chocolate pie with whipped-cream clouds."

"In that case I should mention I brought 'good chocolate' back with me from New York."

"You did?"

"I figured there would be a day it was desperately needed."

Greg reached for a conclusion for both of them. "Tanya is going to show her true colors with time. A dozen years or so from now, you and Ann will probably know which one of you was right. I predict you two will be friends at least that long."

Janelle smiled. "I hope so. I owe her, Greg. I didn't kill Andrew, but the only person who believed that until Ann came along was God."

"God tends to be enough," he replied, thinking back to his time in Pakistan. "You okay?"

"Exhausted, but okay. I'll sleep better tonight than I have, as the past is no longer a mystery. It's one of two things, and I can live with that. I'm ready to close this chapter and move on."

"It gets smoother from here. There's a grief wave still to come, but it will pass."

"A grief wave—you've got a weeping woman ahead of you. That must be very unappealing."

"A good doctor doesn't mind tears," he reassured. "Some people grieve by crying, while others experience a period of melancholy when life loses its color. Sometimes the grief turns into creative expression, like making art that memorializes the people of the past. Yours will find its own rhythm, I'm sure."

"In all of this I've been avoiding saying I truly loved Andrew, and he's gone."

"I've noticed."

"The wrong way to handle it?"

He shook his head. "The deepest loss needs its own space, and for you, Andrew is probably the last and deepest grief you will carry. He was the future you wanted, and instead he's lost forever. You can't recover him. Keeping a mental distance has been a way to talk about him with Ann without shattering. That will shift now, and you'll start to let him go."

"Like your wedding picture on the wall. What you miss from your past. But you've moved on."

"Like that," Greg agreed. He had learned this island gave people time to find their balance, space to move on. It had offered him that too, and it would do the same for Janelle.

Marco joined them, feet wet from dancing in the waves,

threatening the sand creation she'd built. She hugged him with a laugh. "I'd like to watch the last movie on my top-ten list, then call it a night. Tomorrow the sun comes up on another day of freedom. For everything else this has been, nothing takes the pleasure away from the moment when the early-morning sun touches my pillow."

Greg obligingly rose and offered his hand. "Let's go do exactly that."

EPILOGUE

GREG ENJOYED BEING THE SILENT OWNER of Paradise of Pies, for the tables were filled with customers and there was a long line at the front counter. Today's special was apple cheesecake. He greeted those he knew, took time to chat with the oldest island resident at one of the window tables, then slipped through the staff-only door. The kitchen countertop remained half filled with freshly made pies ready to feed the unending demand out front.

Janelle was in the office, reading a book and waiting for him. On Monday and Friday, the offerings in the shop were her own creations. Janelle started making pies in the morning when it was still dark outside, stopping at eleven o'clock. And when they ran out, the shop sign turned to *Closed*. Islanders knew to arrive early. She shared the business with two other bakers, who each took two days of their own. As far as profitable businesses went, this one was a gem. Three ladies baked pies, two sales clerks sold them, and a young man looking to become a manager for Greg one day supervised cleaning the shop each evening and set up for the next morning's baker.

"I brought lunch."

Janelle looked up from her book to consider the sack he carried. "For South Carolina barbecue, I'll pause before finishing the last chapter of this mystery. Have a good trip?"

"The weather cooperated, even if the reason for going turned out to be an opportunity I declined. The food from Carl's Bar-B-Q looks as good as you promised, and the line was as long as you warned. I ordered us both double slabs of ribs and also coleslaw. They foil-wrapped the ribs and ice-packed the slaw, assuring me it all would make it here in good shape. Marco's already angling for a few bones."

Janelle grinned. "Let me heat those ribs and then we'll go find a picnic table."

"Kevin's holding the picnic table out back for us and keeping an eye on Marco." His cousin's son was in town for a few days, hoping to find a charter-boat captain willing to hire him for seasonal work. "They said fifteen minutes under the broiler in the foil packages and the ribs will be like they just came off the smoker."

"That's easy enough." She switched on an oven broiler, opened a cupboard for a tray, unpacked the bag he'd brought, and slid the barbecue packages in to reheat.

Greg gave her a thoughtful study as she pulled out a stool, shook the ice off the slaw container, and opened it. She still looked sunburned, windburned, and happy from yesterday spent out on the water—a good combination on her.

"Want an early taste?" she asked.

"Sure."

She pulled open a drawer to get spoons and opened another cupboard for bowls.

In the last seven months, Janelle had found her footing. She'd moved into an apartment in town, joined this pie endeavor, and become quite adept at the sport of fishing in her off hours. Her smile was the norm now. The bad nights, the lingering grief, were easing off.

Greg accepted the bowl of coleslaw, took a first taste. "Okay, this is incredibly good," he admitted. Though not normally a fan of coleslaw, it did make a perfect side dish for barbecue.

She turned her attention to her bowl, spooned out another scoop. "I don't think the coleslaw will last until the ribs are hot. They're going to need the full fifteen minutes in the oven."

"It's not the first reverse-order meal you and I have eaten. How many times have I started with pie?"

Janelle laughed. "Very true."

Greg went over to explore the refrigerator, opened the caps on two cold root beers, passed her one, and considered the moment safe to tell her a piece of bad news. "Tanya has gotten herself into some trouble with a designer she dated. He says she took part of his upcoming show collection with her after he broke up with her. She says the dresses in her possession were gifts he gave her while they were dating. It's heading to court."

It was the first time Tanya's name had been mentioned in a while, and Janelle paused at the news, her smile fading. "I'm sorry for her—that he broke up with her as much as the dispute."

"Ann thought you'd want to know."

Janelle nodded. "I appreciate your passing it on." She drank part of the soda, then mentioned, "If Tanya's ex-boyfriend does take her to court, wins the case, and he's still alive a year later, Ann should consider changing her opinion of Tanya."

Greg simply smiled. The two women's agreement to disagree about Tanya still held. A wise outcome, he thought. It was likely going to take years for the truth about Tanya to become apparent, if it ever did. "It would still be best if you didn't make contact, didn't send sympathy flowers or a card."

"I've accepted that Tanya and I have permanently parted ways. It's reality that most friendships turn out to have a life-span to them."

Janelle was no longer in touch with friends from before Andrew's death. That was just one of many items she and Greg had discussed in prior months.

Greg tipped his root-beer bottle her way. "While that may be true, I'm hoping ours manages to endure."

She locked eyes with him and smiled. "I do too."

While he'd made it a rule not to date clients, the day was soon coming when she wouldn't need him in that capacity any longer. She wasn't sure if the island was her temporary home or where she wanted to settle long term, but she'd make that decision in the coming months. She needed time. He knew her heart was still letting go of Andrew. She'd been politely dismissing interest from some of the nicer single guys on the island. But she suited him personally. Falsely accused prison time changed perspectives on life in ways it was hard to explain, and that was a big rock to have in common. It created an appreciation of freedom, a contentment to simply enjoy life, a willingness to let go of what would otherwise turn a person bitter. Janelle instinctively understood that and shared those traits with him. And there were numerous small things they treasured in common: a love affair with good food, comfortable chairs and conversation, a preference for doors to remain open, an enjoyment of silence, the delight in a simple glass of ice water, all the way down to an intense dislike for the sound of metal on metal. Janelle thought like him and reacted like him in important ways that no one else had done in over a decade. It made for a vibrant relationship. And he wanted to know where that relationship might lead one day. If she was still on the island a year from now, he planned to ask her out on a real date, see what kind of reply he got. Greg eyed the oven. Those ribs smelled really good.

"Friends tell each other to be patient," she said.

He grinned—she wasn't going to last the full fifteen minutes either. "We should choose our pie before the best ones are gone."

"You'll want the key lime pie." She nodded to the second refrigerator. "Middle shelf."

He found it, cut two thick wedges, and slid over a pie plate. "Dessert course next. It's best served cold." He pulled a folded piece of paper out of his pocket, unfolded it, and pushed it her way. "Not that you need pie before you read it, but another offer came in if you'd like to tell your story in book form. I'm dutifully passing it along." Ann routinely fielded such inquiries directed to Janelle.

She looked at the figure and the offering publisher, balled it up for the trash. "Still not interested."

He wasn't surprised, yet it was useful to see. She'd moved on. The significant shift that always came for a client had settled in for Janelle. She didn't see herself as primarily connected to the past. She now saw herself as connected to the present. She was sleeping soundly, handling relationships, enjoying work, and getting restless when bored. His work was about done.

"Let's go riding this afternoon," she suggested.

"Sure." He kept Monday afternoons and Tuesday mornings open for whatever she wanted to do. They'd probably talk more about the scenery than they would about subjects from her past, which worked for him. It was conversations about the future that were the last part of the puzzle, and those were still a ways off, he thought, for they would come from her own dreams as she caught up with life again and allowed herself to look forward.

She finished her pie, put together picnic plates and silverware, added a roll of paper towels to the basket, then reached for hot pads. "Those ribs smell wonderful—I'm declaring the main course ready to eat. If you'll carry the basket and hold the back door, I'll bring the tray."

Greg nodded as he swallowed the last of his pie. They headed out toward the picnic table behind the shop. Kevin was eagerly waiting, as was Marco. Janelle opened the foil packages and began dishing out the ribs.

The entire year could repeat this kind of day and that would be fine with him. Contentment in life was vastly underrated. He'd found it, and so had Janelle. And if it took life's quirks to bring it about, like a pink pocketknife being bought at auction, and curiosity on the part of the buyer, life was also showing the reality that it was watched over by God. Even impossible situations could change. He'd tasted that in his lifetime, and so had she.

Greg was looking forward to the coming year, to seeing where it took them both. Janelle smiled at him over a rib, like she knew what he was thinking. They had a good beginning to what promised to be an interesting future.

DEADLY ISLE

DANI PETTREY

ONE

HE WAITED, lurking against the buoy's cold, rusty body, awaiting *her*.

He glanced at his watch.

Any moment now.

His breathing shallowed as he focused. He'd only have a few seconds, a blink of an eye to act, and then he'd disappear beneath the murky surface.

Sand and silt tossed up from the storm worked even better with his plan than he could have imagined. Finally, things were turning his way.

Taking another shallow breath, he tried to force his heart to pump harder, his adrenaline to burn. He'd enacted this moment repeatedly in his mind, had swum his escape route more times than his gloved fingers could count. He had this—had *her*.

He spotted movement, her head rolling sideways, barely breaching the waterline for a brief, controlled gasp of air—one of her last. She swam with the current, which would carry her dead body down along the shoals of Henry's Point, where his crime would look like the perfectly painful accident he'd envisioned. But the other one would follow shortly, always a few minutes behind the bend. That was his window to act. His perfect window.

Her arms smoothly stroked in a straight line toward the buoy, her right hand finally reaching out and grasping ahold of what she expected would be a safe resting place. How wrong she was. Her head rose above the surface, and without hesitation, he swung.

|||||||||||

Teni was off her game today. How could she not be after what had just happened between her and Alex? She fought against the storm-driven waves to increase the pace of her stroke, knowing Julia was outracing her, but at this point she didn't care. Sobs threatened to wrack her body, but she fought them off, focusing on her breathing as the painful breakup flashed through her mind. Why on earth had he waited until they'd arrived at their wedding venue, her home island, before breaking the news?

Alex looked down at his feet, then back at her. "I think we've both known something's been wrong ever since the engagement."

"Alex?" He was right. She had felt something was wrong but could never pinpoint what.

He held up his hand. "Let me get this out. You know I think the world of you . . . but that's not enough for a marriage, Ten."

"But . . ." she sputtered. Why had he waited so long? They were only hours from meeting with her pastor about wedding details.

"Give me a hug," Alex said. "I'm going to have Lenny run me back to Annapolis before this storm hits." He glanced at the darkening sky. "Looks like it's going to slam Talbot."

Much as her heart had just been slammed. If she was honest with herself, she felt the same concern as Alex—knowing they

156

weren't right for each other, but she hadn't understood why. She
supposed that didn't matter. Regardless of the reason it wasn't
working, it was over now. And it still hurt.

She propelled forward in the water, swimming with the
current as her mind raced back to the vision of Alex sailing
off beneath the darkening sky, taking her dreams of marriage
with him. To take Teni's mind off the pain, her cousin Julia
had insisted they still make their traditional end-of-season
race out to Barner's Buoy, but she was clearly in no state of
mind to truly compete. She was barely resisting the urge to
ball up and cry.

As she swam she realized she was losing a friend—just a
friend. Losing her fiancé should have felt like losing so much
more.

What was wrong with her?

Why couldn't she find a love like she'd experienced with Callen Frost all those years ago? But did she really want that? That
love had ended in horrible, soul-crushing heartache.

As she reached the buoy, she lifted her head, fully anticipating finding a gloating Julia waiting there. She'd finally beat
Teni to the buoy after all these years of racing, but Julia was
nowhere to be seen.

That's odd.

Teni checked her time. *Twenty-two minutes. Pitiful.*

Typically, she nailed the thousand-yard swim out to the
buoy in around eighteen. Julia was usually around twenty.
Teni should have been a minute or two behind her. Julia had
streamed past her in the inlet. Surely she would have noticed if
she'd passed her cousin during the swim.

She grabbed the buoy and sidled around it. "Jules?" she
called over the burgeoning waves. "Jules? Where are you?" No
way Julia would turn around and make the swim back without

waiting for her to arrive and taking a hefty rest as they always had.

Teni's gaze flashed to the once-white buoy, now a mottled gray, but it wasn't the buoy that garnered her attention, but rather the bright red substance on and surrounding the rusty handhold they always used to grab onto as they rested.

She swallowed, panic slithering through her veins.

A boat approached from the distance, but her focus remained on her cousin.

"Julia!" She ducked under the water but saw nothing—only the white caps sloshing above the surface, muddying the waters several feet below.

Breaching the surface, she took a deep breath, trying not to give in to the panic suddenly flooding her system. Everything was fine. Julia probably just decided to skip the rest and head back to shore because the storm was coming in. And what appeared to be blood . . . She looked back at the red now being washed away by the waves.

Had Julia gotten hurt?

"Julia?" she hollered again, something urging her to stay—to keep looking.

"Ten?"

She stilled at the sound of his voice—the first time she'd heard it in over a year.

Callen Frost. Not now.

Swallowing, she turned to find his boat idling ten feet to her six.

"What are you doing out here?" he called out as rain began falling, wind lashing white caps up and over her chin as she worked to stay buoyant.

"Jules and I . . ."

"Your race?"

She nodded. "What are you doing out here?"

"Collecting my crab pots before the storm rolls in." He gestured to the loosely woven silver-wire pots that suckered the crabs in and prevented passage out.

His dark brows furrowed. Dark brows, dark eyes, the color of the sky at night over Talbot. "Something wrong?" he asked.

"I can't find Julia, and there was something that looked very much like blood on the buoy." She could say that with a good deal of certainty, given her job with the National Resources Police, along with her specialization in underwater investigations.

"You think she cut her hand? I've always told you that buoy is a rust bucket."

Teni shook her head. "That was my first thought, but it was too much blood and not shaped like a handprint."

His eyes narrowed—eyes that used to captivate her. "What are you thinking?"

She swallowed. What *was* she thinking? She was thinking like an investigator mixed with the fact that Julia was a missing family member. Training plus emotion equaled overreaction at times. "Maybe I'm overreacting, but I've got a sick feeling in my stomach. I don't think Jules would have turned back without waiting the extra minute or two for me, especially not if she was hurt."

Callen reached out and looped his hands under her arms, hefting her up to his boat. The first time she'd been in his arms since that fateful day on the beach nearly a decade ago.

"What are you doing?" she asked.

"Helping you find Julia."

"I can find her better in the water." It was where she excelled, and he was the last person she wanted help from.

"In this approaching storm, you really think that's the best way to proceed?"

No. She was reacting emotionally. She needed to calm down, focus. Why did it have to be Callen who came to her aid?

TWO

THE FARTHER SHE AND CALLEN TRACKED BACK, the faster Teni's heart raced—until they were at the boathouse and there was still no sign of Julia. No goggles. No wet footprints. Her cousin's towel still hanging on the hook. No sign of dripped blood.

A lump weighted at the bottom of Teni's stomach. "It doesn't look like she's been back."

Concern deepened across Callen's face. "What are you thinking?"

Why did he always ask her that? And she never got to reciprocate, or at least never got an answer beyond, *About you*. At least until that day . . .

"If Julia got hurt, if she was struggling in any way and she didn't stay at the buoy . . ." Teni thought aloud, pacing, trying to make her mind approach the situation as if she'd been called on the scene. And that was the scariest aspect. So many scenes she'd been called to started out just like this—a missing loved one, only a small clue, a direction, a spot of blood. She swallowed the bile rising in her throat at the thought of how most of those cases ended with her retrieving the loved one's body from the seabed or the bottom of the bay.

"If she were struggling in any way, she is a good enough swimmer to know to let the current carry her . . . and it is pulling toward . . ." She calculated in her mind. Talbot Island had zero cell coverage, so there was no fast way to look up the tides, but she didn't need to, she felt them. . . . "Henry's Point." It was where nearly everything lost in the bay surrounding Talbot eventually washed up, where beachcombers and treasure hunters flocked after a storm to seek their latest token or beautiful shell.

"Back in the boat," Callen said, hopping in and offering Teni a hand.

She grasped hold of the hand she'd held on to so often as they'd run through the white oak and black walnut trees populating Talbot, crunching over acorns and dried leaves, tripping over golf-ball-sized black walnuts, their hands black from cracking them open to eat the goody inside. So many memories wrapped up in one man—the best and the absolute worst.

"It'll be all right," he said, laying a hand on her shoulder and squeezing.

She nodded, fighting the barrage of emotions flooding through her as rain trounced them.

Thoughts of Julia flashed through her mind—her fuzzy socks, purple lipstick that only Jules could pull off, a night of chick flicks and buttery popcorn mere hours ago. Jules wasn't just her cousin, she was her best friend. If anything had happened to her . . .

She swallowed, refusing to let her mind wade there.

The boat ride out to Henry's Point took less than five minutes, but it felt like a lifetime. Why was she so fearful? Julia had probably just cut her hand, was hurting, the waves burgeoning, and she let the current carry her to Henry's Point rather than try to make the swim against the current back to the boathouse. But why wouldn't Julia have waited the minute or two for her? It didn't make sense.

Callen focused on navigating the shoals while approaching

the tiny barrier island—more like sand bar, actually, one they'd spent plenty of summer days on. She blinked through the thickening rain and cloud cover, trying to make out her cousin amid the marsh and sand.

Please be waving to me.

The island was fully visible from their vantage point and there was no one standing on the shore, but that didn't mean Julia wasn't huddled up somewhere in the marsh.

"Jules," she called.

Callen navigated around the shoals, idling just offshore. "I can't go in closer or it'll run aground."

"I'll go in." She dove into the waves and current-driven water without a moment's hesitation. Callen's voice echoed through the water, but it was muffled and she wasn't stopping, if that was what he was suggesting. The rip current pulled hard, but knowing better than to fight it, she let it pull her out before she swam back in at an angle.

She reached the shore moments before Callen did. He was fully clothed and fully drenched.

"What are you doing?" she asked.

"I was worried you were caught in the riptide."

"Thanks, but I've got it." She'd always been a strong swimmer, but he still managed to beat her every time—he always thanked his Pocomoke roots, the island's natives, for the inherent ability. She'd worked at it—to him the gift came effortlessly.

They trudged through the marsh, Teni sinking into the sand well above her ankles, the rain cold on her skin, the one-piece Speedo not nearly enough cover for the deluge they were in.

"Jules?" she called again.

"Julia?" Callen hollered.

They worked their way from the north point toward the south point, and Teni was just about to give up and relax in the thought that Julia was probably safely back at the boathouse now with some cockamamie story about what happened. But then Callen whispered, "There."

Julia. Lying with her face in the sand, her limbs dangling in the marsh.

Teni rushed forward and flipped her cousin over. The side of her head was smashed in, her eyes open and lifeless, sand coating her lips.

Teni cleared Julia's airways and started CPR.

Callen raked Teni up in his arms, holding her shivering body against his sturdy one, engulfing her in a bear hug. "She's gone, honey. She's gone."

"No." She shook her head, tears streaming from her eyes. "She can't be. We were just . . ."

She'd just lost her parents the year before last in a tragic boating accident, and now Julia—her sister for all intents and purposes—was gone. She blinked as tears gushed hot down her cold face. *This can't be happening. . . .*

"I know." Callen cradled Teni's head in his hand, and her gaze shifted back to Julia, her cousin's wet hair mangled with sand, marsh, and seeped blood. Had she hit her head on the buoy?

Teni sniffed and pulled back slightly, looking up at Callen, who sheltered her eyes from the rain by cupping his hand over her forehead. "For that kind of wound, it would have had to have been a really strong wave that slammed her just right against the buoy."

"True, but it could easily happen if she came up and didn't see a wave coming, or some of the damage could have occurred on the rocks of the shoals as the current carried her to Henry's Point. You can already see bruises forming."

Teni nodded and rested her head back against Callen, bawling for the loss of Julia on the one shoulder she never thought she'd rest her head on again.

THREE

"I'LL GET HER," CALLEN WHISPERED. "You wait on the boat."

"No." Teni sniffed, shaking her head.

He frowned. "What do you mean *no?*"

"No. This needs to be documented."

"Honey, she hit her head and drowned. It was an accident."

"But it's my job as an NRP officer to document every incident—accident or not." She'd do this right, for Julia.

"Okay, what do you need to do?"

"I need my equipment bag off my boat. I need to photograph her before we move her."

"Ten . . . ?"

"I'm doing this right."

"Okay." Callen held up his hands, having learned long ago when she wasn't budging. "Let's go back and get your bag."

She shook her head. "I'm not leaving her alone." She looked up at Callen. At six-foot-one he towered nearly a foot over her five-foot-two frame. "Will you please get it?"

Callen raked a hand through his soaked hair. "Sure. Where is it on your boat?"

She explained, and he left her alone with Julia, her heart breaking, the only warmth the tears streaming down her cheeks. First her parents and now Julia. Why was this happening? Why was God ripping everyone she loved from her life?

||||||||||

Callen watched Tennyson Kent in her element. He'd never seen her work a case, but considering the loss she'd just endured, she was managing to document her cousin's accident with impressive focus and proficiency. Poor Teni. First her fiancé left the island—he'd passed Lenny's boat heading away from Talbot as he was heading back in, radioed Lenny for the deets, and learned the engagement had been called off. That was the last thing he'd ever wanted to happen to Teni, but it provided an undeserved second chance to win the heart of the woman he'd always loved but had been foolish enough to let go.

"Okay," she said, slipping her camera with its rain guard back into the case. "We can take her home now."

He nodded and bent, gently lifting Julia's limp body, his heart squeezing, remembering when his mom had made him hold her as a baby. A crying, squirming little thing in his six-year-old arms, but it was Teni's cousin, a new Kent family member, and they all kowtowed to the Kents.

Now she was a limp, dead weight in his arms. He tried not to look in her eyes, for he swore they were full of fear. Had she survived the initial blow against the buoy? He prayed not. Prayed she'd died instantly rather than suffered as the current and undertow dragged her body up onto Henry's Point. Once a place of amazing memories, it was now a place of two terrible losses—first Teni, ten years ago by his thoughtless words after a horrible action that had destroyed their relationship, and now her cousin to the ravages of a storm-surging bay.

He swallowed as he placed Julia's body below deck and covered her up with a sheet from his master bunk. Teni stood watch from the stairwell, gripping the silver rail, her fingers blue. What had he been thinking, or rather, where was his head?

He grabbed the comforter out of the cupboard by his bunk and wrapped it around Teni. "Here, this ought to help."

She clutched it to her tiny frame. "Thanks."

He nodded. "We'll let mainland police know about the accident, but I doubt they'll risk sending someone out in the storm." The nor'easter whipping up the east coast had shifted course midafternoon and was now due to hit them full-on tomorrow. Talbot Island had no police force, so it fell under the jurisdiction of Crisfield—the closest town on the mainland but still an hour's boat ride away.

Teni nodded. "I assumed the same. I'll call the accident in via the landline when we reach shore."

Lacking cell service and cable TV, among other amenities, the island was "lost in time," according to the tourists, but it had its charms—the permanent islanders being cut off from the world after "the season" being one of them.

His experience as an Alcohol, Tobacco, Firearms and Explosives investigator and hers as a National Resources Police officer with unilateral statewide jurisdiction meant they could handle possession of the body until the ME could safely arrive after the storm.

Minutes later they approached the Kents' dock. Well, Teni's since her parents' tragic death. He swallowed against the stark realization of just how horrific Julia's loss had to feel for her, coming so close on the heels of her parents' accident.

He gave Teni the helm and jumped onto the dock as she angled up to it, tying the rig line to the winch. After making sure the boat was secure enough, he jumped back on board and found Teni down below, standing over Julia, sobbing.

He wrapped his arms around her shoulders, resting his chin on the top of her head as he'd done so many times. "I'm so incredibly sorry." For more than he could express.

He heard her swallow, hard, and she turned, wiping the tears from her eyes with the back of her shivering hand. "We need to decide where we will keep Julia until the ME can make it over from the mainland."

"I know. Why don't you let me handle that?"

She shook her head. "She's my cousin."

"Maybe the volunteer fire station?"

"That glorified barn? Hardly a sturdy structure during the storm, and they have no basement or cellar. . . ."

He knew that look in her eyes.

She put a hand to the back of her neck. "The icehouse."

"What?"

"It's underground, so it'll be safe from the storm. It's secure and the cool temperatures will . . . preserve . . . her body." She bit back what looked like another sob ready to wrack her slender body.

"Good idea. I'll carry her there. You call the mainland."

"I'll come with you, and then we can call the mainland."

He nodded, knowing she was going to see this through every step of the way. She was a good investigator and an even better cousin.

Jensen and Maxine, the Kent property's caretakers—*Teni's* caretakers when she was off property—came rushing out of the house.

"Wh . . . wha . . . what's wrong?" Maxine asked as Jensen wrapped his arm around her. Both obviously knew the two girls had gone for the swim, probably saw them off, as always.

"Julia had an accident," Callen said, certain Teni would have a hard time forming the pain-filled words.

"An accident?" Jensen asked as Maxine sobbed.

167

Callen explained as quickly as he could to spare Teni the horrible details and assumptions being repeated. He thought the assumptions right, but until the ME did the exam, they were just assumptions—not facts.

They laid Julia in the icehouse on the cold, stone bench and kept her draped with the sheet.

Maxine ran and gathered a sprig of fall wildflowers, dripping with rain, and laid them on Julia's covered chest.

"Come, Maxie," Jensen said after a short while. "Let's leave them to their peace."

"Peace? What peace?" Teni asked, then blinked rapidly, as if she hadn't meant to say that out loud.

Now was not the time to give her a lesson on God's sovereignty or the peace He'd eventually fill her with. Now was the time for sorrow and grieving, and trusting He'd carry Teni through the days, weeks, and months of mourning ahead. And if there was anything he could do personally, he'd be there for her. He hadn't been once. He'd never repeat that mistake again, if she'd allow him the privilege.

"Do you want me to call the mainland for you?" he offered.

"No. I'll do it. I'll process and report the accident as I would any other. NRP has jurisdiction on this one. I'll call in my ME of choice after the storm—it's our case."

He didn't know all the inner workings of the NRP but had researched the organization when he'd heard Teni had followed in the footsteps of her father and his line, who'd all joined the NRP, starting with her great-grandfather. He was a founding member of the Oyster Police, which, in time, turned into the National Resources Police. He knew she was right about the jurisdiction. The NRP utilized whatever local authorities they needed for their cases, but when it came to the water and any accidents or crimes committed on it—it fell under NRP jurisdiction. It was an interesting unit. One unique to Maryland and its shores and waterways.

Callen followed Teni back to the main house, where she called her superior and informed them of the situation. Then she called her ME of choice.

Jensen cleared his throat, wrinkled hands wringing, clearly at a loss for words. "I'll finish securing the house for the storm."

"I've got it," Callen said.

Jensen looked to Teni.

"Callen and I can take care of it," Teni said. "You two take care of your place."

"Are you sure, Miss Tennyson?"

"Positive, and how many times have I asked you both to call me Teni?"

"Okay, love." Maxine leaned in and kissed Teni's brow. They'd been with the Kents since as far back as Callen could remember. Always a part of the girls' lives—the two cousins growing up nearly as sisters after the divorce of Julia's parents and the remarriages that bumped her all around. Eventually, Teni's folks had taken her in, and she'd grown up on the island with them.

Them.

It always had been them—he and Teni—growing up together. And then he'd destroyed it all in one drunken night on campus, with a group of guys who were never truly his friends and a girl he'd been too drunk to even remember her name the next day. It had been exactly the wrong way to handle his father's death, but the wound was raw, and instead of returning to Talbot to find solace in Teni's arms, he'd remained on campus that weekend and fell into the very wrong ones.

Teni grabbed the toolbox Jensen had sitting on the entrance table. "I've got this. You should take care of your place."

"I did earlier when word of the storm shift first came in. I'll stay and help you. Actually . . ." He took the toolbox from her hand. "You shouldn't be worrying about this now. Let me handle it."

"No." She shook her head, always so stubborn. "I'd rather stay distracted."

He understood the urge to find a distraction during a loss, only too well—and that distraction had destroyed his and Teni's relationship.

FOUR

TENI SLIPPED ONE FOOT into the luxurious bubble-filled claw-foot tub, then her other, the soothing scent of lavender wafting in the steam rising from the tub and clinging to the gilded mirror hanging over the pedestal sink.

Callen had held true to his word, helping her secure the house, and then remained until leaving at nearly ten o'clock, saying she needed to get some rest. Like she'd be sleeping tonight.

She still wasn't sure how she felt about Callen's help. He had crushed her with his betrayal, but his presence today had brought an unexplainable measure of peace and stability amid the storm raging in her.

Slipping to a seated position in the tub, she jerked as lightning cracked nearby, the flash of light casting leaf-patterned shadows across the hardwood floor.

She swallowed. Her momma would scold her for drawing a bath during a thunderstorm, but her momma wasn't here, and now neither was Julia.

As she sank deeper into the water, the bubbles tickled her chin, the aromatic scent of lavender filling her nostrils.

Calm down, Teni. You're strong. You're a fighter. You will not fall apart, and as good as it felt to have Callen near, you don't need him.

She took a steadying breath.

You don't need anyone.

Because no one was fixed—all could be lost in the blink of an eye.

||||||||||

Approaching the house, he noted candles flickering in the master bath window upstairs. Why candles? He wasn't sure why she used candles while the electricity still ran, but any open flame only stood to serve his purpose.

He made his way down the four concrete outside cellar steps and entered the dark, dank basement. Lifting his flashlight, he scanned the space, thankful storm shutters covered the two small windows. He had total privacy as long as Tennyson remained upstairs.

Not wasting any time, he got to work—following the gas line leading from the propane tank into the cellar and along to the hot water heater.

||||||||||

Teni stirred in the tub as the wind rattled something outside. She stilled.

Had something come loose in the storm? Or was she just being jumpy because of her raw emotions over Julia's death, coupled with her earlier argument with Jared Connor about her decision to bring ferry service to the island?

She listened carefully—as still as a mouse caught in a cat's piercing glare.

There it is again. The rattle of something. Had the cellar door or a shutter come loose?

Pulling the plug from the drain, she grabbed the fluffy, white towel off the tub-side towel stand, wrapped it around herself, and stepped from the tub onto the bath mat. And after drying further, Teni pulled on her yoga pants, long-sleeved *Woman Up* tee, and a pair of pink fuzzy socks that reminded her of Julia, then made her way downstairs.

IIIIIIIIII

He glanced to the exposed-beam ceiling and stilled. Something was draining.

Footsteps padded across the floor, catching each ease and creak of the timeworn floorboards. He needed to work faster.

IIIIIIIIII

Teni turned on the kitchen light. The house appeared still, despite the storm raging outside. Maxine and Jensen were tucked away in their cottage. Perhaps the rattling she'd heard had simply been a branch scraping against a window on the first floor, the sound having echoed from below. She was just being overly jumpy—her emotions getting the best of her, and yet . . .

Better safe than sorry.

Especially if a storm shutter had come loose. For the nor'easter hadn't fully hit yet—this was just its outer bands.

Yanking on her yellow raincoat and matching rain boots with whimsical ducks carrying umbrellas, she grabbed the Maglite off the hook by the door and stepped onto the porch, the blustery wind whipping the hair from her damp, lopsided bun.

Her house phone rang and she turned. Probably yet another sympathy call about Julia's loss. The news was already spreading across the island. It was so kind of everyone, but it just made it harder for her—jarring her back to the moment she'd rolled Julia's limp body over and . . .

She swallowed, moved back into the house, and lifted the

phone, shucking out of her jacket and dropping the flashlight on the entry table beside the phone base.

"Hello?"

"Hey, Tennyson."

"Alex."

She turned her back to the entryway table, leaning her weight against it.

"I just wanted to let you know I made it back safely. I should have called hours ago, but I was making sure Lenny got to where he needed to be."

"Lenny?" Hadn't he returned to Talbot as planned?

"He said the storm was moving in swifter than anticipated so he anchored his slip in the marina and is crashing with friends until it passes." Alex cleared his throat. "Look . . ." Hesitation hung thick in his voice. "I know today wasn't easy, but it was the right decision for us both."

After what happened with Julia—which Alex didn't know about, but she couldn't bear to say it aloud one more time—their breakup wasn't at the top of her concern list.

"Thanks for calling, Alex, but I've got to go."

"Okay. You be safe in this storm."

Which one? The one raging outside or the one tearing her apart from the inside out?

"Good-bye, Teni."

"Bye, Alex." She hung up, only to have the phone ring again.

With a stiffening breath, she answered, prepared for another consolation call.

"Hey, Ten," Callen said. "I apologize for calling so late."

She glanced at the giant clock hanging over the kitchen's brick fireplace. Eleven o'clock. Not late compared to some of their nighttime mystery-solving adventures as teens. Good thing her momma had been a patient woman. Teni had tested her more than she prayed her future child or children would ever test her.

"I just wanted to see how you are doing."

Tears rolled down her cheeks at the weight such a simple statement held.

"Ten?"

"Yeah." She wiped away the tears with the back of her hand. "Sorry. Was spacing out. I'm fine."

"You sure? I hated to leave, but I wanted to let you get some rest."

One thing she wouldn't be getting. No way was she going to find rest tonight.

A creaking sound stole her attention.

It sounded close. *Very* close. Gooseflesh rippled up her arms. She stilled, listening, but it stopped.

"Ten?" Callen asked again. "You sure you're okay?"

"Yeah," she said, still trying to listen. "I'm fine."

"Okay. Well—" The line went dead.

She sighed.

Every. Single. Storm.

Resting the dead phone back in the receiver, she moved to make some hot cocoa—her brief moment on the porch enough to spring a chill in her bones, and she could clearly use a bit of relaxation. She was so tense. Old houses creaked, especially in a storm, so why was her heart palpitating like she was in danger? The thought of Jared Connor following her back to her house nestled inside with unease.

Don't let him intimidate you like he used to—bully that he's always been.

It was just the roller coaster of emotions she'd been dragged through today. Jared's threats, Alex breaking the engagement, precious Julia's shocking accident—she was in a sensitive and vulnerable state, but she wouldn't give in to the fear eating at her, despite her intuition screaming otherwise.

‖‖‖‖‖‖

He worked fast, and as silently as possible. He needed to ensure Tennyson didn't smell the gas until it had a chance to fill the basement and hit the blazing pilot light, which she was thoughtful enough to keep flickering by her use of hot water above.

He surveyed the space around him and smiled when his flashlight beam landed on the red velvet Christmas tree skirt in a clear plastic storage tub.

Now to be extra quiet . . .

He crept to the storage tub, opened it, bunched the skirt in his gloved hands, and ever-so-carefully climbed the basement stairs, wedging it into the space between the mudroom door and the floor. Even with her presence in the kitchen—a mere room away from the mudroom—filling the crack would give him the time needed for the gas to fill the small space. And then it was good-bye Tennyson Kent. All his troubles would disappear in an explosion's brief but deadly blast.

‖‖‖‖‖‖

Teni pulled the kettle from the burner and switched off the dancing flames. Pouring the hot water over the dark chocolate Godiva cocoa powder she'd emptied into her favorite *I moose wake up* travel mug, she scalded her hand on the kettle and, jerking in response, managed to splatter chocolate cocoa all over her light gray shirt.

Great. She dropped the kettle back on the burner and held her hand under running cold water until the burn chilled, though a blister was already forming on the heel of her palm. Switching the water to hot, she yanked a dish towel off the stove handle, dampening it in the steaming water, hoping to use it to dab out the stains dotting her favorite shirt before they set.

Lightning struck with a house-shaking clatter, illuminating the tree line outside her kitchen window.

A chill reverberated up her spine.

Was that . . . a man's silhouette? Had Jared returned?

Thunder rumbled in her chest.

Lightning crackled again, this time zigzagging across the black night sky, again clearly illuminating the forest and a fleeing silhouette.

She swallowed. Someone *was* definitely out there. Grabbing her sidearm and flashlight, she shimmied into her raincoat and rushed outside, flipping on the porch light as she went.

The metal flashlight was cool in her still-burning palm as she raced for the tree line. She took one step across the forest's threshold and an explosion rent the air, quaking the ground and propelling her toward the trees in a rush of fire.

FIVE

TENI'S HEAD SWAM, darkness and fierce heat enveloping her. Something was shaking her. She tried to open her eyes, but they were so heavy. So very heavy. And why was it so hard to breathe?

Again the shaking. This time she somehow managed to raise her heavy eyelids. Rain poured down on her, and Callen knelt beside her, leaning in close, his face mere inches over hers, fear flaring in his dark eyes.

Lightning scorched the sky, thunder quickly following.

His mouth moved, but all she heard was ringing searing her ears.

Callen rattled her. "Teni," he mouthed.

She blinked, a cough wracking her shoulders and chest.

"Oh, thank God," Callen said, his voice finally breaking through the ringing as she struggled to breathe.

He pulled her up into his arms.

Flames danced high and fiercely beyond his shoulder.

What was happening?

She blinked. Flames were engulfing her home—her family home.

"No!" She lunged from his hold, her head swirling.

"Teni," Callen said above the incessant ringing in her ears. "Easy now. You're okay."

"But my home." It had belonged to her family since her ancestor was deeded the island in 1767 and had built the first part of the house the following year. And it was burning to the ground.

At least she still owned the land—no one could take that heritage from her. She'd owned the island since it passed to her after her parents' death in the boating accident—the island having passed down through the Kent bloodline, eldest to eldest to her. Owning an island and leasing out the land to tenants seemed strange to many in modern society, but growing up on Talbot, it was all she'd known—her family's island steeped in lore and legacy. A legacy she'd just lost an integral part of.

An expression that showed he understood the crushing blow of losing her family home creased Callen's face. "I know."

Volunteer firefighters were dousing the blaze with hoses, and the rain streaming down in a sheer blanket of cold pellets had to help.

What had happened?

Lightning seared the sky again, illuminating the smoke-smeared faces of the volunteer firefighters.

The silhouette. She'd seen a silhouette.

Had that just been a coincidence? Someone in the woods, someone watching her before her house exploded?

Thank goodness she'd left the house to check on it. If she hadn't . . .

Her head swirled and her legs wobbled beneath her as she attempted to scramble to her feet. Where was her gun?

"Whoa, Teni." Callen grasped her tighter. "I got you. You're okay."

"If I'd been inside . . ."

He swallowed, his Adam's apple bobbing. "I know." To her

surprise, he pressed a kiss to her brow. "But you're safe. I've got you."

Did he really have her? Like he used to? Not possible.

"What happened?" Her head continued to swim as she scoured the debris-strewn ground for her weapon, finally spotting it a solid ten feet away, glistening in the fire truck's floodlights.

"I don't know yet," Callen said, helping her to a fully upright position and bracing her in his steadying hold, "but I promise I'll find out." He directed her toward a red SUV's lowered tailgate. "Paul's going to check you out."

Paul was the town paramedic, when he wasn't on the mainland pursuing his nursing degree. Thankfully for her, he'd taken the semester off to work with his dad and earn some cash so he could return to school in the spring. While on the island, he volunteered with Talbot's fire department, which was composed solely of volunteers, including Callen. Whenever he was on the island, Callen was on call. No wonder he'd arrived so quickly. Or at least it'd seemed quick. One minute everything was hot and black, and the next Callen was rousing her. But she actually had no idea how much time had elapsed between the two.

"Hey, Teni," Paul said as Callen lowered her to sit on the open SUV tailgate. "I'm just going to make sure you're okay."

She nodded, Paul's words muffled over the diminished ringing still assaulting her eardrums.

Paul bent, swiping a small light across her eyes, her burning home painfully visible over his broad shoulder.

Raindrops dripped off her eyelashes as she blinked, struggling to wrap her head around the fact that she'd just lost the home that had belonged to her family for generations. On the same day she'd lost her cousin. And her fiancé.

||||||||||

Callen anxiously paced while awaiting Paul's assessment of Teni. She looked to be in shock, but amazingly seemed okay otherwise. She was strong, always had been. Memories of that day at Henry's Point, him confessing to what she'd already learned through the gossip vine, her usually stiff-in-trauma lips quivering, tears spilling from her teal-green eyes, the same hue of the bay she loved so much.

Pain echoed through his heart, reverberating to his soul. That day had crushed something in them both—all because, instead of running to God, he'd tried to escape the overwhelming pain of his dad's death in the worst of ways, and it had cost him the most important person in his life. Teni.

Clearing his throat, he looked to the team working in unison to douse the flames. For a volunteer team of islanders, they excelled at what they did. Now he just had to wait until the fire was out and the scene secure to begin his investigation. He had a head start, though. It was clear some sort of gas explosion had produced a catastrophic outward blast—evidenced by the debris field stretching out at least a hundred yards, based on what he'd passed as he rushed in to . . .

He swallowed hard.

He'd feared Teni had been in the house at the time of the explosion, feared she'd been killed, and the notion of Teni gone from this world had imploded his heart. He couldn't breathe.

How he'd maintained his fierce pace to the scene . . . he didn't know. It had to have been God moving his legs, keeping him going. The fear had felt paralyzing, but he'd made it to Teni's side and, praise God, she was all right.

Gratitude to God flooded him, and he thanked the Lord she'd been out of the house. But that thought led to a question—one that had been nagging at him since finding her. What had Teni been doing outside in the storm so late at night?

So many questions rattled through his mind, so much

turmoil. The chances that Julia would die in an accident on the same day Teni's house suffered a gas explosion . . . The odds were nearly impossible. Was someone trying to kill off the Kents?

"Other than a good jar . . ." Paul said, pulling Callen from his thoughts as he stepped back to reveal Teni, "she's just fine."

The tension that had been wracking Callen's body released, the adrenaline burn-off searing his limbs. *Thank you, Lord.*

Smoke mingled thick with the fog and dousing rain. Clearing his throat, he said, "Thanks, Paul," in a cracked voice.

The kid nodded. *Kid* meaning he was almost a decade younger than he was—nearly the same age Callen had been when he'd trounced Teni's heart.

He shut his eyes and then blinked. Tonight, God had provided him yet another chance to win back Teni's love. He'd brought her through the fire.

Sinking down on the SUV's open bed, he huddled up against her, an Army green survival blanket draped across her shoulders—no doubt donated by retired Master Sergeant DeBerry during the volunteer firefighters' supply drive. "How you holding up?"

She looked at him, those beautiful teal-green eyes, the same green as Julia's, the same strawberry blond, long wavy hair—the two had always been inseparable and looked more like twins. He stiffened.

"What's wrong?" She coughed, and he rubbed her back in soothing, circular strokes.

"Nothing." No need to worry her with a random thought, though a piercing thought all the same. What if Julia's accident was no accident? What if someone smashed Julia's head against that buoy thinking it was Teni? They looked nearly identical, and Teni always reached the buoy first. The one day she didn't, Julia had died.

If foul play was involved, had Teni been the intended target all along . . . or was someone trying to take out the Kents? First Julia and now Teni?

"Let's get you out of the rain and into some dry clothes." He'd take her back to his place until the fire was out and any work on his part could begin.

She lifted in his hold to a standing position but swayed, so he maintained his steadying embrace—his hands wrapped around her slender, toned arms.

Lifting his chin at Paul, he said, "Tell the chief to send word when the fire's out and the scene secure."

Paul nodded. "Will do."

Teni bobbed along beside him, her head clearly spinning. *Enough of this.* He lifted her up in his arms. The woman was still as light as a bird. "We've got to get some meat on those skinny bones of yours."

"I'd argue I'm fine to walk . . . but . . ." Her head lolled.

"Shhh. Just rest. I've got you." To his amazement, after a moment she did, resting her head against his shoulder and fully giving in to his embrace. She felt incredibly right in his arms—then again, she always had. How could he have been so foolish? Giving in to self-pity and temptation instead of protecting the woman he loved?

They reached the clearing in the forest, his house still dark. He'd just gone to bed when he heard the explosion. He quickly yanked on the closest jeans and shirt and raced downstairs, where he'd pulled on his boots and grabbed his coat off the rack by the door. Within a fog of moments, he was racing through the woods that separated his home from Teni's, fearing the entire time that Teni was dead and he'd never get to tell her how sorry he was and that he still loved her with a consuming love.

Reaching his porch with Teni thankfully alive in his arms, he jiggled his front door open and carried her to the couch, where he gently laid her down. "I'll grab the lights."

As he turned on the tableside lamps, the room and Teni became clearer. She was shivering, soaked, and in shock.

"Let's get you dry." After taking her boots off and setting them by the door, he pulled the soaked blanket off her shoulders and slipped the yellow raincoat from her slender frame. Underneath she wore a long-sleeved T-shirt and mud-covered yoga pants.

Snagging the thick throw his mom had woven for him off the back of the couch, he wrapped it around her shoulders. At least it would be a temporary fix. She shifted to a seated position, swaying as she did so.

"Easy now," he said. He wrapped his arms around her, rubbing hers, trying to warm her, but she was still shivering. "Let me get you some towels and dry clothes." He shifted to move.

She clasped his arm, her hand cold and trembling. "Not yet." She looked up at him, her eyes still wide. "Sit with me for a moment?"

"Of course." He moved back to her side. "I'm right here. I'm not going anywhere." Never again, *if* she'd forgive him. But how could she after what he'd done, and after so much time had passed? Even though the engagement was called off, she'd been about to marry another man. Clearly, she'd moved on.

She leaned into him as she had so many times before. And despite the horrific circumstances surging around them, he reveled in the feel of her back in his arms. Thank goodness, she'd left the house, which led him back to the question . . .

"What were you doing out in the storm?" he asked, unable to help himself.

"I thought I heard a noise."

He tried not to chuckle. It was storming out—blustering winds, shocks of lightning, and rumbles of thunder moving in swiftly across the bay's dark surface. "What kind of noise?"

"I don't know, like a creaking. Like the cellar door was opening or a storm shutter was loose, and then I saw a silhouette of someone in the woods."

He stiffened. "You saw *someone*? Do you know who?"

"I definitely saw someone. I'm not sure who, but . . ."

"But?"

"I had a run-in with Jared Connor earlier."

SIX

"*Ms.* Kent."

Knowing that sneering pronunciation of *Ms.* anywhere, Teni stopped short. Jared Connor. *Not again*, and certainly not right after Alex had broken off their engagement.

She turned to find Jared coming out of Milly's restaurant, where she'd been looking for Julia to tell her about the broken engagement—to cry on her cousin's, and best friend's, shoulder.

"I need a word with you," Jared said, stalking toward her.

Jared's father, Darren Connor, came out of the diner behind his son, wearing his brown shoreman overalls, his everyday attire—every day except Sunday, when he wore his white dress shirt and navy tie. Always the same, but always so sweet—his gray hair combed over and a navy handkerchief sticking slightly out of his shirt pocket, available for anyone in need. He was a kind older gentleman. His son Jared was anything but kind.

"Now, son," Darren said. "Don't go bothering Miss Kent." He looked at Teni with soft blue eyes, wrinkles crinkling around the edges. "I apologize."

"Stop apologizing to her, Dad," Jared replied, his voice

186

heated. "So what if she owns the entire island and leases us our land? She doesn't own *us*."

"It's fine, Mr. Connor," Teni said. Jared always had a mind of his own and an opinion to share—and always a strong one, at that. While Jared was more than a handful of years older than she was, they'd attended the same school for many years. Everyone from kindergarten through high school attended the one schoolhouse on Talbot Island.

While Darren was a hard-working shoreman—a man Teni greatly respected—Jared, though an excellent shoreman, liked to stir up trouble, especially with her.

Darren's wife, Marybeth, stepped to her husband's side—waiting, watching, as she always did. Marybeth clung to her grandmother's ways, holding tight to the superstitions of the elders' ancestors. The eldership was a practice the island's inhabitants had done away with decades ago, but their descendants still clung to it. Marybeth and those like her were always warning other townsfolk about this or that, disliking the few remaining Pocomokes—the original natives to the island, Callen included.

Why Teni's great, great—and so on through the generations—grandfather ever leased to superstitious or prejudiced landholders, or created the eldership in the first place, she'd never know, but among the handful still on the island, many held tight to their traditions—including Jared.

He stopped a mere foot from her. "You've got to stop the ferry service."

Not this again.

"It disturbs the sea life, the wildlife, and pollutes our water, which supports many of our livelihoods. Not to mention, it brings throngs of tourists traipsing on our shores. They don't respect the land or our ways."

Throngs was an exaggeration. Yes, the island had tourists, but their impact in any negative way was minimal, and on the positive side, they brought lots of money to the island. "As I've explained numerous times, lots of the residents on Talbot rely on the tourists and the income they bring for *their* livelihood."

"Because you've made them dependent on it. I mean, seriously, look at the pathetic shopkeepers giving away our local treasures to the mainlanders."

"They aren't giving them away. They are being paid for their beautiful crafts and local food items."

"At least you got the *local* part right."

"Jared, I appreciate your perspective and concerns, but the ferry system on the Chesapeake is one of the best. It only runs Memorial Day through Labor Day, and only two days of the week even then." To be honest, she preferred the island when the ferry stopped running and Talbot became solely inhabited by the locals again, but many of the locals—especially the younger people—had stepped away from living off the bounty of the Chesapeake Bay, and they needed a way to support themselves. The tourist season—minimal as it was—provided that much-needed source of income.

Teni had made the decision to allow the ferry service only after a vote, and it was made for the sake of the townsfolk, not her personal preference. Her grandfather had taught her that owning an island and leasing out the land was a *huge* responsibility—one that required dedication, business sense, and respect.

"So that justifies selling out our island?" Jared asked, his foot tapping an anxious melody on the leaf-strewn ground.

"I'm not selling out anything."

He took a step closer, getting in Teni's face, as he often had when she was young. But she was no longer a little girl waiting for Callen Frost to swoop in and rescue her from a bully. She was a police officer, working for National Resources. Her livelihood was *literally* to protect and safeguard Maryland's waterways. No one cared more about preserving the bay than she did.

"You need to rethink your position," he said, his tone gruff, his glare harsh.

She folded her hands rather than fidget with them. "I've already given it careful consideration."

"So you're saying you won't reconsider?" he asked, his tone growing more heated, urgent. The distance between them evaporated as his angry face grew ever closer to hers until she could feel his breath on her skin.

She held her ground, refusing his attempt to force her to step back, to cower as she had as a child. Jared was a bully then and he was a bully now. She squared her shoulders. "That's correct."

"This. Isn't. Over," he snapped, his posture rigid.

"I'm afraid it is."

"Or so you think."

Her eyes narrowed. Was that a threat? "What's that supposed to mean?"

He smiled, but there was only cruelty in it. "You'll see." He turned, striding into the woods before she could reply.

"I'm so sorry about him," Darren said. "The boy's just—"

"No need to apologize, Mr. Connor," she said quickly, stopping his unnecessary apology. "Jared's his own man and free to express his opinions." But certainly not a veiled threat.

"Thanks, Miss Kent. You have a good day now." Darren lifted the brim of his hat in a courteous gesture. Always the gentleman.

"Mr. Connor, how many times must I ask you to call me Teni?"

He smiled and turned back to the diner while Marybeth moved closer—lines spidering out from her tight, pale lips.

"Jared's not wrong, you know," she nearly hissed, so gritted were her teeth—her hatred for Teni no secret. "You're threatening our way of life."

"I'm sorry you feel that way. We held the decision to a vote, and the majority voted in favor of the tourist business during the summer."

"The vote wasn't unanimous, and you allowed *everyone* to vote."

Teni's gaze narrowed. "So?"

"So, it should have been limited to the original settlers' families. To the elders' families."

"*All* of the families on Talbot are descendants of the original settlers and locals. Or . . ." She linked her arms across her chest and cocked her head. They'd had this argument before. "Are you suggesting those of Pocomoke descent—those who were here first—shouldn't get a vote?" Hard to believe anyone was that backward in their thinking, but sadly, she knew that was the case with Marybeth.

"That's precisely what I'm saying." Marybeth sneered.

"That's beyond wrong."

"You only think so because of that Frost boy. Half-breed that he is."

Had she seriously just referred to Callen as a half-breed? Who talked like that anymore?

"I'm saying that because it's right. *Everybody* deserves a vote," Teni said, trying to simmer her heated response to Marybeth's cruel words.

"Elders and their descendants used to decide. It should be that way again."

"That's not going to happen." It never should have happened in the first place.

"We won't just sit by and watch you destroy our traditions, our home." Marybeth wagged her bony finger.

"What are you implying?"

"I'm not implying anything. I'm giving you some friendly courtesy advice."

"Really? And what's that?"

"You'd better watch that pretty back of yours."

"Are you actually threatening a police officer?"

"Of course not, dear." Marybeth smiled, her teeth stained and crooked. "It's a courtesy. Not a threat. I'm looking out for you."

Why did she find that so incredibly hard to believe?

Marybeth turned and hustled back inside Milly's.

Well, that had been a fun addition to the day.

Trying to shake off the odd chill of foreboding racing down her spine, Teni stepped into the orange-and-red leaf-covered wonderland leading back to her home, the crack of sticks and the crunch of leaves sounding beneath her. The leaves rustled in the breeze coming off the bay, and she inhaled the sweet, salty air deep in her lungs.

The sensation of being watched suddenly raked over her. She turned, surveying the expansive woods. "Hello?" she called out, knowing the woods could be filled with any number of people at any time. Or had Jared Connor lingered behind? She was in no mood for a second argument. Could he really not see she'd invited the ferry in for the locals' benefit?

The woods stilled, the only sound the whistling wind streaking through the leaves overhead.

Okay, she was being foolish. She refused to give in to fear— even if her emotions were taking her for a ride on the loopty-loop today.

She continued. Another dozen steps or so into the woods a stick snapped about sixty yards to her right.

Pausing, she surveyed the woods again. "Hello? Anyone there?"

Again, no answer, and an uneasy fear trickled through her.

Fear was foreign in these woods since she'd become an adult, so why was she suddenly so uneasy?

The sense of being watched wouldn't abate, no matter how she quickened her pace. Fear clung to her like tree sap sticking to her fingers.

Finally breaking past the wood's edge, she turned, staring into their depths.

Movement swiftly shifted in the leaf-shadowed distance.

She narrowed her eyes but couldn't make out if it was an animal or a person, the full foliage masking whatever or whomever it was. But someone or something *had* been there.

Another shiver shot up her spine.

She hurried inside her house and locked the door for the first time in forever.

What on earth was happening with her today? Had she seriously let Marybeth and Jared Connor get under her skin? Or was she just in an overly vulnerable state due to the broken engagement?

She stared out her kitchen window overlooking the woods—still feeling someone's presence—someone watching. Had Jared followed her home? Was he stalking her now?

SEVEN

"DO YOU THINK THE SILHOUETTE you saw could have been him?" Callen asked as Teni shivered beside him after catching him up on the conversation she'd had with Jared.

She rubbed her arms, swallowing, her coloring paler than he liked. He wrapped the throw more tightly around her. "I don't know. Maybe," she said.

"Do you think he was in your house? That he was the creaking you heard?"

"I don't know. I just heard some sounds and then saw someone outside. I can't be sure who. Then I went to look and . . ." She swayed.

"I got ya."

She swallowed. "I'm still trying to wrap my brain around it, and it's so frustratingly fuzzy."

He didn't want to push her, but this was important. *Very* important. "And you didn't see his face or anything that might identify him?"

"No. Just a silhouette as lightning streaked the sky. I flipped the porch light on and chased after him. Seconds later I felt an explosion, and the next thing I remember is . . . *you*." She looked up at him.

She'd flipped a switch and the house had exploded. Had the house been filling up with gas and the light switch ignited the explosion, or had the gas simply reached the pilot light? Most likely the latter—a light switch typically didn't spark to light a flame.

"Did you smell gas in the house? It would smell like rotten eggs."

"No." She shook her head, then clearly regretted the motion as her hand braced her forehead. "Why? What are you thinking?" she asked, shivering in his hold, her clothes underneath the blanket damp at best, soaked at worst.

"That we'll figure out what happened." He'd make certain of it, but he needed to be careful, not question her too much. Not yet. "We need to get you dry."

She nodded.

"Are you okay here while I go grab you some warm clothes?"

Again, she nodded.

He gathered towels, a brush, dry clothes, and anything else he could think of, then helped her up to his bathroom, where he'd placed all the items on the countertop.

He studied her a moment. "Are you going to be okay on your own?" he asked, half afraid she might topple over. She was strong, but she'd been knocked hard.

She bit her bottom lip and placed a stabilizing hand on the countertop. "I'll be good."

"I'll be right outside the door if you need me."

She nodded, the movement slight, her head clearly tender.

A handful of minutes later, she emerged wearing one of his T-shirts and pair of sweats, rather swimming in them. Her hair was pulled up in a side thingy with the hair band that had been on her wrist. She handed him the folded towels and blanket. Leave it to Teni to focus on the details amid a crisis. No doubt that focus made her such a great investigator.

"What do we do now?" she asked.

"We hunker down." He clutched her arm and guided her through the hall and back down the stairs to the sofa, where he again gently helped her sit. "Until the fire is out and the scene secure, I can't begin my preliminary investigation."

She shifted on the couch. "You're the fire expert, so what are you thinking happened?"

He rubbed his hands together. "With an outward blast and a wide-reaching debris field like that, it was a gas explosion."

She scrunched her face, her button nose upturning the way it did whenever she was putting the pieces of a puzzle together. "Gas explosion?"

He nodded. "I just need the scene secure, like I said, to determine the cause."

"The cause?"

"Was something faulty, was there a malfunction . . . ?"

Her beautiful eyes narrowed. "You don't think the silhouette . . . the noise, that someone, possibly Jared, intentionally did this?"

She read him so well, even when that was the last thing he wanted.

"It's possible, especially given you saw someone right before the explosion."

Her lashes fluttered. "If you think foul play might be involved . . . and I was supposed to be in the house . . ." She tensed, her shoulders growing rigid. "Do you think Jared might have been trying . . . to *kill* me?" Her chest rose and lowered in quick repeat, her breathing growing shallower, her hands fluttering about as she spoke. "If he tried to kill me, what about Julia? What if her death wasn't an accident?" She swallowed. "Did he kill my cousin too?"

Callen scooted closer against her, and taking her waving hands into his, holding them tight, he gazed into her eyes. "We'll figure this out—*together*."

195

She pulled her hands back, moving them as she spoke. "I know Jared was frustrated about the ferry, but could he be frustrated enough to kill?"

"I don't know. We don't even know for certain that it was foul play." But his gut sure said it was, especially if she'd seen someone in the woods. Plus, the odds of Julia's "accident" happening and Teni's house having a gas explosion the same day . . .

"I can see it in your eyes. You believe it was foul play."

He raked a hand through his drying hair. "It's a gut instinct, but those can be wrong."

"I don't know. They're often spot on."

She was right. That'd been his experience.

She stood, flinging off the blanket. "Julia!"

He frowned. "What?"

"The explosion. What if it reached the icehouse? What if . . . ?" She grabbed her rubber boots—with yellow, umbrella-carrying ducks on them—sitting by the door. Sliding them on, she pulled her raincoat off the hook where he'd hung it next to his.

"What are you doing?" he asked. She shouldn't be going anywhere. She needed to sit, to rest. To be safe.

"Going to make sure Julia . . . her body is okay . . . that the explosion . . ."

Hadn't reached Julia.

Knowing Teni would never rest until she was certain nothing had further harmed her cousin's body, he slid on his coat and boots, grabbed the lantern off the table, and followed Teni back out into the storm.

EIGHT

THEY TRAIPSED BACK UP the slippery muddy slopes
leading from Callen's home to hers, or what was left of it.
Her rain boots did their job in keeping her feet dry but didn't
effectively grip the shifting ground beneath her, so Callen sta-
bilized her by keeping a hold on her arm. She tried to ignore
how good his touch felt, but it was undeniably amazing. She'd
been so battered by the day's events she'd let down her guard
and fallen back into his arms. It was the wrong message to send.
The wrong person to rely on, but he was here and . . .

And she couldn't think much beyond that now, other than
the fact that she had to keep the guard around her heart better
fixed in place, even if it was breaking.

Rain splattered her nose, but the tree canopy overhead provided some measure of protection from the deluge.

As they reached the wood's edge, she saw her home—or what
had been her home—was now a skeleton of charred remains
with the fire nearly out.

Devastation raked through her as she stared down at a remnant of a charred and splintered cedar shingle by her boots.

How would she ever rebuild?

"Hey." Callen wrapped his steadying arm around her shoulder, his strength holding her up. "It's going to be okay."

She wished she could believe him, but after the year she'd had—the last two years, actually—it was hard to believe. She seemed doomed to tragedy, and she was sick of it.

Enough!

She wanted to yell at heaven, but she restrained herself, knowing the depth of Callen's faith in God's providence and sovereignty. He believed nothing could touch her without first going through her Father. If that was true, why did she want to be in a relationship with God at all?

Callen glanced over at her, worry blanketing his face. "You okay? I can have Paul take you back to my house if this is too hard."

She stared at the pitiful remnant of her house and the dwindling flickers of the last of the fire, doused by hoses and pouring rain.

My home.

Her chest squeezed.

She could rebuild, but she'd be starting with barely a foundation. So many memories gone in an instant—memories of her and her parents, and Julia . . .

She rested her palm on the thick, gnarled trunk of a black walnut tree for stability and flinched as something sharp pierced her hand. Yanking her hand off the tree, she tried to shake the pain away.

Callen frowned. "What happened?"

"Something sharp . . ." She held her hand flat, open to his inspection.

He lifted the lantern. "A shard of a shingle," he said. "We better have Paul stitch that up."

She nodded, walking with him back to the paramedic's SUV.

Though the fire was nearly out, the acrid odor of smoke still hung thick in the air, threatening to choke her lungs.

Callen sat with her while Paul started working on her hand, but after announcing the fire was fully out and ordering the firemen to erect tall poles with bright lights to illuminate her home, the fire chief, Sam, waved him over.

Callen rested his hand on her shoulder. "Let me talk with Sam, and then we'll walk out to the icehouse."

She nodded, knowing full well she couldn't sit and wait.

Callen joined Sam and the two began walking the perimeter of her home. She waited until Paul finally left her side, and she slipped away, hurrying around the decimated shed that had sat twenty yards from the house and down along the winding path that led to the icehouse. She should wait for Callen, especially if today's tragedies had been intentional—but surely Jared wouldn't . . .

She continued through the woods. It wasn't that far, and she could take care of herself. Callen had more important matters to tend to—like figuring out what had caused the explosion.

||||||||||

Callen strode at Sam's side, taking in the devastation now fully illuminated with the pole lights, the threads of rain heavy in their glare.

"I want to start with tracing the main gas line leading into the house," Callen said.

Sam's bushy brows furrowed. "What are you thinking?"

"Teni said she heard something that didn't seem like typical storm noise and then saw someone's silhouette outside her house right before the explosion. That's why she went outside—to investigate."

"Are you saying someone might have entered her basement

and compromised the line?" Sam's broad shoulders stiffened. "You think this might have been intentional?"

Callen swallowed. That's exactly what he thought, but he'd refrain from bringing Jared Connor's name into it until they had more information. "We both know it was a gas explosion by the way it exploded outward. I believe it originated in the basement and the shockwaves rippled up to the main part of the house, blowing debris outward"—he looked back to the forest he'd raced through, praying all along Teni had somehow survived the blast—"at least a hundred yards."

Sam nodded, and the two headed for the gaping cellar stairwell, the concrete steps surviving the blast, the doors long gone.

Tracing the line from the propane tank, Callen found what he was looking for, what he had feared. He pointed to the cut line with his gloved hand and looked up at Sam.

Sam centered the orb of his flashlight on the amateur incision. "I'd say we just found our source."

Someone *had* tried to kill Teni.

|||||||||

Callen and Sam's voices echoed through the wooded hollow as Teni passed pieces of her home. Charred shingles, splinters of wood, and tin roof littered the winding path to the family's icehouse.

Please don't let any further damage have happened to Julia's body. She's been through enough.

A crack sounded off to her right.

She stilled and surveyed the forest, the rain a mere drizzle under the thick leaf canopy.

"Hello?"

Nothing.

Shake it off, Teni. You're just being paranoid. Jared is not stalking you, and if he is, you're a cop now, not a scared little kid.

The path dipped and rose as she continued to the icehouse.

She stepped carefully across the narrow creek to the other side, and a splash echoed along the creek to her right.

She swallowed. "Callen, is that you?" If he looked to Paul's vehicle and found she wasn't there, he'd be right behind her, but no answer came.

Should she turn back or keep going?

She was closer to the icehouse than the house she'd just lost. Better to just go forward.

Her eyes scanned the darkness as she moved, the floodlights creating a halo of fog through the trees. She stilled, listening.

Silence, but something told her she was not alone. She increased her pace, only ten yards to go, but heavy footsteps sounded behind her. Not Callen's. Was it Jared? Was he back to harm her?

Breaking into a run, she hollered for Callen.

Make it to the icehouse. You can barricade yourself in.

The icehouse was close, its structure low and nearly blending with the forest floor like a rock sitting upon the bumpy earth.

The footfalls increased. Was that someone breathing? Was he *that* close?

Gooseflesh rippled along her clammy skin.

A part of her argued to stop and turn, to face her follower, but she was unarmed.

Reaching the icehouse, she fumbled with the lock, only to find it had been busted open. She flung open the doors and slammed them shut behind her, grabbing a shovel from its place on the wall and slipping the wooden handle through the door handholds.

She took a step back, wishing she'd brought her weapon with her, but she'd given it to Callen to hold since the sweatpants he'd given her didn't seem a secure place to holster it.

The icehouse door rattled, the musky scent of a man's cologne lifting on the wind, seeping through the slight crack in the door.

She hollered again for Callen and stepped forward to see if she could identify Jared's face through the small slit between the doors. A knife blade stabbed through the slit, missing her eye by less than an inch.

She stumbled back, looking for something to defend herself with and praying Callen had heard her hollers.

The doors rattled again on the frame, the knife slicing in again, then wriggling to pull back out for another stab, but one didn't come.

Silence ensued.

Had he left, or was he simply trying to fool her?

Footsteps echoed nearby and approached again. Was he coming back?

The door yanked hard, and her heart squeezed, her chest compressed.

"Teni!" Callen shouted, and her tight chest muscles relaxed. *Thank you, Lord.*

"I'm in here. Hold on." She slipped the shovel out of the door handles and pushed upward on the right-side door. Callen lifted as she pushed, and it swung upward and out. Callen rushed down the stairs toward her. "What happened?"

She explained.

"But you didn't see who it was?"

She shook her head.

"I'd say we comb the woods, but he could be anywhere, and right now keeping you safe is my priority." He rubbed her back, exhaling. "Do you think he'd been here in the woods all along, watching?"

"I don't know." She moved to Julia and lifted the sheet . . . only to find grain bags underneath. Shock riddled through her. "Julia's not here."

"What? You don't think . . . ?"

"He must have removed Julia's body, saw me coming back, and . . ."

"Thought he'd take you out in the process."

She shook her head. "What do you think he did with Julia?"

"Perhaps stashed her somewhere. We could call in cadaver dogs from the mainland, but with the storm . . ."

"Lines are down."

"So you didn't hang up on me," he said.

"What? No. Of course not. Why would you think I'd hang up on you?"

"I just thought you ended the call abruptly."

"No. The line dropped." A thought danced through her head. "You don't think he took out my phone lines too?"

"Probably down from the storm, but we can check them when we get back to my house."

"But what about your investigation?"

"We already located the cause."

She waited.

"Compromised gas line."

"Compromised . . . as in?"

"As in, someone definitely rigged your house to blow."

She swallowed. "With me in it?"

He nodded. "I'm afraid so."

NINE

FRIENDS AND NEIGHBORS, having heard the explosion, having seen the blaze, came to check on her through the night. Maxine and Jensen were the most fretful, but she assured them she was all right, though it was a bold-faced lie. She was anything but all right, but she wasn't focusing on self-pity any longer. Rather, she intended to throw all her energy into finding the culprit and seeing him behind bars.

As morning approached, Callen, with ash smudged on his face and the acrid odor of smoke clinging to him, graciously offered her the use of his guest room. "So, you're done with your investigation?" she asked as they walked back through the woods to Callen's place.

"The preliminary provided more than enough evidence to prove the cause of the explosion, but I'll do a second walk-through in the daylight for procedural thoroughness. Daylight always reveals things darkness attempts to shroud."

She hoped he didn't start with his Christian talk about the beauty of God's truth and light, because from where she was standing, all she saw was engulfing darkness.

Focus on the case. "So . . . your findings definitely showed . . . ?"

"Conclusive evidence that the gas line was tampered with—cut, actually. The explosion occurred in the basement when it filled with enough gas and hit the pilot light, sending shockwaves rippling up to the top floor."

He'd already said it had been intentional, that someone had tried to kill her, but the deep realization squeezed her chest, choking the breath from her lungs.

"You want to talk about it, Ten?"

She shook her head.

"Look, I know you're strong. One of the strongest women I know, but you're also tender. I'm probably the last person you want to talk to, but I'm here, and I promise I'm a good listener."

He promised? She'd heard that before, and she'd believed him beyond measure—right up until he'd squashed that out of her. After that day on the beach, after hearing him confirm the truth of the rumor she'd heard from Everett Jones, she'd vowed never to allow someone the power to harm her like that again—not even Callen Frost.

Even if he had attempted to fight for her, to beg her forgiveness, and even if she'd somehow managed to find that forgiveness in her, things would never be the same. How could they be?

"What?" he asked, studying her as they stepped out of the forest and his lit home bade them in from the storm.

She frowned. "I didn't say anything."

"No, but your entire body just tensed, like something struck you suddenly."

She shifted her thoughts off Callen and back on what she'd been thinking earlier in the night. "What if . . . ?"

He unlocked the front door and held it open for her.

She stepped inside, hanging her dripping rain jacket on the coatrack, rivulets of water drizzling down the slick material, beading at the bottom, then plopping to the thick, black mat beneath the rack. She watched as the same occurred on Callen's hung coat.

He kicked his boots off, leaving them by the door, and she followed suit.

"Sorry. Didn't mean to ignore your question. Just wanted to get you inside, where it's dry and warm. You were saying . . . What if . . . ?" He gestured to the sofa.

She took a seat on the couch, one leg bent beneath her. "I know everyone on the island, which means I know whoever tried to kill me, assuming he's from around here." Jared Connor was foremost in her mind, but would Jared really go to such lengths over the ferry? Though his anger with her ran so much deeper—always had. He hated her, hated her family, for owning the island. Was he trying to take out the remaining Kents—few as they were—one by one?

She exhaled. Was she reaching way too far in her thoughts regarding Jared? Instinct had always served her well. Or maybe it hadn't. She thought back to the times it had let her down— the best example standing five feet from her.

Callen clicked the heat on—probably deciding it best not to make a fire, despite the exquisite stone fireplace on the opposite wall—and then hunkered down beside her. "I know it's extremely unsettling to think it might be Jared—or if not him, it's probably someone else you know."

Hold *unsettling* and try flat-out *terrifying*. She *knew* Julia's killer, and her would-be killer.

She rubbed her arms as a chill shot up them, crawling around her shoulders and encasing her in gooseflesh.

"What?" he asked. He had the most annoying habit of doing that, of knowing when she was upset or thinking or . . . anything. He *knew* her. After all these years.

"I'm just trying to wrap my mind around why he'd steal Julia's body."

Callen raked a hand through his hair. "I don't know, unless . . ."

"Unless he was worried the ME would find something proving it wasn't an accident once she did the autopsy."

"Like . . . ?" Callen nudged her to work it through from the killer's perspective.

"Evidence she was murdered, or . . ."

"Evidence that could identify him as her murderer," he said, finishing her thoughts.

She swallowed hard. "Yeah."

Where was Julia's body? As foolish as it was, she actually prayed, prayed they'd recover Julia's body so she could have a proper funeral and be buried in the family plot by her parents and Teni's.

She inhaled. So much loss.

||||||||||

He'd screwed up, gotten greedy. Not only had he snatched Julia's body in hopes of preventing the medical examiner from ruling her death a murder, he'd attempted to kill Tennyson on the same night. Of course the witch heard him. He should have known she wouldn't blame any noises he made on the wind or the storm like a normal person. No, she was an investigator, and today those skills had served her well—but not for long.

He'd watched as they'd discovered Julia's body washed up on Henry's Point, and rather than collecting her and preparing her for a funeral, Tennyson had turned it into a working crime scene. The witch always had been trouble, and now she stood markedly between him and his agenda.

Rowing with adrenaline-fueled arms, he cut his camouflaged raft swiftly through the water, the storm muffling any sound the oars might make. He steered into the dark cove, tied the anchors to Julia's body, and rolled her overboard.

No one, not even Tennyson Kent, would find her this time.

Rowing back with a smile of pride and accomplishment on his face, he pondered finishing his work tonight as planned, but attacking Tennyson would be foolish, especially while she was staying at Callen Frost's home. Of course he'd be involved, and have to be an investigator as well. No, he'd have to impatiently bide his time again—at least until tomorrow. Until she was alone in the woods. She always was at some point during the day. And he'd be waiting.

She was so confident in her skills, but her pride would prove her downfall.

He'd attack fast and without mercy, and this time, she wouldn't escape his grasp.

Tennyson Kent would be dead before the nor'easter passed.

TEN

"YOU SHOULD GET AT LEAST a couple hours rest," Callen said, handing her a steaming cup of hot cider with a cinnamon stick. "We'll go talk with Jared after I confirm my findings at your house."

"Okay, I'll rest. Just not ready quite yet." Sleep would elude her or be filled with nightmares, she suspected.

"Okay, if you are sure." He grabbed a yellow legal pad and a pen from the table and placed it in front of her.

She scrunched her face in curiosity. "What's that for?"

"Start by writing down the names of everyone who came by after the fire. I've found most arsonists like to revisit their work."

"That's sick."

"But unfortunately true." He exhaled. "Together we can write down all the locals' names, and then we'll compare lists and see if we can come up with a narrowed-down suspect pool."

"Great. Okay . . . so the purpose of this is . . . ?"

"We start with every possible suspect on the island and then narrow it down. For example, we know it was a man, so we'll highlight the men's names."

"Why not just write down only men's names?"

"Just because you saw a man in the woods doesn't mean he worked alone or for his own purposes."

"Meaning someone could have partnered with him or hired him?" Could Marybeth have ordered all this for her son to carry out? Her hatred for Teni ran even deeper than Jared's.

"All things are possible at this point. I know you had a fight with Jared, but what about your ex-fiancé?"

Of course he'd heard. Everyone had by now. Gossip ran rampant on the tiny island. "Alex?"

Callen rubbed the back of his neck. "Surely he's upset about your broken engagement."

Teni grimaced. "Sure, he's upset, but he is the one who called it off."

Callen's eyes widened a bit, and she could tell he had questions, but she didn't want to go into her relationship with Alex at the moment, so she just said, "We both had concerns, but he initiated it."

"But he could still be bitter about it, or maybe he expected you to resist his suggestion you break it off. If he married you he'd own this island with you, right?"

"Yes . . . ?"

"I'm sorry. I know I sound cold asking these questions. I don't mean to be insensitive. It's just an investigator's training, which you understand full well."

She nodded. She understood, but it didn't make it pleasant. "I get it," she responded. What Callen said was plausible, but he didn't know how much Alex loathed Talbot—always said it would make a better golf course and expensive resort. He had tried to talk her into selling it more than once. But she'd put an end to that idea at their engagement party, when he went as far as introducing her to an interested developer who was friends with his father. But surely, he wouldn't go so far as to . . . What would he gain? Revenge? "It couldn't be Alex. Lenny took him back to Annapolis before the storm blew in."

"Are you sure he made it back?"

"Yes. He called, said Lenny had anchored in the marina and was bunking with friends until the storm passed."

"Did he call from his cell?"

"I have no idea."

"So he could have called from a landline somewhere on Talbot before the storm knocked the lines out." Callen had in fact confirmed the lines were out—at least at his and Teni's places.

"Theoretically, yes. But if Lenny stayed in Annapolis, how would Alex even get back to Talbot?"

"Are you positive Lenny stayed in Annapolis, or are you only going off what Alex told you?"

"What Alex said, but . . ."

"After you rest, we can go to Lenny's and confirm. See if his boat is tied up for the storm."

"Fine, but if Lenny's gone then we cross Alex off the list."

"He could have turned around after Lenny left the docks and hired someone else to bring him right back to Talbot."

"But the storm?"

"A strong mariner could handle this. It's just the nor'easter's outer bands for now, and if the price was right, you'd be surprised by what a lot of down-on-their-luck sailors are willing to voyage through for the right price."

Could it really be Alex? Did the man she'd dated for seven months possess the heart of a killer? "But even if you're right that he's upset about it . . . killing me doesn't get him the island."

"No, but if he views it as a major loss, and you as the reason he lost it . . ."

That was a startling thought.

"Just out of curiosity, would Julia be next in line to inherit after you?"

"No. Our cousin William, as his dad is second oldest of the brothers."

"William's parents wouldn't inherit?"

"His dad died of a heart attack and his mom isn't eligible."

"What do you mean?"

"The inheritance only goes through Kent blood. If I was out of the picture, Talbot would go to my uncle's only child, William, and then it would go to—"

"Julia?"

She nodded. "Correct."

"So, it doesn't sound like an issue of inheritance. I was thinking if it went to you and then Julia, maybe . . ."

"If that was the case and it was an issue of inheritance, we'd need to warn William."

Callen shifted tentatively, like he had something to say but didn't want to voice it.

"What is it?"

He raked a hand through his wet, spiky hair. "Probably nothing."

"Just tell me." Things could hardly get any worse.

"You and Jules look so much alike, and you're normally the faster swimmer. What if Julia . . . ?"

Teni swallowed, hard. "Wasn't the intended target. What if it was supposed to be me and since I was swimming slowly, poor Julia was murdered in my place?" The thought was sickeningly engulfing. Hot tears stung her eyes.

"Come here." Without waiting for an answer, Callen pulled her into his embrace. "You can't think like that."

"But what if it's true?" What if she'd caused Julia's death?

ELEVEN

TENI ROLLED OVER, fighting the urge to pray, the pillow a squishy sponge beneath her tears.

Why would someone want to kill her, and could it really be Alex, as Callen suggested?

It seemed impossible that the man she'd been engaged to would want to kill her, and yet there was a gnawing in her gut that whispered not to dismiss the notion outright.

She released a huff and punched the pillow, trying to get comfortable but knowing comfort would elude her.

If it was true, it certainly wouldn't be the first time she'd neglected to see a character flaw in someone. Of all the people she would have vowed she knew to the core, Callen Frost had been first on the list.

They'd been nearly inseparable ever since they'd met that fateful day in church. She'd run into him, *literally*, in the hall during service. Hymns played softly in the background as she retraced the hallway, looking for her favorite, sunshine-patterned hair ribbon, which she'd managed to lose on her way in. And there he was, bending to pick it up. She'd heard of Callen Frost, the fastest kid on the island. Of Pocomoke descent on his mom's side, he traced straight back to the natives living on the island when it was deeded to her great—multiplied by so many numbers she couldn't keep track—grandfather.

She was only six at the time, but she still recalled that day, and the odd stirring sensation that had raked through her, like somehow she'd known Callen all her life. They'd surely seen one another prior to that day, as small as Talbot was, but that was her first memory of him—of *them*.

From that day on, they were inseperable, meeting up in the woods for mystery-solving adventures. Then, fast-forward through years of joy and off he went to college . . . and within months smashed her heart.

She squeezed her eyes shut at the horrid memory of that day, then opened them.

If Callen, a man she'd known practically her entire life, had surprised her with a heart-wrenching character flaw, how could she be surprised when anybody else did?

Had her breakup with Alex been God's way of protecting her from a man whose character flaws—one as extreme and depraved as being a murderer—hadn't been revealed yet?

But Alex was the one who'd broken off the engagement. If he was so angry with her and wanted to own Talbot, why call off the wedding? Why not marry her and kill her afterward? Because the inheritance would never go to him upon her death. Ownership would continue through the direct Kent line, and she had made it abundantly clear that she'd never sell.

Perhaps he really was angry and was using the breakup and a supposed trip back to Annapolis as his alibi. It was a beyond-unsettling thought.

She exhaled, turning to face the window—rain pelting it in a relentless cascade.

Then there was Jared Connor. She wasn't looking forward to interrogating him, but if he'd killed Julia, she'd do whatever was necessary to see her cousin's killer behind bars.

She stiffened, unable to find any measure of rest. The day to come would hold its own challenges, and for the first time since before her parents' death, she hungered for God. Deeply hungered for the connection she'd cut off. His presence would never leave her, according to His Word, but she'd done her very best to ignore Him—the easiest target for the hurt and anger eating her up inside. Maybe she'd been wrong. Maybe she'd spurned the only true source of comfort, peace, connection, and wholeness. Maybe her relationship with Him was what had been missing, leaving her feeling so empty all these years.

|||||||||

Teni opened her eyes to a pine-paneled ceiling and blinked. Callen's guest room. She was in Callen's place. His mom still lived in the family home, but she'd heard through the gossip mill on Talbot that Callen had purchased Old Man Miller's place when he passed on and had spent the past three years renovating it on weekends. The two-story, New-England-style house with weathered, gray-painted cedar shingles, traditional tin roof, and green trim was gorgeous. It was so like her ancestral home, apart from the shingle color—hers a maritime blue with glossy white trim—the nautical colors soothing her soul whenever she'd spotted it.

Thoughts of the loss of a home that had been in her family for generations broke her heart anew.

She rolled to face the window. Rain pelted, bouncing off the double-pane glass. Light filtered through the white gossamer curtains, signaling it was time to get up. She glanced at the clock on the nightstand. 8:38. She should have been up at dawn, ready to continue the investigation that had started with finding Julia on the beach. Flashes of her cousin's body tracked through her mind, and she grabbed her stomach at the sudden onslaught of nausea. She squeezed her eyes shut, saying a prayer for her cousin, and for once, not second-guessing why. Julia deserved as much, and Teni . . . She'd come to the end of herself. She was tired and worn and had nothing left to give. She surrendered in that moment, crying out to God to forgive her anger and to engulf her in His arms as He had so many years ago.

I've been here all along, resounded through her mind, whispering words of deep comfort to her crushed soul. *I have loved you with an everlasting love.*

A deep peace amid the horror of her circumstances swelled inside, not erasing the pain, but cushioning her in it.

I will hide you in the shelter of my wings.

Truth continued to flow through her, and she sat in silence, letting it flood her being.

Thank you, Jesus, for never leaving me. Though I do not understand why all this is happening, I will trust you in the trial. Forgive me for turning my back all these years. I've come to the end of me and I need you. Help me find Julia's killer and my attempted one. And please guard my heart. It feels as though Callen and I have never been apart, but I don't understand how that can be. What are you trying to tell me? Surely not to trust him again? He hasn't even apologized. And why am I worrying about my relationship with Callen during a time like this?

Because outside of God, Callen had been her rock—her constant for most of her life. She'd never really recovered from that sudden loss of someone she loved so deeply, and being in his presence again, all the feelings she'd had for him were flooding back. Was he the reason she'd never fully connected with Alex? Somewhere deep inside, did she still love Callen Frost?

Shaking her head, she rolled over, yanked the covers off, and stepped on the cool floor. Enough of that line of thinking. The temperatures had definitely dropped with the storm surging in, and the cloud cover smothered out the sun, leaving the sky a charcoal gray mixed with patches of light, but still predominately overcast. If her grandpa Pete's lessons in reading the skies were any indication, they had less than twelve hours before it fully hit Talbot head on. She wondered what the official weather reports were saying, but she'd learned never to doubt a mariner's ability to read the skies and smell the air to determine a coming shift in the weather.

Red at night, sailor's delight. Red at morn, sailors be warned.

The adage had been drilled into her head since her earliest memories.

She tiptoed out of the bedroom, hoping to make it to the bathroom and have some semblance of not looking as disheveled as she felt before greeting Callen, but two steps into the hall, she heard his door creak open behind her.

"Morning," he said.

She turned, praying she didn't look as awful as she felt.

He leaned against the doorframe, arms crossed, a soft smile curling across his handsome face, which was smooth as could be. He blamed his Pocomoke roots for his inability to grow facial hair, but he loved his roots and his family's traditions. He was proud of his heritage—both as a Pocomoke and a native Talbot islander—despite the fact he lived and worked in DC. What a culture shock that had to be—Talbot compared to DC. It was cool he fit with both, just as she did with her life in Annapolis and Talbot.

Not bothering to try to rake a hand through her tangled knot of hair, knowing it would only draw more attention to it, she simply responded with, "Morning."

"I left some towels, toothbrush and paste, brush, etc. on the guest bathroom sink for you. I'm thinking that after I finish my investigation of the fire, we should head into town and grab you some clothes that fit at Jones's before we get started on our search."

The Jones family's general store—which sold everything from clothes to food to deicer to premium-priced gasoline—had been in their family since their original settling ancestor, who had begun it as an apothecary shop selling necessities on the side. It still held the original pharmacy, though restored many times over, and Teni still loved the antique dark walnut apothecary cabinet full of tiny drawers, which had once held the only type of medicine available to the locals—tinctures brought over from England and herbs grown on the island.

"Sounds good, but we should stop by the boathouse too. I always keep an extra outfit and some toiletries in the bathroom there. We can run by and grab them before we head into town."

"Only if you promise to stick by my side this time."

This time? She'd stuck by his side for years, until he'd severed the bond that day on the beach—or at least it felt like the bond had been severed. Though, being back with him now, she felt the bond resurrecting in a way she hadn't thought possible.

He pushed off the doorframe. "Deal?"

Just standing by while he finished his arson investigation would be difficult—but she wanted his investigation to be completed asap, so the findings could be documented and proven beyond a doubt.

"Deal," she finally said.

"Good." He smiled. "I like having you back by my side."

She swallowed, unsure of what to make of that statement.

He stepped closer, slipping a strand of her hair behind her ear. His touch felt so good, so comforting. She'd thought she would never feel that again.

He swallowed, inching closer still. "I never apologized the way I should have for what I did. I was just so embarrassed, so ashamed of what I'd done. I felt there was no way I deserved you any longer—no way you could possibly forgive me."

They were doing this now? She fought to stem the tears threatening to fall. "You didn't even give me the option. You just said you'd messed up horribly, you were sorry, and you'd stay out of my life. That was it, and you were gone." Hot tears tumbled down her cheeks. "You never even tried."

"I know, and I'm so sorry. It was the worst mistake I'd ever made on top of the already worst mistake. That night, I was trying to drown the sorrow over losing my dad with alcohol, and one of my roommates was slipping something in the drinks. I saw it go in. I knew better, but I drank it anyway. Next thing I know I'm waking up in bed with some girl and I don't even remember what happened. Before I could get out of bed, Everett came in and saw us.

"I stopped hanging out with those guys that day, switched dorm rooms, and turned my life back around. But all that is beside the point. The point is, I know I'm a decade late, but after everything that happened . . . After I heard the explosion and thought you were . . ." He swallowed. "I knew I needed to tell you how sorry I am. And if there's any way you can find it in your heart to forgive me, I'd love the chance to win you back, to love you the way you truly deserve."

She stood there dumbfounded—all the emotions of the last day wrapped up in a knot in her stomach. She'd finally heard the words she'd longed to hear from Callen for over a decade. But . . . how did she? How did they . . . ?

"Look, I know that's a lot to spring on you." He backed up and she regretted his withdrawal the minute he moved. "I'll go make us some eggs while you get freshened up."

"Okay." She nodded awkwardly, still stunned.

He headed for the wooden stairs, ducking under the low ceiling at the top of them before proceeding down.

She rushed into the restroom, shut the door behind her, and then leaned against it for support as her legs wobbled beneath her.

What do I do with this, Father? I feel like you just answered my prayer, but where do I go from here?

Collecting herself, she pushed off the door and braved a glance in the mirror.

Yikes!

Her hair was a tangled, tousled strawberry-blond mess— half still loosely in a braid, half all over the place. Mascara, what hadn't come off when she'd washed her face last night, clung in little flecks about her eyes, and she looked as pale as a sheet of paper. Of course, she'd be the one person on Talbot Island with fair skin—even fairer than Paul and his entire redheaded family.

She brushed her teeth and washed her face, scrubbing it hard and pinching her cheeks for a little color, and then tackled her hair. Finally confident she didn't look a total wreck and telling herself to keep the circumstances in perspective, she headed downstairs—how she looked was the last thing she ought to be worried about.

Callen turned and smiled at her, an iron skillet in hand. "Eggs?"

"Please." She'd been too upset to eat much of anything yesterday since breakfast.

Yesterday when she awoke, life looked so different. She was headed out with her fiancé for Talbot Island to discuss their wedding with her pastor. Now the engagement was broken, but that was the least of her worries. Someone had tried to kill her, and Julia was dead and her body missing. She hurried her pace, anxious to get started asking questions and searching the island. She wouldn't rest until she retrieved her cousin's body for a proper burial.

"Easy there," Callen said. "We'll get started soon enough." He sat across from her and added salsa to his eggs.

"How can you sound so nonchalant?" He'd always been that way, once something was fixed in his mind.

"I'm not taking this lightly at all, but you need to eat. You need to take care of yourself."

"Not now. Not while someone has Julia's body."

TWELVE

CALLEN COMPLETED HIS INVESTIGATION in the pouring rain, but he confirmed the gas line had been cut on purpose, and her house had been rigged to explode with her in it. Thankfully, she'd heard a noise and gone to investigate or she'd no longer be alive—which made her realize that life was too short and that no one ever knew when their last breath was coming. It made her decision to respond to Callen's questions and apology much easier. Between that realization, the time spent with him over the last day, and a strong direction from God as she prayed, she was ready to forgive him and to move forward again.

As they skirted her property down to the boathouse, she took hold of his hand and stopped next to the tree where he'd carved their initials when their friendship shifted to a romantic love in their teens.

"I still remember the day you carved this," she said as rain fell around them—though they were sheltered somewhat by the trees. She pointed to the carved lopsided heart with Callen's and her initials inside.

"We had a picnic at its base"—he looked up—"and I got walloped on the head with a black walnut."

She chuckled. "That's right. I'd forgotten that part." Back then all she'd seen was Callen.

He chuckled as thunder shook the ground. "There I was, trying to be all romantic at what . . . ? Seventeen? My idea of a grand gesture was to pack cold-cut sandwiches and Doritos. What was I thinking? God probably dropped that walnut on my head to try to knock some sense into me."

"I think it was very romantic," she said, stepping closer to him as wind and rain swirled around them.

His brows arched as pleasant surprise shifted across his handsome face. "Is that so?"

"Yes." She hovered closer still, tilting her head to look up to him, rain sprinkling across her eyes, its full force softened by the leaf canopy overhead. "And don't forget the Hershey's kisses."

"My lame segue into our first kiss."

"It wasn't lame and the kiss hardly was."

His gaze locked on hers, and the storm raging around them faded as she focused on the feel of her heart beating in her chest, her breathing rising and lowering, the blink of Callen's thick lashes . . .

"And I took to heart what you said this morning," she continued as his face lowered closer to hers. "I forgive you."

A weight visibly lifted from his countenance, hope springing in his deep voice. "You do?"

"Yes." She nodded, glancing to his lips and then back to his eyes. "I'd like to try again."

He swallowed, his Adam's apple bobbing. "You would?"

"Very much."

His lips descended on hers before she could blink, and he enveloped her fully in his strong arms. The feel of him against her was like she was home again. Why had she ever thought she could get over so deep a love despite the crushing betrayal that had tested them for far too long? That was in the past. This was the present, and she wanted her future to be spent just like this. She'd been attempting to force a relationship with Alex when her heart, unbeknownst to her, had still been deeply tied to another—to Callen. But now the years they'd lost faded away as he deepened the kiss—his hands spreading through her hair, massaging, pulling her closer still, until it felt as if no space existed between them.

All time evaporated until somehow—she wasn't sure how much later—they managed to disengage from the kiss and take a step back. Then, just as shockingly to Teni, she managed to walk straight, for the most part, to the boathouse, despite her jellied legs.

Excusing herself, she stepped into the boathouse bathroom and changed into a pair of yoga pants, a T-shirt, a fleece, and running shoes. She tried not to think about how only hours ago she'd been here with Julia, laughing at Julia's attempts to make her smile despite the breakup with Alex and the harsh confrontation with Jared and his mother.

Julia's attempts at humor always worked, and she'd managed to make Teni belly laugh as they slipped on goggles, preparing to dive into the deep greenish-blue water and race. Teni braced her palm against the white paneled wall for steadiness. How could her cousin be gone?

"You okay?" Callen asked outside the door. The man had a sixth sense when it came to her—always had.

"Yep." She wiped the tears from her eyes, attempting to resist the encroaching sadness threatening to swoop in and engulf her afresh. Her life had changed, yet again, in the blink of an eye. She took a steadying breath, slowly releasing it and repeating the pattern until her heart began to slow back into a normal rhythm. "I'll be right out," she managed.

Taking another deep breath, she tucked her toiletries bag

under her arm and opened the door to find Callen waiting with that I'm-not-buying-it expression on his face. His skin was smooth—the color of light molasses. His eyes the dark, deep brown of rich chocolate, his hair the shade of a bold cup of coffee but cropped shorter than the shoulder-cresting haircut he'd had when they were teens.

Callen was ruggedly handsome, and she'd always been a fool for his stunning good looks, but it was the man inside—the intelligent, funny, strong, bold, adventuresome man—that she'd fallen in love with all those years ago. He had her heart and soul, apparently never letting go despite how it appeared on the surface.

She exhaled, her shoulders dropping as her mind flashed back to Julia and their last moments in this very place—such a roller coaster of events and emotions. She didn't know whether to laugh at the pain threatening to consume her or cry from the joy she felt being back with the man she loved but was too foolish to realize she still did until today.

Callen held his arms out, and she rushed into his hold so forcefully he swayed back for a moment. "She and I were just here together," she said as tears tumbled down, her emotions raw and bleeding at the surface. "We were goofing off before the race, like always. Jules smiling, her freckles dancing the way they did."

"The way yours do." He caressed her cheek, and she leaned deeper into his hold.

"It's not fair." None of it—her parents, her cousin, her house . . . so much gone in the blink of an eye.

"No, honey, it's not. Everything you've been through hasn't been fair."

"Then why does it happen?" *Why did God allow it?*

"Because we live in a fallen world with fallen people. Evil exists and tragedies, unfortunately, happen here. But nothing touches us that God hasn't allowed or equipped us through His Spirit to endure, and when tragedies like this happen it reminds us that our home and our hope is in heaven. There everything is fair. There are no tragedies, no death, no separation, and no sorrow."

She inhaled the scent of cedar always swirling about him, and exhaled slowly. "I wish we could just be swooped up and taken there now."

"Me too—a lot of the time—but I'm still here and I know that means God's got more for me to do, more for me to become, more time to grow into Jesus' image and serve Him."

"Do you really think *I'm* serving God?"

"Absolutely. As an NRP cop, you save lives and you put criminals behind bars. You combat evil. I absolutely believe you're serving God, and not just there, but here."

"Here?"

"You steward Talbot like a champ. You care about preserving our way of life, while also making sure everyone is taken care of and has a source of income. You care about this island, about everyone on it. Even the Connors. I can't fathom why you haven't kicked them off after all the trouble Jared and his mom have made—though, I guess that wouldn't be you. You're too kind. You put up with their anger and threats because you realize this is their home too. But if Jared is behind all this he belongs behind bars, and he'd better get there quickly because if I lay my hands on him . . ." His face tightened.

"But you were saying . . . ?" His assurance about her role on Talbot was a balm to her weary soul.

"Talbot's our home, and God would never put you in charge of such a huge responsibility if He didn't know you would take care of His people on the island. There are many believers here, and many more to share the love of Christ with."

She'd never considered that before, but what Callen said

made sense. Had God made and equipped her for this very role and place?

|||||||||||

Callen steered his red Tahoe along the cobblestone street, one of the few roads on the island that wasn't a dirt path. The woods filled the bulk of the island—the houses along the fringes of the shore and marsh. Most destinations were easily walked to in good weather, but the Connors lived on the far side of the island, and it was still pouring rain, so she and Callen decided to drive. Of the islanders who owned cars, most, like Callen, had four-wheel-drive vehicles, but many islanders used dirt bikes or ATVs to get around the small island.

They stopped in town to pick up clothes for Teni before proceeding on to the Connors. Though, it was more a quaint village than full-size town. There were two restaurants, Milly's and Steve's Grill, Jones's General Store, and Nancy and Bill Carter's laundromat.

Then there were the tourist stores that showcased the work of various island artisans—homemade island recipes, spices grown on Talbot, and handmade crafts. Most of those shops closed at the end of the season.

A few other businesses were run out of folks' homes, such as Max Harper's mechanic shop and Alice's Alterations. Whatever couldn't be found on Talbot meant a trip to the mainland—close to an hour by boat to the nearest town.

Other than a few stops to briefly receive condolences about Julia's death and Teni's house explosion, their trip inside the general store was quick and to the point—just what was necessary to get by until she returned to Annapolis and could bring new supplies with her to Talbot. But where would she stay while on Talbot until her family home was rebuilt? Callen would likely offer, but with everything pointing to them being fully back together, that wouldn't be appropriate. She could stay at the B&B, but after a while that would add up. Perhaps her friend Becky would let her crash at her place, or she could do a combo of the two.

"How long until I can rebuild?" she asked Callen as rain so thick it was nearly blinding at times pelted her raincoat.

"My guess would be within a month, so you might be able to get the framing done before the winter, but it'll definitely be spring before you can be fully back in."

Yet another legacy she'd lost—she'd never missed celebrating Christ's birth in her ancestral home, and it sounded like a new home built before Christmas was going to be too big of a task.

After tossing the bags containing her purchases into the back seat, they headed for the Connors' property, which consisted of three houses—the parents', Jared's, and his brother, Jacob's—and a few ramshackle outbuildings.

"Ready?" Callen said, as he shifted into Drive after opening the Connors' property gate.

She nodded, praying God would equip her, for who knew what lay ahead.

THIRTEEN

CAESAR, JARED'S PIT BULL, met them as they pulled
up to Jared's house.

"Great." She rolled her eyes. "This ought to be fun." She
loved dogs—she really did—but Jared always trained his dogs
to be vicious. She'd already had one encounter in the woods
with Caesar, where she'd ended up with massive stitches and
nearly lost an ankle. Mainland animal control told her she
had the right to sue, but she didn't want the dog put down—
just better managed—so she hadn't pressed charges. Of course
Jared hadn't said a word of thanks, had instead blamed her for
"riling up" his dog.

"I'll get out first—get Jared to put Caesar in his pen."

"It's okay." The last thing she wanted was Jared Connor
thinking she was intimidated. "I'll be fine."

Taking a deep breath and saying a prayer for safety, she
stepped out of Callen's Tahoe the same time as he did.

Caesar immediately flew to her side, barking and jumping,
but she held her ground, her knee poised to jab forward if
necessary.

"Shut up, Caesar," Jared said, stepping out under the covered
porch in a pair of well-worn Levis and a black T-shirt featuring

a band she didn't recognize. At least the electric guitar etched in gray gave that suggestion. "Oh, it's you," he said, taking a swig of his beer.

Teni looked at her watch. Drinking before lunchtime?

He wiped his nose with the back of his hand and sniffed. "What do you two want?"

Callen stepped toward him, and Caesar shifted in his direction.

"Go on!" Jared hollered, and Caesar scampered off into the woods adjacent to the Connors' property—Jared's house sat on the southeast edge of the acreage. "Now, what is it you two want? I've got a Terps game to watch."

"We need to ask you some questions."

His chin dipped and jutted back. "Such as?"

Marybeth's hunter green Volkswagen station wagon pulled up.

Great. Her presence would make things go so much smoother.

"What are they doing here?" Marybeth asked, pulling her black raincoat tightly about her as Jacob rode up on his ATV.

Wonderful. A family reunion minus the one Connor Teni truly liked—Darren. He'd offered his condolences on the explosion, when they'd run into him entering the general store as they'd left. He was probably still there. His presence would have made this much easier.

"What's up?" Jacob asked Jared with a lift of his chin as he joined him on the porch.

"The investigators are here with some questions," Jared said snidely.

Jacob looped his thumbs in his jeans' waistband. "Is that right?"

Jared nodded as Marybeth—scowling at Teni and Callen the entire time—made her way over to join her boys on Jared's porch.

Callen gestured for Teni to head up and out of the rain. She did so, ignoring the glares of the Connors.

But cover felt good. The rain was so heavy, fast, and thick, it felt like fingers jabbing hard into her flesh.

Jared took another swig of his beer before saying, "Let's get this over with so we can get back to the game."

Jacob had carried a twelve-pack of beer up on the porch, and he now set it on the wire-spool table before moving to stand beside his brother. Marybeth set a slow cooker and bag of rolls on the table beside the beverages. They'd come prepared for the game, apparently.

Since he wasn't formally arresting Jared, Callen didn't need to Mirandize him, but Teni assumed for procedural accuracy and to be overly cautious, he did. Then he asked, "Where were you last night between nine and midnight?"

"You don't have to answer their questions," Jacob said. "He just said it could be used against you."

"You can answer now and get it over with, or we can haul you in to the closest mainland police station as soon as this storm passes. Your choice."

He exhaled. "I was here with my ma, watching a movie."

He'd spent Saturday night watching a movie with his mom? Teni would have loved to still have the option of watching movies with her mom—whatever night it fell on—but Jared hardly seemed the type to spend the night with his mom over his brother or drinking with friends. Word was, they played a lot of poker and gambled for some strange things—fishing lures, weird nighttime dares . . . The list went on.

"That's right." Marybeth jumped straight on the party line. "He was home with us."

"Until midnight?"

"Yes. We got started late. After dinner."

"What movie did you watch?"

"*Dunkirk*," Marybeth said snippily. "Rented it once it was a decent price and available to rent from here."

"What'd you think, Jared?" Callen asked.

"It was fine." Jared shrugged.

"Have a favorite part?" Teni asked.

"Nah." He took another swig.

So this was off to a great start, and when they wrapped up twenty minutes later, they'd learned little else. With Marybeth and even Jacob backing up Jared's alibi, there was little she and Callen could do, unless . . .

"Stop the vehicle," she said as Mr. Connor approached Callen's SUV from the base of the long driveway weaving up from the still-open gate.

Callen did so with a smile.

Teni jumped out in the strengthening wind blowing so hard she almost expected it would lift her feet from the ground. Had to be over sixty miles per hour—the storm due to fully hit late tonight and on into the early hours of tomorrow morning.

Teni waved Darren Connor down, and he slowed his old orange Chevy truck to a stop beside Callen's SUV.

"What are you two doing out here?"

Teni shielded her eyes with her hand cupped along the brim of her raincoat hood. "We just had some business with Jared and Marybeth, but I was hoping I could ask you a quick question."

"Oh . . . okay?"

"What did you and Marybeth do last night?"

"We had a family dinner with the boys and then watched a movie."

"What movie?"

"*Dunkirk*. It was good. Have you seen it yet?"

"I did. It was awesome." She shifted to see better, her back to the wicked wind. "And the boys watched it with you?"

"They did."

Teni's heart fell. If Jared wasn't trying to kill her, who was? Could it possibly be Alex, as Callen posed?

"But Jared wasn't feeling well, so he headed to his house about halfway through."

Oh, really? He and Marybeth had neglected to mention that little tidbit.

||||||||||

"So Jared lied to us," Teni said as they pulled away from the Connors' property. "Think that's enough to get a search warrant for his place? To look for Julia's body hidden somewhere on their property, or evidence he took her?"

"I'd say. Call your superior and see what you can do regarding Julia, and I'd do the same regarding the arson investigation. But with the phone lines down . . ."

"Great. We're stuck until the storm passes and the lines are back up or the ME we called shows up." She shook her head. "It's not soon enough. Jared probably realizes we are on his trail, and if he has Julia's body stashed somewhere, he'll more likely get rid of it fast."

"He knows we're watching him. No way he'll do anything. He'd have to be a huge fool. I'm not sure . . ."

She tilted her head.

"We both know Jared's not the brightest bulb in the pack, and . . ."

"And what?"

"I just don't know that he's smart enough to orchestrate all this. Jacob, maybe, but he's not the one who threatened you."

"What if they are working together?"

Callen inhaled. "It's a possibility, but let's confirm Lenny never returned to the island with your ex, and then we'll go from there."

"After Jared and Marybeth's threats, you really think it could still be Alex?"

"You said he wanted you to sell Talbot. If he'd married you

233

and you had sold Talbot to a developer, he'd have been set for life."

"So he tries to kill me out of spite?" Even if . . . "Why Julia?"

"He probably thought she was you. You look alike, especially in the water, and you're always the first to the buoy."

"I knew it." Tears welled in her eyes. "It's my fault she's dead."

"*No. It. Isn't.* It's the fault of whoever killed Julia. Not you."

"But if I'd been on my game, Julia would still be here."

"Honey, you can't think that way. You aren't the one who killed her. Whoever is behind all this did, whether that be Jared or Alex or someone else. They did this. Not you."

She nodded, knowing in her heart if she'd just pushed harder, had swum faster, that Julia would most likely still be alive. How did she let go of that? But Callen was right. It was the murderer who chose to take Julia's life, and at this point they were just assuming it was a mistake and Teni had been the intended target.

Looking out the window at the gushing rain and wind swells swirling the downpour into erratic funnels, she closed her eyes and prayed.

Father, you know who killed Julia and why he is trying to kill me. Please give us clarity. Help us discover who it is and put him behind bars. And help me deal with this overwhelming guilt I feel over Julia's death. Please guide Callen and me through what the next day holds. Keep us safe in this storm.

It seemed only fitting a massive storm raged around them while one raged so fiercely inside her.

She shifted uncomfortably as they pulled up to Lenny's house and found his boat docked at the pier. Alex *had* lied to her. The implications of what that could mean knocked the air from her lungs.

FOURTEEN

CALLEN LOOKED OVER AT HER as he rolled to a stop and shifted the Tahoe into park, pulling up the emergency brake. He didn't say anything, just stepped out of the vehicle and came around to open her door. No reason to attempt an umbrella. With the winds as high as they were, it'd be more struggle than help.

He locked his arm with hers when she stepped out, and together they strode against the blustering wind toward Lenny's front door.

Callen knocked, Lenny answered, and Teni's heart dropped. Alex had definitely lied to her.

"Hey, Len. Can we come in?" Callen asked.

"Oh, sure." He stepped back. "Come on in. Ignore the mess."

Lenny's house proved he was a bachelor, and not a tidy one at that. Magazines and old soda cans were strewn about the living room, along with discarded sweatshirts and jackets tossed over the recliner and other pieces of furniture.

"What's up?" Lenny asked.

"Did you take Alex back to Annapolis yesterday?" Teni asked, her heart pounding in her chest.

"Yep."

"And then . . . ?" Callen asked.

"And then I headed back. I toyed with the idea of anchoring in Annapolis, but with it just being the storm's outer bands, I figured I'd rather be home for the weekend."

"Did Alex come back with you?" Callen asked, and Teni held her breath, trying to wrap her mind around the implications Lenny's answer could hold.

"Nah. He was happy to be back in Annapolis. He wasn't much of a fan of Talbot, other than wanting to sell it. Couldn't believe he actually told me that. What a loser."

"Tell me about it," Teni said, irritation sparking through her. How insensitive could Alex be to tell a local he was pushing for Teni to sell Talbot? "He told you I refused to sell, right?"

"Yeah, said you were a fool for not selling, that you were shortsighted." Lenny stepped a few feet into the kitchen and grabbed a Coke from the fridge. "You guys want one?"

"Sure. Thanks," Callen said.

"I'll take one too. Thanks," Teni added.

"So to your knowledge, Alex didn't come back to Talbot?" Callen asked.

"Not that I know of, but I just dropped him at the docks with his suitcase and ran in for a quick bite before heading back."

"Thanks, Lenny," Teni said.

Lenny's blue eyes narrowed. "What's this all about?"

Callen explained just enough.

"Whoa. That's crazy, dude." Lenny shifted his gaze to Teni. "I'm real sorry about Julia."

"Thanks."

After a few parting words, Callen and Teni hurried back to the shelter of Callen's SUV, and once inside and settled, Callen turned to her. "Well, we know Lenny didn't bring Alex back, and since Lenny toyed with the idea of staying, maybe Alex didn't know he decided to return, so maybe he didn't lie to you after all."

"He said Lenny had anchored and was crashing with friends. Maybe he just assumed because Lenny said he was considering staying, but it sounded like he knew that's what had happened. Honestly, I don't know what to think."

"I think we should head back to my place and hunker down for this storm. It's just growing stronger, and I don't think there's anything else we can do until the phone lines are back up and we can get a warrant."

Great. They had to sit and wait while Jared did who knew what with Julia's body. It could already be buried or dumped somewhere by now. The thought of not giving her dear cousin a proper burial weighed heavily on her heart as they made the drive back to Callen's.

||||||||||

Knowing they had to wait for the phone lines to return, time passed slow as molasses. But at the same time, it flew fast as a locomotive racing down the steel rails with a *clickety-clack* by just being in Callen's presence. They made up for lost time, and it wasn't long before it was midnight and she made her way up to bed.

She'd just crawled under the covers when Callen's floodlights shifted on, the bright light slipping through the interior full-length shutters. Moving for the window, she pulled back the heavy hunter-green shutter and searched the ground as lightning zigzagged across the black, rain-drenched sky, illuminating the tree line . . . and a fleeing figure.

Teni's chest compressed, and she swallowed hard. He was back.

Lightning flashed, striking a tree and snapping the majestic thirty-five-foot black walnut tree in a lopsided half.

Thunder shook the earth and sparks shot from the tree, flaming shards of wood raining down like ash.

Her eyes scanned the perimeter, and his movement caught her eye again—he was racing deeper into the woods.

She hollered for Callen and sprinted from the room, smacking straight into his bare chest in the darkened hallway—her hands pressed to his abdomen, his muscles toned and sculpted beneath her fingertips.

"I saw him," she managed to blurt out.

"What?" His voice was deep with sleep.

"I saw a man outside, again."

"You wait here. I'll go check it out." He flipped the light switch in his room and rushed in. Pulling on his shirt, he slid on his side holster, slipped in his Glock, and grabbed a walkie-talkie.

"Not happening," she said, rushing back to the guest room to grab her own Glock in her still-bandaged hand. Not having her waist holster, she kept it lowered at her side.

Moving back into the hall, she nearly collided with Callen a second time.

"*Please* stay here," he said, desperation clinging to his tone, concern creased across his brow. "I don't want anything happening to you."

"I appreciate that." His concern was genuine and evident. "But I'm going." She wasn't the wait-and-see kind of girl. "I'll be careful." Or at least attempt to.

He arched a brow. "Tennyson Marlena Kent, you haven't been careful a day in your life."

So she lived by instinct. So far, it had served her well, at least as an investigator. "We're wasting time," she said. Racing down the steps, she slipped on her coat and boots and grabbed her banged-up-in-the-blast-but-still-working Maglite and sped out the door before Callen had time to argue.

He hurried after her, quickly reaching her side and sticking to her like fly paper. "Where'd you see him?" he asked.

"At the break in the tree line, there." She pointed to three o'clock. "Then, when I stood at the window and lightning hit the tree, he fled that way." She shifted her arm, pointing to their twelve.

"All right, let's go, but please stay by my side."

"We can cover more ground if we split up."

"Ain't happening, sunshine."

He hadn't called her that in a decade.

He was ridiculous when it came to protecting her. "You are so stubborn," she hollered over the storm.

"Stubborn?" He smiled. "Pot. Kettle," he said. The sound of Sam's fire siren blared dimly in the distance but grew louder the closer it drew.

"I radioed Sam on the walkie-talkie system we use when the lines go down," Callen said.

She prayed that siren didn't scare the intruder off before they could catch him, but it was the right decision. The tree fire—small as it may be in comparison to the one that had ravaged her home—needed to be extinguished quickly to keep it from spreading despite the rain.

Mud oozed beneath their boots as they entered the forest, clinging to them as they tracked in the direction the man had fled, the beams of their flashlights spreading out in an arc, clearly illuminating a few feet out, then fading into a faint glimmer of light in the distance.

"Wait!" Callen hollered, halting her in place with a strong arm across her torso.

"What?" she called over the storm.

He jiggled his flashlight at the muddy footprint in the damp but mostly sheltered part of the woods, thanks to the leaf-covered canopy.

"I'm going to guess a size ten," Callen said, hovering the sole of his size-eleven boot over the print and finding it less than an inch shorter.

Teni illuminated the path of the prints tracking forward. "Now we know the direction he's fled."

Callen carefully moved around the prints, carving a quick mark in the tree so they could come back and process the prints properly. Since there was no cell service on Talbot, no one bothered carrying their phones, so there'd be no quick picture-taking until they went back to Callen's to retrieve a camera. But they'd never stop midpursuit to process evidence.

The manhunt came first and foremost, so they rapidly continued, following the boot prints until the canopy opened up and the prints faded into mashed squishes of mud under the rain's heavy fall.

Terrific.

Something snapped on their left.

They shifted their flashlights, their beams landing for a moment on a man dressed in black, ski mask included.

"There!" Teni shouted, racing forward as he quickly moved out of her flashlight's beam.

"Teni, wait!" Callen hollered. "We're near the underground cave system. With this rain—"

He spoke a moment too late, for the ground gave way in a rush, yanking her down a cascading mudslide with a whoosh. Branches prodded and poked into her flesh as she fell through the muddy opening in the earth—no doubt brought on by the flooding rains. She'd been so fixated on catching the man, she hadn't thought ahead to what she might be headed into. The ground beneath her was cold and slick.

She blinked as Callen bent over the opening, more than a dozen feet above, the beam of his flashlight shining down. "You okay?"

She lifted her head and nodded. "Yep." Just embarrassed she hadn't watched her step better, and now whoever had been outside of Callen's house was getting away.

"Let me get you out," Callen said.

"No." She shook her head as she propped herself up on her elbows. "Go after him."

"Ten? You can't be serious. I'm not going to just leave you here."

"Please. He's getting away. I'm fine."

"Ten—"

"Please."

"Fine. Stay put," he said.

Like she was going anywhere?

Callen's footsteps echoed away, sloshing through the slick mud above.

She scrambled to her feet and examined the pit she was stuck in.

Rain pattered in, turning the earthen walls to slippery mud, but tree roots poked through the far side, and she had thick branches surrounding her.

Shoving branch after branch into the side of the pit, she fashioned a climbing wall and, after a few struggles, slips, and missteps, finally clawed and crawled her way over the edge and back onto level ground.

"I should have known you'd figure a way out," a male voice growled—one familiar despite his obvious attempt to muffle it.

No, it can't be.

She swallowed, attempting to turn and face the man, but he quickly grabbed her from behind, pulling her into a chokehold, stealing her breath away. While she suffocated and wriggled to break free of his ironclad grasp, he jerked her gun from her bandaged hand with a painful jab.

"Finally separating you two gives me the opportunity I need." His hot breath tickled the nape of her neck, making her skin crawl.

He squeezed tighter on her neck, so tight and forceful he was close to crushing her windpipe.

Focus, Teni. Concentrating all her effort, she wriggled enough to elbow him hard in the solar plexus, then stomped on his instep as he shifted. When he loosened his hold, she took full advantage, quickly spinning around and thrusting the heel of her palm up into his nose with as much force as she could muster, his nose cracking loudly upon impact. She'd definitely broken it.

"Teni," Callen called from what sounded like a hundred yards away, but closing in.

"You'll pay for this," the man said, regaining his composure and lunging to retrieve the gun he'd dropped during her onslaught.

Teni spotted it on the ground as lightning flashed and dove for it. They collided and wrestled for the weapon.

She managed to grab hold of his ski mask, yanking it off as the gun fired.

"No!" Callen hollered, closer than she expected.

She stumbled back in a crablike crawl—the bullet having entered her shoulder in a hot rush of heat. "William?" She swallowed. Her *own cousin* was trying to kill her? He wasn't even supposed to be on the island. Why?

William scrambled to his feet and darted into the darkness as Callen approached.

"He went that way," she said. "William went that way."

Shock echoing her own crossed Callen's concerned face. "William? Your cousin?"

She nodded, then winced, her eyes heavy.

His face tightened. "You okay?"

"Yeah. He just . . ." Darkness engulfed her before she could finish her sentence.

FIFTEEN

TENI WOKE TO A BRIGHT LIGHT OVERHEAD and a
table or some hard surface beneath her.

Paul stood beside Callen, both gazing worriedly at her.

"Look who's awake," Paul said.

Paul? What was he doing here? And where was she?

Pain ricocheted through her right shoulder as she sat up,
searing down her arm to her fingertips.

Callen rushed to her side. "Easy now, sunshine. You took
quite the hit."

"You mean that was real?" Her cousin William had shot
her? *He* was the one trying to kill her? Had he killed Julia and
stolen her body too?

"I'm afraid so," Callen said.

"But . . . why?" What had she ever done to William to make
him want to kill her and Julia?

Paul cleared his throat and shifted for the doorway.

She gazed around. She was in Paul's kitchen. It'd been years
since she'd last been here, but she recognized the seashell-print
wallpaper.

"I'll give you two some privacy," he said. "Holler if you need
anything. And, Teni . . ." Seriousness overtook his expression

243

and tone. "You best listen to Callen and take it easy. The bullet missed a major artery by only this much." He demonstrated, holding his thumb and forefinger very slightly apart.

"You took the bullet out?" She glanced from him to her bandaged shoulder.

"My dog got shot by a hunter not too long ago. I had to remove the bullet or Oberon would have died."

"And?"

"Obby's alive and well. Crashed up on my bed snoring as we speak. Don't worry. Between paramedic and nursing training, you learn a whole heap of a lot." He tapped the white door-frame with his long, slender fingers. "I'll be upstairs if you need me. Like I said, just holler. Oh . . ." He paused in the doorway. "I gave you a good dose of pain meds. They should start numbing the pain soon, and I'll send some home with you."

"Okay. Thanks," she said, still feeling as if she were in a dream.

Callen moved closer, taking up his stance by her left side and placing a gentle hand on her shoulder as Paul's footsteps echoed up the stairs.

"I was terrified back there," he said, moving his hand to cup her face, his palm warm and sturdy. He exhaled with a tremor, gazing into her eyes. "Terrified I'd never get to tell you that I love you." He swallowed, his Adam's apple bobbing. "I always have. Always will."

She swallowed, elation filling her despite the pain. The emptiness she'd carried since their breakup disappeared, her heart pouring forth in her words. "I love you too." A breath escaped her lips as his descended on hers. Time evaporated as their kiss deepened, but finally, using restraint beyond her measure, she broke the most majestic kiss of her life.

"What?" he said, breathless as he caressed her cheek.

She exhaled, every fiber of her being screaming, *Stay in the moment*, but they had a killer to catch. "William," she managed, surprised she could speak, let alone think coherently, after *that* kiss.

She'd never considered she was being hunted by a family member—a family member who she'd celebrated holidays with, who she'd played with as a kid, and who she'd looked after at family events, being five years older than him.

Apparently, none of that mattered to him.

How could he have tried to kill her? He'd most likely killed Julia too. What was wrong with him?

"I radioed Sam and had him call in the Talbot Search and Rescue volunteers," Callen said. "We've got a manhunt before us."

"One we need to wrap up before the nor'easter passes, or William will be able to slink off the island and we might never find him." She slowly slid off the table they'd turned into a surgical table, the movement deepening the ache throbbing in her shoulder.

"Easy now, sunshine."

She loved the sound of his nickname for her dancing on his delicious lips.

"I can't believe William killed Julia and keeps trying to kill me. What does he want? To inherit an island he's never cared about?"

"You said he's next in line."

"Yes, but he's never cared about Talbot. So why now?"

"Maybe he feels he deserves it and has been planning this for a while, or maybe he's suddenly desperate for money and plans on selling it."

"Like Alex wanted to do. . . ."

Callen's dark brows furrowed at her pause. "What?"

"Alex and William really hit it off at the engagement party."

He arched a brow. "The party where Alex introduced you to a developer?"

"Y . . . e . . . a . . . h." She narrowed her eyes, no doubt thinking the same thing as he was. "You're wondering if Alex told William about wanting to sell Talbot to a developer?"

"The thought crossed my mind."

"You think they could be in this *together*?" It was a horrible thought—her cousin and her at-the-time fiancé planning her death. Horrific, but not altogether improbable.

William was into business dealings, start-up companies . . . Not unlike Alex. And neither understood the beauty of Talbot or appreciated her family's legacy.

Alex's ambivalence, she got. William's, she never had. It was *their* family's island. She couldn't help who the deed passed to. Her great, great, great and so on grandfather had set that in motion when he'd been given the island.

Had William secretly wanted the island he seemed to never care about so badly that he was willing to kill Julia and her? Or was Callen on to something? Was it all because William and Alex had joined forces? Alex finding the buyer, and William getting her out of the line of inheritance. Then he'd sell Talbot and what . . . ? Pay Alex a hefty broker's fee for finding the buyer, connecting them, making sure Teni made it to Talbot. Had it all been a setup they would use if she refused to sell to the buyer Alex had chosen?

She shook her head. She'd loved them, thought they loved her. Could they both care so little about her and her very life?

SIXTEEN

"I IMAGINE WE SHOULD START the search at William's place, though I doubt he'd actually stay there if he wishes to remain hidden," Callen said.

"Agreed." She nodded.

"So be thinking of any other places on the island William might stay—with a friend, possibly?" he asked. "Though it seems more likely he'd want no one to know about his presence on the island," he added.

"That makes sense. There is . . . *was* an old fishing cabin on the northern tip of Talbot where he and his dad used to go. Pretty sure it's uninhabitable, but it's worth a shot."

"Sounds like a strong possibility. He could also be hunkered down in a tent somewhere—on Talbot or on one of the barrier islands."

Henry's Point was one of three small barrier islands surrounding Talbot, the others being Wilson's Key and Evan's Marsh.

Callen stared at her with eyes narrowed. "I don't suppose there is any way I can talk you out of this. You just had a bullet taken out of your shoulder. Paul said the damage was minimal,

247

but I can't . . ." He shook his head. "I could ask Paul to search with me, and you can hang out with Oberon."

"Not even a little chance. This is my fight. Besides, Paul needs to stay close to the radio in case there is a storm-related injury." Her shoulder still throbbed, but the pain wasn't too bad. The meds appeared to be doing their job. She was a bit loopy but confident she could hold up her end of the search.

Callen took a deep breath and appeared resigned. "Okay, let's start with William's house, then the cabin, and if need be, we'll go from there."

They were right in their initial assumption—William wasn't at his house, nor did it appear he'd been there in a while—so they rode out to the northern tip of the island.

Rain lashed hard in the stinging, hurricane-force winds, which also pelted sand through the air.

Battling the wind and rising water level—already mid-calf high as they climbed out of the Tahoe—they trekked to where Teni recalled the cabin had been, though it was nearly impossible to make out much of anything through the blanket of pummeling rain.

"I think it's that way," she hollered over the storm's roar.

Callen nodded and followed, the two wading through the rapidly rising waterline. The chill of the bay water, mixed with the dousing rain, seeped through Teni's pants and down her legs. As the water rose to mid-thigh level, she wondered if they wouldn't make better progress swimming.

"There," she said, barely making out the brown clapboard structure that sat as close to the shoreline as possible while still being on the island. The roof and four walls shockingly remained in place, though the front porch was crumbling, the porch roof nearly caved fully in.

Faded orange storm shutters covered the windows, and water swirled half a foot up the matching orange door.

Wading toward the front door with weapons drawn—Teni using one of Callen's since William had stolen hers before fleeing last night in the woods—they paused before stepping onto the porch.

Callen indicated for her to wade around back in case William was inside and attempted to flee. He clearly did not like the thought of her being around back alone—though competent, she was not in tiptop shape. She knew he respected her skills, but she also knew he'd always be protective of her, especially when she was nursing a bandaged shoulder, which a bullet had just been pulled out of.

|||||||||

Callen hated Teni being out of his sight for even a moment, but the back needed covering.

William, being the weasel he was, would most likely take the coward's way out and use a rear window to flee. But he felt better about Teni covering the windows than he did about having her break down the front door. He'd be the one to face William's reaction to the startling intrusion, if he was in fact inside.

Exhaling, Callen kicked in the door and rushed in, water flowing in after him. Noise rustled in the back, but it was so dark with the storm shutters in place he couldn't make out the source.

A squeak sounded off to his left. A door opening and closing. Callen raced toward it as wood cracked and splintered from inside the room.

"He's coming out the northwest side of the cabin," he hollered to Teni.

William cussed as Callen broke through the door and found him halfway out the open window. Teni waited to greet him with a gun aimed at his head from outside.

Callen grabbed William by his shirt, hauled him back in, and aimed his gun at William's center mass. "Ten?"

"On my way in," she said, rounding the cabin, unable to climb up through the window with her injured shoulder. No pressure or weight should be put on it, Paul had said.

A few moments later, she entered the room behind them.

"Hold the gun on him while I cuff him," Callen said.

"With pleasure," she said.

Callen waited until Teni was in position before cuffing William and reading him his rights. Now to restrain him somewhere until the nor'easter passed and he could be moved to a precinct on the mainland.

"Where is Julia's body, you sicko?" Teni asked, fury resonating in her tone.

William smiled smugly. "I'm not saying a word until I speak with my lawyer."

"You're definitely going to need one," Teni said as they hauled him out into the storm and on to Callen's house, where they'd hold him until the police arrived to work in conjunction with NRP on Julia's death, and with ATF on the attempted murder of Teni via arson.

One vital question remained in Callen's mind—was Teni's ex-fiancé part of William's scheme to kill her off, and if so, how would they prove it?

SEVENTEEN

IT WAS A LONG, TENSE NIGHT, with Teni and Callen both remaining on high alert while guarding William, who held insufferably true to his word, refusing to say anything until he spoke with his lawyer—literally not a word. But thankfully, his expressions and body language confirmed many of Teni's suspicions.

She taunted, questioned, and prodded, and William's smug expressions or flutter of his eyes or flush of red up his neck gave away the answers he refused to give audibly.

By eight the next morning, the storm finally died out, and Callen and Teni got calls out when the lines came back up several hours later. It wasn't long after that they received a call back letting them know the mainland police were headed out to take William into custody. They'd planned to send an ME to collect Julia's body, but her body still hadn't been found. Unfortunately, facial expressions wouldn't give up locations— unless Teni named the right one and William reacted in some way, but clearly she hadn't guessed the right location yet, or he'd simply managed to maintain a stoic expression throughout that specific round of questioning.

By one o'clock, the Crisfield police officers arrived at Callen's front door. After once again Mirandizing William Kent, they took him into custody and transported him via boat back to their precinct.

Teni and Callen followed in his boat.

Flooding had swamped a good portion of Talbot, and once the waters receded, the extent of coastal erosion would be revealed. There would be much damage to repair and deep wounds in Teni, which would require deep healing, but her eyes were finally open to the only true source of healing—her Father in heaven.

Callen clasped her hand as he helped her from the boat, his hesitation to let go of her hand apparent on his face.

After a tight squeeze and a gentle kiss on her brow, he said, "We've got this."

Inhaling and then exhaling in a slow, soothing stream, she nodded, praying God would give her the strength and forbearance to remain professional and not to react in any way that would provide William with even the slightest amount of pleasure. He wasn't in control of this conversation—she'd be when it was her turn.

She and Callen watched William's interrogation by one of Crisfield's detectives from behind the viewing glass. Though William only responded once his lawyer finally arrived, even then, every answer he provided was clipped and devoid of emotion.

"Let us have a crack at him?" Callen asked the precinct chief out of courtesy, because technically, both he and Tennyson had jurisdiction under the circumstances.

"Be my guest," the chief said, gesturing them toward the room.

The interrogating officer looked up as they entered the room. He nodded and stood, excusing himself, giving them the room.

William's jaw tensed along with his entire frame. He looked

to his lawyer, anger flushing his cheeks. "I won't speak with them," he gritted out.

"You don't have to talk, but you do have to listen," Callen said. He proceeded to lay out all the charges against William and the evidence they had to back up said charges—Teni's processing of Julia's body on Henry's Point before moving her to the icehouse, along with the photographic evidence taken of the bruises forming along Julia's right cheek, where she'd been struck with what appeared to be a fist, perhaps a gloved fist, but still a man-sized fist. Then there was the cut gas line and his fleeing the arson scene. Not to mention his shooting Teni in the shoulder in the forest.

William's lawyer grimaced. "Please give me and my client a few moments to confer?"

"Absolutely," Callen said as he and Teni stood, exiting the interrogation room and moving back into the viewing one.

It didn't take a lip reader to translate what was occurring. William's lawyer was laying the cold hard facts out for him and urging him, quite vehemently it appeared, to cop a plea.

Teni prayed she was right because she already had recommended terms in mind—a full confession, naming of any accomplices—though she still couldn't fully wrap her mind around the possibility of Alex being one, even though he had been fixated on selling the island.

But the most important of the terms to her was that William reveal where he had hidden Julia's body.

It took hours for the DA to solidify the terms, and William and his lawyer even longer to try to barter out of some of them, but the DA, thankfully, held firm. A maximum punishment of life in prison in a moderate-level facility that was neither hard-core prison nor the type that more resembled a country club than a jail.

Finally, the agreement was struck, though reluctantly on

William's part. He confessed to the charges against him—killing Julia, attempting to kill Teni, first by arson and then by shooting her. His motive was as she and Callen had suspected. William wanted Talbot for himself and was willing to do whatever it took to obtain ownership of it.

The final admission on William's part, and by far the most shocking to Teni, though clearly it hadn't been to Callen, was Alex's role in it all. Alex had brokered the deal between William and the developer to take place once the island was legally William's. He'd even gone so far as informing William of when he'd be leaving Teni alone, and at what time she and Julia had their swim planned.

How could a man she'd loved, at least as a friend, a man she'd so foolishly almost married, want her dead?

EIGHTEEN

AFTER THE POLICE LEFT TO ARREST ALEX, William finally gave up the fact that he'd "disposed" of Julia's body—his cruel word—by anchoring her down and dropping her off the side of his raft in Hunter's Cove. Thankfully, the cove was sheltered from the raging nor'easter far more than the open bay, and the cove was relatively small.

Anxious to dive in and attempt to recover her dear cousin's body, Teni and Callen headed for the precinct door, passing a handcuffed Alex on the way in.

He refused to look at her, but Callen didn't waste the opportunity to block his path and force him to look him in the eye. "You're going to pay for what you've done."

Alex offered a smug smile—one Teni had rarely seen before. "I haven't done anything," he said.

"That's exactly what William said . . . *at first*." Callen smiled.

Panic flashed across Alex's face. "What *did* William say?"

Teni smiled and waggled her fingers good-bye as they exited the precinct, confident that Alex would get what he deserved. She trusted the DA to see to it.

Now to find Julia.

||||||||||

Thankfully, the bay settled quickly after the nor'easter dissipated. Hunter's Cove was calm and sheltered. Callen tried to talk Teni out of diving, given her recent injury, but she didn't need both arms fully functioning to dive. Her shoulder was sore, but her arm was moveable. She was an underwater investigator. Locating and retrieving bodies was in her wheelhouse. She was going under. Paul joined the conversation, but after finally realizing she wasn't backing down, he relented only by getting her to agree to signal for help if she found Julia's body, rather than trying to carry her cousin to the surface herself.

Her gear in place and regulator in her mouth, Teni slipped off the dive deck on the rear of Callen's boat into the water. Four other divers on the island and, of course, Callen had volunteered to help her search. The six of them spread out in a grid pattern they'd established before going under.

A half hour into the dive she began to despair, until something reflecting in her dive light caught her attention.

She swam toward it and discovered her sweet cousin tied with sailor's rope and anchored with metal diving weights.

She photographed the scene with her underwater gear, then cut Julia free, grabbing hold with her good arm. Callen spotted her waving her dive lamp and came to help her, taking Julia from her and carrying her in an arm-around-the-waist backward hug up to the surface.

Callen lifted Julia to Paul's outstretched arms as he knelt on the edge of the dive platform on Callen's boat.

Callen climbed up and waited until Teni was on board before carrying Julia's body below deck once again, laying her on the same bench as when they'd found her at Henry's Point.

The ME Teni had personally requested arrived within hours.

An autopsy would be needed to officially determine Julia's cause of death, but William had already confessed. Now they could have a proper funeral, and although Julia had been taken from their lives so young, at least they'd retrieved her from an unknown grave, and she could be buried alongside her parents in the Kent family graveyard, where Teni could place Julia's favorite flower—purple tulips—as often as they were available.

EPILOGUE

THREE MONTHS LATER

Teni watched Callen nail the final beam in the frame of her home restoration.

It had taken more than a month for them to begin reconstruction, due to pending structural approval of the safety of the original homestead's foundation and load-bearing support beams, which had been of such quality they had withstood the explosion and fire. Being able to rebuild around the heart of her ancestral home made Teni happy, but not as happy as her renewed relationship with Callen.

They'd spent a week of uninterrupted time together after William's arrest—she on bereavement and "injury" leave, and Callen on long-overdue leave time.

Then they'd spent every free day since working on rebuilding her home, despite winter coming on. They'd been blessed with the gracious help of a fabulous gang of local friends and neighbors, who worked together in solid but rapid fashion, reminding her of an old-fashioned barn raising.

During this time, she'd been bunking in Becky's parents' guest room. Now that the threat to her life was over, Callen was comfortable with her being out of sight . . . at least for the night. But they'd been spending every other minute of their days together—attending church on Sunday mornings, watching movies on Saturday nights, taking long walks in the woods, which, at Callen's side, had once again become a place of great memories.

"All right, everybody. Great work," Callen said, setting his hammer back into his toolbox. "Let's take an hour lunch break and meet back here at one." They still had a ways to go, but it was a strong start, and if the weather turned and they had to break until spring, they had at least gotten a head start and could begin again when the weather warmed.

Everyone dispersed for lunch, leaving her and Callen alone.

"Come with me," he said, holding out his hand.

She pursed her lips. She'd seen that mischievous twinkle in his eyes before, and it always spelled trouble in the most delightful way.

"Where are we off to?" she asked, clasping her hand in his.

"You'll see." He winked.

"Will we be back on time?"

"Close enough." He smiled as they trekked through the now leaf-barren forest down to his house and around to the front, which faced the bay.

Then, leading her down to his lowered rowboat, he smiled again as she caught sight of the two plaid wool blankets—one on each bench seat—and an old-fashioned wooden picnic basket nestled on the floor between them.

"A December picnic? On the bay? Isn't it a little chilly?"

She clasped hold of his outstretched hand and stepped into the boat, awaiting an answer.

"Don't worry. I'll keep you warm."

Already warming at his mere words, she took a seat on the rear bench and draped the wool blanket across her lap.

Light flakes of snow began falling as Callen settled into the seat opposite her and rowed them toward Wilson's Key.

She looked at him, questioning. "Why Wilson's Key?" It was the largest of Talbot's three barrier islands, on the west side of Talbot.

"Since we're making a fresh start, I figured we needed a new island hangout for making new memories together."

She smiled as he anchored the boat, grabbed the basket and both blankets, and offered his hand. "Ready?"

"More than ready," she said, placing her hand in his.

He smiled and squeezed her hand as they stepped onto the island's snowflake-laden shore.

Callen laid out one of the blankets, set down the basket and the other blanket—clearly to drape over their laps as they ate—and then pulled her into his strong, sturdy arms. "I'm glad you're ready. Because, you know, we've got a lifetime ahead of us."

She bit her lip, excitement racing through her. "Is that right?" A lifetime spent at Callen's side. Nothing, absolutely nothing, sounded more amazing.

"Yeah. I'm thinking three or four kids, a dog, and maybe even a Volvo."

"A Volvo? No way."

His smile spread wider. "Prefer being a minivan mom?"

"No. I mean, nothing against them, but I'm just more a Jeep kinda girl."

"No," he said, snuggling her tighter and tipping up her chin, "you're *my* girl." He pressed his lips to hers.

CODE OF ETHICS

LYNETTE EASON

"On my honor, I will never betray my badge, my integrity, my character, or the public trust. I will always have the courage to hold myself and others accountable for our actions. I will always uphold the constitution, my community, and the agency I serve."

—Law Enforcement Oath of Honor

ONE

"GET HIM TO SURGERY, ASAP! OR NUMBER FOUR."

Dr. Ruthie St. John followed the gurney down the hall to the elevator that would take them to the second floor. As a trauma surgeon in a busy city, she wasn't often bored. This shift proved to be no different. "Go, go! How's his blood pressure?"

"Low, but he's stable right this second. Bleeding is slowing."

Another team hurried past them with Dr. Hugh Stancil working on the woman in the gurney next to her patient. He glanced at her. "I've got room four."

The elevator doors opened and she raised a brow. "Not if I get there first."

The doors shut on his scowling features. Ruthie wasn't worried. She knew room three was open and he would be directed there. Everyone just seemed to like room four. For her, it was because it was where she'd performed her first surgery. For Hugh, it was a matter of putting her in her place. Something she did her best not to let him get away with.

They continued to monitor the patient on the ride up. He blinked up at her. "What happened?"

"You were shot."

"Who are you?"

"Dr. Ruthie St. John. I'm going to take that bullet out of your shoulder."

"I'm fine."

She patted his arm. "You will be."

"No, seriously," he slurred. "I can't . . . have to . . . people trying to kill . . ."

Then the medicine took over and his eyes closed, shutting off whatever protest he was trying to form.

When the doors slid open, the surgical team met them and whisked him off to the operating room. Ruthie ripped off her gloves and tossed them in the biohazard bin. She nudged the faucet on and began to scrub in. Working quickly, she followed all procedures before entering the room where she'd do her best to repair his shoulder so he wouldn't have any lingering aftereffects. Granted, he wasn't knocking at death's door, but bullet wounds were sneaky. "What's his story?"

"Police officer," she heard over the speaker. "Isaac Martinez. A detective, actually. He responded to a domestic disturbance and caught a bullet for his trouble."

Ruthie wondered if her law enforcement family knew him. "Did someone call the chief?" she asked as she entered the OR, sterile hands held in front of her.

"Don't know." Her attending snapped the gloves over her hands.

Tabitha St. John, Ruthie's mother and the Chief of Police for the city of Columbia, South Carolina. Any time there was an officer-involved shooting, the chief was informed. She'd probably show up at the hospital before they were out of surgery.

No matter. It wasn't her problem. His wound was, and it was time to do her stuff. "Is he under?"

The anesthesiologist nodded.

"Vitals?"

Meg, the nurse on duty, called them out to her.

Ruthie inhaled the cleansing deep breath she always took and let it out slowly behind the mask. Then she picked up the small forceps tool that would allow her to extract the bullet. "Let's get this done." Working quickly, she established that the bullet was lodged in the space between the clavicle and the first rib.

Amazing.

She looked up at the nurse. "I guess if you have to get shot in the shoulder, that's the place to do it."

"No messy bone fragments," Meg said.

"Doesn't appear to be." She removed the bullet and dropped it in the pan Meg offered to her. It would be turned over as evidence. Ruthie checked the surrounding tissues for any bone fragments or bleeding, then nodded to her resident. "You can sew him up."

|||||||||

Isaac heard the voices, but for some reason he couldn't force himself to respond. His eyes wouldn't open, his limbs refused to move. And who'd set his shoulder on fire?

He had to focus, had to wake up. Or was he already awake? Or dreaming? But the voices sounded so real. And became clearer with each passing moment.

". . . very fortunate. The bullet didn't hit any bones. I simply had to remove it, repair some damaged tissue as best I could, and stitch him up. He's also on antibiotics to ward off infection. Fortunately, there's no serious damage, but he'll definitely need to take it easy while he heals."

Isaac liked her voice. It was soothing and warm. Smooth like silk, low but feminine. Professional, yet filled with compassion. He wished she'd keep talking.

"Thank you."

Isaac stilled. He knew that second voice. It didn't soothe him at all. His sister, Carol. Who'd called her? Why was she here?

Well, okay, she was probably here because she'd heard he'd been shot, and she was on his emergency contact list. Right. But the fact that she'd bothered to come surprised him. No, the fact that her husband, Officer Brent Olsen, had *let* her come surprised him. Maybe Carol had grown a spine in the last few months since he'd seen her.

"When can he go home?" Carol asked.

"We'll observe him tonight, but I would say as long as he doesn't start running a fever, he can go home tomorrow."

"Okay, thanks. I'll pass this on to my family."

"Is there anyone who can stay with him? You?"

"Ah . . . no, probably not me. I doubt he would want me here. But our mother might come stay. She works the night shift at a twenty-four-hour pharmacy and was trying to get someone to cover for her. As of twenty minutes ago, she hadn't left the pharmacy."

Isaac didn't want his mother here. As much as he loved her, she would hover. He couldn't take that right now. Just the thought of it sent dread shooting through him. Yeah, that wasn't happening. He could take care of himself. Would insist on it. If he could get the words from his brain to his lips.

Footsteps faded, and the darkness pulled at him once more. He fought it. If he slept, he couldn't fight back. He drifted anyway.

||||||||||

Ruthie dragged the pair of gloves from her hands and tossed them into the trash. She needed a vacation. Yesterday. She was supposed to be gone already.

Headed to her little cabin in the woods that was off the grid. No cell service, no internet, no . . . nothing. Just her and nature and a good book. She hadn't decided if she was in the mood for a romance or a mystery, so she had packed both in the bag sitting in the back of her car. All ready and waiting. But the waiting was almost over.

She made her way to the private family room, where she found her mother with the detective's sister. "Hi, Chief St. John. Did you need a word with me?"

"Yes, please. Excuse me."

Carol nodded, and the chief followed Ruthie into the hall. "How's Detective Martinez doing?"

"He'll be fine."

"Good. Good. I'll see him when he wakes. How are you? Ready for your vacation?"

"Trying to be."

Her mother hugged her. "I'm so proud of you. You know that, right?"

"Even though I'm just a lowly surgeon and not on the streets fighting crime?"

A laugh slipped from her mother. "Even though, darling." She turned serious. "You're here to patch up the ones hurt by crime."

"True."

"All right. I'll see you later. Have someone let me know when he wakes."

"I will."

"And enjoy that vacation. You'd better get out of this place while you can."

"As soon as you say good-bye."

"Good-bye. See you when you get back."

Ruthie watched her mother leave, then sighed as she snagged her wayward dark hair into a neater ponytail. She walked to the nearest nurses' station and opened her laptop to enter her notes. Hospital life continued around her. Time passed.

"Hey, Ruthie, how you doing?"

Startled, she looked up to find her brother Derek leaning

against the wall, arms crossed, lips twisted into what he probably thought passed for a smile. "Hey, I'm fine. Just finishing up some notes. What are you up to?"

"Thought I'd just come by to see you. Say hi." He held up a green-and-white bag. "Bring you some donuts."

Her mouth watered, but she wasn't falling for it. "Uh-huh. Spill it. What's on your mind?"

"I can't just come see my favorite sister?"

A laugh burst from her before she could stop it. She snagged the bag and pulled out her favorite. Chocolate-covered with cream filling. "Thanks for some post-op humor."

He raked a hand through his dark hair. "Oh, all right. You know how you have that little cabin in the woods reserved?"

She shot him a wary glance even as she relished the sweetness on her tongue. "The one you told me about? The one I've been talking about for the past eight weeks, four days"—she glanced at the clock—"six hours, ten minutes, and forty-two seconds? The one I'm getting ready to spend the next week in all by myself?"

"Yeah. That one. Are you going to use it?"

"Are you blind, deaf, and certifiable? Yes, I'm going to use it." She frowned. "This must be horn-in-on-Ruthie's-vacation week."

"What are you talking about?"

"Chloe wanted to use it for a day, too." Their sister Chloe also worked with the police department with her K-9 partner, Hank.

"No, she beat me to you?"

"I told her no way."

"Just listen to why I want it and if you still want to say no, I understand."

"Ugh. . . . Okay, why?" She took another bite of the donut. A big one.

He sighed. "I'm going to ask Elaine to marry me. She saw the brochure and went nuts over it. Said that's where we needed to have our honeymoon. I thought it would be a nice romantic touch to ask her to marry me there, then go back for the honeymoon. That is, if you're not going to be present. That might kinda kill the mood."

Ruthie swallowed, gaped at him, then snapped her jaw shut when his expression didn't change. "Boy, you've got some nerve, don't you? I thought y'all were broken up."

"We were. Now we're not."

"And you're not going to share that story?"

A slight smile tilted his lips. "It's not a big deal. We just had to come to an understanding on a few things."

"Like what it really means to be married to a cop. Especially one who goes undercover a lot?"

"Yeah. Something like that. It's a miracle, but our schedules wound up exactly the same for the next two days. I requested the third day off and so did she. And I don't need it for the whole week or anything. Just the first few days so we can have a romantic dinner by the fire, go hiking in the woods, play Phase Ten, and just hang out together. So, *please*?" He drew the word out, clasping his hands together in a gesture that made him look like a teenager begging for his dad's car.

Ruthie groaned and sighed. The things she did for her siblings. "Does she know you cheat at that game?"

"What? I do not!"

"Liar."

He huffed a laugh. "If I confess, will you say yes?"

She scoffed. "No, you can't confess under duress. It wouldn't be admissible in court."

"Are you a lawyer or a doctor?"

Ruthie laughed—a tired laugh, but at least she managed it. "I'm a pushover."

"You are?" Hope flickered.

"Argh!" When he stayed silent and just looked at her with those pleading, sad eyes, she shook her head. "I would probably be bored out of my skull anyway, with nothing to do but sit on the dock by the lake reading a book for seven straight days."

Derek's eyes lit up. "Seriously?"

He'd missed the sarcasm. Or ignored it. She rolled her eyes. "Yes, seriously."

"Yes! Thank y—"

She held up a finger and he snapped his lips shut. "But," she said, "I get the latter part of the week, so don't even think about trying to extend your time."

"Of course!"

"And if you tell Chloe, I'll hurt you. Big time."

"I won't tell her, short of having a gun to my head."

"That's not funny." Derek was often undercover with some of the most dangerous lowlifes in the city. Having a gun held to his head wasn't unheard of.

He bounded over and wrapped her in a hug that squeezed the air from her lungs. "You're definitely my favorite sister."

"Then let your favorite sister breathe, please," she squeaked.

Derek let go and grinned. "We don't actually need it until tomorrow afternoon. You could go for the night."

She might just do that. "Call me before you head out, in case I decide not to go, and I'll give you the code to the box that holds the key."

"Thanks, Ruthie. If you ever need anything, just let me know."

"Of course. And if you don't come through, I'll just tell Izzy you said I was your favorite." Izzy and Derek were twins, and it was a well-known family fact that nothing and no one came before the other.

His glee turned to horror. "You wouldn't."

"Not today."

Derek hugged her again. "Thank you, thank you! I won't even threaten to tell Chloe you gave me the cabin instead of her."

"Derek!"

He kissed her cheek and took off, his jaunty steps echoing in the tile hallway. Ruthie pursed her lips. "You're welcome," she muttered.

"Hey, I thought you were supposed to be taking a vacation."

She turned to see Meg Worth, her favorite OR nurse. Meg had been in the operating room while Ruthie had worked on Detective Martinez. "I am."

"Well, what are you doing still hanging around this place? Get your behind in gear and get out of here. You've got a whole week off, remember?"

The pretty African American woman had spunk that made her patients smile. And while she was a complete professional around the patients, she knew she could speak her mind to Ruthie—oftentimes without a filter.

"Trust me, I remember," Ruthie said, "but plans change."

"Not unless someone changes them. Changed to what?"

"To me not telling anyone else that my plans changed and turning part of my vacation into a bit of a staycation."

"You're going to stay at home?"

"Just for the first part of the week."

"No cabin in the woods?"

"Eventually." She told the woman Derek's plans.

"Girl, you are too much. Who gives away their vacation cabin? Even to a brother? You're crazy." She planted her hands on her trim hips. "You have totally lost all sense the good Lord gave you. Honey, you *need* this vacation."

Ruthie grimaced. Leave it to Meg to tell it exactly like it was. "I agree. But the cabin's not happening for me until a little later in the week." Or later that evening. It was only a two-hour drive. She smiled. Truly, she was thrilled Derek and Elaine had worked things out. She pointed a finger at the woman in front of her and scowled. "But not a word to anyone, understand?"

Meg held up a hand in surrender. "You know you don't have to worry about me saying anything. You go rest so you can bring those magic fingers back, ready to save more lives."

Ruthie smiled then frowned, regret slugging her. "Couldn't save that car accident victim yesterday," she said softly.

"No one could have saved him, hon. He was gone before he got on your table. He just didn't know it yet."

True, but . . . "Doesn't make it any easier."

"No, I guess it doesn't." Meg hugged her. "Take it easy, doc."

"Yes, ma'am. You too."

Meg left, and Ruthie sat on the bench to tie her tennis shoes. She wouldn't need scrubs for a whole week. The thought exhilarated her—and slightly depressed her. She loved her job. But Meg was right. She really *did* need this vacation. She grabbed her purse and slung it over her shoulder.

But first, before she could start enjoying her days off, she had a patient to check on. The detective should be in a room by now, and he was probably just fine. She still couldn't believe the bullet had hit where it had, entering about as close to perfect as one could get. Someone was looking out for him.

She made her way down the hallway, nodding to those she knew, intentionally keeping her stride purposeful, not inviting anyone to stop and chat. At the nurses' station, she took Detective Martinez's chart and read through the latest information. Nothing of note, except that he'd awakened and asked for something to drink. There were no relatives staying with him.

"Still here, I see."

Ruthie spun to see Meg. "I thought you were leaving."

"Mm-hm. I thought the same about you, but I figured you'd be back here to check on the detective one last time."

"So you're here to make sure I really leave this time?"

"I am." Meg crossed her arms. "Go on and check on him. I'll be here to escort you to your car when you're done."

Oddly touched, Ruthie laughed. "All right. I'll just be a minute."

Ruthie slid the chart back into its slot and slipped down the hall to room four. She pushed open the door and came to an abrupt halt. A young man dressed in green scrubs held a syringe, ready to push it into her patient's IV. "Excuse me. Who are you?"

The person turned and shot her a small smile. "I'm the new night nurse. I was just getting ready to give Mr. Martinez here his medicine."

"I just read his chart. He's already had it."

But the person had already turned back to the port. He inserted the needle.

Ruthie gasped. "I'm his doctor and I said stop!"

He continued to ignore her. Fear for the man in the bed overrode anything else. She lunged forward and shoved the nurse away. He stumbled backward with a surprised cry while the syringe fell from the port and tumbled to the floor.

He shot to his feet. His dark eyes glittered, menace emanating from him. Chills enveloped Ruthie. He was no nurse. He sprang at her and wrapped his fingers around her throat.

She let out a scream before his grip tightened and cut her air off.

Realization finally hit.

This man was here to kill her patient.

But he was going to do his best to kill her first.

TWO

ISAAC WOKE AT THE SOUND of the scream. Instinct had him reaching for his weapon only to find his hand flailing uselessly at his side. Sounds of a scuffle reached him and he tried to speak. A crash sounded. Another scream.

"What's going on in here?"

A curse.

Then scrambling, running footsteps.

"Security! And I need a doctor! Ruthie, are you okay?"

Isaac worked himself into a sitting position, hating the weakness and the flashes of pain. The door opened and several hospital workers rushed in.

"Ruthie!"

Isaac looked down to see a woman on the floor and another woman squatting in front of her. "Hey."

The first woman, dressed in street clothes, scrambled to her feet and focused on him. "You need to lie back down. You don't want to move wrong and tear that wound open." She sounded hoarse.

He waved a hand. "I'm fine. What happened?"

"You're not fine, you've been shot. And had surgery. Don't

mess up my work." She touched the bandage on his shoulder. "No blood, that's good. How do you feel?"

"Like I've been shot. Who are you?"

She jolted and snapped her gaze up to meet his.

And that's when he noticed the red marks that would soon turn to bruises. He blinked and reached out to stroke the side of her neck. She flinched away. "Who choked you, and why?"

"I'm Dr. Ruthie St. John, the surgeon who removed the bullet in your shoulder earlier today. As for who tried to choke me, I'm not sure. But he was trying to jam this into your IV." She held up a syringe. "I managed to knock it out of his hand, and he got a little angry." Ruthie stretched her neck and winced. "Fortunately, he didn't have a very good grip, and with a little self-defense move, I managed to get loose."

"And then I came in and the man ran off," someone to his left said.

Isaac finally took in the other woman. A nurse. He recognized her. He'd been awake when she'd come in earlier. Meg something. "Anyone call security?"

"Yes, they're on the way." Ruthie waved the other onlookers out of the room. "We're good here. Thanks for coming to the rescue."

They left. Reluctantly. But he was finally alone once again with Ruthie and Meg.

"I'm going to need my shirt."

Ruthie gaped at him. "What? You can't go anywhere. You could break that wound open and bleed to death."

"And besides," Meg said, "your shirt has a hole in it. Not to mention the fact that you bled all over it."

"Fine, get me a scrub top. Anything."

"Are you not listening?" Ruthie asked, stepping toward him. "You can't leave."

"No, you're not listening," Isaac said. "If I don't leave, I'm a dead man."

"Why didn't you have protection on your door?" Ruthie asked softly.

"What?"

She sighed. "Usually when a cop's life is in danger, he has officers on his door for protection. There's been no one on your door, no one watching your back."

He nodded. "Usually. But there won't be any cops here. They don't care if I live or die."

Ruthie straightened and narrowed her eyes. "I don't believe that. The chief wouldn't tolerate that kind of behavior from her officers."

He shrugged, then winced. "Sounds like you know the chief."

"A bit. I also know if she knew what was going on, she'd have an officer here."

"Maybe, but I'm better off without one than with one who thinks I'd be getting what I deserved if I wound up dead. Because if you know the chief then you know that while she keeps her finger on the pulse of the city's finest, she doesn't always know the details of each and every one of her officers—or how they feel about one who snitched on a brother, especially one who is denying everything and looking like he's going to get away with it. The only way to prove I'm right—and get my career back—is to stay alive. If I can't find the evidence I need, I might as well resign." He tried to stand, but slid to the floor, his IV tube clanking against the pole, reminding him he was still trapped. He reached for it and stopped when warm fingers closed over his. He met Ruthie's eyes.

"You snitched on another cop?"

"Yep."

"I see." Her expression didn't change, but he could feel her judging him.

He sighed. "No, you don't. Nobody does."

"Hm."

278

"It's like if you see another doctor taking drugs from the pharmacy and you ask him what he's doing. He says nothing and puts them back. But now you're suspicious. Then you find out it's a regular thing going on. What do you do?"

"Report it," she said softly.

"Exactly." He pressed a hand to his shoulder and grimaced.

"You're going to run, aren't you?" she asked.

"I am. But only so far. I'm really close to proving that there are some cops in my department who are giving the good ones a bad name—and others who are helping them cover that up. There's one person who can make this all go away, but he went off the grid. I've got to find him and the evidence he has and convince him to do the right thing."

"They're trying to kill you because of that?"

"Apparently. And while I know that not every cop in the department is bad, I don't know who is and who isn't anymore. My uncovering this one situation has led to something huge, and it's up to me to stop it." He drew in a deep breath and blinked at the stars swimming in his vision. "Now . . . I've got to go. I can't be a sitting duck in this hospital bed."

For a moment, she simply watched him. "If you move wrong, you could tear open that wound and cause some serious bleeding."

"Will it kill me?"

"Probably not. At least not quickly. Your biggest threat is possible infection."

"No, my biggest threat is the guys who want me dead. And there's only one way to stop them."

"By finding the guy with the evidence."

"Exactly."

"Where is he?"

"On the run. But he's got a sister in the mountains of North Carolina. If I can track her down, I can probably find him."

"Don't you think the guys who tried to kill you can find him, too?"

"Yes. Which is why I need to find him first. He's not answering his cell phone or using his credit cards or social media. He's disappeared completely."

Her gaze never left his. "Once the pain meds wear off, you're going to be hurting."

"Won't be the first time."

Another sigh slipped from her, and he wished he could read the thoughts going on behind those blue eyes. She gave a decisive nod. "All right, then. I can see you're about as stubborn as they come. Can you give me about fifteen minutes so I can gather some supplies to send with you? To take care of the wound?"

He started to protest but could see she was probably just as stubborn as he was. "Fine. Fifteen minutes. No longer."

She started to turn, then whirled back to him. "They're probably watching, aren't they? The room, the hospital?"

He hesitated, then nodded. "Yes. Probably."

She turned to the nurse, who'd been observing the whole conversation. "Meg, you stay on the door. Don't let anyone in here. No doctors, no staff, no one. And especially no cops. If anyone asks, tell them he's taken a turn for the worse and is being moved to ICU."

Meg's eyes went wide, but she simply nodded.

"Good. Come on."

The two ladies stepped outside the room, and Isaac wilted back onto the mattress, his head spinning, nausea churning. It had been all he could do not to show any weakness in front of them. Now he was debating the wisdom of trying to leave.

But, like he told the very pretty doctor, if he didn't, he was a dead man.

‖‖‖‖‖‖

True to her word, Ruthie had gathered supplies and shoved them into a backpack she'd borrowed from the lost and found. Next, she'd grabbed an empty gurney, which she now rolled toward the room where she hoped Isaac still waited.

A short breath of relief puffed from her lips when she rounded the corner and found Meg pacing in front of the door. Ruthie rolled the gurney to the door and Meg held it while she pushed her way inside. Isaac sat on the bed, looking pale. She tossed a set of scrubs on the bed next to him. "Let's get you changed."

He looked up and blinked. "Huh?"

"Well, you can wear the gown if you prefer, but I thought you might like everything covered up for our little ride."

"What ride?"

"The one where you play dead."

"Good idea. Then what?"

"You tell me where you want to go, and I'll take you there." He hesitated and she raised a brow. "You really think you have the strength to do this on your own?"

His sigh echoed hers. With a quick look at her, then Meg, he finally shook his head. "No. I know I don't."

"So you do have some common sense," Ruthie said.

He shot her a dark look. "Occasionally, I give in."

"Perfect. You need some help getting dressed?"

"I can dress myself." He glanced at his shoulder. "The pants anyway. Turn around."

Ruthie wasn't sure he could, but she turned her back to him without argument. Meg did the same with a roll of her eyes that would have done a teenager proud.

With a few low groans through clenched teeth and a bit of careful maneuvering, he managed to get the pants on.

"You're not in danger of passing out or falling or anything, are you?" Ruthie asked. She couldn't help but glance over her shoulder. She'd rather cause him a bit of embarrassment than have him fall on the floor, reinjuring his shoulder and possibly adding a head injury to his assortment of wounds.

"Close, but I'm managing."

Not the answer she expected. "Let me help you."

"No. Turn around." He shot her another dark look and she quickly turned her head back to stare at the far wall. But the image of his olive complexion, dark eyes and hair—and muscular chest—stayed with her. The only reason he wasn't on the floor unconscious was because he was in tip-top shape. Not that she had a personal interest in that. It was just a professional observation.

Right. A grunt had her turning.

"You know you're being silly. I'm a doctor."

"Don't care. You're also a pretty lady. Eyes on the wall."

That shut her up. She ignored Meg's snorting laugh and focused on her patient's voice. He sounded breathless and done in. "Can we turn around now?"

"Yeah."

He'd gotten himself on the gurney and lay there, chest covered in sweat, dragging in deep breaths. "I probably should have let you help."

"Not going to argue with that."

"I couldn't get the top on."

Ruthie handed the shirt to Meg, then the two of them worked together to put it on him with as minimal movement of his shoulder as possible. Pulling the sheet up to Isaac's shoulders and locking eyes with him, Ruthie said, "Catch your breath, concentrate on keeping your breathing even, but shallow. We don't want the sheet to move up and down since you're supposed to be dead."

"Got it."

"No talking, no moving, no doing anything that makes it look like you're alive."

"Come on, doc. I got it, I promise."

"All right, then." She pulled the sheet up the rest of the way and gave a satisfied grunt when he didn't move. She really couldn't even tell that he was breathing. With one last look at Meg, she nodded. "Let's roll."

THREE

ISAAC LAY UNDER THE SHEET, his shoulder throbbing, mind whirling, while he tried to keep his breathing shallow. He was riding blind and he didn't like it one bit. The vulnerable position caused his nerves to itch and his heart to pound. Used to being the one in control, this new situation rankled him.

And, whether he wanted to admit it or not, it scared him senseless. Relying on someone else was something he usually avoided at all costs.

And now he found his life in the hands of a surgeon.

Once outside in the hallway, Isaac listened to the commotion. Then he was rolling, hand twitching, wishing for a weapon. Where was his Glock? Cole probably had it. No matter how he felt about Isaac, his partner wouldn't have left it on the kitchen floor where Isaac had dropped it when the bullet slammed into him.

Footsteps passed him. Paused. Then headed back his way.

"Ruthie?"

The deep voice sounded much too close. Isaac tensed as the wheels squealed to a stop.

"Lee." Ruthie's brief, professional response impressed him. "How are you?"

"I'm fine. But what are you doing?"

"Taking this patient down to the morgue. What does it look like?"

"That's not your job. That's what the flunkies are for."

Flunkies? Isaac supposed he meant the transport unit employees.

A chuckle escaped his pretty doctor, albeit the sound had a harsh edge that made Isaac lift a brow.

"See, that's the problem with you, Lee," she said. "You think you're too good for things. Doing stuff like this keeps your head the right size. You ought to give it a try."

"Such a do-gooder, Ruthie." The bass voice caused Isaac's head to pound harder. "You're not going to make chief of surgery with that kind of attitude."

"Maybe not. Now, do you mind? I've got other things to do than stand here and swap career advice with you."

Admiration for her warmed him throughout. She was spunky. He liked that. He was starting to think she might just help him stay alive after all.

Would they really come after him like this? Because he'd reported something that he'd had no choice but to report?

Yes, he admitted grudgingly, there were a few who might take it this far. He should have known, should have been prepared, but he'd been so busy focusing on stopping them, he hadn't prepared well enough to keep them from stopping him.

And he should have. After all, even his partner had given him the cold shoulder. He'd even gone so far as to tell Isaac he'd better have his own back, because after filing his report, no one else would.

And now this.

Isaac replayed everything from the call to the arrival at the house. Three cruisers had responded. Six officers. He and Cole had gone in first. Had it been a setup? A way to get rid of him? Teach him a lesson? If he'd died, who would question the report by the other officers? Chilled at the thought that his own partner would go so far as to risk his life, he bit the inside of his cheek.

Elevator doors swished open. She rolled him in and the doors shut. "We're in a service elevator," she said, her voice barely more than a whisper. "It will take us down to the basement, then I'll find a wheelchair and we can roll you out to my car. I've got one more stop to make. You need meds."

He assumed they were in the elevator alone and wanted to demand she not make any more stops. He could live without pain meds. But he clamped his lips tight and worked to control his breathing.

Dead men didn't talk—or argue.

||||||||||

Ruthie hated that she'd caught the attention of Dr. Lee Porter. Of all the people to run into, it had to be him. With a grimace, she slid her hand under the sheet and found her patient's fingers. "Squeeze my hand if you're okay. You're doing this dead thing way too convincingly."

The strong grip reassured her, and when the doors slid open, she pushed him out of the elevator. "Almost there," she said softly.

Things should be relatively slow at the moment down here. Hopefully. Then again, it wasn't like she came to the morgue on a regular basis.

Hospital security officer Brad Channing saw her coming. "Evening, Dr. St. John. What brings you down here?" He swept a hand toward the gurney. "Other than the obvious."

"That's about it. I didn't feel like waiting on someone to transport him, so I thought I'd do it myself."

"I can take it from here if you like." He stepped forward to take her place.

"Ah . . . no, that's all right. If you'll just get the door, I'll roll him in. I've . . . um . . . got some paperwork I need to fill out before I'm finished."

She tensed, hoping he wouldn't insist. When he simply shrugged and opened the door for her, she exhaled a slow breath of relief. "Thanks, Brad."

"Any time."

And then they were alone.

Where was Christy? The morgue technician was usually on duty for second shift, but right now the place echoed emptiness, which worked great for her purposes. Moving quickly, she unlocked one of the cabinets and found bandages, tape, and items she would need for stitching. Once she had everything signed out according to protocol, she stuffed the items into the bag she'd packed in his room and set it aside.

"What are you doing?"

Ruthie spun to find her "dead" patient sitting up and pressing a hand to his wound under the sling. His pale features belied his "I'm fine" attitude. "Gathering a few more supplies you're going to need. You better lie down and pull that sheet back up before someone walks in here and realizes you're not dead."

"What's the plan?"

"To get you out of here. Then figure out how to keep you alive long enough for you to heal."

"Good plan."

"Thanks."

"But I'll have to take it from here. If you get involved further, you could get hurt," he warned.

"Well, if you don't let me get involved, you could die."

He raised a brow. "A slight exaggeration."

"Maybe. In the medical sense. But I think you need someone looking out for you. Someone who has your back."

His jaw tightened. "I've gotten pretty good at watching my own back."

"Right. That's why you have a bullet hole in you. The truth is, you won't get far on your own. If they're willing to go this far to kill you, they probably have people at every exit watching for you."

He stilled. "You think like a cop."

"It's second nature."

"Why's that?"

"It's not important." She walked to another cabinet and pulled an item off the top shelf. "Right now, our priority is getting you somewhere safe."

"What did you have in mind?"

"Can you stand up?"

"Of course."

He managed, but even she could tell the effort it cost him and moved fast, laying the bag on the gurney. She unzipped it.

"A body bag," he said.

"Yes. Now get in."

|||||||||

Isaac swallowed. He wasn't superstitious or even terribly claustrophobic, but the thought of being zipped up in that black bag turned his stomach. He'd seen too many bodies carted off in those things. Instead of airing his fears, he settled himself on top of it, and she wrapped it around him.

The rasp of the zipper sent chills along his nerve endings. She stopped when she got mid-chest. "I won't zip it all the way if you prefer. I can leave you a finger hole at the top. You'll be able to get out if you need to."

"Thanks." He didn't recognize the huskiness in his voice. Fatigue and nausea had taken over, and he wondered if he might pass out. At least if he was unconscious, he wouldn't be worried about being zipped up like a dead man. The fact that she'd picked up on his internal angst surprised him. He thought he

288

was better at hiding his emotions. Then again, he'd been shot, had surgery, had almost been killed in his room, and was running from those who wanted him dead. A little noticeable angst was probably normal.

The zipper continued its journey up over his face and then stopped at the top of his head. True to her word, a sliver of light filtered through the small hole she left. Knowing he could get out without a massive struggle allowed him to breathe a little easier.

"All right, here we go," she said. "Should be a piece of cake from this point on."

The gurney rolled. The whoosh of the doors and the rise in temperature told him he was now outside the hospital.

"Hey, doc, hold up a second."

The gurney stopped. His heart rate kicked it up a notch at the voice. Cole Guthrie, Isaac's partner—the man who'd made his life miserable for the past three months. Cole had made it clear he thought Isaac was betraying the badge and the men and women behind it by pushing to find a fellow cop guilty of something he couldn't prove. The conversation hadn't gone well.

"*Let it go, Isaac,*" Cole had said. "*He put the money back.*"

"*He did. This time. But I feel certain that wasn't the first time he's taken some, and if I don't do something about it, it won't be the last.*"

"What are you two doing back here?" Ruthie asked, jolting Isaac back to the present. "This is a restricted area."

"Well, we're cops. We're pretty free to come and go where we please. I'm Detective Cole Guthrie and this is Detective Paul Sullivan."

"I see. Nice to meet you guys, but I'm sort of in the middle of something here. What can I do for you? And while you're talking, could you open the back of that ambulance?"

Isaac heard the sound of footsteps, then the door opening.

"Kind of odd for a doctor to be moving a body all by herself, isn't it?"

Ruthie went still. He couldn't see her, but he felt her. Heard the hitch in her breath. "Odd? No, not so odd when the person was someone I cared very much about. So much so that I volunteered to oversee the transfer personally. Why is everyone so surprised that I'm willing to help out?" She sounded truly baffled, and Isaac began to think she might just pull this off.

But he'd give anything to have his fingers curled around a weapon right now.

"Where's the driver?" Paul Sullivan asked. Isaac liked him about as much as he did Cole.

A huff left the doc's lips and Isaac almost smiled. "Gentlemen, what's this all about?" she asked. "I've got things to do after I get this man to the crematorium. If you'd like to give me an escort, I'll take it. And the driver is in the cafeteria, grabbing a snack. He should be back shortly. But while you're here, you want to help me get him inside?"

"Ah . . . yeah. Sure."

And then he was moving again.

Finally, Ruthie seemed satisfied that he was settled. "Thank you."

"No problem," Guthrie said. A pause as they all left the back of the ambulance. "Are you the one who did surgery on Detective Martinez?"

"Yes. He should be in recovery, if you're looking for him."

"We are," Cole said. "And he's not in recovery."

"Then I guess they moved him after he was attacked."

"You know about that, huh?"

Ruthie gave a light snort. "You bet I do. I was in the room when it happened. But don't worry, he was okay by the time I left."

FOUR

RUTHIE STIFLED HER FRUSTRATION and did her best to keep her nerves under control. Would these guys never leave? Isaac didn't want his partner to know he was okay. The fact that someone tried to kill him in the room had convinced her he might have good reason to want to hide out, and she was going to help him. Now she just hoped she didn't do something stupid and mess it up.

Her heart pounded so hard she thought for sure they'd notice. *Stay calm, Ruthie. Act normal. You've got this.*

The officer to her right, Detective Guthrie, had sharp blue eyes that seemed to cut their way into her very soul, chipping away at her half-truths to expose the lies dripping from her lips.

But instead of calling her on them, he shot one last look at the black bag that held his partner and shook his head. "All right. Come on, Paul. Let's head back to recovery." He dipped his head at Ruthie. "Thanks for your help, doctor."

"Any time."

Ruthie's shoulders wilted for a split second before she grabbed her car keys from her pocket. The driver, Ben Carlisle, really had gone to the cafeteria to grab some coffee and a snack. But he'd be back before too long. "Oh boy," she said, "that was nerve-wracking, but they're gone. Stay put until I get my car and pull it around, okay?"

"All of this is being caught on camera, you know. They'll figure it out."

Having a voice come from the body bag was incredibly creepy. "I know. It's okay. By the time they watch the security footage, we'll be long gone."

"You could get in a lot of trouble for helping me. I'll take it from here."

"I'm not worried about trouble. Stay still until I come back."

"And if the driver of this ambulance gets back before you do?"

She sighed. "Let's not worry about that until it happens. Seriously, stop talking. I'll be right back." Without waiting for his response, she took off for the doctor's parking lot. It wasn't far, and if Ben stayed true to his routine, she had a good ten minutes left to get her car, get Isaac, and leave.

She clicked the fob to unlock her gray Honda Pilot and climbed into the driver's seat. Where was she going to take him once she got him in the car? Backing out of the space, she pulled around to the ambulance and found things just as she'd left them. She opened the door and gasped. Isaac had freed himself from the body bag and was sitting on the gurney, pale and shaking. "Come on, you," she said. "Can you walk?"

"I hate to say it, but . . . maybe."

"Only one way to find out." She looked back over her shoulder. "We're running out of time."

"I'm coming." He made his way to the edge of the gurney, then lowered himself to the floor. She grabbed his good arm and helped him into the passenger's seat of her car. "The body bag," he gasped. "Don't leave it in there."

She snagged it and threw it in the back of the Pilot. "Ready?"

"Yeah."

"Hey, Ruthie, what are you doing back here?"

She gave a low groan, and Isaac winced as he turned his head to look out the window.

"Nothing, Ben," she said as she turned, trying to block his view of Isaac. "Was just on my way home and had to come back and get something."

"Thought you were going on vacation."

"Wow. It's the topic of conversation around the hospital, huh?"

"Don't think you've taken a vacation since I've been doing runs." His brows rose. "And that's been two years. So, yeah, your vacation is ranking pretty high up there in the gossip mill."

"Well, I'm off to start enjoying it. Have a good night, Ben."

"You too, doc."

Ruthie pulled away, and Isaac let out a low huff of relief. "So," he said, "can you head west on 26?"

She shot him a tight smile. "Was planning on it."

||||||||||

Ruthie drove with an expert hand that allowed Isaac to relax a fraction. "Do you know everyone in the hospital? Like, well enough to have a decent conversation with them?" he asked. "I didn't think we'd ever get out of there."

"Pretty much."

His shoulder throbbed with an intensity that set his teeth on edge, but taking something for it would have to wait until he was sure they were safe.

"Lean the seat back," she said. "You'll be more comfortable taking some of the pressure off that wound."

He did so. And she was right. The throbbing eased slightly and his eyes wanted to close. He forced them to stay open. He couldn't sleep yet, not until they were away from the hospital and out of danger. At least for the moment. "You know where we're going, right?"

"The mountains of North Carolina." She pulled a brochure from the dash and passed it to him.

"Nice."

"Yes. It's lovely. My brother Derek talked me into booking it." A pause. "So . . ."

"So?"

"Why was that guy trying to kill you, and why didn't you want your partner to know where you were? Can you fill me in while we ride?"

How much should he tell her? He didn't even know her, much less feel like baring his soul. "I'm not exactly the most popular guy in the house right now."

"Not if you squealed on a cop."

"I didn't squeal. I reported a fellow officer trying to steal cash from the evidence room. He says I misunderstood, so now I'm *persona non grata*—at least until I prove otherwise."

"Ah. Now the pharmacy analogy makes sense." She paused. "You're the guy."

"The guy?"

"I've heard about you. And not everyone hates you. Some of us actually think you did the right thing. If it happened the way you said it did."

"It did. There was no misunderstanding. And who is *us*? Better yet, who are *you*?"

"Ruthie St. John."

"Yeah. My doct—" Oh. Wait a minute. "Not St. John, as in—"

"'Fraid so. My mother is Tabitha St. John, Chief of Police."

Isaac wished the seat would open up and swallow him. "Oh man. That is so messed up." He laughed, ignoring the pain it caused. "Of all the surgeons in the hospital, I get you."

"Hey, I'm a good surgeon."

"It's not that. It's just that your whole family are cops. There's no way you can understand what I'm doing."

She blew a raspberry. "That's about the dumbest thing I've ever heard. And I'm sorry you see it that way. The good news is, no one's expecting me back to the hospital for a while, and my nosy family will probably leave me alone—at least until one of them watches the security footage. We have some time to figure out what to do with you."

"What do you mean what to do with me? I'm going to find the guy I'm looking for, then convince him to do the right thing and hand over proof that cash and drugs have been disappearing from the evidence room for a while now."

"What kind of proof?"

"Doctored evidence logs and original security footage that's been altered to look like no one was in the evidence room when the stuff disappeared. Whoever is doing this is going straight to the cash and the drugs. They don't bother with the weapons." He shook his head. "Someone has to stop it. Because if I don't, the cost of their betrayal is going to be much higher than just some missing money. While that's wrong and a crime in itself, there's no telling where those drugs will end up. Maybe the schools. And then we'll have dead kids turning up left and right. That's not going to happen while there's breath left in my body. And it starts with stopping whoever's stealing from the evidence room."

"Can you narrow it down to a shift? A certain person working? A certain time of day?"

"No. If I could do that, I could find the person responsible. These are guys who know how the system works, and they've found a way to circumvent it. Everything looks legit. Nothing looks like it's missing. But the evidence tech who was helping them pull this off is now missing."

"How did you figure it out? How do you know for sure what's happening?"

"I had entered some evidence. Then, a couple of hours later, one of the guys who'd picked up the stash and delivered it to the evidence room said he'd found another bag that had fallen out on the ride to the station. I was heading inside and volunteered to take it in for him."

"Nice."

"I can be." He shot her a faint smile. "Anyway, I went back to the room and told the guy what happened and signed that bag in to be added to the stash. There was a new evidence tech on duty; Howard had just switched out with this guy. When he took me back to the locker and opened it, at least half of what I'd brought in was missing. I asked him where the rest was and he said that was it. I asked to see the logs and he showed me. It matched up with exactly what was in the locker. I didn't say anything else—simply put the rest of the drugs in the locker and shut it. But it didn't sit right. I knew what I knew. So I investigated Howard's background, and he came back squeaky clean. Still, like I said, I knew what I'd brought in. I wondered if other stuff was going missing, so I started checking after that. One of those times, I caught Officer Lansing stuffing some cash in his shirt."

"His shirt? That doesn't sound right."

"Didn't look right, either. I confronted him and he said it was all a misunderstanding, that he was going to sign it out for a sting operation. Usually, I wouldn't have thought anything about it, but after the missing drugs, I checked the records and no sting operation was in the works."

"And you reported it."

"I did. And Officer Lansing got called on the carpet. He denied everything, of course, and started turning others against me, blowing the whole thing out of proportion." He sighed and shook his head. "I almost let it go. But the missing drugs bothered me. I couldn't let that slide. I kept up my own investigation, and I guess word got around. And then Howard went missing—he's the evidence tech I'm looking for."

"How do you know he's still alive?"

"Because he has to be."

She raised a brow, then sighed. "Okay. I see what you're saying. And I understand you've got to find this guy. But for now, why don't you rest? You're awfully pale."

He snapped his lips shut and wished he could turn off his mind as easily as his words. He wanted to protest, insist that he could take it from here, but the fatigue and the pain pulling at him said he wasn't going anywhere. So he took her advice and closed his eyes.

The chief of police's daughter. Great. He couldn't remember how many siblings she had, but he was quite certain she was the only one who hadn't gone into some type of law enforcement. He forced his eyes open. "So, what are you? The black sheep in the family?"

"Yep." She huffed a laugh. "That's me. I rebelled."

"But you think like a cop."

She grimaced. "The fallout of growing up in my family, I'm afraid. But medicine has always fascinated me."

She started to tell him about going to med school, and as much as he wanted to hear it, he knew he was going to fade. With his head propped against the headrest, he slipped into the beckoning darkness.

FIVE

RUTHIE STOPPED at the little gas station on the side of the road. She was the only vehicle in the area and quickly filled up while her patient slept on. Deeply. Silently. She checked her phone, then wondered if she should get rid of it since whoever was after him would be sure to check the security footage and figure out he was with her. But before she did that, she needed to make a call.

Slipping to the back of the store, but next to a window so she could see the car, she dialed her mother's private number.

"Hello?"

"Hi, Mom."

"Ruthie, everything okay?"

"Actually, no." She proceeded to tell her mother everything that had happened at the hospital, including hijacking her patient to the mountains with her. "But I think they'll come after him."

"Mary Beth mentioned something about an incident at the hospital. She didn't tell me you were involved."

Mary Beth Dean, her mother's assistant.

"She may not have known. But, Mom, there will be hospital

video footage of Isaac leaving with me. Whoever's looking for him will figure it out pretty fast if they haven't already."

"Which puts you in danger, as well. You need to bring him back and let us put him in protective custody."

"If I can talk him into it. He was pretty adamant about getting away to find some guy who has proof of who's behind the evidence-room thefts. And truthfully, he needs time to heal."

"Is there anything else you can tell me?" her mother asked.

Ruthie sighed. "I don't think so, but I don't think I've got the whole picture. He's the one who caught an officer stealing cash from the evidence room."

"I know that situation well. Heath Lansing was the officer. He denies any wrongdoing, and there's no evidence to prove he did what he's being accused of." She paused. "And you say someone tried to kill Martinez in the hospital?"

"Someone definitely did." She'd left out the part where the guy had gotten his hands around her throat. Moms didn't need to know everything. Not even chief-of-police moms. She raised a hand to touch the bruises she knew were there. It was a good thing the air was turning chilly. She was going to need turtlenecks for a while.

"I'm going to send Derek to stay with you. He can help keep an eye on things."

"Um . . . no. Not Derek."

Silence. "Okay. You want to tell me why?"

"He's got plans."

"Involving . . ."

"Elaine."

"I see."

She probably did. "What about Brady?"

"Yes, I'll send him. Give me the address and give me a second to get ahold of him."

Ruthie did.

"Okay, I've got Brady on the line," her mother said a few moments later. "Hold on." A click sounded. "Brady, are you with us?"

"I'm here, Mom. What's going on?"

"You've got a new assignment effective immediately."

"Fill me in."

Once it was all arranged, Ruthie hung up and rubbed her eyes. As a surgeon, she was used to going without sleep, but fatigue dragged at her. They had about thirty more miles before they'd be at the cabin. She knew Isaac wanted to head straight to his guy's place, but he could barely function, much less chase someone down.

She turned her phone off and dropped it into the nearest trash bin. Rats. She really liked that phone. Ah well, it was worth losing in order to help someone stay alive.

Back in the driver's seat, she glanced at Isaac. Still asleep. She placed her fingers on his wrist to take his pulse, and his right hand shot out to encircle her wrist. She gasped. Okay, not asleep. "Don't break it, please. I need it."

He released her as quickly as he'd grabbed her. "Sorry," he said. "I'm really sorry. It's reflex these days. I've been sleeping with one eye open."

"I understand. I ditched my phone. We probably need to toss yours, too."

"I have a phone, but it's not traceable. One of the first things I replaced when things started getting hairy."

"When was that?"

"When Lansing spread the word I'd reported him, that I was jealous of his upcoming promotion, and that I needed to remove myself from the force."

"Right. Sounds like good reasons to be on the alert. Okay, so we've got about thirty more minutes. You need a pit stop?"

"No. I think I'm okay."

"What about pain meds?"

"No thanks."

"Ibuprofen?"

He quirked a brow at her. "You think that would make a difference?"

"Maybe a slight one." That was a big maybe.

"I'll try it."

Once she got him dosed and as comfortable as he was going to be for the remainder of the drive, she put the SUV in gear and pulled back onto the two-lane road that would take them up the mountain.

IIIIIIIII

Isaac wanted to kick himself for overreacting to her touch. The truth was, just like he'd told her, he'd been sleeping with one eye open since Lansing had started running his mouth. And two nights ago, he'd awakened to three guys in his bedroom wearing masks and carrying baseball bats.

Only the fact that he'd had his weapon on the floor next to his bed had saved him from a beating. Or maybe even death, now that he thought about it. He'd rolled out of bed, grabbed the gun, and aimed it. *"You've got five seconds to get out before I start shooting. You're in my home, in masks, with bats. Who do you think is going to be in trouble for this one?"*

They'd run. And he'd installed a home security system.

Isaac had also continued to do his job, taking the heat from the other officers and letting it roll off his back. He'd done the right thing in turning Lansing in. He knew it and they did, too, but getting back in their good graces would be next to impossible until he had irrefutable evidence.

And now someone was mad enough to try to kill him in the hospital?

Truly, wanting him dead really didn't make sense. Sure, he

expected the shunning and the refusal to partner with him, but to flat-out want him dead? It didn't jive.

And frankly, he just wanted to find a bed and sleep rather than worry about it.

"Brady's coming to help," his pretty doctor said.

Isaac whipped his head to look at her. Dizziness hit him. Whoa. Moving fast wasn't good. He swallowed against the surge of nausea. "Where?"

"At the cabin. We need help. You need help."

"Wait a minute. Cabin? No, I need to get to Sally Peterson's house."

"I can get us there, but what are you going to do? Catch Howard with your web slinger? Come on. You're not a super-hero. You can barely stand."

She was right, of course. He just had to pray his call from the hospital had been warning enough for Sally to get away from her brother and into hiding.

Her words penetrated. "Brady St. John? Your brother? A cop who probably hates my guts like all the rest of them?"

"Not a chance. I have a feeling you two are actually a lot alike."

"I'll reserve judgment on whether or not to take that as a compliment."

She shot him the first real smile he'd seen since he'd met her. "It's a compliment. He's big on doing the right thing no matter the cost."

That simple statement brought an unusual lump to his throat. He decided it was better than the nausea. "You believe me?"

"The guy who tried to kill you in your hospital room was a big influencer in swaying me to your side." She paused. "I believe you."

"Thanks." His husky voice earned him a quick glance and

a short nod. "I need to call and have someone go out to Sally's house and make sure she's okay." With effort, he made the call and received assurances someone would go check on her and call him back. Silence settled in the SUV and Isaac closed his eyes, desperately needing healing sleep.

The next thing he knew, they were stopped and Ruthie was rubbing his bicep. "Isaac? Can you wake up?"

"Working on it," he grunted.

"Good. Let's get inside and you can have the nearest bedroom."

Sounded good to him. He opened the door, then immediately slammed it shut. "Turn the overhead light off, please."

"Of course."

He liked she didn't have to ask him why.

Once he was sure he could open the door without making himself a target, he shoved it open. Cold air blasted him, dispelling the lingering drowsiness and bringing him to full alertness.

"Go easy," she said. "Wait for me to help you."

"You do realize that if I fall, you'd better just let me hit the ground rather than try to catch me."

She snorted. "I'm stronger than I look."

He took a look around while she made her way over to him. "Nice place."

"I thought so."

"Lots of places to hide, though. Good places for a sniper."

"Yep. You are *definitely* a cop." She paused. "But the good thing is, it's dark right now. A sniper's going to have to wait until it gets a little lighter to get a good shot, right?"

"Maybe. Unless he's got special equipment."

"I give up. Can you get my gun out of the glove compartment?"

He stilled. "You have a weapon?"

"Yep. And it's legal."

"God bless you," he breathed and opened the glove compartment. He checked the weapon and found it perfect in every way.

"Let's go." She held out a hand, and he grabbed it to let her help pull him to his feet. Weakness invaded him, and he wrapped his good arm around her shoulders while she gripped his waist. "You realize this is doing severe damage to my ego, right?"

"You were shot. You get a pass this time. When we get inside, I want to check the stitches."

All he could do was offer a low grunt.

Once inside the cabin, he absently took in the simple yet lovely decor while he let her lead him to the ground-floor bedroom.

Sinking into the mattress, he closed his eyes.

||||||||||

That was the first time Ruthie had ever seen anyone literally asleep before his head hit the pillow. She arranged the covers over him and went to get the stuff from her car. Back in the cabin, she grabbed her stethoscope and headed into the bedroom to find her patient still sound asleep.

Maybe. Remembering his lightning-quick reflexes, she gave him a light poke in the arm, then stepped back.

He didn't move.

She slipped the ends of the stethoscope into her ears and placed the disc over his heart. Then his lungs. She wished she could flip him over and listen to his lungs from the back, but she would have to be satisfied that all seemed well in spite of their crazy flight from the hospital. Since he had on a V-neck scrubs top, she was able to get a clear look at the bandage. No blood had seeped through yet, so maybe they were all right.

She set up the nightstand with the rest of the supplies so she could change his bandage when he woke. For now, he just needed to sleep.

Back in the den, she grabbed her bag, hauled it to the other bedroom, and set it on the bed. Since she'd planned to be away for a week, she'd brought everything and more.

A low buzzing caught her attention and she hurried into Isaac's room to grab his phone from the end table. A swipe across the screen connected her. "Hello?" She slipped out of the room.

"This is Officer Clark. I'm looking for Isaac Martinez."

"He's unavailable at the moment. Could I take a message?"

"Let him know that I went to see Mrs. Peterson. She answered the door with a crying baby on her hip and said everything was fine at her house. I thought she looked a little harried and asked to come inside, but she said I'd woken the baby and she needed to get the little guy back to sleep. I insisted and she agreed to let me in. I walked around the home and all looked quiet to me."

"All right, I'll pass the word on to Isaac." She paused. "Could you just sit outside for a little while and make sure? We're worried about her."

"I can do that. At least until I get another call."

"Thank you."

She hung up and then remembered Derek and Elaine. With a sigh, she grabbed the landline phone and dialed his number.

His sleepy voice answered on the second ring. "What?"

"You can't bring Elaine here to ask her to marry you."

Silence. The rustle of bedsheets. "Ruthie?"

"Sorry to be the bearer of bad news, but you can't come up here tomorrow. I've got a patient here recuperating, and I can't move him for the next few days."

"Have you been drinking?"

"Derek!"

"But, Ruthie, I had it all planned."

She ignored the whine in his voice and explained the situation, as well as the fact that Brady was on the way.

A heavy sigh greeted her. "You need me to come help?"

A smile curved her lips. She knew she could count on him, no matter what. "Nope."

"Because I will, you know."

"I know, but I don't think that's necessary." She paused. "However, there might be one thing you can do."

"Sure. What's that?"

"I want to know what happened with the domestic disturbance where Isaac ended up getting shot. I want to know what the story is there and if there was more to it than meets the eye."

"What did he tell you about it?"

"Nothing yet. But someone tried to kill him in the hospital. If they'd succeeded, I have a suspicion that even with an autopsy it might have looked like a death caused by the gunshot wound. Even though it wasn't the most serious one I've ever seen, it still did damage, and it wouldn't be unheard of for him to die from it." He still wasn't completely out of the woods. There was still the risk of infection, a missed bone fragment, a blown stitch . . .

The list could go on. She could only pray none of those things happened and he would heal just fine. "I haven't heard what was in the syringe, but that might be a good place to start."

"I'll look into it. I know Isaac, and he's a good man."

"Even though everyone seems to think he's lying?"

Derek fell silent. "I'll be honest. I wasn't sure what to believe at first, but why would he lie about it? He had no beef with Lansing. As far as anyone else knew, they were friends. No, if he really saw what he said he saw, then he had no choice."

"I knew you'd see it that way. His partner, Cole Guthrie, was at the hospital along with another man by the name of Paul Sullivan. Do you know them?"

"Yes. Guthrie is a piece of work. Sullivan's not much better. But I'll talk to them."

"Isaac didn't want them to find him. I think he suspects they're involved in whatever—and whoever—he's trying to bring down. Don't trust them."

"I understand. I'll be in touch."

"Thanks. Oh, and I had to ditch my phone, so call this number or Brady if you get something."

"Will do."

She hung up with only a twinge of guilt at ruining her brother's engagement plans, but it couldn't be helped. Isaac needed a safe place to recover and right now, this was it.

Back in the kitchen, she opened the refrigerator and a sigh of relief slipped out. She'd paid the extra money to have it stocked. *Thank you, Lord.* Her patient needed protein and veggies. But nothing that would upset his stomach. Soup. Crackers. Tea or ginger ale.

She also pulled out grilled chicken, broccoli and carrots, and a baked potato with butter, sour cream, and bacon bits. He might not eat much depending on how he felt, but at least it would be there. She'd recommend the soup and crackers first, then he could move on to the other stuff, as long as his stomach behaved. And they could do leftovers, because while she didn't mind working in the kitchen, she had no plans to do it day in and day out.

While he slept, she cooked. And while she cooked, her mind spun, trying to process everything that had happened in the last few hours.

Just as she finished with the chicken, the phone rang. She grabbed the handset mid-ring and tucked it under her chin. "Hello."

"It's Derek. I found out what happened on that DD."

"Tell me."

"The call came in around six o'clock last night. A woman screamed that she needed help, that her husband was threatening to kill her and her kids. She rattled off the address and the phone went dead."

"Was anyone else hurt?"

"Yeah. The wife. She grabbed a gun, shot her husband, and kept firing. One of the bullets got Isaac before she passed out from loss of blood. The wife was also shot and brought in around the same time as your guy."

The woman on the gurney, no doubt, the one Hugh had been working on. "Did the husband make it?"

"No, but she did."

"Okay, thanks, Derek."

"Welcome." He paused. "I saw the hospital security footage, Ruthie."

"Thought Mom was going to try and pull it."

"She wasn't fast enough. Someone got to it before Mom or me, because Miranda said something about it being a popular piece of video." Miranda with hospital security.

"Great."

"It's obvious you're the one who helped Martinez leave the hospital."

"I figured it would be."

"Apparently, as soon as you took off, two officers requested to see all footage of anyone leaving the hospital."

Isaac's partner and the other man with him flashed into her mind. "I'm sure I can guess who. Cole Guthrie and Paul Sullivan."

"You got it on the first try. I'm still looking for them so I can have a word. I'll get back to you when I know anything else."

"Thanks."

She hung up and turned to find Isaac standing behind her. She gasped and slapped a hand against her racing heart. "Whoa. That's mean sneaking up on a girl like that."

"Sorry." He held his wounded arm by the elbow, even though

it was cradled in the sling. And he sounded anything but sorry. "What was that all about?"

"That was Derek. He was doing some research into your shooting." She passed on what she'd learned.

"I would have told you that."

"You were sleeping. Want a pain pill yet?" The white outline of his lips and the flared nostrils said he needed one.

"No."

"Pretty please with sugar on top?"

His lips relaxed into a small smile for a brief second. "No, but thanks. I need to keep my wits about me."

"I discovered I have some Toradol. It's good for the pain, but it won't knock you out since it's not a narcotic."

He hesitated. Then nodded. "Sure, that would be fine. I think I've taken that before."

"I should have suggested it earlier but forgot I'd thrown it in with the other stuff. I found it a bit ago when I started unloading everything." She found the bottle and dumped one of the pills onto his outstretched hand. "You're very fortunate, you know."

"I know." He swallowed the pill without water.

"Good. You hungry?"

"It smells good in here."

"That's because I'm a good cook."

"I should probably try to eat."

"Probably."

They settled at the table with the food Ruthie had prepared. "Will you tell me your side of the domestic disturbance shooting?"

"The call came in, and my partner and I were two of the responding officers."

"I didn't think detectives took that kind of call."

"Not normally, but we were one block over. We couldn't just sit there."

"Of course."

"So, we arrived, went in, and the wife grabbed a gun. She started firing at her husband and didn't have the best aim."

"But she managed to hit you."

"That she did."

"Are you sure it was her bullet?"

He stilled. Finished chewing a bit of the chicken and swallowed. "Why do you ask that?"

She leaned forward. "It's obvious someone wants you dead. Could the domestic disturbance have been a setup?"

For a moment he didn't move. Then he gave a short nod. "I've thought of that."

"I see."

"Ballistics will tell one way or the other where the bullet came from and which gun it came from. Until then, I'm laying low . . ."

"Wise decision."

". . . while I track down Howard."

She rolled her eyes.

He finished off the soup and crackers and the rest of his piece of chicken, then leaned back. "I'd better stop there."

"I'm glad you felt well enough to eat that much, but it's back to bed for you."

"I just got up."

"You're telling me you're not ready for more sleep now that you've eaten and the pain is under control?"

He hesitated, then sighed. "Fine, but as soon as I wake up, we've got to get going. I need to check on Sally, find out if she's seen Howard."

"Sounds like she's okay at the moment." She told him about the phone call from Officer Clark.

"Good."

Isaac made it to the couch and stretched out.

By the time she got the blanket over him, he was asleep again.

SIX

ISAAC BLINKED AND SAT UP. The blanket pooled at his waist, and he realized he was still on the couch and the sun was coming through the east window and spilling across his face.

The room was empty, but his nose detected coffee. He swung his feet over the side and pushed himself into a sitting position. A glass of water and two pills sat on a napkin at the edge of the coffee table.

Take the Toradol when your shoulder wakes you up. The other pill is your antibiotic.

He downed the pills. Taking inventory, he determined that while his shoulder was on fire once more, he could stand without weaving.

In the kitchen, he found two mugs and poured the coffee that had just finished brewing. With one hand, he hooked the handles and carried them to the open back door.

Ruthie sat on the screened-in porch, book in hand, feet propped on the little plastic table in front of her.

Shouldering the door open, he stepped outside.

She looked up and smiled. "You look like you're feeling a bit better."

"A bit."

She took the coffee from him. "How'd you know I like it black?"

"There's no cream or sugar set out."

"Hm. Observant."

"Occasionally."

"The shoulder?"

"Hurts."

"The pills?"

"Taken."

She laughed. "I like you, Isaac Martinez." Then she sobered. "What are we going to do about the men trying to kill you? I think it's only a matter of time before they track us here."

"I know. Which is why I've got to leave."

A frown dipped her brows. "You're not strong enough to leave."

"I don't have a choice. I'm a dead man if I stay. And not only that, I'm endangering you, as well."

"Brady's here. He got here last night after you passed out."

"Fell asleep." Her "passed out" description was probably more apt. The fact that he hadn't heard a thing scared him.

A lot.

She gave a longsuffering sigh. "Whatever."

"Where is he now?" he asked.

"Checking the perimeter." She nodded to the radio next to her. "He said he'd let me know if he found anything." She lowered her bare feet to the porch floor. "For now, there's nothing to be alarmed about."

"I'm alarmed you feel like you can sit out here in the open. Come inside, please."

"It's not exactly open."

"It's a screened-in porch. Not exactly bulletproof."

She frowned, but she didn't argue further and let him lead the way.

He took a seat on the couch, letting out a low grunt when

he jarred his shoulder. "Did Brady have anything to say when he got here last night?"

"No, not much, other than that the syringe our attacker at the hospital had was filled with potassium chloride, and I could have picked a worse place to harbor a fugitive."

"Hey, now. I'm not a fugitive. At least not in the usual sense of the word. It's only the bad guys who're after me, not the law."

"They're one and the same this time, aren't they?"

He stilled. "I don't want to believe it, but yeah, I think so."

"They don't like that you ratted one out without the proof to back it up. That cop code thing is strong."

He blew out a breath and raked a hand through his hair. She wasn't telling him anything he didn't already know. "Yes. It is." He paused. "Even my family has turned against me."

"I noticed your sister was rather . . . um . . ."

"Unconcerned?"

"No, actually, she was very concerned. She seemed like she wanted to stay but couldn't for some reason. She was torn."

He could see that. "Her husband's a cop. He probably forbade her from having anything to do with me."

"And yet she came to the hospital to check on you."

"True. We were close, once upon a time." He took a drink of his coffee. "Potassium chloride, huh?"

"Yes."

"That's bad."

"Very. If he'd managed to get that in you, you wouldn't be here."

He nodded.

"You must have some suspicions about your partner," she said.

"Cole."

"And his buddy, Paul? I didn't care much for either of them, even though they were friendly . . . in an intimidating sort of way."

"They didn't seem to bother you any."

She laughed. "I have three brothers. I've learned to hide my pounding heart and stand up to bullies."

"Your brothers bullied you?"

"I would have said so at the time, but looking back, they were just big, annoying teases."

His spine stiffened as a footstep creaked the wooden boards on the porch, and his fingers curled around the weapon he never left far from his reach.

She peered through a crack in the blinds. "It's just Brady. One of my bullies . . . er . . . brothers."

If he wasn't so tense, he'd have laughed.

After a light rap on the door, her brother stepped inside. His eyes went straight to Isaac. "Glad to see you awake."

"Thanks."

He switched his attention to Ruthie. "Heard you say something about bullies."

"Just that you have to stand up to them—and big brothers, too. Did you see anything out there?"

He frowned. "I'm not sure. Could be residents of the other cabins around here, or it could be someone trying to figure out which cabin to target."

Isaac stood with a grunt. "That's my cue to go. I've got to find Sally Peterson. She can help me find Howard, who has the evidence I need to prove my story and clear my name. He was going to give it to me, then decided he'd rather make money off it, the jerk. Fortunately, Sally doesn't live too far from here."

"You can't go tracking someone down with your shoulder like that," Brady said.

"I don't have much choice. I'm worried about her."

The window behind them exploded, sending Brady and Isaac diving for Ruthie.

SEVEN

RUTHIE LANDED ON THE FLOOR, the back of her head smacking the hardwood with a painful thud. Stars danced in front of her eyes, and for a moment she couldn't move.

The need for oxygen outweighed the fact that someone was shooting at them. She shoved. "Get off. I can't breathe."

Isaac had been faster than Brady. She must have caught him in his wounded shoulder because he gave a gasp of pain before rolling onto his good arm. He scurried to the shattered window, her weapon gripped in his right hand.

Brady was right behind him. "Stay down, Ruthie."

The order was unnecessary. She had no intention of offering her head as a target.

Several more bullets blistered the side of the cabin.

Brady returned fire, then ducked back against the wall.

Another crack sounded, but this time no bullets entered the room.

Silence.

The radio crackled. "Clear! Shooter's down!"

Ruthie raised her head. "Derek?" Her gaze swiveled to Brady. "You called in reinforcements?"

"I did. Aren't you glad?"

"Thrilled." She sounded nonchalant, but she had to curl her fingers into fists to hide the trembling.

"I need to get out of here," Isaac said. "Obviously they know where I am now."

Brady pulled a bag from beside the sofa. "I'll take you wherever you need to go. Ruthie, you go home and stay out of this."

She laughed. "You're out of your mind, right?"

Brady blinked at her. "How so?"

"That's how so." She pointed at Isaac, who'd slumped into the recliner, looking pale and shaky once more. "He's my patient and in no shape to go chasing after anyone. Someone has to make sure he doesn't tear his stitches open. He's only"—she glanced at the clock on the mantel—"twenty-six hours post surgery. He should be resting in a bed, not chasing killers."

Sirens sounded in the distance. "Guess Derek called in the cavalry," Brady said. "He'll take care of things here. Let's go."

"You fired your weapon," Ruthie said. "Don't you have to stay here and make a statement?" She shook her head. "Why am I telling you this? You're the cop, and you're not going anywhere."

"Then Derek."

"You mean Derek who shot the guy and will have to make a statement, too? Come on, Brady. You're both stuck here."

"You stay here, too, Ruthie," Isaac said.

"Not happening." To her brother, she said, "We'll be fine. We'll stay in touch and make sure you know what's going on."

Brady sighed and frowned. "I can tell I'm not going to change your mind."

"No, you're not."

"Fine. You guys are going to have to take off, and I'll catch up to you in a little bit. Where exactly are you going?"

"To find Sally Peterson," Isaac said. He rose with a grunt. "Thanks, Brady. I owe you."

"Yeah, remember that, and don't let my sister get killed because she's helping you."

"Brady!" Ruthie slugged him in the bicep. He didn't even blink.

"He's right," Isaac said. "I can handle this on my own if you'll let me have the keys to your car."

"Then we'll be pulling you out of a ditch because you fell asleep at the wheel. Or some family will be planning their loved ones' funerals because you lost consciousness for a brief moment."

He flinched.

"I'm going," she said. "I like my car too much to let all that happen."

Brady let out a low whistle. Isaac laughed before he winced and held a hand to his shoulder.

Ruthie bit her lip and shook her head. "Let me grab my bag and the keys. Brady, pack those leftovers for us, will you? I brought a cooler. It's on top of the refrigerator."

"Ruthie—"

"Do it!" He raised a brow, and she drew in a breath. He wasn't one of her interns to boss around. "Please. I'm going to Sally's with Isaac, and I would like to eat when I get there. But first, I'm going to get the medical supplies in the bedroom." She pointed down the hallway.

"Fine."

Within minutes, they were in her car and headed down the road in the opposite direction of the sirens. "I'm sorry about this," Isaac said.

"Don't worry about it. And I was just kidding about liking my car that much. Truth is, I like you and don't want to see you get hurt." She glanced at his shoulder. "Well, hurt any more than you already are."

"Thanks, Ruthie, I appreciate that."

"Welcome. Now, put Sally's address in the GPS and let's get this over with. You need to eat something and sleep while I drive. The cooler's in the back. There's a sandwich on top for you. Bag of chips, too."

"Bossy little thing, aren't you?"

She stiffened, then huffed a low laugh. "Sorry, operating room training, I guess. It's become a bit of a habit."

"They're not bad orders. I think I'll follow them."

"Good."

Once she had directions, it didn't take her long to find the highway and set the cruise control. They'd be there in a little over an hour.

||||||||||

The yard was cute and well kept, even though it was littered with toys. Isaac couldn't remember how many kids Sally had, but if the toys were any indication, she had more than one.

They parked across the street and down two houses in order to be able to observe. "I just want to watch for a bit. See if anything shakes loose."

"You think Howard is here?"

"I don't know. I think it would be stupid of him. He'd be putting them all in danger. Then again, he has evidence implicating these guys in the thefts and he tried to blackmail them. I'm thinking stupid might be his middle name."

"Whoa."

"I know."

"You left that part out."

"Didn't seem important at the time."

"So, he may not be real interested in giving up that evidence."

Isaac shrugged with his good shoulder. "I don't care if he's interested or not. It's the only proof out there about what's happening. These guys stealing from the evidence room are super careful. The only reason Howard got the drop on them is because they trusted the wrong guy—and Howard wasn't interested in justice. He just got greedy and wanted a bigger cut."

"How well do you know Howard, anyway?"

"Well enough. He's a big Civil War buff and so was my grandfather. Howard would talk about the latest book he'd read or about some reenactment thing he was going to be in. He's nice enough, and I enjoy our conversations, but we aren't close friends or anything."

"How is it that they haven't tracked down his sister? You did without any trouble. Seems like they could do the same."

"I don't think so. I think Howard and Sally have been estranged for a while. He said something about that one time during one of our conversations. Something about how she thought his fascination with the Civil War was stupid, and he shouldn't spend so much money on the paraphernalia. When I asked about her, he just shook his head and said they didn't really talk. Then he changed the subject. The only reason I was able to find her is because I was sneaky."

"How so?"

"Since I knew something was happening with the drugs and money in the evidence room, I'd kind of been keeping track of the guys who work in that area. He was one of them. I followed him to a restaurant thinking he might be meeting someone. Instead, he got on the phone, and I heard him mention something about coming into some money and bragging he had a plan. When he mentioned blackmail, I knew I was onto something. So I went over to his place later that night, started asking him questions, asked him to help me figure out what was going on."

"Bet that went over well."

"He kept his cool. I was impressed. Said he didn't know what I was talking about and that he couldn't help me."

"He wanted his money."

"Exactly. He'd left his phone sitting on the kitchen counter, and I snagged it on my way out. He ran the next day, but it was too late. He'd already made his blackmail demands. His place was shot up that night. If he'd been in there, he would have been Swiss cheese. My taking his phone probably saved his life. But it also allowed me access to information that the people he's trying to blackmail don't have—like his sister's info."

"Wasn't there a passcode on the phone?"

"Yeah, but I'd watched him punch it in when we were talking." He shrugged. "Most people aren't too careful about that. And then when he left the phone sitting on the counter, just begging to be swiped . . . well . . ."

"What makes you think this time will be different? If he wasn't willing to help you before, why now?"

"I plan to be a little more convincing." Movement caught his eye. "The garage door's opening."

Within seconds, a Honda minivan backed out. The garage door shut and the van disappeared around the curve.

"Did you see the truck in the garage?" he asked.

"I did."

"That belongs to Howard."

She reached into the back and grabbed the bag Brady had sent with them.

"What are you doing?" he asked.

"I'm the closest thing you've got to backup. You're not going alone."

She pulled a weapon from the bag and smiled. "Good. Brady thought ahead. It's registered to me and I know how to use it. And when not to use it. Don't worry."

"Don't worry?"

She checked it like an expert and shoved it into the waistband at the small of her back, then pulled the hem of her T-shirt over it.

He blinked. "You look way too natural doing that for some-one who's not a cop or a criminal."

"I grew up playing cops and robbers. In my family, I had no choice. We graduated from pop guns to paintball. I had to be good at whatever we were playing, or I would always be the one getting shot. That didn't sit well with me and my competitive spirit. Then we moved on to the shooting range. I can shoot with the best of them, including Mr. Hotshot Sniper Derek St. John. It irks him to no end."

"I can imagine." Isaac's heart wanted to puddle at his feet. He was falling for this incredible woman he was just getting to know, and he had no business doing so when he had no guarantee he'd make it through the day alive.

But once this was over . . .

"Exactly how many guns do you own?"

"Seven."

"Seven. And you're a surgeon."

"I am."

"Okay, then. Well. That makes total sense." He pointed toward her back. "Only pull that as a last resort, okay?"

She nodded.

"Promise me, Ruthie, please. And hang back."

"How far back?"

"As far as you will. I can't have you getting hurt. Please."

"That's the second time you've said please in the last five seconds."

Man, she was stubborn. "I mean it."

"Fine. I'll leave the gun where it is unless one of our lives is in immediate danger. I promise. How's that?"

"It'll have to do." He drew in a deep breath. "All right, let's go knock on the door and see who answers."

||||||||||

While Ruthie was confident in her ability to shoot bull's-eyes on paper targets, taking aim at a human being was another thing altogether. However, she simply couldn't let Isaac face down a potentially dangerous man all by himself. Not that he hadn't done it before, but she hadn't been there during those times. This time, she was.

Isaac walked up the front steps and rang the bell.

And waited.

She stayed at the bottom and watched the windows. Ruthie had been the "bad guy" in enough training exercises with her brothers and sisters that she knew what they looked for when confronting a suspect.

When no one answered after the third knock and repeated punching of the doorbell, Isaac growled.

"Don't think he's here."

"Maybe. Or he's hiding."

"What now?"

"I find a way in."

"Um . . . isn't that kind of like breaking and entering?"

"Kind of like it, yeah."

"So, maybe you shouldn't?"

"Probably not."

But he was going to do it anyway.

"He might be hurt," he said.

She raised a brow at him. "He might be."

"Those guys could have caught up with him and his life could be in danger."

"You're stretching for exigent circumstances, aren't you?"

"I am."

"Still, it could be possible. I mean, we don't know who was in that van. We just assumed it was his sister and her kids."

He jerked and real worry filtered into his gaze. "You're right."

"I am?"

"Yes, actually." He tried the knob. Locked. "Sally? It's Isaac Martinez. You in there?" When he got no response, he touched the etched-glass window pane next to the door, then made a fist.

"Go through the garage window if you're thinking about breaking that," she said. "The door leading into the house is probably unlocked."

He stared at her for a moment. "You really missed your calling."

They made their way around to the side of the house where the garage window was low enough for him to climb into. He reared back to smash it, then stopped and gave it a shove upward. He shook his head when it slid on the tracks high enough for him to fit through. He looked at Ruthie. "I suppose you're going to insist on coming."

"You really have to ask?"

He helped her through the window.

Once inside the home, Isaac let his gaze wander around the kitchen. "Nothing looks out of place in here."

The kitchen opened up into the den, which had toys strewn from one end to the other. A bag of diapers spilled over in the corner next to the television. As though someone had grabbed a handful in a hurry?

With his weapon gripped in his right hand and his left arm hugged up against him in the sling, Isaac made his way down the hall. Ruthie stayed behind him, watching to make sure no one popped out and shot him in the back.

Her palm itched to pull the weapon resting snug against her skin, but she'd promised. And so far, she had no reason to need it. Thank goodness.

They finally stepped into the master bedroom, and Isaac drew up short.

"What is it?" she asked.

"Howard's already had visitors."

Ruthie stepped around him to find a man on the floor next to the bed. The bullet hole in his forehead suggested his visitors hadn't liked him very much. A sheet of paper lay next to him, but she couldn't read the writing from the doorway. Even though she could tell by looking at him that he was dead, she hurried over, knelt, and pressed her fingers against his throat. Like she'd thought. No pulse.

She looked up at Isaac. "Stab wound in his right hand, but I don't see any more. That didn't kill him. Most likely it was the bullet in his head. Now what?"

"I have a bad feeling you were right."

"About what?"

"About who was in that van."

"Why would whoever did this take a woman and her children?"

"For leverage."

"With who?"

He sighed and pressed his thumb and forefinger against his eyes. "Me." He held up the paper that had been on the floor beside the body.

Turn over the evidence or they die.

EIGHT

"YOU?" RUTHIE LOOKED BACK AT THE DEAD MAN and groaned. "He told them *you* had it?"

"I don't know. Most likely thought it would buy him some time, not a bullet."

"But how did they find him before us? They just finished shooting at us at the cabin. How in the world did they get from there to here and . . . wait a minute." She frowned and touched the dead man's cheek. "He's cold to the touch. Lividity has already set in." She lifted the edge of his shirt. "Blood is pooling in large patches beneath him," she muttered.

"Time of death?"

"Wish I could take his liver temp, but I'd say he's been dead at least twelve to fourteen hours. I could be off, but not by much."

"So he was dead before we even left the hospital?"

"Maybe. Or shortly thereafter. How'd they know to come here?"

He pinched the bridge of his nose and closed his eyes. "Me, maybe?" he whispered. "I called Sally from the hospital landline. I had to chance it when I realized how serious these guys were. My phone was with the rest of my stuff, so I had no way of . . ." He shook his head. "I'm an idiot. Of course they'd check outgoing phone calls from my room. I should have used a different phone."

"So, you expected someone to try and kill you in your room?"

"What? Of course not."

"Then I would think it was perfectly legit to think you'd be safe in making the call." She frowned. "What did you tell her?"

"That some bad people were after her brother and she needed to get as far away from him as possible."

"So they sent someone to her place and someone else followed us to our cabin."

"No, I'm guessing once they realized who you were, they had someone watching your brothers and sisters—maybe even your mom. When Brady—and Derek—took off, they probably followed one of them." He shrugged. "I guess it doesn't matter now how they found all of us. We just have to deal with the fallout and save Sally and her kids."

"We need to get a BOLO put out on that minivan," she said. "And an Amber Alert on the kids."

"No. They'll get rid of them if we do that."

"Then what now?"

"They'll contact me. Somehow." His eyes landed on the telephone hanging on the wall. "Because if we're right and they think I have the evidence, they'll have to give me instructions on how to deliver it."

"But you don't have it."

"Nope. Which means I have to find it. And I have a feeling time is short."

The home phone rang as if to mock him.

"Don't answer it," she said.

"It's them."

"And if you answer it, time is going to get even shorter."

"But if I don't answer it, they might hurt one of the hostages."

326

She huffed. "They can't even know we're here. It's probably not even them."

He met her gaze. "It's them. They knew we'd wind up here." He glanced at the window nearest them. "And they're probably watching."

Isaac reached for the phone.

||||||||||

Ruthie waited, her gaze darting from the window to the door.

"Hello." A pause. "Yeah. Now? I don't have it." Another pause. "Well, he lied. . . . Right. Got it. . . . Yeah, yeah, no cops. . . . I want proof of life. What?" His gaze landed on the closet. "Hey! Don't hang . . . ugh." He dropped the phone and darted to the closet. Opened it and dropped to his knees. "Sally!"

Ruthie nudged him aside and pressed her fingers against the woman's neck. "She's alive."

"I can't carry her." His frustration echoed in the small space.

"Move out of the way, please." He did, and Ruthie slid her arms under the woman's armpits and pulled, easily removing her from the closet. "She doesn't weigh enough. Could use another ten pounds."

"Probably lost some due to the stress of having a husband run out on her."

"Stand-up guy, huh?"

"Yep."

Ruthie began her examination and found the reason for the woman's unconscious state. "They knocked her in the head."

"Can you get her to wake up? We've got twelve hours to figure out where Howard hid the proof and turn it over to them . . . or they kill her three children."

Ruthie closed her eyes. "They wouldn't, would they? I mean, it's just a bluff, right?" She grabbed the picture from the end table. "Look at this. The date says it was taken last month. The oldest can't be more than ten or eleven. The youngest is still in diapers. Who can kill babies?"

"People do it every day." He scowled. "We're going to have to tear this place apart."

"Brady's going to be calling soon and asking where we are."

"We'll have to ignore him. The guy on the phone said they're watching and if anyone else shows up, the kids will start losing fingers and toes."

"I'm going to throw up."

"You'll have to get in line."

"Did you recognize his voice?"

"No, he used some kind of voice distortion machine or app." Isaac looked around. "Where would you hide evidence that could save your life if it was hidden well or get you killed if someone found it?"

"I wouldn't hide it here." She grabbed the lamp and flipped it on, then bent back over the woman to examine her pupils. "She's got a concussion."

He sighed. "How long before she wakes up?"

"No clue."

"Does she need a hospital?"

"I wouldn't mind a scan of her skull, but she's breathing fine. Pupils are equal, but larger than normal. I think we just need to watch her real close."

"We'll get that opportunity, because she's coming with us."

The woman groaned.

"That's a good sign, right?" Isaac asked.

"Yes, it is. Sally? Can you hear me?"

She didn't answer, but blinked and groaned again.

Isaac paced. "Where would Howard hide it? We don't even know if he had it on him when he ran. He could have hidden it at his place." He stopped, then gave a short nod. "That's where we need to be. His place. He would have hidden it and then run."

"Why?"

"Because it would buy him the time he needed, should they track him down. A chance to escape if they had to transport him somewhere."

She glanced back at the dead man. "I don't think that worked out like he planned."

"Yeah." His frown deepened as Sally opened her eyes again and this time kept them open. "Sally? Can you hear me? We really need you to wake up. We need your help."

She raised a hand to her head with a wince. "I . . . maybe. What happened?" Then her eyes flashed. "My children! Howard!"

"The people who were here took them," Isaac said, "and we're on a time crunch to find them. So you can't get hysterical."

"Took them? My babies!" Sally's voice rose, and she seemed to be headed straight toward hysteria when she pressed a hand against her head. "I'm going to be sick." She rolled to her feet and stumbled into the bathroom.

Ruthie followed her.

Once Sally had emptied her stomach, Ruthie placed a cold rag on her head and led her to the den. "Lie down on the couch."

Isaac sat beside her and held her frozen fingers.

"I know your voice," Sally said. "Isaac? You were right. Oh my goodness, you were right. I should have run. Why didn't I run?"

"Hey, I need you to stay calm. Just listen, okay? And think. Did Howard give you any hint of where he might have stashed whatever these guys are looking for?"

"No. I mean . . . I don't know."

"Please, Sally. Think."

"I'm trying! Don't you think if I knew something I'd tell you? They have my babies! They killed Howard!" Her eyes darted past him to the bedroom. "Oh, Howard." Tears fell.

"I know. I know. Calm down and catch your breath. I need your help. Your children need your help. Please."

Harsh breathing and hiccupping sobs wrenched Ruthie's heart.

Sally finally got herself together and flipped the cloth to the cooler side. "I . . . I asked Howard why people were after him." She sniffed. "He said he had something they wanted. I told him to give it to them, but he said it was his retirement paycheck."

"What else?"

"I was scared, so I told him to get out of my house, but he said it was too late. Someone was on the way to bring him the money."

"Go on."

"Um. A guy got here and they argued. I was going to get the kids and leave, but there was another man blocking my exit. He wouldn't let me go." Her voice broke and she cleared her throat. "Then, when Howard said he didn't have whatever they wanted, that he wasn't stupid enough to bring it with him, the guy pulled out a knife and stabbed Howard in the hand." Her last word came out on a squeak.

"Why did they shoot him?"

"Because Howard pulled a gun and tried to shoot the guy who stabbed him. The other guy shot him instead. Then the two started yelling at each other."

"So, what made Howard tell them I had what they were looking for?"

"I ran over to him, screaming at him to tell me where it was so I could give it to them. He was just gasping, trying to breathe, but he apologized, said he should have known better. The guy

330

who shot him kept demanding he tell him where it was or he'd kill me. And Howard said, 'Tell Isaac it's in plain view. He can find the evidence hidden in plain view.' And he died. He died, and they took my children," she whispered as sobs wracked her thin frame. She raised a hand to her head. "My head. He didn't have to hit me so hard."

"I've got some medicine in the car. Let me go get it." Ruthie ran to the vehicle and snagged one of the pain pills she'd brought just in case Isaac caved and decided to take something stronger. He hadn't, and she could tell he wasn't going to. But it would benefit Sally. Ruthie ran back inside, grabbed a cup of water from the kitchen, then returned to the den, where Sally lay on the couch. "Are you allergic to any medications?" Ruthie asked.

"No, not that I know of."

"Good, then take this."

"What is it?"

"Lortab."

"It'll make me sleepy."

"Yes, but it will also help your head. Just take it."

The woman grimaced, but did so. Then she started to weep again.

"What are we going to do?" Ruthie asked Isaac.

"Whatever it takes to rescue them." He scowled. "This is Howard's fault. I can't believe he told them I could find what they need."

"I keep coming back to one thing," Ruthie said. "Howard said it was hidden in plain sight."

"I didn't miss that. I just have no idea what he's talking about."

"Where's your husband?" Ruthie asked Sally.

"Tennessee," she said on a sob.

"I'm assuming he's not going to be any help."

"No." Sally used the rag to wipe her face and catch her breath. "He won't be any help. He's a walking cliché." She waved a hand. "Walked out with his secretary. Fortunately, I suspected something was going on and opened my own bank account, then siphoned a lot of our savings into it. I was trying to plan, to make sure my kids and I were taken care of if he pulled something like he did. But I sure didn't count on this." Tears welled again. "How am I going to get my kids back? Nick's just a tiny little guy. Barely a year old. They've got to be so scared." She stuffed her right palm into her mouth and choked back a sob.

Ruthie rubbed Sally's shoulders and looked at Isaac. "What now?"

He already had his phone out and was dialing. "We call this in and then get out of here."

With the crime-scene unit on the way, as well as local law enforcement, Ruthie and Isaac headed back to her vehicle with Sally in tow.

Sally stopped. "Wait! I need my cell phone. They may try to call me." She whirled and raced back inside, returning within minutes, purse over her shoulder, phone in hand. She staggered a little when she reached the car. The pill must have been taking effect.

"Normally, I wouldn't advocate running out on a crime scene," Isaac said, "but I've got to figure out what I'm looking for."

"I know." Ruthie pulled the car away from the curb. "Can you call Brady and let him know what's going on?"

"Of course." Isaac leaned back after maneuvering his seat belt around himself. "I don't believe this."

"I think we need to go to Howard's house," Sally slurred from the backseat.

"Can you get in?" Ruthie asked.

"Yes, of course. He keeps a key under a brick on the top step of his front porch."

"And you think he hid whatever it was at his home?"

"I can't think of any other place he would hide something."

Ruthie nodded. "Then we're going to Howard's house. To see what he hid in plain sight."

NINE

ISAAC'S PHONE RANG AND HE SNAGGED IT. "Yeah?"

"Where are you?"

"Don't shout, Brady. We're on the road. Where are you?"

"I'm shouting because I'm worried. And we're at Sally Peterson's house. With a dead man and a missing family."

"I was just getting ready to call you. Sally's with us. The guys who killed Howard took her kids, but you can't let on that you know. Meet me at this address." He rattled it off.

"Where am I going?"

"Howard's house."

"I'm on the way," Brady said. "And we've gotten an ID on the shooter Derek took out at the cabin."

"Who?"

"Officer Jay Harrison."

Isaac shut his eyes, easily picturing the large, redheaded, jovial man. "I never took him for a killer."

"I don't know what you've stumbled on, but it's a doozy. The chief has called for an audit of the evidence room and has pulled random footage from the security tapes to be viewed. She's assigned officers she trusts implicitly for this job."

"Who?"

"Izzy and Chloe and a couple others."

"Your sisters."

"Yeah."

"You don't think that's a bit biased?"

"Absolutely."

Isaac let out a short laugh, then flinched when his shoulder protested. He'd taken more medicine, but fatigue and nausea dragged at him.

"But," Brady said, "it's bias based on fact. My sisters and the others are good, honest cops. My mom knows without a shred of doubt that she can trust them. If there's anything to find, they'll find it."

"Thanks. When you get to Howard's, don't be obvious. They'll probably be watching. If they think I've called in reinforcements, they may act on their threats. I don't know. But I know I don't want to be the cause of those kids getting hurt."

"I know. We'll be sure to stay hidden, but keep your phone on so I can hear what's going on. Can you do that?"

"Yeah. I'll call you when we get there."

He hung up and noticed Ruthie pressed the gas a little harder.

"They're going to know you told the cops," Sally said. She'd been asleep when he'd taken the call. His talking must have awakened her. "They're going to know," she said, "and they're going to kill my babies." The tears that had momentarily stopped when she'd fallen asleep now flowed with renewed vengeance.

Careful not to jar his shoulder, Isaac turned in his seat. "Sally, listen to me. Listen." He waited for her to look at him while she wiped away her tears. "The guys doing this—they're cops. I can't go up against them alone. They're not going to hurt your kids. They're just using them, understand?"

She nodded, but he could tell she wasn't entirely convinced. He sighed. "They want me. If it comes down to it, I'll offer myself in exchange for your kids. I'm *not* going to let them hurt them."

Sally shook her head. "No. You can't do that. I don't want you hurt, either."

"I'm hoping it won't come to that, but just know that if it does, I'll make sure your kids are the priority."

Blinking against more tears, she drew in a shaky breath and nodded. "Thank you," she whispered.

He caught Ruthie watching from the corner of her eye. A frown furrowed her brow, and he wondered what she was thinking. If he had the energy, he'd ask her. "Keep your eyes on the rearview mirror. I'm going to have to sleep for a few minutes."

"I thought you might need to. It's fine. I'll wake you if I notice anything off."

He nodded and shut his eyes.

||||||||||

Ruthie was pretty sure they hadn't been followed but couldn't guarantee it. There were a lot of ways to track someone these days, but she'd done the best she could. Arriving at Howard's home, Ruthie pulled to a stop at the curb, then nudged Isaac awake.

Sally, who'd fallen asleep once more thanks to the medication, sat up and rubbed her eyes.

Isaac's eyes opened, but he didn't move for a few seconds. Neither did Ruthie. Then he blinked and drew in a breath. "We're here."

"We are. I drove around the block twice and haven't seen anything suspicious. I'm sure they're probably watching the house, though."

He gave a short nod. He palmed his cell phone and dialed. "Yeah, you getting close? Uh-huh. Good. The phone's on."

He dropped it into his pocket. "Brady will be right behind us looking for whoever's watching, so we can get started. He'll be here in about ten minutes. Stay here while I clear the house."

"You think they're waiting inside?"

"Wouldn't be surprised. They killed Howard. They want me to find the evidence, but I'm sure they're looking, too, and this is the first place they'd come when they didn't find it at Sally's house."

"But you can't go in there by yourself," Ruthie said.

He rubbed his eyes. "Let me just case the place. If I need help, Brady will be here shortly."

Ruthie gave a reluctant nod. "All right. But I'll be watching, too. If I scream, that means duck."

He gave a low laugh. "Okay."

She scowled. "I'm serious."

His smile faded. "Okay."

"Good."

"Lock the doors and be ready to get out of here, understand?"

"I understand, but I still think you should let me come with you."

"Ruthie . . ." He flicked a glance at Sally.

"Oh. Right. Okay." Maybe. There was no way she was going to leave him alone. Then again, she and Sally might be a distraction if he thought he needed to rescue them. "I'll take care of us. You worry about you. And don't do anything stupid."

"Like what?"

"Like think you can win a fist fight."

He pursed his lips. "Stay put."

Weapon gripped tight, he approached the windows and tried to peer inside. With a shake of his head, he slipped around the side of the house.

And Ruthie waited. Fingers clamped around her steering

wheel, doors locked. The minutes ticked past. Her nerves popped with visions of him being shot. Or hit from behind. Or . . .

It was all she could do not to burst from the vehicle. But she couldn't leave Sally alone.

"I'm going in there," Sally said as she gripped the door handle.

"Not yet. Just give him a couple more minutes."

"No one is in there," she said. "We're wasting time. Time my kids might not have."

"And if you go rushing in there, you could set off a trap or something and get yourself killed. Then where will your kids be?"

Sally sat back with a defeated sigh. "You're right. I'm sorry."

Finally, Isaac came back into view and waved that it was all right to exit the car. He walked up the front porch steps and waited for Ruthie and Sally to join him.

Sally retrieved the key and handed it to Isaac.

A low hum caught Ruthie's attention. "What's that?"

Isaac cocked his head, listening. The hum faded, and he frowned at her. "Not sure. Let's get this done."

He opened the door and they stepped inside. Ruthie paused a moment to take in her surroundings. The foyer led straight into a den area. To the right was a large eat-in kitchen and to the left was a hallway that led to the bedrooms. A small home, but it was neat and tidy. In the den, a large-screen television dominated the space over the fireplace and surround-sound speakers hung from the corners of the walls.

"He was a movie buff," Sally said. "Especially anything that had to do with the Civil War or the Underground Railroad." She shrugged. "History in general, but mostly the mid to late 1800s."

A chess set sat between the two recliners facing the television on the wall. Two bookcases on either side of the fireplace were full but well organized and neat.

Sally sighed. "What am I going to do with all of this?" She sniffed as tears began to fall again. "And why do I care when someone has my children?"

"I'm sorry," Ruthie said.

The woman shook her head. "Howard's always been greedy. He had a love for money and the desire to have more and more. I'm grieved that he chose this path, but I'm not surprised he wound up dead because of it." Her eyes, still red from her tears, hardened. "I don't know if I'll ever be able to forgive him for this. He's betrayed everything our parents tried to instill in us. And now my children are in danger because of his actions."

Ruthie had nothing to say to that. Sally was right. She squeezed her hand and turned to find Isaac scanning the room.

"In plain sight," he said. "I really have no idea."

Sally bit her lip and frowned. "Howard was notorious for wanting to get the last laugh on someone. What would it take to get that?"

"Hiding the evidence where no one would see it unless they knew it was right in front of them."

"So, we know it's right in front of us, but where?" Ruthie said. She walked over to the bookcase and scanned the titles. Some were self-help books, but most were about the Civil War. There were even a few fiction titles. Two of which she'd read.

They made their way through the house, opening drawers, scanning shelves.

In the bedroom, Ruthie found more Civil War collectibles and more books. Again, everything was neat and tidy. She pulled his gym bag out from under the bed and went through it. Nothing but clothes, a clean towel, and a pair of expensive tennis shoes. And a receipt for a locker at a local gym.

Sally entered the room and sat on the bed. "What happens

if we don't find what they want?" she asked in a low voice and with a glance over her shoulder. "Will they really hurt my children?"

Ruthie hesitated, then joined the woman on the bed. "I don't know, Sally. I really just don't know. I *do* know one thing. After spending so much time in Isaac's presence, I've learned quite a bit about him."

"Like what?"

"He's stubborn and smart and means what he says. If he says your kids are a priority, then they are."

The woman bit her lip and nodded, then winced and held a hand to her head. "I've got to stop doing that. Thank you."

"Sure. Why don't you rest while I keep searching?"

"I can help."

"No. You're under a lot of stress right now, and that concussion has got to feel awful. Just find a comfortable spot and rest."

"I can rest later."

After twenty minutes, they convened in the kitchen, quiet and morose. Tears stood out in Sally's eyes. "I'm sorry I'm not more help. I just don't know where to look. Howard and I haven't talked in forever and I . . ." She pressed fingers to her shaky lips.

Isaac raked a hand through his hair. Ruthie could see the fatigue in his eyes and the effort he was making to hide the pain. "I'm just going to take another look in his bedroom," she said.

Something niggled at the back of her mind. Leaving the two of them in the kitchen, she wandered back down the hall to the master bedroom. She went to the bookshelves. Running her fingers along the spines, she noticed the titles were in alphabetical order. And there it was. The title she'd skimmed over, but her subconscious must have caught. She pulled the book from the shelf and went back into the kitchen.

Before she could tell them what she thought she'd found,

the hum she'd heard earlier returned and she went to the door. "What *is* that?"

"A drone," Isaac said. He lifted his phone. "Brady, they've got a drone flying overhead. Can you figure out where they're controlling it from?" He lowered the phone and drew in a breath. "All right. Brady's on that. Let's get our thoughts together and figure out where to go from here."

Ruthie held up the book. "I think I may have found—" A noise caught her attention. "Did you hear that?"

Isaac frowned. "What? The drone?"

"No. Your phone. Someone's yelling."

He lifted it and hit the speaker button. "What is it?"

"Find a place to hide and get down! Now! Away from the kitchen!"

TEN

ISAAC IGNORED THE THROBBING in his shoulder and pointed the women to the hallway. "Go! Go! To the hallway."

Gunfire sounded. The windows in the kitchen shattered one after the other. They made it into the hallway as the bullets continued to pelt the house. "Brady! Who's shooting?"

"It's the drone. We're going to shoot it down."

"Hurry!"

Isaac wasn't sure how long the rain of bullets lasted, but it felt like years.

And then silence.

"Got it," Brady said over the speaker. "Stay put."

"They shot it down?" Sally whispered. "Now they'll know we called for help. Now they're going to kill my kids."

"No, they won't," Isaac said. "They still don't have what they need."

Ruthie stared at him. "But they were willing to kill us. To destroy this place. So maybe they *do* have what they need."

He shook his head. "That was just a warning. I think. Somehow they knew Brady and the others were out there."

His phone beeped, indicating another call. "Brady, they're calling me. I'm going to have to take it." He switched over. "Yeah?"

"That was stupid. Get rid of the cops or one of the kids dies. There won't be any more warnings or chances." A picture came through via text. A gun against a small child's head. Isaac's nausea returned in full force.

He had to swallow before he could speak. "I got it. What do you want us to do?"

"Find what Howard hid."

"I'm working on it, man."

"And you're running out of time."

The line cut off. He sighed and swiped a hand across his eyes. What was he going to do? "We're going to have to lie about finding it," he said.

Sally gasped. "What? We can't do that!"

"The only way to end this is to meet with them."

"But won't they demand some kind of proof?" she asked. "What happens when they realize you lied?"

"I'm hoping it won't come to that."

"No," she said. "We can't take that chance. They'll want to watch it or something first."

"I know. But it will be a distraction."

His phone rang again. "You keep calling and interrupting my searching, I'm going to have to ask for more time."

"I haven't seen the cops leave," the distorted voice said.

"Give me five minutes and you'll see them go. I'll make sure they're visible. You can follow them or whatever makes you feel better."

"Do it. When they're gone, call me back."

Click.

"Isaac?"

He looked up to find Ruthie holding a book. "What is it?"

"*Hidden in Plain View* is the title. It's about the Underground Railroad." She flipped the cover open. Cut into the pages was a small hole. Just big enough to hide the flash drive resting inside.

Sally gasped and jumped to her feet. "I should have known. I should have thought he'd use one of his stupid books."

"It's okay. We've got it now." Isaac stood, pulled the flash drive from its hiding place, and studied it. "Nice job, Ruthie."

"Now what?"

"I want to see what's on this, but first, we come up with a plan to get Sally's kids back."

He dialed Brady's number. "You've got to clear out, and they have to see you leaving. That drone firing on the house was just a test to smoke you out, and we fell for it."

Brady fell silent. "We'll leave, but we won't go far. I'll call you when we're clear."

"Fine. And we found the evidence."

"You found it?"

"We think so. I need a laptop to know for sure, but we're going to act as though this is what they're looking for and now we're going to use it."

"For?"

"A trade."

After he hung up on a still-protesting Brady, he dialed the number that would connect him to the men who'd decided to betray the badge.

"Yeah?"

"They'll be clearing out any minute," Isaac said.

"Good, we're watching."

"I found the evidence. How do you want me to deliver it?"

A slight pause. "So it really exists."

"It does."

"The three of you get in the car."

"Why all three? I've got the evidence. You don't need them."

"All three. Anyone gets left behind, they die."

Isaac didn't like it.

"Stop thinking about how to leave them behind and just do it."

344

"Now?"

"Now. Then, I'm going to tell you where to go and you're going to throw your phone out the window. Understood?"

"Won't I need it to stay in touch with you?"

"No. Because once I give you the directions, if you don't show up in the allotted time, the kids die."

"You don't have to keep saying that," he snapped. "I know what the consequences are."

"Just making sure."

Isaac motioned for them to head toward the car, phone still pressed against his ear. Ruthie frowned but palmed her keys and headed for the door. Sally followed.

Isaac climbed in the passenger seat and Ruthie slid behind the wheel. "We're in the car," Isaac said.

"Now, we're going to meet at a place that's wide open. The only car I want to see is that Honda Pilot the doctor drives."

"What's the address?"

The man gave it to him with explicit directions—to make sure Isaac didn't need a GPS, no doubt. Using a pad and pen he'd grabbed from the kitchen, he wrote down the directions.

ELEVEN

RUTHIE TIGHTENED HER GRIP on the steering wheel and glanced in the rearview mirror at Sally. The woman looked done in. No doubt the pain meds were helping her headache, but she couldn't be comfortable. Still, the tight jaw said she was determined to keep it together for her kids. Her eyes slid shut and she leaned her head back.

"Where are we going?" Ruthie asked Isaac. When he tossed his phone out the window, her blood ran cold.

He glanced at her. "We're heading to a very remote area about thirty minutes from here."

"Where?"

"Someplace that's going to be hard for anyone to sneak up on, but I think I heard a baby crying in the background, so we know the little one is okay."

Sally made no response from the back, and Ruthie realized she'd dropped back off. It was probably for the best. Her traumatized brain needed to heal.

With Isaac giving her directions, Ruthie drove. "Brady's not going to be able to follow us, is he?"

"I don't think so. Unless he gets creative."

"What are we going to do?"

"*We* aren't going to do anything."

"Isaac—"

"I mean it. I'm going to find the kids, and you and Sally are going to stay hidden."

"They said for all three of us to be there," Ruthie said.

"Yeah, well, they're getting ready to find out that sometimes you have to compromise to get what you want."

Thirty minutes later, they arrived at the rural edge of a town. An empty lot with a trailer at the back of the property loomed before them. Trees surrounded the area, and Ruthie's hopes rose. It might actually be possible to sneak up on the trailer from the back through the woods. Somehow. Maybe. But they'd probably have a lookout.

Isaac directed her where to park, then took the flash drive and pressed it into her hand. "Hold on to this. They're not getting it until we know the kids are safe. Y'all stay put until help gets here, okay?"

"I'm going," Sally said. "My kids are in there. There's no way I'm staying behind. If you go, I'll just follow you."

Isaac's jaw tightened. "I can't keep you safe if you're with me."

"I'm not asking you to keep me safe. I'm telling you I'm getting my kids with or without your help."

"Sally—"

"I'm going." Sally climbed from the vehicle, purse clutched under her arm.

Isaac gave an exasperated growl and pointed a finger at Ruthie. "Can you at least stay here with the flash drive? And find a place to hide if you see anyone coming?"

"I can do that."

Sally shot a frantic glance back at Ruthie, and Ruthie hoped the woman could keep it together. At least until her children were safe.

From her position behind the wheel, she looked down at the flash drive, then drew in a deep breath and started praying.

||||||||||

Isaac kept his weapon out of sight and his good hand on Sally's lower back. He led her along the tree line. Somehow it made him feel less of a target, even though they could have someone planted out of sight, ready to pick them off. The door to the trailer opened and Paul Sullivan stepped out with a weapon trained on him and Sally.

Isaac pulled to a stop. "Why am I not surprised? Cole in there with you?"

"Cole? That do-gooder? No way, man. Get in here."

To say he was surprised to hear Cole wasn't involved was an understatement. "Why the voice distortion?"

"It was fun to use it."

"Right."

"Where's the other one?" Sullivan asked. "The doctor?"

"She's here," Isaac said as they walked into the trailer.

"She's in the car with the flash drive," Sally said. "Now where are my kids?"

Isaac winced. She obviously wasn't thinking clearly. He prayed Ruthie had listened to him and had gotten herself to a place to hide.

"They're fine. In the back room. Help yourself and stay there. Don't come out until someone comes to get you."

Sally turned on her heel and disappeared down the hall. Isaac heard a squeal. "Mama!"

At least the kids were safe. Now he just had to find a way to get them all out. "Where's your partner?" he asked.

"Busy. Where's your backup?"

"It's likely they're trying to find us but probably not having much luck. We did what you said. It's time to let Sally and her kids go."

"You let me worry about Sally and the kids. Put your weapon on the floor and kick it over here."

Isaac didn't bother to argue. He removed his weapon, placed it on the floor, and gave it a shove with his foot. It slid under the couch.

Sullivan rolled his eyes. "You always did have lousy aim." He held his weapon on Isaac and lifted his phone to his ear. "Check the car. The doc has the flash drive." He looked at Isaac. "That was clever using the body bag and the gurney."

"Ruthie's idea." He paused, ears tuned, trying to figure out a way to get his gun and shoot his way out. The only problem was that he felt sure Sullivan wasn't acting alone. Someone else was here. Somewhere. "How much did Howard want to keep quiet?"

"A million."

"Wow. And you didn't want to pay him off and avoid all this?"

"Wouldn't have had to if you hadn't caught Lansing stuffing his shirt. Howard got scared it was all coming to an end and wanted a big payoff. He planned to disappear somewhere tropical with all that money. Unfortunately, we weren't interested in funding the trip."

"Speaking of Lansing, I assume he's here somewhere?"

"Somewhere."

"Who else?"

"Me, Lansing, Harrison, and Howard. Too many people means smaller pieces of the pie."

Why didn't Isaac believe that?

Sullivan's phone buzzed, and he lifted it and checked the incoming text. His eyes hardened on Isaac, his jaw tightening. "Where is she?"

"What do you mean?"

"She's not in the car."

||||||||||

Ruthie made her way to the back of the trailer. She simply couldn't sit in the car and do nothing. She had to at least make sure Isaac and Sally didn't need her and the extra weapon she carried. Two of the windows were covered, but the third gave her a view into the back bedroom. She could see Sally sitting on the bed with her three children. The woman held the smallest one and the other two leaned against her.

There was no way to get them out of the room through the window, so they would have to wait. It didn't look like they had anyone guarding them at the moment—at least not inside the room.

Footsteps sounded, leaves crunched, and she ducked, then darted back to the tree line to huddle behind one of the larger tree trunks. A man she didn't recognize walked the perimeter of the trailer, his steps crunching the fallen leaves. Had he heard her own steps in her race from the trailer? Seemed like he couldn't have missed them.

He swept a weapon over the area and continued the trek. If he'd heard the crunching leaves, he didn't seem concerned. Then again, maybe he wasn't listening for her or expecting anyone to be back here.

Once he was out of sight and looking like he was heading back toward her car, Ruthie ran a shaky hand over her hair. What should she do? Wait for the guy to leave the car and go find help? No, they were looking for her now. Eventually, they would do something to one of their hostages when they realized they couldn't find her. Ruthie shuddered.

She needed a plan. A distraction.

She pulled the weapon from her waistband and fired a shot into a tree.

||||||||||

350

Isaac dove headfirst into Sullivan's abdomen when the man jerked at the gunshot. The loud crack had provided the opportunity Isaac needed to get the drop on him.

Sullivan's breath whooshed from his lungs, and he went to a knee. Isaac moved in with a hard punch to the man's face. He kept swinging, staying on the offensive, because working with one arm, if he let Sullivan get the upper hand, Isaac would be toast.

"Don't move!" Ruthie's voice came from behind him.

Isaac landed one more punch on Sullivan's jaw, and the man's eyes rolled back in his head.

With his good arm, Isaac pushed himself to his feet and turned to find Ruthie with her weapon still trained on the unconscious Sullivan. "There's another one out there," she said.

Isaac nodded. "I need something to tie this guy up with. Then we can worry about the other one."

"Do you know who he is?"

"Probably Lansing. I'm not sure that it was just the three of them. There may be more."

"I haven't seen anyone else."

"We'll figure that out in a minute. Grab his phone and call Brady." Isaac grabbed a lamp cord and yanked it from the base of the light. He used his good arm and feet to roll Sullivan to his stomach, then held the cord out to Ruthie. "Actually, I'm going to need your help first. Help me get his hands behind his back." She did, then bent the man's knee and attached his ankle to his wrists. He would be miserably uncomfortable when he woke up, but Isaac really didn't care. "Nice job."

"Thanks, but I don't see the phone anywhere," she said. "Where is it?"

He looked around. No phone. "Check under the furniture."

"What's going on? What's happening?" Sally cried from the hallway. Her eyes landed on the man trussed up and unconscious and she gasped.

"Get your kids and get out that back door," Isaac told her. "Run into the woods and find a place to hide. Take a blanket just in case this takes a while." He tossed her one from the sofa. "Ruthie, go with her while you can. I don't know how long before the other guy gets back."

"But—"

"Help her get her kids to safety. I can take care of this. I'm not leaving just yet. I'll find the phone and call Brady. Just go. Hurry."

Ruthie pressed her lips together and looked at Sally. "What did they do with your phone?"

"Um. I have it. In my purse."

"They didn't take it?"

"Yes, but I found it in the bathroom a minute ago."

"Okay." She shot a look at Isaac. "Are you sure about this?"

"My concern is the kids. And not letting these guys get away with this. You have the evidence. Make sure it gets into the right hands. And stay away from the vehicle. They probably have someone watching it."

Ruthie nodded. "All right, come on, Sally. We'll call for help once we make sure your children are safe."

Sally started to say something, then bit her lip, spun on her heel, and disappeared back down the hallway. In seconds, she had all three children with her—baby on her hip, the other two trailing behind, eyes wide, scared.

Ruthie held her arms out to the little girl, who looked to be about four years old. The child let her pick her up. Ruthie nodded to Sally. "I'm ready when you are." The five of them slipped out the back door and headed to the woods.

Just then, Isaac heard a footfall on the step outside the front door and raised his weapon.

TWELVE

RUTHIE FOLLOWED SALLY THROUGH THE TREES, trying not to trip on the undergrowth. Heart pounding, she hugged the little girl close to her and pulled up short when Sally turned off onto a well-worn path.

Then the woman stopped in front of a small shed and threw open the door. "Here, we can hide in here."

The inside held a twin bed, in addition to various work tools including a lawn mower, and what looked like a bathroom off the back. "How did you know this was here?"

Sally blinked. "I didn't. I just saw the path and took it, and it led here."

Made sense. Ruthie set the little girl down on the bed. The older child sat next to her and pulled her into her arms like she'd done it a hundred times before. "Okay, you guys stay here. Sally, I need your phone. I'm going to call Brady and make sure he knows where to come."

Sally pulled the phone from her purse and handed it to Ruthie. She swiped the screen. "What's your password?"

"Nine, five, one, zero, zero, zero."

When the phone opened, Ruthie dialed Brady's number. And waited. Then realized it wasn't ringing. She glanced at the screen. "Ugh. No signal." She tried again. Ruthie glanced at Sally, back to the phone, and walked toward the door. "You guys stay here. I'm going to see if I can get a signal outside."

Back among the trees, she tried again. This time it rang. Once. Twice.

Something hard pressed against the back of Ruthie's skull. She froze.

"Hang up. Now."

Ruthie did.

"Don't move. Don't cry out. Don't breathe if you know what's good for you."

A hard ball formed in Ruthie's gut. "You deserve an Academy Award."

"I was the lead in our high school play. Drop the phone."

Ruthie did so.

"Now your weapon. Nice and easy with no funny moves. Give it a toss, too."

Ruthie followed the orders, then turned to face the mother of three. "Why, Sally?"

"A lot of reasons."

"Such as?"

She huffed a short laugh. "Such as a loser husband who only cares about making kids, not raising them. Such as never having enough money because he's buying some trinket for his latest girlfriend. Such as watching my children go without because I can't afford to get a job because I can't afford the childcare I'd have to pay for. Such as—" She drew in a breath. "It doesn't matter anymore. We're taken care of now. That's all that's important. I've done what I had to do."

"You were unconscious." Ruthie nodded to the woman's wounded head. "That's a real concussion you have there."

"Yes. And I plan to take that issue up with Heath when I see him. And then I'm going to hurt him as bad as I possibly can without killing him. Or maybe I'll do that, too."

"Was Howard really your brother?"

"Yes, he really was. But just like my husband, he's been a loser all his life. Not to mention a weak and sniveling coward. And one who spends money like it's an endless supply. Do you know how much credit card debt he managed to rack up? He was my big brother. He was supposed to help *me*." She shook her head. "I go to him after years of not speaking and ask him to pay my mortgage for one month. One lousy month. And he says no. He's broke." Tears dripped down her cheeks and she sniffed. "Whatever. He got what he deserved. And I'll finally get what I deserve."

"What's that, Sally?"

"My happily-ever-after."

This wasn't adding up for Ruthie. "When you ran back to the house to get your phone, you got the gun, too?"

"Sure did."

"And just how are you connected to all of this? Who's going to give you this happily-ever-after?"

"Paul Sullivan. The man I'm going to marry just as soon as this is all over. He's going to take care of me and my kids from now on. No more scraping by on government assistance. No more begging my ex for child support payments. No more pressure to take care of three kids all by myself." Her last words ended on a sob.

Ruthie's mind processed the woman's words even as she was calculating possible escape scenarios. "How did you two even meet?"

"The kids and I used to spend a lot of time at Howard's place after my husband took off—and before Howard decided he was tired of having us around. Paul would come over a lot. One thing led to another, and I fell in love with him." She wiped the tears from her cheeks, but the weapon never wavered. "But I couldn't figure out the connection between Paul and Howard.

They sure weren't friends—they argued too much. So I started spying. And found out they were stealing drugs and money from the evidence room. Howard was real nervous about everything. Then he got paranoid and was scared they were going to get rid of him."

His paranoia hadn't been too far off.

"One night, I was in the back of the house with the kids, and Howard was ranting about fixing the video, saying that they needed to be more careful. I walked in and talked to him until he calmed down. Paul seemed really impressed and brought me up to speed on everything. Later, he pulled me aside and kissed me." Her eyes darkened, and a small smile curved her lips before she blinked and her expression hardened once more. "Then that cop caught Heath stealing and reported it. Paul was livid. Howard said they had to back off, take things easy for a while, but Paul insisted that everything was fine. Howard was terrified they were going to set him up to take the fall for everything."

"So he made sure he had the evidence he needed to ensure that didn't happen."

"Yes. I'm the one who told Howard to get it and hold on to it."

"For what?" It hit her. "Wait a minute. You're not sure Sullivan isn't just using you, right? It's occurred to you that he was only interested in you because of what you could get Howard to do. The control you had over him."

The woman's eyes flashed and her jaw tightened. "You're very smart, aren't you?"

"I'm a woman. In your shoes, it's how I would think."

"It occurred to me. Only Howard got more stupid than even I could deal with. Once he realized his cash flow was about to come to an end—thanks to your boyfriend in there—he decided it would be wise to blackmail everyone involved. I was all for having the evidence, but blackmailing the others? Stupid. And he paid for it with his life. But I'm not going to let that stop me from getting what I've worked so incredibly hard for."

"Is this really the legacy you want to leave for your children?"

"My children are the reason I'm doing this. They're going to have everything I've never had."

"Not sure how that's going to work with you sitting in a prison cell."

Sally laughed. A harsh, guttural sound that scraped across Ruthie's nerves. "Prison isn't an option. Now, we're going to walk back to the car and get the flash drive, because I'm assuming you don't have it on you."

"You would assume correctly."

"Then you would have left it in the car. Or somewhere nearby. Walk."

The woman was smart. "What about your kids?"

"They won't leave the shed. They'll be fine."

Ruthie took three steps toward what she thought was the right direction, then stopped.

"What are you doing?" Sally asked.

"I just want to know—did you kill your brother?"

"No. Paul did. Finally."

The woman was cold. Dry-ice cold.

"Now walk."

"Where am I going?" Ruthie asked.

"Up that hill then down the other side. The car is at the bottom."

Because she had no choice, Ruthie obeyed. As they headed toward the car, she realized that the only thing keeping her alive at the moment was the fact no one else but her knew where the flash drive was. She wasn't a cop. She had a basic understanding of self-defense, but she wasn't sure she could go up against a woman with a gun and come out the winner. When she'd managed to get the attacker off her in the hospital, she'd been going strictly by instinct. She still wasn't sure how she'd managed to get loose from him.

This was different. She had too much time to think.

And yet she may not have a choice. She went as slow as she dared up the hill. At the top, she could see the vehicle just as Sally said.

Ruthie let her gaze skim the SUV and the empty street beyond the drive. No sign of help. Dread hardened into a knot in the center of her belly. But Sally didn't know that just before she'd placed the weapon at the base of Ruthie's head, she'd shot a text to Brady. What if he hadn't gotten her message? What if help really wasn't coming?

With a cry, Ruthie spun and slammed her forearm against Sally's outstretched arm. Sally cried out and dropped the gun. Ruthie scrambled for it, lost her balance, and went to the ground. Then found herself tumbling down the steep hill.

||||||||||

The door opened. "Yo! Sullivan! Where are you? You here?"

Isaac pulled back into the first bedroom off the hall and glanced at the man he'd managed to drag in there one-handed. His head swam and his shoulder throbbed, but he had no choice but to ignore the weakness and just do it. And fast. Unfortunately, he still hadn't found the phone.

"Sullivan!"

Where was the cavalry? Surely Ruthie had had time to call Brady—or someone?

Heavy steps headed toward the hall. He stepped out of the room, weapon held ready, waiting for the man to come around the corner.

"Sull—"

"Sullivan's out of commission right now. Get your hands up."

358

Lansing scowled but lifted his hands. "Martinez? Now what?"

"Now we wait for the good guys to get here so we can haul you and your buddies to prison."

"I don't think so."

"So, what are you going to do? Go for your weapon?"

"You'd really shoot me?"

"Three times. Center mass." He shrugged with his good shoulder. "Don't think I'll miss from here."

Lansing paused, then gave a nervous chuckle. "Come on. We're both cops. We can just forget this and be done with it."

"We're both cops? Really? You still see yourself as a cop? Let's get something straight here, Lansing. You're not a cop. You're a traitor. You've betrayed everything the badge means and made the rest of us look bad. You're not a cop. Not by a long shot. Now, why don't you head back into the kitchen and have a seat? Then we can discuss what being a real cop really looks like."

Lansing backed up slowly, his gaze never wavering from Isaac's. "You're making a huge mistake, Martinez."

"Only you would look at this as a mistake. Speaking of mistakes . . . was that you in my bedroom a few nights ago? You and Sullivan and Harrison?"

A smirk tilted the man's lips. "It was."

"Thought so. Were you there to scare me or kill me?"

"Does it matter?"

"Not really."

Lansing reached the couch. Then spun and dove out the still-open front door.

||||||||||

Ruthie's roll down the steep hill ended with a bone-jarring halt at the bottom. The world tilted around her, her equilibrium momentarily destroyed. She struggled to her feet, and a gunshot sent her scrambling. The bullet pinged off the ground beside her, and she dove behind the back of her vehicle while her head settled. Sally must have recovered the weapon.

Great.

As the second shot sounded, a chopper flew into view. Three law enforcement vehicles roared up the street, and Ruthie wanted to cry.

But Sally was still shooting, so that was going to have to wait. She dodged another bullet that hit her car.

Then the shooting stopped.

Sally had to be running back to get her kids. Doors slammed as officers exited their vehicles.

"Brady!" Ruthie waved, caught his attention, then spun to run back up the hill.

She heard him calling to her but had no time to stop and explain. She couldn't let Sally get away. And she couldn't let the woman use her children as hostages. The only thing she could do was lead the officers to the shed.

More shots. Ruthie ducked behind the nearest tree before she realized the bullets weren't coming her way. Brady was getting closer, so she continued her run down the path.

Brady finally pulled up beside her.

"There," she gasped and pointed. "In the shed. It's Sally. And Paul Sullivan. And Heath Lansing. But there are three kids in there, so don't go in shooting." But someone had been shooting. Where had those shots come from and why?

"Isaac!" Where was he? Had he found Lansing and fired the shots? Or had Lansing found him? Fear pumped her blood even faster.

Brady and the others passed her, and she backed up. She caught sight of Cole, Isaac's partner, and felt bad for assuming the worst about him.

"Police! Freeze!"

Ruthie spun to see Sally on the ground, her hands being cuffed behind her back. "Let me go! I didn't do anything! You can't do this! I have children!"

The oldest girl tried to push the arresting officer from her mother. "Let my mama go!" She kicked him, and another officer held her while she wailed.

The two smaller kids stood with a female officer, crying.

Her heart broke for the children, but it had to be. And now she had to find Isaac. She took off down the path that would lead her back to the trailer. Only to have something slam into her back. She fell to the ground and rolled. Lansing looked down at her. "Get up."

〡〡〡〡〡〡〡

The bullet had missed Isaac by inches. Lansing had fired at him as he'd come out the door of the trailer. Then Lansing had escaped around the side of the home and into the woods.

"Give it up, Lansing!" Isaac hollered.

Fleeing footsteps were his only answer, but other officers were right behind him. Shouts and orders filled the air, warning that the man was armed, but Isaac kept going.

And pulled up short when he found Lansing with his back to a tree and an arm around Ruthie's throat. "Let her go."

"No way, man. She's my ticket outta here." He started backing toward the front of the trailer, down the path toward his truck. Ruthie grabbed at his arm, digging her nails into his flesh. He growled and moved his arm to the back of her head.

Other officers had their weapons trained on Lansing and Ruthie, but no one would shoot. Not while Lansing had a gun to her head. The man now had a tight hold on her hair. "Put it down, Heath. You and I both know you're not getting out of here."

"I'm not going to prison."

"So, what are you going to do?"

"Leave. It's really that simple. Let me get in the car and leave, and I'll let her out somewhere not too far from help. I don't want to kill her. I just want to get out of here."

Isaac wished he could believe that. Not that he would even consider it, but he wished he could believe the man wouldn't hurt Ruthie. The look in his eye and his body language belied his words. Isaac shifted his gaze to Ruthie.

Her pale face told him how scared she was, yet her blue eyes spit fire and determination. "Isaac, I don't want to die."

"I know, Ruthie. I don't want you to die, either."

"Then scream."

He blinked. "What?"

"Remember what I said about what to do when I scream?"

Oh yeah. His gaze sharpened. "Yes."

"Shut up, you two." Lansing hurried backward, dragging Ruthie with him.

Isaac caught Brady's tight features watching everything play out. A sniper had to be in place. Could probably get Lansing in the back. But would the bullet penetrate him and hit Ruthie?

Isaac screamed.

Ruthie went slack, pulling Lansing off balance.

Isaac fired.

THIRTEEN

RUTHIE ROLLED AWAY FROM THE MAN who now lay
on the ground. Isaac's bullet had hit its mark. Trembling, she
reached out and pressed her fingers against his neck. A faint
pulse beat. "We need an ambulance!" She wanted him to live. So
he could face a lifetime in prison. Death was too easy for him.

Paramedics who'd been given the green light to approach
rushed over and dropped next to Lansing. "I'm a doctor. Get
me his vitals." Ruthie shouted orders as though she were in
the comfort of her operating room. The paramedics worked
quickly and got Lansing loaded into the ambulance.

They took off, and Ruthie found herself enveloped in a one-
armed hug, her nose buried in Isaac's hard chest. For a moment,
she simply stood there and soaked in the comfort being offered.
"I should have gone with him."

"No, they'll take care of him."

"They can do everything I could have done if I was with
him, right?"

"Yes, Ruthie."

She sucked in a deep breath. "I think I might be a little rattled, but I'm entitled, aren't I? I mean, I did get held at gunpoint

several times today. Surely I get a pass—no, I should have gone with him."

He gave her a light shake. "It's okay. You did all you could. They've got it."

"Right. Of course."

"So. Are you okay?"

"I think so. Yes." She glanced at her hands and grimaced. "I would prefer not to have that man's blood all over me, but yes, I'm okay."

He waved a paramedic over who'd just driven up in a second ambulance. "You have something she can wash the blood off with?"

"Yeah. Hold on a second."

When he returned, Ruthie scrubbed her hands and arms, then used the proffered towel to dry them. "Thanks. That feels so much better."

Isaac hugged her again like he didn't want to let her go. She found she was okay with that idea.

"Ruthie?"

She looked up to find Brady standing next to them, eyeing her and Isaac. She slipped out of Isaac's embrace to wrap her arms around her brother's waist. "You got her. You got them all, right?"

"We got them."

"And the kids? I could hear them crying. I hate that they had to see her get arrested."

"They'll be all right. Social services is on the way. I heard someone say something about grandparents in Florida. You know the drill. While they're waiting on the relatives to get here, they'll have the kids see a counselor immediately and will let them see their mom as soon as it can be arranged."

"As weird as it sounds, I think she was a good mother. She really seemed to love those kids."

Brady scowled. "If she loved them, she wouldn't have made the choices she made."

"You really believe that?"

He sighed. "Some days. Other days, people like her just confuse me."

"I think her motivation was in the right place, but everything else was mixed up."

"You're a softie, sis."

"Maybe so."

"Ruthie?"

She turned to see Isaac, face pale, hand pressed to his shoulder. "Yes?"

"I think I may have pulled my stitches loose." When he removed his hand, his palm was covered in blood.

She gasped. "Oh no!" She hurried over to him and grabbed him by his good arm. "Let's get you in the back of the ambulance so I can take a look."

In the ambulance, Ruthie helped Isaac remove the sling and his shirt to expose the wound. It didn't look nearly as bad as she'd feared. For that much blood, it must have been seeping for a good while. "Looks like you popped three. I can fix that right up." She grabbed the nearest suture kit, disinfectant, and other items she needed. "Lie down. I'm going to give you a couple of shots to numb the area, and then we'll take care of this."

"What? Here?"

"Yep. Now be still."

Brady appeared. "You have the flash drive?"

"I buried it," she said.

"Where?"

Ruthie directed him where to find it. While she waited for the numbing medication to take effect, she watched her brother dig up the flash drive. He blew the dirt off and returned to the ambulance with a laptop. Nodding to Isaac, he inserted the drive into the USB port. "I figured you'd want to see this."

"You figured right."

"Is it all right if I sew while you watch?" Ruthie asked.

"Sure."

A few clicks later, a video popped up on the screen. Brady and Isaac watched it while she worked.

"There." Brady pointed at the screen. "There's Sullivan slipping cash into a bag, and there's Lansing doing the same. It's all security footage that was scrubbed. I guarantee that if we went back and looked at the time stamps on the other footage, we'll find it's repetitious."

"They made a loop," Isaac said, then grunted when Ruthie tied off the last stitch.

"Yeah." He removed the flash drive and turned to Isaac. "You did it."

Isaac ran his good hand over his face and nodded. Then he looked at Ruthie. "We did it. I couldn't have done it without your help."

She smiled at him. "Always glad to support the blue."

"You did a good job, Ruthie," Brady said. "I don't like that you put your life in danger, of course. And when Mom finds out the details—"

"Um, we don't have to tell her those."

Brady's right brow shot up. "You really think you're going to keep this from her?"

"We're in North Carolina. She's a chief in South Carolina. I think it would be very possible to keep this from her."

He laughed. "You can try, but she's got friends all over this state."

Ruthie's shoulders deflated. Brady kissed her cheek. "Now, I've got to go deal with Sullivan, that turkey Isaac trussed up."

Brady left and Isaac let out a low, mournful sigh. "You know, when I took that oath all officers take when they decide to risk it all every day of their lives, I never once thought I'd be arresting those I considered my family—people I would have died for."

"I know." Ruthie brushed a stray lock of hair from his eyes. "It's heartbreaking that there are those who'll betray the badge, but those are few and far between." She gave him a light nudge. "But you're a hero. You just potentially stopped those stolen drugs from getting back out on the streets and in the schools."

"That's what it's all about." He nodded and gave her a half smile. "Being one of the good guys."

"Exactly."

But she knew this would hurt for a long time, especially when the media got hold of it. They would magnify the four who'd betrayed their oaths of honor and most likely play down the roles of those who'd risked their lives to bring them to justice.

It wasn't right and it wasn't fair, but she knew those who wore the badge would do it all over again tomorrow, regardless of their portrayal in the media. Then again, maybe the media would surprise her.

Brady led Sullivan from the trailer, the lamp cord replaced by cuffs. Sullivan favored his left leg, limping, his lips twisted into a tight grimace as Brady pointed him toward the police cruiser. Sullivan's eyes caught hers, and he glared. She lifted her chin and narrowed her eyes, refusing to let him intimidate her.

Isaac's hand wrapped around hers. She looked at him and smiled. "It's over."

"Yeah. It's over, and I have one question for you."

"What's that?"

"Will you go out with me?"

EPILOGUE

Ruthie looked around the table at the piles of food that would soon be consumed by her large family. Love swelled, bringing tears to her eyes. She blinked them back and snagged the bowl of rice Brady passed to her. "You all right, sis?" he asked.

"Of course."

Isaac sat at her right, his sling now gone, shoulder healed. He was officially back on duty. He leaned over. "You're sure you're all right?" he whispered in her ear.

She passed the bowl on to him with a smile. "I'm more than all right. Grateful to be sitting here. Just feeling incredibly blessed."

Isaac's eyes landed on his sister, her husband, and his niece who sat opposite him. "I know what you mean."

She squeezed his fingers, then went back to the food. It had been four months since the day she'd been held hostage with a gun to her head. Twice. Four months of healing.

She glanced at Isaac. Four months of getting to know the man she'd rescued from a killer. And who, in turn, had rescued her. A man she loved more with each passing day.

Isaac had been exonerated, the bad guys had been put away, and life had returned to normal—only better, because he was in it. Apologies had come in left and right as soon as the story broke, and he'd been hailed a hero by the department and the public.

Chloe, Ruthie's younger sister, and Hank, her detection K-9, sat with her fiancé, Blake MacCallum. Blake's daughter, Rachel, laughed with Ruthie's cousin, Penny. The two girls had been victims of a human trafficking ring that Blake and Chloe had busted a year ago. It was good to see them smiling and acting like teens.

Derek and Elaine sat at the opposite end of the table, their smiles rivaling the brightest star in the sky. Engagement agreed with them.

Ruthie had hopes of joining those ranks one day soon. Maybe. Isaac had hinted he was thinking about it. She'd hinted that it was fine with her.

Brady and Derek argued about something, and she knew neither one would drop the subject until someone else changed it. She didn't care. It was just the way her brothers worked.

She enjoyed the bantering with her family, loved that they could all manage to make time to come together to share a meal and catch up. And she'd enjoyed getting to know Isaac's family. At first, she'd been wary, especially after Carol's attitude in the hospital, but Isaac hadn't held a grudge. And Ruthie supposed she could understand that the woman's first loyalty lay with her husband. And, finally, Ruthie loved that her family was always willing to welcome others to the table and into their hearts.

"So, Ruthie," Derek said, "now that you've had some time to think about it, are you giving up surgery to join the rest of us in law enforcement?"

She rolled her eyes. "Ha ha. Not likely."

"She totally could," Isaac said. "You would have been seriously impressed."

"Come on, guys." She glared at Derek. "Why do you bring this up every time we get together?"

"It's fun to push your buttons."

"Yeah, well, my answer's still the same today as it was last month. I was scared out of my mind. I could never do what you guys do."

Isaac squeezed her hand again. "You did what you had to do. That's all we do every day."

"Well," her mother said, "until you decide to head to the academy, let's leave the cop stuff to the ones who are trained for it."

"Works for me," Ruthie said with a smile. Her mother now knew the details of everything that had happened. She'd read the report, then found Ruthie at the hospital and hugged her for a good five minutes.

Then she'd sighed and cupped Ruthie's face in her palms. "I love you, Ruthie."

"I love you, too, Mom."

"Please don't go chasing any more bad guys."

"Yes, ma'am. I promise."

"Thank you." Then she'd kissed Ruthie's forehead and walked toward the exit, head held high, back straight. But Ruthie knew the woman was mush on the inside.

Ruthie scowled at her brother. "Let it go, Derek. You've beat this horse back into dust."

"Hey." Isaac's voice in her ear made her jump.

She turned. "Hey."

"Wanna take a little walk?"

"Sure." He pulled her away from the table and onto the back porch. Spring was in the air, but the weather was still chilly, especially at night. They sat on the swing that hung from the roof, and Ruthie snuggled next to him.

"I love you, Ruthie."

She stilled. He'd never come right out and said the words quite like that. "I love you, too, Isaac."

"Good." He released a breath that sounded as if he'd been holding it for an eternity.

Ruthie chuckled, then turned serious. "I admire you so much. I have to be honest, though. I never really saw myself falling for a cop."

"What? You're kidding."

"Nope. I've always thought I'd meet someone at church or the hospital. Another doctor or an administrator or something."

"Well, we did meet at the hospital."

She laughed. "That we did."

"So, I guess the thought of spending the rest of your life with a cop doesn't make you want to run away?"

"No. Not much anyway. The cop culture is as much a part of my life as the medical one."

He kissed her temple. "That gives me hope."

"About what?"

"That we could make it. Too many law enforcement marriages end in divorce."

"I know."

"But your parents have done it. Izzy and Ryan, Chloe and Blake. They all are willing to take the risks."

"Yep. Cops marrying cops. I don't know if that's a good thing or not. Could get volatile in their households."

"They'll be fine. They just have to work out their priorities."

"Yeah," she said softly. "I don't understand how cops who take the oath to honor the badge and everything else can simply turn their back on that."

"I think, sometimes, officers just get so sick of seeing the bad guys win that their focus becomes shifted. They lose sight of the fact that they're doing good and get overwhelmed. Mindset can be a powerful thing."

"True."

"That's not an excuse for criminal behavior, though." He paused and looked up at the sky. "I love this."

"What?"

"Sitting here with you. Being surrounded by the darkness, holding you in my arms with the stars as a nightlight."

Ruthie's love for this man took her breath away. While she couldn't breathe, she might as well take advantage of that. She leaned over and kissed him.

With no hesitation, he wrapped his arms around her and lifted one hand to cup the base of her head. Ruthie lost herself in the moment and the man, while a tiny part of her thanked God for the good that had come from such evil.

Isaac lifted his head and pulled her closer. "Will you marry me, Ruthie?"

"When?"

"Tomorrow?"

"Okay."

His laughter rumbled against her cheek and she grinned. Then sobered. "Wait. Are you going to be okay being married to a trauma surgeon? Someone who has to work all hours of the day and night?"

"You mean like a detective? I think I can handle it."

"What about kids?" she asked.

"I want them. Do you?"

"Yes. Very much so." A pause. "Just maybe not as many as my parents had."

Another chuckle. "Then we'll work out the details. God's brought us together. As long as He's in the midst of us, we'll be fine."

"We'll have to work to keep Him there," she said softly. "It's not easy when life and distractions get in the way. I've watched my parents, and while they love each other, they've had their ups and downs. It takes real commitment to stay together through it all."

He hugged her close. "I know. No marriage is perfect." He kissed her temple, then chuckled.

"What?" she asked.

"I'll probably get on your nerves."

"Probably. And I'll most likely cause you to pull out a few hairs."

He rubbed a hand across his full head. "I think I can spare a few. I'm game if you are."

"Yeah," she smiled. "I'm game."

"Hey!" Derek's voice reverberated behind them.

Ruthie jerked and turned to shoot him a glare. He stood in the doorway that led back to the den where the rest of her family sat watching football. "What?"

"Are you two lovebirds going to stay out there all night? We're getting ready for a rousing game of Phase Ten. Now, move it. Please." That last word was tossed over his shoulder as an afterthought.

Ruthie groaned and dropped her head back against the swing.

Isaac laughed. "What is Phase Ten?"

"The most frustrating game on the planet. I stink at it, or rather my cards always stink. That's the only reason Derek wants to play. So he can beat me. Because"—she raised her voice—"he can't beat me on the shooting range."

"I can beat you. You just cheat."

"Do not, brat!"

"Do too, bigger brat!"

Ruthie ducked her head while Isaac laughed. Then he kissed her again. "Come on," he said. "I've got to see this."

"We won't scare you away?"

"Never."

"All right, then. You can protect me from them."

"Who's going to protect me?"

"Good point."

Yet, he followed her willingly—almost eagerly—to the family dining table, and they slid into their chairs. Ruthie couldn't keep the smile from spreading. "Just know that Derek stacks the deck."

Derek scowled. "Do not."

"Do so."

"Here," Isaac said, "let me deal."

"Yes," Ruthie said. "Let Isaac deal."

"But I always deal first," Derek said.

She crossed her arms and glared. With an offended huff, he passed the deck to Isaac, who began to deal the cards.

Ruthie sighed with contentment. She loved her life. She picked up the first three cards.

She loved her family. Grabbed the next three.

And she loved Isaac. She snagged the last four while she pictured herself in a white dress walking down the aisle of the church she'd grown up in. Of course, her father would walk arm-in-arm with her, ready to give her away.

With another prayer of thanksgiving, she picked up her hand . . .

. . . and groaned.

ABOUT THE AUTHORS

Dee Henderson is the author of numerous novels, including *Threads of Suspicion*, *Traces of Guilt*, *Taken*, *Undetected*, *Full Disclosure*, and the acclaimed O'MALLEY series. Her books have won or been nominated for several prestigious industry awards, such as the RITA Award, the Christy Award, and the ECPA Gold Medallion. Dee is a lifelong resident of Illinois. Learn more at www.deehenderson.com or facebook.com /deehendersonbooks.

||||||||||

Praised by *New York Times* bestselling author Dee Henderson as "a name to look for in romantic suspense," **Dani Pettrey** has sold more than 400,000 copies of her novels to readers eagerly awaiting the next release. Dani combines the page-turning adrenaline of a thriller with the chemistry and happy-ever-after of a romance. Her novels stand out for their "wicked pace, snappy dialogue, and likable characters" (*Publishers Weekly*), "gripping storyline[s]," (*RT Book Reviews*), and "sizzling undercurrent of romance" (*USA Today*). Her ALASKAN COURAGE series and CHESAPEAKE VALOR series have received praise from readers and critics alike and spent multiple months topping the CBA bestseller lists.

From her early years eagerly reading Nancy Drew mysteries, Dani has always enjoyed mystery and suspense. She considers herself blessed to be able to write the kind of stories she loves—full of plot twists and peril, love, and longing for hope and redemption. Her greatest joy as an author is sharing the stories God lays on her heart. She researches murder and mayhem from her home in Maryland, where she lives with her husband. Their two daughters, a son-in-law, and two adorable grandsons also reside in Maryland. For more information about her novels, visit www.danipettrey.com.

||||||||||

Lynette Eason is the bestselling author of the WOMEN OF JUSTICE series, the DEADLY REUNIONS series, and the HIDDEN IDENTITY series, as well as *Always Watching*, *Without Warning*, *Moving Target*, and *Chasing Secrets* in the ELITE GUARDIANS series. She is the winner of two ACFW Carol Awards, the Selah Award, and the Inspirational Readers' Choice Award. She has a master's degree in education from Converse College and lives in South Carolina. Learn more at www.lynetteeason.com.

If you enjoyed *The Cost of Betrayal*, you may also like . . .

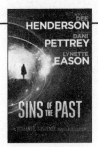

In this collection of gripping novellas from three beloved masters of romantic suspense, sins of the past lead to danger in the present. The collection includes Dee Henderson's "Missing," Dani Pettrey's "Shadowed," and Lynette Eason's "Blackout."

Sins of the Past

More from Dee, Dani, and Lynette

While Detective Evie Blackwell and her new partner, David, investigate two missing-persons cases in Chicago—a student and a private investigator—their conviction that "justice for all" is truly possible will be tested to the limit.

Threads of Suspicion by Dee Henderson
AN EVIE BLACKWELL COLD CASE
deehenderson.com

Private Investigator Kate Maxwell never stopped loving Luke Gallagher after he disappeared. Now he's back, and together they must unravel a twisting thread of secrets, lies, and betrayal while on the brink of a biological disaster that will shake America to its core. Will they and their love survive, or will Luke and Kate become the terrorist's next target?

Dead Drift by Dani Pettrey
CHESAPEAKE VALOR #4
danipettrey.com

After being dumped by her fiancé, K-9 officer Chloe St. John decides to focus all of her attention on her job. When she is assigned to team up with US Marshall Blake MacCallum to take down a trafficking ring, they must race against time before another girl goes missing. Can she move on from her past? And can he trust himself around this firecracker of a woman?

Called to Protect by Lynette Eason
BLUE JUSTICE #2
lynetteeason.com

More Romantic Suspense

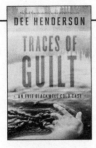

State Police Detective Evie Blackwell is launching a new task force dedicated to reexamining unsolved crimes in Illinois. While looking at old evidence for a couple of missing-persons cases in Carin County, she pulls out a few tenuous leads—with startling implications.

Traces of Guilt by Dee Henderson
AN EVIE BLACKWELL COLD CASE
deehenderson.com

When modern skeletal remains are discovered at Gettysburg, park ranger and former sniper Griffin McCray must confront his past if he, his friends, and charming forensic anthropologist Finley Scott are going to escape this web of murder alive.

Cold Shot by Dani Pettrey
CHESAPEAKE VALOR #1

When police officer Isabelle St. John's partner is murdered, she must work with Detective Ryan Marshall to solve a case that may force her to choose between family and justice.

Oath of Honor by Lynette Eason
BLUE JUSTICE #1
lynetteeason.com